The Inhuman Condition

S P Whitehead

First published 2007 by Scott Whitehead, Palmerston, Northern
Territory, Australia.

ISBN-10   0646494740

ISBN/EAN-13   978-0-646-49474-6

Hard-copies of this book can be ordered online at
www.cafepress.com/moncom and the eBook can be
downloaded from various online eBook stores..

About The Author

Scott P Whitehead was born in Adelaide, Australia, in 1970, and moved with his parents to Darwin in the Northern Territory in 1976. There he finished Year 12 at school, matriculating in 1987. After a year at University in a Bachelor Of Business degree, he left to work as a Computing Assistant for the Northern Territory Government, and from there went commercial fishing for a few years, living on a beach near Finniss River, and again at Croker Island, off the coast of Arnhem Land.

Moving to Palmerston NT in 1993, he worked at various administrative jobs, fruit picking, Web Designer and Internet Consultant, and some labouring jobs.

Gaining advertising income from online discussion forums he built (www.moncom.net World Forums), it was then that he began to write on a regular basis. He first self-published 'The Inhuman Condition' in 2007.

He continues to moderate his online forums daily, which now attract millions of visitors each year. He continues to write daily, between riding his motorcycle about, going fishing, and creating new websites. He is also a carer for a friend with throat cancer. And at the beginning of each wet-season he can be found picking mangoes somewhere south of Darwin in the Northern Territory.

When a beacon was detected in a distant solar system Gerry Handley assumed, along with every other employee involved, that an automated probe had malfunctioned. There would be a simple explanation, definitely human involvement.

However, there was something else. Events Gerry and his crew could not explain. Something that would strip him of his old life forever. A discovery that would make him dangerous.

And as his knowledge grew, so did the gulf between himself and humanity.

Dedicated to Georgina Louisa Talbot

ONE

'... Crying everyone's tears...'
Sade' – King Of Sorrow

In an unusually quiet suburban street of Darwin, most people were in their gardens, the warm breeze preferable to the sweltering heat indoors. They were enjoying an ideal Sunday afternoon in the humid Northern Australian city, the comforting sound of distant lawnmowers and children's laughter floating in softly from over the rooftops. Lightning flashed on the horizon, the distant storm clouds flickering with a picturesque violence.

A large, though somewhat gaunt man turned into the street, staggering slightly as he pushed an old motorcycle up the slight incline. To the people that glanced in his direction, nothing seemed out of the ordinary. A patron of the pub around the corner it was assumed, his last money spent on a beer, deemed more important than fuel at the time. Either that or a bike thief, they thought. There certainly hadn't been any shortage of thieves or drunks about lately.

He was muttering as he made his way up the street, though not loud enough for anyone nearby to piece together a meaningful sentence. A good thing, considering the number of creative expletives that rolled from his tongue. Veins bulged in his forehead, face bright red with the exertion.

He didn't have far to go, but Gerry wasn't too sure if he'd make it without a rest-stop. He had to get the motorcycle home with him, being over 130 years old and almost certainly the only one of its model left in the world, a breeze to hot-wire and very valuable. They made them to last back in the year 2054, but security was a different matter. The early owners lived in a different world. No vehicle could be left on the side of the road now. It would be missing or vandalised within hours. Though relatively quiet during the day, except for the occasional yelling from every neighbourhoods collection of wife-bashers or drunkards, the suburban streets were seething with degenerate activity after nightfall. The human garbage seemed to find

1

strength in the darkness. Perhaps it was the relative anonymity that set them free to make life so difficult for everyone else here. Though it was his hometown, Gerry had long ago lost all respect for the degenerate society he had spent most of his life within. If he were to be robbed by another hardcore junkie or accosted by another violent part-aboriginal moron, he was worried that he would lose control of his own actions, something he had never before done as an adult. He would have to get out of the suburbs soon if he wanted to stay out of trouble with the law.

The Government had lost control of the intellectually-disabled hoards for over fifty years now, and had given up even attempting to do so, but if someone such as himself took it upon themselves to put a stop to one of the violent drunks or such, they would find themselves in a whole heap of legal trouble. And only the demented low-life that faced him in court would have a lawyer, paid for by the Government. He would get no help himself. Civilised people didn't get any breaks here in the Territory. For almost a century, the Northern Territory was known as the place where the only decent people that lived there were those who hadn't yet saved enough money to leave.

Gerry had decided that it was now his turn to escape this terrible place, but he'd been telling himself that for almost twenty years. He wasn't even sure what it was that had been holding him here. Maybe it was the great fishing and warm weather. Or possibly the women that he had known. But all that just wasn't enough any more. The Government had recently reinstated the highway speed limits too, so now he couldn't even get out onto the highway on his motorcycle, and enjoy himself as he distanced himself from the degenerate suburbs at high speed. An elderly female politician had just decided that high speeds were dangerous on the long, straight highways that the Territory was famous for. For herself, it certainly would be dangerous to travel at near three hundred kilometres per hour on a motorcycle like Gerry had been doing for most of his adult life, but she had decided to force her own physical limitations on everyone that lived here. There really wasn't anything keeping him here any more. He decided he that he would decide on a destination tonight. This time he really would turn his back on this miserable hometown of his.

With determined effort, he forced himself and the machine up onto the footpath, turning up an alleyway almost hidden by the branches of overgrown trees that bloomed from the front yards of the houses at either side. Taking advantage of a downward slope, he jumped onto the bike, hoping the momentum he was gaining as his speed increased would get him home without any more effort on his part. Slipping expertly between the fence and the car barrier at the end of the alleyway, Gerry let the bike roll out onto the street without slowing. Not willing to touch the brake, he took a gamble that there would not be any vehicles moving up the street and emerged without having time to look for oncoming traffic.

He was relieved that a car had not ploughed into him, but Gerry was accustomed to relying on chance to get by. In an instant, Gerry decided that in all probability there were most likely no vehicles on that street at the time, and yet again put his life into the hands of a mathematical statistic. As always, the dice rolled his way. He grinned while he sat upon the rolling motorcycle, thinking of all the effort that his risky manoeuvre had saved him from. He would be able to get most of the way home from here just by keeping his bike moving downhill, determined to avoid using the brakes.

Someone he could not remember had once told him that he lived a charmed life. Gerry always thought on it after he had done something risky and it had paid off. His good fortune certainly had not stopped both himself and others making his life very difficult for him though. It didn't seem to matter if most things he wanted fell into his lap, his certain ability to lose what he had just gained was turning into a lifelong trend. A stable income and an ordered existence were what he wanted, but in reality six months of the same was too much for him, and he would force a change. It had never occurred to him that maybe he couldn't be happy living either way, but knew that he would always illogically follow the belief that the grass was greener on the other side. Like most people, he found solace in keeping himself busy, the more rushed the better, though always striving to get back to where he had already been.

In the long run his many and varied lifestyles worked to his advantage, a jack-of-all-trades being a rarity in a society blooming with new information and new technology. It seemed to take longer and longer over the years to get a grasp of even the minor subject and to truly specialise in one of them could take more than a lifetime. Gerry had a stronger than average backing in most of the sciences, more practical experience than theoretical, and this made him useful.

Though skilled enough to take his pick of well-paying jobs on Earth, Gerry took his expertise off-planet as often as possible.

He would quickly learn to operate the scientific and military equipment that was available to him on missions with very little instruction, and with human error being so expensive out there, it was this strength that was valued most of all by his employers on scientific expeditions. He had kept injured shipmates alive with his medical skills and could repair faults with the electronics and computers on the craft. He was one of only a few men alive who was confident piloting a hyper-speed interstellar ship on manual control if there was ever any reason to deviate from the programmed flight path or carry out a manoeuvre of which the computer was incapable, though both were very rare occurrences.

He had been of extra value when their destination was a very hostile environment, where his engineering abilities were tested in the construction of a base that would withstand the heat, wind, and dangerous fauna. With pride he'd heard two years later that his structures still stood, and had played a big part in keeping dozens of expeditions fatality-free in a very dangerous place indeed. His reputation had been given a boost on that job, allowing him to pick and choose from employers ever since.

And on the last job he gained experience in culling a species, which was not something he'd put on his resumé, though he'd had job offers since which were in much the same vein. He would never carry a gun again if he had any say in the matter. No one had ever been in a situation on an interstellar trip that required defending themselves with a firearm. So far they had only ever been used offensively on other species. There was also a risk that a stressed-out space farer would flip out and take advantage of the weapons availability to main or kill one of his innocent shipmates. This was reason to keep guns off interstellar craft, as far as Gerry was concerned.

Work in space wasn't sought by many now. It had lost a lot of the glamour it held in the early days, being relatively commonplace but even more dangerous, mainly due to the

4

insanely high speeds they would attempt, and the unpredictable nature of far-flung solar systems. Nevertheless, it paid very well, the high pay rates being a necessary incentive if measurable progress was to be made in the race to make off-planet trips more safe and comfortable for future generations of explorers and settlers.

Gerry had been off-planet nine times now, each time longer than the last. Being so isolated from home and from 'regular' people would never be a very comfortable experience for him, but the pangs of homesickness did diminish in frequency over time. A six-week job in space was simply a novel way to earn some good cash as far as Gerry was concerned, and he always impatiently counted down the hours to the return trip. There was no doubt that the best part of his job was getting back to Earth and spending his pay on beer, cigars and motorcycles.

Back in Earth's gravity now, Gerry was feeling the strain on his weakened body. At least this unplanned exertion would speed his recovery from his last mission, he thought to himself. There had been synthesised gravity on board the ship, but not enough to allow him to keep muscle tone.

The bike rolled even further than he'd hoped, still having enough speed to mount the driveway and continue down the footpath next to his little single-bedroom unit, where he gently squeezed the brake, pushing the side-stand down when it came to a halt. Climbing wearily from the motorcycle, Gerry took the keys from the ignition and walked to the front door. It was locked, and assuming no one was home as he let himself in, he was suitably surprised to see his girlfriend standing in the kitchen.

She was more of a part-time girlfriend, disappearing for weeks at a time into a trashy existence she had cultivated as a barmaid years before. There was no half way. Gerry couldn't stomach her drunken, drug-addled acquaintances, so it was a choice of them or him. She chose to take turns, living two separate lives. Like Gerry, she too knew how to get what she wanted.

He smiled at her as she turned around on hearing him enter, but he was just too tired to stop to trade pleasantries.

'Hello Janet,' he said simply, walking past her to the bathroom. Turning on only the cold as he showered, he could feel the oppressive tropical Australian heat running off of him, gurgling down the drain with the water. Leaning against the tiled wall he sighed deeply and wearily. He'd spent much of the past year in low gravity and needed more time to regain his Earth-legs.

Even near total exhaustion, his thoughts kept returning to the past. Still the scenes played before him, his eyes barely open and his senses doing cartwheels, his visions of what had gone were sparkling clear, and far too shocking to simply be forgotten, or even pushed to the back of his mind for more than a few minutes at a time.

The violence he had witnessed, even worse, the violence he had played an active part in, was taking its toll now. He'd taken weapons with him to a friendly planet and helped decimate a species. He was not a soldier, and resented being forced to carry out the duties of one to earn his wage.

People on Earth felt they were slightly safer after what he and his crew had done, though the cost was the 'disappearance' of an intelligent, though somewhat primitive species. There was never any reason to perceive them as being a threat to our lives, only a threat to our people's lifestyle on the remote planet.

The species they had found were labelled pests soon after military scientists discovered that it was likely that they would be a never-ending hazard to research and business ventures on the planet. The people back on Earth would lay judgement of course, over ninety percent believing newspaper reports, which suggested a small animal on a distant new colony was wreaking havoc with structures at the camps, risking the lives of their pioneering heroes. Some of the stories were correct, with some materials being torn from a dormitory complex under construction, and parts were sometimes removed from power generators and other pieces of mechanical and electrical equipment. In reality, humans actually living on the colony found the pilfering to be little more than an inconvenience.

The technological success of the indigenous species was obviously in part due to their strong sense of curiosity and ingenuity, which was also to be their downfall. Men with an eye to the future used it as leverage against them. Their intelligence was used to instil general sense of trepidation, the implication that an alien species plotting against humankind bringing to the surface a primitive fear. Public opinion on Earth was on our side, even if those opinions were based on lies. Humankind's first off-planet military assault was to be put to the test. The benefits were

6

too large and obvious to ignore. The American President said their 'interests were being threatened', and that we had God on our side. Most of the leaders in the western world had agreed that a heavy-handed response was in order, though this was expected.

Some blame the perfection of genetic engineering for the worldwide lack of respect for species deemed 'less than us', though a slow desensitisation was surely just as much to blame. With a few scraps of their tissue we could bring them back from extinction at a point in time we deem best for them, and best for us. Discovering a new species could be exciting, full of possibilities, but at times it was more of a reminder of our own vulnerability. Humankind proved to be very dangerous when a threat was perceived, even if a civilisation was only remotely likely to ever disadvantage our carefully ordered society. Our ability to put a species 'on ice' was a godsend.

There had never been a journalist out so far. The cost of distant space missions was huge, as they had always been. A few photographs of Earth's first intergalactic soldiers slaughtering thousands of scared, almost defenceless aliens would have been worth the billions of dollars in transport costs to a newspaper company, though it would be very doubtful if the photographs, hard-copy or entangled-particle transmission, would make it back to Earth. The United Nations and individual Governments had the resources to stop any material of that type being published, just as they'd always had. The ship and its occupants 'disappearing' was not a risk to be ignored even by the most determined of reporters. It seemed that taxpayers were content with paying the government to keep them ill informed and naïve. Ignorance is bliss.

Gerry had personally slashed through the throat, or something that they had been instructed was a throat, of one of the last living specimens. And, not for the first time, he'd felt the revulsion, the sense of horror that came with slaughtering an intelligent being, a being that knew pain, and understood that death was to be feared above all else. An utterly harmless creature without a will to protect itself, with the means to do so, but an innate decency toward others that the gentlest of men would have had difficulty understanding.

The last specimen alive was restrained without a struggle. It had stood immobile during the culling, like many of the others,

7

unable to believe what was happening to what once must have been their equivalent to family, friends and neighbours. It stood in what was probably the village centre, watching the carnage in seeming passive resignation. Its head flicked left and right, witnessing the death of its companions to every side. Gerry remembered the way it then focusing intently on a stone sculpture in front. It was as if the stone held as much importance to it as the blood-letting. So weathered it was impossible to make out any recognisable features on the stone, only the symbols carved at the base showed in was created by an intelligence and was not a natural formation. To Gerry, it was ample proof that these were intelligent beings. He was sure it was a religious icon of some sort. Though people had rid the Earth of most religious groups, it was not long ago that many people believed the world had been made in six days. As far as Gerry could tell they had a society that was advanced as ours was only a few hundred years ago, though less materialistic and lacking the greed that ruled a capitalist society such as that which was so entrenched on Earth.

Gerry passed over a cable-tie, which was adeptly slipped over the tiny hands and pulled tight. So tight, that a trickle of blood ran down the little creatures arms, though it seemed oblivious to the pain. Gerry still hoped that they didn't feel any, though he knew better.

He had ignored their soft chirping and squeaking as he fired a round into them with his sidearm. They made the sounds incessantly anyway. There was nothing else obvious in their actions or appearance that was recognisable to their exterminators as fear or pain.

It made their job much easier. Most of the soldiers saw the situation in the same light as if they were killing rats in their basement back home, removing a 'pest' which could cut into their countrymen's quality of life. Those in command decided no one warranted any counselling after this mission. Even the American soldiers skipped their usual session on the couch with a therapist. Killing fellow human beings was known to affect the mind adversely, but the destruction of a vermin was nothing out of the ordinary for the average person on Earth, let alone a trained soldier well versed in the ethics of what they were doing by those in command.

8

It was different for Gerry though. He had gone on the mission as a Research Assistant and the ship's Maintenance Engineer. Then they received the order that every available hand be shuttled down to assist with the culling.

Previous attempts had been made to eradicate the creatures. Traps had been designed by engineers back on Earth, though it involved a great deal of guesswork. Humans had managed to find a way of trapping and studying all other species that we came in contact with so far without too much difficulty. But the attempt to keep our hands clean, and kill by remote means a being that was perhaps almost as intelligent as us, was unprecedented. Here, using a creature's basic instinct against it was not a complete solution. There was a need to find an understanding of very complex communities and lifestyles. Poisoning some of their water supplies was pointless, as only a few hundred would be eradicated before their incredibly effective communication system was put to use. Bombs were not an option on planets other than Earth, the high costs involved in getting them or their component materials off of one planet and delivering them to another making it infeasible for now.

A more hands-on approach was required. Another attempted extermination involved loading up a human envoy with a menagerie of new viruses, engineered by scientists on Earth for maximum infection rate and targeted with perfection at the weaknesses in their biological make-up. Special Services staff employed by the United Nations were used to gain possession of five of the target specimens that were required in the final testing of the viruses. They worked beautifully in the lab, and everybody concerned was justifiably proud of their flawless work.

But when it came to using the diseases against the target species, they proved utterly ineffective. They obviously were quite adept in the biological sciences or had some powerful natural medicine in their flora, and had a serum to render all seventeen bugs ineffective, widely available in less than twenty hours. Not that it mattered. The infected targets and any that they had come in any contact with were quarantined so early that the viruses were given no chance to spread. The final frightening blow came when they also cured the infected individuals. There was not a single death.

9

The final attempt was bolder by far, but turned out to be almost too easy. A few dozen UN Special Service personnel were dropped into each of their colonies, instructed to annihilate the species without undue damage to their fabrications. Military officials were concerned about the possibility that the species had deduced the virus infections to be an aggressive act against them, and may have put together some defensive mechanisms, or even retaliatory ones. Nothing of the sort was implemented. Some close study in the ensuing months by anthropologists showed why.

These small beings had developed survival mechanisms that were far different from those of any Earth-born creature. Violence toward other species was never required as a means to survive and procreate. They could never have foreseen a meeting with a creature like Man. They were technologically advanced, and could have put together a very strong defence system, but obviously assumed it unlikely to have an encounter with something with such a destructive urge as ours. Sitting ducks.

Gerry thought about his actions far too long and hard to be capable of living the soldier's life. Obsessive was not too strong a word for it. Not being one for discipline, in fact being actively opposed to it, made it difficult to follow orders blindly and without personal judgement.

These things weighed upon him. His own kind felt the fate of an innocent species on a planet far from home was less important than economic and political gain on Earth. At times he was ashamed to be human.

There were very few species discovered that used tools or even communicated with each other effectively, let alone posed a military threat to Earth. Probability said the day would come eventually. As long as we survived to continue the search of the galaxies, we could be certain that there were other species out there looking for us also. Would they take us at face value or judge us by our past. Which would be more just?

It was these sorts of problems that weighed upon Gerry's mind. Things he couldn't change, yet felt some responsibility to try. He felt their weight even as he dried himself and lay back on his bed to rest. It was impossible for him to feel anything close to contentment while being so aware of what his country and his species had done, and were still doing, to each other. Their

10

callous sense of justice assumed the ends justified the means. This combined with the attitude that might was right was a volatile mixture. Maybe it was just a bad attitude on his part, but Gerry couldn't shake the feeling that he had been an active participant in something very, very wrong.

Back here on Earth, billions of kilometres from the scene of the crime, Gerry was still paying the price. His memory had become his enemy.

His exhaustion soon gave him respite though, helping him fall quickly into a deep and dreamless sleep.

TWO

'Fear will stop you loving;
Love will stop your fear...'
Morcheeba – Fear & Love

It was dark when Gerry awoke. A distant streetlight cast enough light through the open window to see by as he sat up and glanced about the room. Janet wasn't next to him, and in a corner of his mind there was a faint hope that she had left again. He enjoyed her company, but he also valued his solitude very highly. Spending much of his life over the past few years crammed into the tiny rooms aboard interstellar craft with a group of stressed work-mates had given him an appreciation for a quiet and relaxed lifestyle.

The clock radio showed 8.26pm. As he was getting out of bed he heard a noise and looked up to see Janet opening the bedroom door. In some ways he was happy to see her, and smiled genuinely as he stood to greet her. She had a lit joint in her fingers, which she held out to him. He shook his head.

'I might have drug tests sometime soon for work, it stays in the system too long. It wouldn't stop them employing me, but it'd be another black mark on my record I don't need.'

She smiled, took one large puff and put it in the ashtray next to the bed. 'I wish had a little bit of that willpower.'

As they hugged she knew she had been welcomed back again. If he was angry about her leaving for a month without an explanation, he wasn't showing it. It irked a little, the thought that maybe Gerry just didn't really care if she left. She was an optimist though, and knowing him as well as she did, assumed it was simply his sense of self-reliance, not being the type of person to give control of his feelings to another.

Immediately relaxing with each other, their lips locked together firmly. She parted her lips slightly, pressing her tongue between his lips, to make him do the same. He complied, and tasted sweet smoke filling his mouth. Without a second thought he slowly inhaled as she gently breathed the smoke into his lungs.

12

When she was done, she broke the kiss and looked up into his eyes.

He placed his hands softly on either side of her face. 'Everyone's willpower has its limits. Self-control isn't really my strong point either.'

She smiled seductively. 'Good, if you knew what was best for you, you'd find a good girl to spend your time with, so I'd hate it if you could resist this.'

She said 'good girl' as one word, with a touch of negativity in her tone. Gerry knew that she was either jealous of other women's ability to limit the number and nature of the joyous experiences that were available to them, or truly felt a life limited by morals distasteful. Gerry didn't care either way; he thought both attitudes valid.

Janet pulled her black sports-bra off over her head and threw it aside, while Gerry took the liberty of reaching out and slipping his thumbs under the waist of her pants, peeling the skin-tight Lycra downwards. He found a lacy black g-string underneath, which he also pushed down to her ankles, forced to sink down to his knees to do so, being careful not to break the flimsy piece of cloth.

She took a step backward out of the clothes Gerry had helped remove, and was standing naked before him. As always, she was very conscious of her fine physique and as he looked up at her she lifted her arms to pull a thin leather tie from her hair. Her breasts were thrust outward as she worked the knot, her nipples hardening quickly, a visual clue to the desire they both felt. Gerry watched the skin around them tighten, stretching under the inner pressures to what looked like a painful size. They looked as hot and hard as Gerry knew they would be to touch.

Gerry gazed up at her softly-lit form before him as she gently shook her head, letting her long black hair fall freely about her shoulders.

'Very nice,' he muttered, then realising it an understatement he added, 'What did I do to deserve this?'

She only gave him a quick, coy smile, the prettiness of the gesture quickening his pulse further.

Janet's fitness routine involved nothing more than dancing and fucking, her diet consisted of a beer breakfast and a similar 'liquid lunch', a couple of sandwiches for dinner, with drinks to wash it down. And here was the proof that a mildly hedonistic lifestyle worked well for some people. Her tight little abdomen showed a sensuous pattern of toned muscles. Her skin was softly tanned almost everywhere, only two very small patches of pale white skin showing on her body. The little untanned triangular shapes around her nipples helped to accentuate them, and made one wonder how she could have possibly kept her breasts contained in such a tiny piece of cloth.

Moving past him to the bed, she pulled him down with her. Lying on her back, her legs slightly apart, Gerry was impressed by the sight before him. She had the style, the lustrous black hair and the petite body that Gerry found stunning, and to him she was something very close to female perfection.

For the most part he appreciated her party-girl nature, and at least for the moment, there was no outward sign of her love for the bottle. She could be a handful sometimes, but at moments like these he was glad he had been patient with her. He wasn't one for conversation, which could make things difficult for him with some women, but with Janet he had a silent understanding. There was a bond between them that made words unimportant; the fact that they knew exactly how the other felt seemed to be enough.

Kneeling on the floor at the end of the bed, Gerry gently pushed her knees apart and kissed and licked his way along her thighs. He could feel her body heat on his face as he neared the mound of her sex. The way it glistened with moisture in the soft light betrayed her longing.

Running his tongue slowly along either side, and then softly over the top of her partly opened folds, he felt her back arch and heard her sigh a beautifully feminine sigh. Flicking his tongue lower, he pushed it slowly and firmly into her. His lips and chin were instantly slick with her wetness, which aided him as he parted her with his mouth. Hands clenched in his hair, forcing his face harder against her, her slim hips swung left and right to give him access to every part of her, making sure his tongue missed nothing.

Gerry could tell she was close to going over the edge, and pulled back, teasing her, leaving her impatient for more. Moving further onto the bed, he took his time kissing her belly, her breasts, her neck, and finally her lips. His desire heightened yet

14

another notch as she licked her own softly scented moisture from his face.

More than an hour passed before they finished with each other.

Afterward, lying on his back, looking up at the ceiling as Janet dozed beside him, Gerry was lost in his thoughts. He was thinking about today, a day that was looking to be very grim, if it had followed in the fashion of the first few hours.

After waking in a foul mood, which he was not normally prone to doing, and having no explanation for the cause, he had gone for a fast ride on his motorcycle. He was free to do as he pleased for the day. The weather was great, if a little hot, and he had no obvious reason to be sitting about the house on his own on the edge of boredom.

But more than a little over-exuberance with the throttle put a sudden stop to his revelry. He recognised the source of the metallic howls and thumps that the motor suddenly produced, having had the misfortune to have big end bearings let go in a few of the vintage machines he had owned. He pulled up at the kerb, bringing the bike to a halt just as the motor turned over one last tortured time and went dead with a final loud thump. It was expensive damage and his newfound enthusiasm for the day had been quickly dashed. And then he had to get the damn thing home again, which was easier said than done.

Towing companies were so expensive they weren't even an option for most people, their usual customers being injured in the back of an ambulance, in no state to look for a cheaper company or dispute price. There was easy money in concussed people, people very recently injured in a traffic accident and those near death. Gerry had heard somewhere that even some of the deceased would get a bill in their letterbox where they'd last lived. To Gerry they weren't an option. It was against his nature to help line the pockets of people whose actions he resented, even though it meant making his life more difficult.

There had been a small chance he could have found one of his friends at home if he had rang around, but finding someone who had a utility on hand at the time would have been unlikely. Anyway, it was not in his character to make chores for his friends just to make one lighter for himself. Before he had even stepped off the vehicle he'd resigned himself to pushing it all the way home again. And he did so, all 180 kilograms of metal and plastic for a distance of 12.4 kilometres. He knew this without doubt; he'd watched the odometer turning over, so excruciatingly slowly while he'd pushed.

'Stuff that,' Gerry said out loud, the memories making him cringe. Remembering where he was, he looked quickly to his right, checking to see if he had woken Janet.

'Well', he thought, 'at least I know I'm still fit.' He was still coping with Earth's gravity after his last stint in space, yet to finish building his body back up. He wasn't feeling too energetic just now though, and he fought off a wave of tiredness, tempted to stay where he was and allow himself to doze off again. Janet was still breathing softly and slowly next to him, probably still asleep.

Standing carefully, trying not to wake her, Gerry found an old pair of shorts on the floor and pulled them on. A flannelette shirt hung from a chair, which he put on without buttoning up. Walking slowly across the darkened room, he opened the bedroom door and stepped into the hallway. Finally able to see, he walked into the living room, where he'd left his helmet on the couch. Reaching inside, he removed a tattered packet of tobacco and a disposable lighter.

Feeling relaxed in the quiet aftermath of an arduous day, Gerry sat on his front doorstep and rolled a cigarette. His lifestyle had been close to ideal lately, he thought, knowing by experience though that it wouldn't last. But he knew better than to sour the moment with pessimism. His bank balance was enough to ensure he had something to eat and a roof over his head for at least six months more.

He still wasn't sure, though, whether he should treat himself to a holiday with the remainder of his money, or invest it towards his future, which appeared more uncertain every time he contemplated it.

He glanced at his motorcycle, mentally cringing when he thought of the time and money it would take before he would have it running again. Engine parts for something of its era just weren't available anymore. Vehicles like his were banned from the roads in most countries, so there wasn't much money in producing engine parts for them. He'd have to machine his own, or pay someone to do it for him. He wasn't prepared for an expense like this.

'If its not one thing it's another' he muttered, but immediately felt that sitting about feeling stressed by the string of annoying events he'd lately endured was pointless. 'Damn. Bloody negative thoughts again.'

These were uncertain times. Peace-of-mind was something only the richest, or the simplest of people, could enjoy. Gerry was sure it had always been this way for most, but there was an air of urgency behind people's lives now that confounded him. It was as though they rushed to end a race, though what was beyond the finish line was anybody's guess. Personal progress demanded all of a person's time and energy. The feeling was contagious, and though he felt himself an onlooker, a separate entity from the dim-witted hoards that filled the cities on Earth, he felt driven by their collective mindless enthusiasm.

He felt that getting quickly back to work was more of a requirement for him now rather than a choice. At the very least he would constantly feel as though he was missing out on something. God knows what, but he knew the feeling alone would push him into calling a few people for a job soon. Fairly modest in his wants; his ideal lifestyle didn't come at a very high cost to maintain. But he was stunned to find that even when all of his needs, and wants, had been met he could not relax. There was always something else that needed doing, another step to take.

Drawing deeply on the cigarette, he was thinking how much nicer it would be if it were a cigar. A Cuban would be more fitting on an evening as pleasant as it was. The sky was suffused with a soft pink light, typical of a very humid night in the tropics. He'd have a beer or two before bed. It was too early for him to think about sleeping yet, and his afternoon nap had revitalised him some.

Deciding that it would probably be raining sometime tonight, Gerry rose and wheeled his motorcycle underneath the shelter offered by his veranda. He liked having it closer to his front door anyway, so he would have a chance of hearing something if anybody tampered with it or tried moving it during the night.

Walking inside he took a beer from the fridge and went to the living room where he clicked on the television and sat down.

Using a small keyboard on his lap he flicked past more than twenty channels of mindless drivel before he gave up, switching then to the Internet.

He soon had one of his employment agencies web-page's in front of him, where he set the computer to search for jobs suiting his location and experience. The list of available positions held over four million entries when it came back. He had to narrow down the search. Just out of interest, under LOCATION he selected OFF-PLANET and a new list of only forty-seven positions appeared.

Many of the positions were for labourers aboard the International Space Station, where hundreds of young adventurers worked in the precision-bearing factories, or if they were lucky, in the science labs as assistants. Working in zero gravity wasn't as fun as imagined, and Gerry had the misfortune of being stuck on the station for a tedious six month stint once before. There was no way of getting out of an employment contract early when you got out there. You simply wouldn't be given a seat on any of the shuttles until your time was up.

'Never again,' he said to himself, scrolling down the list.

One of the vacant positions caught his attention most of all, as it wasn't a publicly advertised position. It had been sent directly to him. Someone had obviously recommended him as a potential recruit. It was for an Assistant Supervisor/Researcher aboard a vessel headed three hundred and sixty-two light years away. The destination was Clavus 3, a moon that had hit the headlines on Earth six months ago.

Gerry knew it to be shrouded in a mist of adenine clouds, a ball of various liquids with a small iron core, with no solid ground to land a vehicle. With no sun near enough to warm it, the moon gained heat energy from its tidal motion, the chemical soup churned by the massive gravitational pull of the dense planet it circled, as well as by the two other moons that orbited with Clavus 3.

The moon had never been observed first-hand before, all of the information on its properties being gleaned from images taken by roving telescopes. One of these passed through the galaxy six years ago, travelling at many times the speed of light, close enough to collect detailed data on the very faint radiation it emitted. Strangely, Gerry thought, they still hadn't bothered to

18

name the planet. It seemed that only one of its moons, Clavus 3, was of any importance as far as scientists and government officials were concerned.

It had recently been decided that there was good potential for life to make an appearance there, with all the necessary building blocks available. The copious amount of adenine the moon floated amongst would ensure a healthy kick-start to life, being one of the four main components of DNA. Life evolved on a moon would be interesting indeed, the lack of a substantial atmosphere and land mass likely to force its inhabitants down a very different evolutionary path to ours. The moon had therefore been earmarked for a visit by one of the surveying and research teams.

And then a light signal had been detected. There was no doubt it had originated from the moon, a mining probe passing within two light years of the system picking up a strong signal. If it hadn't been passing at the time it might have been many years before the transmission had reached the nearest human settlement or another passing spacecraft.

The news had stirred people's imaginations, which was good for exploration programmes worldwide, a surge in investment making extra missions possible. An Australian company was set to have a closer look. And here was Gerry's chance to make some big money, and surely the mission's high profile could only help his future prospects. There was certain to be strong competition for any place on this flight, but Gerry's application would have some extra clout. His character references held the signatures of some very influential people, most of them previous employers for whom he went far beyond the call of duty. Trillions of dollars had been invested in the few off-planet trips he'd been a part of. Fortunes could be won or lost upon one split-second decision. He had earned his pay, and with it the high regard of the men and woman who pushed the buttons back at home.

'No harm in getting my name on the list,' he muttered, and clicked on the LOAD RESUME' and then the SUBMIT APPLICATION button.

Janet walked in, looking half-asleep.

'What was that you were saying, baby?' she asked, reaching over the couch from behind him, wrapping her arms softly around his neck.

'Just talking to myself.'

Janet was studying the screen. 'Working on a Sunday night. That's just like you.'

Clicking on DISCONNECT, Gerry turned and effortlessly pulled her over the soft back of the chair. She ended up lying with her head in his lap, looking up at him.

'Desperate to get back into the rat race, huh? Why are you already looking for work, you've hardly had any time to relax?'

'There wasn't anything worth watching on TV so had a look at some job ads. I put in an application, but I won't be too worried if they don't call back. I might not even go to the interview if they offer me one.' It was definitely the truth. Spending the next few months locked up here with Janet and a fridge full of beer seemed a lot more preferable right now.

'You know the odds of something going wrong are too high if you go on those long trips too often.' Her concern seemed genuine, which surprised him. 'You're pushing it.'

'I don't think so. It only seems that way. Each time a person goes up is an independent event. Just because I've been out a few times before doesn't mean I'm more likely to get hurt if I go up again. The opposite, really. The experience I gained on the other jobs should help keep me safer than ever before.'

It made sense to her and she nodded. 'I suppose'

'It's damn dangerous here on Earth anyway. The engine in my bike seized today. It gave me a bit of a scare when the back wheel locked up half way round a fast corner.'

'I suppose there's no way I can get a lift home tonight then?' Her smile told him she didn't mind.

'I could ring you a taxi if you like, but you're welcome to stay the night.'

Pulling herself up so that their eyes were level, she said 'Thanks', and kissed him firmly. She then stood up and went about switching off the lights and ceiling fans. It was Gerry's cue to rise and lock the doors, and a couple of minutes later the house was dark and silent.

The two just held each other when they got into bed, both revelling in their closeness, ignoring the sweat that a warm Darwin night laid slick between them.

'I'm starting to like you a little too much, Gerry. I've been missing you the past few weeks.' He knew there had been something she'd wanted to say to him. There was a subtle difference in the way she had acted this afternoon.

'You know you don't need to get clingy with me. I'll always be here if you want to see me, and I'm certainly not interested in settling down with anyone other than you. I just need to make a bit more money before I can think about taking care of someone else. My lifestyle as it's been for the past few years just wouldn't sit well with you.'

'I know, it already riles me. Can I hand in my unit though, it's expensive, and anyway it seems pointless to live apart.'

'You'd better not, just yet. It's given you a place to go if we start to get at each other's throats. Best not to burn any of your bridges too soon. If I have to travel for work though, I'd be grateful if you could stay here and mind the place for me.'

'And when you get back?' She really was thinking ahead.

'We should probably be doing a little more than playing about like teenagers. I realised the other day that I've never even taken you out to dinner. At the very least, that little oversight of mine will have to be seen to.'

'Yeah.' She wriggled in closer to him, kissed his chest, and he felt her relax in his arms. 'It pissed me off years ago when we were first seeing each other. I thought you were just using me and didn't think I was worth spending any money on or spending any time with unless it was in bed. But after a while I realised the real reason was that you were just too bloody busy and in your own head to see when a girl wants more. You're lucky I'm so patient.'

'For sure' he said to her, meaning it. He stroked her cheek softly with the back of his hand.

He lay for a long time with his eye's open in the darkness, listening to the intakes of her breath grow deeper and the spaces of time between grow longer as she fell asleep.

He was sure he should be happy now, but he was not, and he could not put his finger on why. Maybe when you didn't know what you wanted out of life it was difficult to appreciate what you ended up with.

Gerry wished he could be more like most people he was acquainted with, not think everything through so thoroughly. He knew it did him no service. He truly needed to accept his place in regular suburban life. Why couldn't he shake the feeling that settling into the accepted daily routine, the weekly routine, the year-by-year routine, was a complete waste of a lifetime.

He had long ago made a conscious decision to avoid slipping into the rut. This made his life difficult though. Going against the grain of an ordered society took its toll on a person. And now, if he were to cement his relationship with Janet, he would be dragging her through the same troubles and torment that he had willingly bought upon himself. She could not know what she would be getting herself into.

Gerry did exactly as he pleased, and had done so for most of his adult life. He would rather be destitute than live in a manner that restricted his options and his sense of self-reliance. There was little security in his life because of his ideals, and he felt it would be cruel of him to allow Janet to become mired in his struggle.

Gerry decided that his lonely fight for total self-determination at all costs would have to remain just that. Lonely. At least until he had tried and tested more of those rarely trodden paths and found a way of life that would make them both happy. After trying his hand at hundreds of different short-term jobs, living in dozens of very different locations, and even leaving the planet altogether on a number of occasions, Gerry still hadn't found a way of life that sat well enough with him for it to be long-lasting, secure. He always seemed to get itchy feet within a few months, no matter what he was doing or where he was living. He was in his thirties now, and had less idea of what he wanted for his future than he did when he was eighteen. Janet should not have to witness his despair, feel the overwhelming stress that he had been placing himself under for so long in his rush to find something better, something that might not even be there.

He was a realist, not at all pessimistic, but his future and everybody else's was a constant source of concern for him. He met people every day that seemed quite happy with their lot in life, but when you got below the surface, talked with them a while,

22

they would often prove somewhat ignorant. It seemed to Gerry that most just didn't have enough facts to know any better than to be resigned to the fact that they could change nothing. Intelligent people, their lives mapped out for them by their Governments and their forefathers, their beliefs and ideals mercilessly shaped and restrained by others. Acceptance of the limitations imposed on their self-determination was much easier than rebelling against it. Most were left no option but to accept that their way of life was the correct one, taking the line of least resistance. Most had only as much understanding of the world that they lived in that they could glean from a trashy, biased newspaper article or websites filled with misinformation. Or their brain was full of chemicals. Close to half of the adult population were on drugs to treat anxiety or depression. The other half relied on liquor stores and illicit drug dealers to bring a fleeting happiness into their lives.

Relatively speaking though, Gerry thought to himself, he was very lucky with his lot. There were many places in the world where people did not have the luxury to be as critical about the conditions a modern life put upon them. He was at least free to continue searching for a path through life that he could respect and sustain.

With this in mind, along with hopes for a more secure future, Gerry closed his eyes and after a while drifted off to sleep.

THREE

'Too fast to live, too young to die…'
The Eagles – James Dean

As the fourth and last door in the airlock tunnel slid shut behind him, Gerry realised how mentally unprepared he was for this expedition. He momentarily considered how ridiculous it was for him to again be heading out, so soon after the weeks of hardship he'd endured during and after the last job. He was at his best in stressful situations however, which was one of the many reasons he had been picked to be part of this crew. At least this trip wouldn't involve decimating an intelligent species. Purely research this time.

No one on the high-speed flights had a very high sense of self-preservation. The statistics were known by all, and new recruits would find out early whether their will to live to a ripe old age was stronger than their desire to be a famous, pioneering space traveller. The glossy exterior view of a high profile, high paying job would always be a draw-card, but once a potential candidate was faced with the realities of the work more often than not they would decide on a career change. There were positions available on many of the craft that serviced outposts and mining sites within the solar system. These were lower risk, high paying jobs for the right people.

Gerry did not show any hint of unease as he walked. It wasn't difficult, simply making a conscious refusal to worry about anything that he now had no ability to change, and besides, he certainly wasn't prone to trembling in fear. This was just another job. The type of job that he needed to feel more alive, to feel as if he was doing something worthwhile. He would cherish the distance he would be putting between himself and the self-serving political and social infighting that shaped people's lives back on Earth. Gerry considered this a time for him to de-stress, to not care for a while. Research mission's light years from Earth necessitated the full concentration of everyone involved, and Gerry could do with a respite from the negativity that urban existence bought out in him. He wouldn't be given much time to think, which suited him just fine.

The layout of the craft was just as he mentally pictured it to be. This gave him some comfort; the hours spent labouring over the plans paying off already. The lights flickered off and back on again three times in quick succession, signalling three minutes until launch. There was a metallic clang behind them, the sound of the shuttle that had brought them here from Earth undocking.

Glancing sideways at his Supervisor, who was walking alongside, matching his fast pace to the cockpit, Gerry grinned, 'So this is what we live for.'

'Must be fucking crazy,' was his bosses reply. 'You would think we would have learned our lesson after our first few flights, but here we are again, gluttons for punishment.' He smiled broadly when he'd finished speaking, showing plainly he was quite happy with what they were about to do. As always, there was a feeling of nervous excitement in the air that couldn't be ignored. Knowing that their chances of surviving until retirement were suddenly much lower for them the moment they'd stepped on board, and that they'd made the choice willingly, gave people some feeling of nobility. There was also an overriding sense of patriotism for some, especially the American crew, though Gerry had always considered that type of mindless pride for one's country of birth to be illogical, in the realms of racism. He was sure everyone on missions like this could only be here for very personal reasons, and the fact that they were possibly doing something for their country, and their entire planet, was only a happy coincidence. The aspiring crew member with a personality type that simply craved the adulation of others were pushed into jobs more suiting their attitude rather than kept in the space programmes. More often than not they wouldn't need to be pushed though. There was many a disenfranchised recruit in the entertainment industry.

'Yeah, some weirdo's get tattoos and piercing because they enjoy the pain. Self-castration without painkillers is still thought of as big-time fun in some circles. There's even a self-amputee club in the States. We probably fit into a special little group right next to that lot,' Gerry said.

The Supervisor laughed, 'Maybe I should have gone and got a nipple-ring and a Prince Albert instead.'

25

It was then that they entered the cockpit, where everyone had to be seated while under hard acceleration. Everyone was already there, and the Supervisors face reddened slightly when he realised he was the last to arrive when he should really have been first. Gerry had met the crew before, and got to know them a little in the group briefings. He gave them each a smile and a nod as he seated himself.

Seconds after Gerry slipped his arms under the chairs restraints, and felt them tighten automatically, he felt the force of the tiny ion jets that pushed the ship to a position calculated to be safe by the computer for ignition of the faster-than-light drive. The burst of gamma rays exiting a main drive this powerful would kill anything in its path for over 800 light years behind the ship. The computer used calculations upon thousands of coordinates to decide when it was safe to fire the main engine. Behind them there was a region of space set aside for the radioactive blasts of ships such as this. It was a no-mans-land, where pilots could fire their engines confident they were not doing any damage or risking any lives.

'We'll be strapped into our seats for about twenty-five minutes. Get comfortable.' Calling then for Darren to accelerate under 70% thrust, the Supervisor clenched his jaw and held the armrests tighter. Gerry did the same.

The viewing screens lit up suddenly, space turning from the deep black emptiness to a brilliant lime-green sea of energy. Now they were really moving.

There was no mistaking the feeling of hyper-acceleration when it came. Gerry felt his innards moving, slipping toward his backbone. It was a sensation only experienced at such an intense level by those leaving the solar system. One had to be very fit to handle these trips. There was very little thought to comfort placed in the design of any of the interstellar craft. Luxury just wasn't worth the cost. Even just transporting some extra padding in their flight seats hundreds of light years would have used phenomenal amounts of energy, not all of which could simply be freely tapped from the vacuum they flew through. Gerry couldn't help but grin despite the pain. It was always an exciting part of a mission.

Energy from solar winds, and radiation of many types was converted to fuel used by the main drive. At the speeds attained, the ship passed through trillions of energy streams every second. Some of this boundless energy was directed to the front of the ship, where what could only be referred to as a computer-controlled black hole sat centimetres from the tip of the nose cone. If the ship did not need to carry humans, and to do so quickly, it would not need this huge man-made mass hovering at the front of the ship. It was required, however, to keep the people on board from being torn apart by the massive g-forces involved in accelerating rapidly enough to cover a useful distance in a feasible time-span. It would also give them gravity aboard the vessel for their journey. Constant discoveries and developments in the properties of quantum gravity over the last one hundred years had made all this possible.

The ship actually sat in a field of negative energy that emanated from this bright sphere of potentially momentous energy and mass. A black hole couldn't swallow everything that came near it without giving a little bit back. It had laws of it's own to abide by. The resulting field of negative space stretched around the ship, which enabled the faster than light travel. The ship and the space that encompassed it, in effect repelled each other. It was as though the universe was trying to spit them out. And while not truly part of the universe, it was possible to ignore most restraints imposed by our universe's physics on faster-than-light travel. The main drive, combined with the synthetic black hole, made for a formidable vehicle.

Anyone viewing the launch from nearby space would be in for an awesome sight. At speeds where the ship was still visible, the red sphere of intense light could be seen floating a few metres from the pointed nose of the ship. As the craft accelerated it visibly stretched, until there was just a streak of red light shooting off into space, as far as the eye could see. Within minutes this would dim, until it had faded away entirely, the craft and its occupants already travelled vast distances. The mass that held the vessel together would darken slightly and shrink, becoming a true black hole, under human control. A solar system, in effect, pressed into the size of a tennis ball, its unusual properties and violent energies tamed and bent to an engineer's will.

The show wasn't over then, the ship's wake hitting them suddenly, a strong burst of mostly ultraviolet light, which could be seen as a blinding red glow suffusing the viewing screens for

27

anything up to three hours. The observers would be in a sea of ultraviolet radiation, which was the energy released as both matter and normal cosmic radiation was dragged inward toward the accelerating ship; sucked toward the unnatural mass that burned in front of the ship, which was itself glowing like a burning ember.

The radiation blast from the main drive had a lethal side effect. The streams of high-energy radiation jetted by these vehicles were so destructive that laboratories on Earth regulated every firing of one of these drives. Any drive fired up while exhausting toward a stellar object within range of its lethal energy would be switched off by remote within milliseconds, if the ships onboard computers didn't prevent it from starting in the first place. This system was developed for the protection of people on earth, way before the chance effect on neighbouring solar systems was investigated. The real worry was that a country using one of these drives would one day use it as a weapon.

Leaked government papers had showed that the possibility was under consideration by some very idealistic governments. The United States government spokesmen frightened people worldwide with their candid responses when queried on the goals behind their own research into the military uses for this new engine.

'We have to keep one step ahead of those who may take advantage of the killing power this device makes available,' it was said. Yet again in the name of peace they were expanding their military advantage, thereby destroying the status-quo that kept us safe. And then there was their Nazi-styled 'First Strike' policy, which made them doubly dangerous. They had murdered millions of people using the pretence that their enemy was attempting to develop weapons of mass destruction. The hypocrisy was lost on them, and they continued to develop these weapons themselves, and were the only people in history to actually use them against their opponents. The availability of hyper-speed drives was more difficult to obstruct though, and every developed country owned them.

The possibility of being able to aim a high-energy drive at a country from space, killing every occupant, and then claiming 'Oops, one of our craft fired its engines at a bad time, sorry folks,' would be a constant temptation for some military officials. Who could say for certain it really wasn't a mistake? Surely it wouldn't be wise for anyone to retaliate, starting an all-out war. Very few organisms on the planet would survive a world war now with all the destructive power on tap, though an attack using a hyper-speed drive was rumoured to be written into U.S. military strategy documents as a plan of last resort.

Sites scattered all over this galaxy claimed to be on the lookout for suspicious activity by the high-powered craft. They could shut down the engines on these craft within a tiny fraction of a second after they had been instructed to fire, though many wondered if these few milliseconds might be all it would take to kill them. Thankfully, the effects of a momentary blast of the energy equivalent to that jetted from a supernova hadn't been tested on a human being yet. It had long been theorised that the dinosaurs had met their end in a blast of gamma rays ejected from one of the nearby supernovas. Another more recent theory, which seemed more likely as time went on, was that a thoughtless alien species aimed a high-energy drive in our direction. We now had the power to do this to ourselves, and to others.

Gerry thought of none of this as they accelerated. He was too busy trying to stop the spittle, which had a habit of dribbling from the corners of a person's mouth when their cheeks were stretched back hard under g-forces. The people seated at the rear of the cabin were usually the victims when this happened, so Gerry was extra careful. It wouldn't be a healthy start to his relationship with his new boss, whom he could hear grunting in the seat behind him. Grunting would help you handle the G's, and would stop you passing out too easily. The worst effects came when the main drive and the ball of compressed matter at the front of the ship would become slightly out of sync. Jumping back and forth from a red-out to a blackout a couple of times a second would happen on some trips. It was the number one reason crew-members resigned from the Interstellar Club. Some people were never the same after being shaken and squeezed so violently, some of who had been forced to endure hours of this torture in the less sophisticated craft of old.

The gravity ball, the main component in the variable-mass engine could easily be modified to cancel out all of the force that was pressing them painfully back into their seats, and the crew could feasibly then walk about the ship while under hyper-speed acceleration, but the side-effects of this were extreme. The crew

29

on the first few high-speed spacecraft did exactly that, and many were injured. There were high-frequency changes in acceleration of the ship and its occupants, so many thousands of changes per second that the vibration would often not be felt. But the brain was being damaged irreversibly, literally shaken until it was bruised and bleeding. So now crew were to endure the massive G's, but the constant thrust would actually help to hold their bodies together, and generally dampen the vibration throughout the ship.

If the forces of acceleration were not enough, the radiation would be the cause of more major problems for travellers. Some of the damage to cells in the human body during high-speed travel was irreversible. The radiation would destroy DNA, so no humans have yet been born, or even conceived outside the solar system. It was an impediment to the proliferation of the human population that seemed to be insurmountable. Even sperm and eggs stored in the most impenetrable of shielding ever designed would be rendered useless. This was only one of many mysterious effects produced when enveloped in a strong field of negatively charged particles. The same mechanism that fired them through space with such huge force would be devastating the biological matter on board the ship. Pregnant women were not allowed on these types of flights of course. Experiments involving rats showed the chance of having a normally functioning baby after even the shortest of high-speed trips was exactly zero. Gerry, like every one else who had travelled at these speeds, was destined to take a pill every morning for the remainder of his life or the effects would catch up with him. Without their medication, they would be riddled with cancers within days.

Gerry would have looked almost relaxed to anyone observing, reclined with his eyes closed, seemingly asleep. His mind was firmly on the job though. He was going through what little information he had been given in the pre-flight briefing. This was a purely scientific mission, he had been told. The fact that the pilot along with one of the scientists on board was on military payrolls wasn't lost to Gerry. The mission was to pinpoint the exact source of the light pulses, and to find a reason for them. He was employed to maintain most of the systems that made up the craft. The smooth running of the computers, the electronics, the safety equipment, and even the mighty engine were all his responsibility, but his roles extended far beyond even this. It did not make sense to have people specialising in only one field out here, where moving people, and anything else, was so expensive. There were plenty of very capable people on Earth with exceptional skills, and the temptation for them to chase the big money and get the chance to find something really new was great. Plus there were the people who had been into space once when young, and were predictably rendered infertile by the effects of the journey. Many would feel as if separate from rest of society when they returned, unable to make a family of their own and even a changed attitude toward what was important to them hampered them in their efforts to fit back into a world they once knew. They would often look for the chance to head back out to where they hoped to again feel comfortable, giving them a solid reason for the damage they had done to their lives and their bodies.

Gerry had been interviewed in private after the group briefing, and had been quietly offered a pay-rate higher than the Mission Supervisor. If things were to get out of hand, Gerry would be able to exercise extended powers. The Mission Supervisor was in command of the team as long as circumstances fell within his expertise. He was trained in organising a scientific research team, was a researcher with numerous degrees and flawless scientific method, and could pilot and navigate a hyper-speed craft, along with others. Gerry had been given a copy of his resume to memorise. It held an impressive list of successful missions he'd headed, and he was obviously a very capable man, but those in the offices back on Earth had obviously decided to maximise their chance of success. Gerry couldn't help but wonder why they were taking so many precautions on such a straight-forward mission.

Everybody on board thought they would find something rather benign when they reached the moon. Strangely though, the pulses of light were of random spacing and duration. There was no discernible pattern picked up within the three minutes the pulses were recorded by the passing ship. It was unknown anywhere in the mapped universe that a natural celestial object would act randomly in any manner. There were always patterns.

This new phenomenon excited scientists, but they were expecting to find a simple natural mechanism to account for it. It

31

seemed unlikely for an intelligent organism to attempt contacting something outside its solar system without transmitting information at the same time. Why not put some obvious pattern to the signal that showed there was intelligence behind it, and maybe to make your intentions known for sending the signal in the first place?

It seemed most likely to Gerry that the signal had originated from a man-made device, refuse from man's many journeys into distant space. The by-products of man's forays were strewn as far as humans and their machines had travelled. He would put money on the source of the signal being found to come from a discarded disposable module from a hyper-speed research craft, or the wreckage of a lost one. A wayward automated probe was also very likely to be the culprit, he thought. No spacecraft Gerry knew of were fitted with lights powerful enough to emit the signal received by the passing probe, but a malfunctioning main drive could hypothetically radiate visible light, though they had never been observed doing so.

And surely the light, seemingly coming from the beacon, taking thousands of years to get to us, could have actually have been emitted from the doomed craft long before it hit the moon. It could have been emitting light while in the same space they were now in, on its way from Earth to the distant moon, Gerry thought. The possibility that they may be in exactly the same programmed flight-path as a doomed earlier mission made him slightly uncomfortable. Wouldn't everybody know about a failed mission to Clavus 3, if in fact there were one?

Some of the myriad automated tools carried by the research and mining probes were classified as secret, and thereby only a few people knew some of these devices existed. Gerry suspected a component of this type had malfunctioned and was shining what was akin to a giant spotlight into space. The radiation picked up was all in the visible spectrum, which meant that the signal was only moving at the speed of light. It would have been over one hundred and fifty years before the light blasts that originated from Clavus 3 would have reached Earth, and only a little less time for it to reach the outstations nearest to the solar system the signal originated from. Whatever sent the signal couldn't have been in a hurry for a reply. The chances that it had been received by a passing craft so soon after it had left the moon were infinitesimally small.

Gerry opened his eyes slightly to observe an effect that he had always enjoyed. Looking down at his arms, which was difficult when your head was tightly pinned back against the chair, Gerry watched them slowly getting shorter. His legs were doing the same thing. After a few minutes his forearms had disappeared utterly, leaving impossibly stubby hands that stuck out from his elbows. His knees seemed to protrude from his hips. He no longer had a lap.

Chuckling at this, Gerry twisted his head as much as he could to get a look at his companions. The sight was more than he had expected, and he laughed hard and painfully. Darren was a true caricature of himself, his short stocky body distorted wildly. He looked over at Gerry with big bulging eyes and reproached him with great effort. The pressure on their chests made speaking difficult.

'You've got no reason to be laughing, dopey. You're just lucky they don't put mirrors in these things. And I mean Dopey as in one of Snow Whites little men.' He twisted in his seat to look around the cabin at the others, as far as he was able, and pretty soon he was laughing hard too. Darren too had obviously never tired of witnessing this modern-day freak show.

The two females aboard didn't appreciate their humour, Gerry getting an icy warning look from Charmaine. The visual effects of their massive rate of acceleration spared no one, and the girls were not putting up with any gawking while they were looking their worst.

Gerry turned his eyes to face the viewing screen directly in front of them, letting his head again relax in the restraints. It wasn't just out of politeness, looking anywhere but straight ahead was hard on the neck. There was nothing to see on the screen but a few sensor readings, the external cameras picking up nothing but a bright green glow.

Knowing that this would be all they would see while they accelerated, Gerry closed his eyes and tried to relax. He used the time to mentally run through a list of tasks that he'd have to complete before they reached their destination.

He was just thinking he might have a chance of getting time for a short nap to relieve the boredom when a chime sounded that bought him fully alert instantly. He quickly looked over the screen before them. Nothing unusual, there was no change.

Out of the corner of his eye, Gerry saw Darren thumb a switch in the arm of his flight seat, and the uncomfortable weight upon him gradually lifted. He was decreasing their rate of acceleration, and within five minutes, the ship was steadily cruising through space. The hum from the main drive had ceased, and the soft whisper of the air-conditioning was the only sound. A glance at the small panel of data at the bottom of the screen told Gerry they were still moving at almost incomprehensible speeds. The numbers showed they were travelling at around 5500 times the speed of light, and had not deviated at all from the programmed flight path. They had safely reached cruising speed.

Gerry leaned forward in his seat when the restraints built into it released him automatically. He smiled at the crew seated around him as he casually assessed their physical condition. Everyone was conscious and starting to move in their flight seats, waiting for the circulation to return to their arms and legs.

He broke the silence. 'I wish all the ships I've been on had such sweet motors. That wasn't too bad at all.'

'Yeah, it'll make the whole mission more enjoyable knowing we've got an easy ride back.' It was Charmaine, who was also thinking positively. She was a little dishevelled after the flight, but Gerry wasn't the only one who noticed that she still looked damn good. Darren's eyes follow her butt as she stood; sweat had stuck the fabric of her suit tightly to her buttocks. Only half an hour into the mission, Gerry thought, and we're acting like we've never seen a woman before. She certainly was a stunning woman though. She reminded him in some ways of Janet back home. She had the same feminine poise, a sultry elegance to her movements.

'At the speed we're moving we'll have to strap in again for deceleration in about forty-seven hours, is that right?' Her mind was very sharp. Gerry knew this for a fact after reading her personal file. High qualifications in a number of scientific fields, including mathematics and physics, and a huge reputation back on Earth for flawless scientific method had earned her a place on this research team.

Darren glanced at the instruments in front of him. 'Yeah, forty-seven hours and seventeen minutes to be exact.'

34

'Fine, I'm off to check on my equipment. Some of the instruments weren't really designed with that sort of shaking in mind.'

Darren and Gerry glanced at each other, both with the same thought. They both laughed softly to themselves as she walked from the flight deck, wondering if the innuendo she'd produced was intentional. The way she turned to flash them a light-hearted grin told them it had been. A rare beauty who also just happened to be a top-notch scientist. Quite a travelling companion, Gerry thought to himself.

The others rose also. Darren headed for the bathroom, and Jennifer headed in the direction of her private quarters. Gerry was left alone with the Supervisor, and used the chance to ask him a few questions that had been playing on his mind.

'Are we picking up any useful data as we're approaching the moon?'

'Nothing detailed yet, just some general stuff about the solar system. The radiation our sensors are picking up from directly ahead is amplified quite a lot just because we're moving through much more of it per second than we would be if we were stationary on Earth, or flying past like the high-speed survey telescopes do. The images we're receiving should have been intensified the same way. Let's have a look.'

They both turned to the main viewing screen as the Supervisor tapped some keys. An image of a dark, lonely looking planet filled the screen. A tiny sun could be seen in the background, not much brighter from this distance than Venus looked back on Earth. The computer had overlaid colours to signify temperatures, and this planet was a dull grey, as cold and as dead as the vacuum of space it floated in.

'These are the best pictures we've managed to get up till now. The computer's sending them back to Earth as we speak. We're using one of the latest entangled-particle data transceivers. No lag at all, they're getting everything live back on Earth the very millisecond it happens. Of course the picture we're getting now is of how the planet appeared hundreds of years ago, though.'

'There's something comforting about having these new data links,' Gerry added, 'We probably have thousands of people and computers looking out for us back on Earth.'

The planets only visible companion in the darkness was a moon. It too looked dark and lifeless. Clavus 3. Though right now something on its surface would be shining out at them, the light would not be visible for more than one hundred and fifty years at their current position.

'Let's have a look at the more recent images that the mining probe captured for us' the Supervisor said, bringing one of them on-screen.

Gerry and his Supervisor glanced quickly at each other and then back to the screen. The feelings invoked when something unexplained and very unusual was being observed were the same for these men as it had been for humans for millions of years. Gerry could feel the hairs on the back of his neck standing up, and his Supervisor shifted uneasily on his feet in an attempt to shake off the sensation of something cold running down his spine.

The light was visible in this picture. As it passed through the adenine clouds that engulfed the moon it was given a bluish tinge. The piercingly bright beam of light appeared to taper out as it reached clear space, headed in a direction they now knew to be Earth's solar system.

The Supervisor touched a key and a chart appeared. Gerry recognised it as a visual representation of the levels of radiation in all the spectrum's. He then zoomed in on the part of the chart that signified levels of visible light, which they looked at closely for a few seconds.

'I don't know how accurate these readings are, but I think we can be sure the source isn't from an incandescent light. It's not any type of light bulb, but we wouldn't really expect it to be. There's not much energy on that little moon other than tidal and chemical energy, and there are ways that this could be converted into light energy naturally. The idea that we're seeing light jetted by explosions of gases from under the liquid surface is looking likely. The force of the undersea explosions would jet upwards from the surface, clearing a tunnel for the flammable gases and the flashes of light we're seeing to travel through. That might explain the random nature of the pulses too.'

Gerry nodded, grateful his Supervisor was willing to keep him informed, though not quite convinced there were enough facts to support his deductions. He did not have any extra concrete information to give so he kept his scepticism to himself. Gerry knew more than he was letting on, but not enough to jump to any conclusions. Before leaving Earth, he had been quietly advised that there was very likely to be some human involvement.

'We'll soon know anyway, I had a look at some of the sensing equipment we're carrying. It's the ducks guts, must be worth billions.'

The Supervisor smiled, 'Yeah, the company might know something we don't. They sure invested a heap of money in this trip, so I'm sure they must think they have some way of making it pay.'

Gerry thought he should get busy, and told his Supervisor as much, 'I better get on the computer and do a check on the ship. It's almost certainly already been done for me back on Earth, considering the instantaneous data transfer, but I'll have a look anyway just to be sure, unless you have something else you need me to do.'

'No, you know what you're doing. Have a close look at the data link though; we've got to be sure not to lose contact with Earth.'

'No problem.' Gerry turned and walked down the hallway, on his way to his new workstation, which would also be his accommodation. He hadn't seen it before, but when he lifted the latch and slid the door open he knew what to expect. It was just as he'd imagined it'd be after he looked over the craft's plans, similar to most of the rooms he'd stayed in on other jobs. Form suited function, not comfort.

Seating himself at the desk immediately, Gerry flipped up a section of the tabletop to reveal a glowing colour computer screen. He preferred to run the diagnostics manually as he sat and watched as the results of the checks were displayed. He wasn't keen on letting a computer programmer back on Earth decide what information was deemed suitable to bring to the crews attention, so he checked over everything himself. An event the computer deemed unimportant might very well be very important to those on-board in some situations. Bugs were constantly found in the software they were using, which is why it was updated as often as twice a week. Gerry didn't want to discover a new one at an inopportune time, so he was very thorough. The new entangled-particle communications system took his full attention for a time, as it was in early testing stages, and was obviously prone to previously undetected problems.

He focussed intently on the screen for the next forty minutes, studying the figures that flicked up at him. When satisfied that he had checked on everything that was relevant to the smooth running of the craft, Gerry folded the screen away and spun around on his chair. One look at the dull brown walls that surrounded him made him feel suddenly restless and he rose from his seat. Before he even realised what he was doing he was stepping out in to the hallway, off to see if there was anything interesting happening elsewhere.

He passed Darren's cabin and all was quiet within, so Gerry didn't bother knocking. He'd probably be back at the flight deck or checking the engine room. A few steps further took him to the entrance of Charmaine's room. The thumps and scrapes emanating told Gerry she was moving her laboratory equipment about.

Knocking softly, he called 'Need a hand in there?' The noises ceased, and in a moment, the door slid open.

'Not really, but if you have nothing better to do than interrupt me you might as well do something useful.' She stepped back to let him through.

He was stunned by the amount of scientific equipment she had at her disposal. He knew she had claimed the largest room, but he'd assumed it was just her good looks that had swayed the mission planners. She would be very difficult to say no to, he thought. Now it was obvious why she needed the extra space.

There were machines in here he had never laid eyes on before, the nature of their uses eluding him. There were usually clues to a device's application, but not here. He took a few minutes to walk about and have a closer look. After completing a lap of the laboratory, Gerry counted five devices for which he could ascertain no obvious function.

'Some amazing stuff you have here. You're certainly keeping up with new technology.'

She was leaning against the wall watching him, a perplexed smile on her face, obviously surprised at the way he had so closely gone over the room. She nodded, 'For sure. Only the best for us.'

He pointed to one of the machines that had confounded him. 'What's that, or aren't I allowed to know?'

'It's part of the probe that we'll be sending down. That part will plug into the camera on board, to filter out any frequencies other than those we select to record, and also gives the data transmission signal a boost so the chances of us receiving quality data is higher.'

'Thanks.' Gerry was grateful, and could tell she enjoyed what she was doing, her enthusiasm showed in her voice and she had suddenly become more animated. She was lovely by anyone's standards, and what he knew of her outstanding professional background made her even more attractive to him. He realised he had been staring at her for a moment, but luckily she hadn't seemed to notice.

'Can you grab those two boxes in the corner and put them up on a bench for me. Pull the parts out of them too. I'll test them now and again after deceleration to see how they stand up. The designers of some of those components paid an arm and a leg to get an idea of what effect hyper-speed has on their inventions. Some substances just don't transport well. And you can imagine what the G's under acceleration do to delicate sensors, and the radiation punches tiny holes through the silicon in some of the older electronic components.' Turning then to the computer screen, she was quickly back to work.

While Gerry did what she had asked, Charmaine busied herself updating her report, though the only new information was a few hazy photographs and radiation frequency scans of the solar system. She didn't want to get behind with it this early in the mission though. If things started happening she didn't want to waste valuable time catching up on what should already have been done in the quiet, uneventful moments.

'Mmm...this is looking more interesting all the time.' Charmaine was talking either to herself, or to Gerry. He didn't know which, so he spoke anyway.

'What's new?'

'It could be nothing, but the frequencies of the light flashes that the mining probe picked up don't quite match what we'd expect after being filtered through the clouds of chemicals we know surround the moon, and most of it's solar system.'

'The boss noticed there was something odd about the flashes picked up by that probe too. What do you think the data might point to?' Gerry wanted to know the line her thoughts were taking.

'I'd only be guessing at the moment. I'd rather wait for a bit more information. It could just mean there are some chemicals we don't know about in the clouds of matter around the moon. We know it's mostly adenine, but there could well be other stuff filtering the signals we've been picking up.'

'Couldn't we ascertain what's in the interstellar clouds by the frequencies of light passing through them?' Gerry was sure this was how gases in distant space had always been analysed, and still were.

'Not in this case. It's too dark down there. The adenine clouds even block most of the radiant heat. And because of that, we're not sure which frequencies are entering the clouds in the first place. Once we get closer and find out what is emitting the light signal it won't be a problem, but as things are now we'd be forming conclusions on too little information.'

'I suppose we'll know soon enough. It would be a bonus to have more of an idea what we were likely to find, and knew exactly which tests were going to be required. I might be going down to the surface, and I don't even know what to wear.'

Gerry was to drop down onto the moon and take samples manually if the data they gathered with automated testing vehicles and on-ship probes gave inadequate information, either because of a malfunction or environmental conditions unsuitable for the test vehicles stipulated a human touch was required. The atmosphere was very thin, and old data showed it composed of mostly nitrogen with traces of oxygen and hydrogen. There was little air-turbulence, even with the massive tidal surges on the surface. The atmosphere was just too thin to allow any significant thermal activity. The liquid surface though would likely be churning with massive waves and whirlpools created by the powerful currents. It was somewhere amidst these violent seas, that mysterious beacon which had brought them here. If Gerry needed to go down there, it would likely be in the submersible two-man shuttle he knew was latched onto the bottom of this craft. If they discovered that there was not any reason to go below the surface there was a possibility he could use a jetpack to get down to the surface, wearing a buoyant suit.

It was very likely though, that the automated probes would do the job just fine on their own. They would be very busy, programmed to collect as much information about the region as possible. They would leave no stone unturned here. Even if the beacon turned out to be nothing of real scientific interest, the entire solar system was important in the minds of many people back on Earth and in the remote colonies. Conditions existed there that were unique to any solar system previously discovered, even as humans had relentlessly scanned the Universe for anything new, or of some resource value.

'I'll leave you to it then. I am feeling a little like the spare prick at an orgy. My job doesn't really begin until we get there, if everything goes smoothly until then that is.'

'OK then.' Charmaine turned back to the computer screen and Gerry thumbed the door switch and exited.

Walking back to his own room, Gerry felt relieved that the others on board were sharing what they knew with him voluntarily. It was not always like this, scientists were sometimes too covert on missions like this. They were often in the pocket of big business back on Earth. Tiny pieces of information could be worth millions to a mining company or to the company that employed the scientists and sponsored the exploration. These were good enough reasons for new discoveries to be kept under wraps if possible, people strongly representing their employers needs over those of their companion crew. There were obvious safety reasons for a free flow of any new data or information. The computers in every cabin could be used to access all data available to any of the crew. There were no private files kept here.

Feeling tired enough to sleep, Gerry set his computer to wake him if there were any changes to the craft's engine performance or life support systems, and on lying down fell into a deep, dreamless slumber.

FOUR

'...I think somebody somewhere is tolling a bell...'
Meatloaf – Bat Out Of Hell

Six hours had passed by the time Gerry arose. He flicked through a few screens of information on his computer terminal, finding everything to be running smoothly, with nothing important in the Event Log.

Yawning as he stood, Gerry went through a half-hour exercise routine, something he did every day without fail. The gravity on board this ship was the same as that on Earth so it was not so vital to exercise here, unlike his last voyage, which had been carried out in almost zero gravity for five months. He was physically wasted after that trip, but he had kept his bone density up near normal, which necessitated exercise with electromagnetic bands around his arms and legs that simulated weight. Arm-wrestling an invisible, electronically controlled force could be a good way to reduce some of the pent-up stress as well.

He did it regardless, only self-discipline left over from his last violent mission keeping him motivated. He now felt that he needed to keep fit. His job description stipulated so, but he did it for personal reasons.

He would not even be here if he weren't in top physical and mental form. It was vital he be ready for any circumstance where his skills were required. The other members of the crew had been trained for emergencies to a certain extent, but none matched his ability when a big problem arose. Only on the larger craft with higher numbers of crew was there usually a safety concern. There would always be a small percentage of people who suddenly found their mission too much for them. Stress could make a person dangerous in these environments. Physical violence towards another was a minor incident compared to the problems that came from mistreated equipment or fiddling with the ships vital systems. Whether the ship's Maintenance Engineer or Assistant Supervisor, it was expected that they protect the vessel's integrity at all cost. Gerry knew that it paid to be ready, to expect

42

to be forced at any moment into a situation that was more than a match, mentally and physically, for him.

Completing the exercises he left his room, going to the cockpit, which was only fifteen paces from his room. It was this lack of space aboard that was so detrimental to a space farer's physical fitness. Gerry felt much better after the exertion, fully alert.

The Supervisor, Jennifer and Darren were peering into a panel of small screens when he strode into the flight control room.

'Hi there, hope I haven't missed anything.'

'Just checking out some of our new data. We're picking up a bit more as we get nearer.' It was Jennifer who spoke. The other two turned to him and nodded a greeting, turning quickly back to the screens. Charmaine wasn't here, probably still back in her cabin working or getting a little sleep.

Gerry went to his seat and swung a small keyboard up from underneath his right armrest. The main viewing screen was off, so he switched it on with a quick tap of a finger. The green glow was all to be seen, the normal visual effects of light at these speeds. He flicked it over to another screen, which showed a simulated view of the planet they were approaching. The details on the huge grey lump of rock were much clearer now. Gerry could make out a surface covered in craters.

Another click on the keyboard changed the view again. This time Gerry was looking at the third moon, it too a clear, high-resolution image. The others had looked up from the smaller instrument screens now. Their faces were lit with the glow of a piercing spot of white light on the moon's surface.

Gerry zoomed in, the computer amplifying the image size by ten times. The detail wasn't too bad, even at such a high magnification. The seas that covered the moon would be very dark in reality, Gerry knew. There was not enough light from the distant sun to cast even the faintest glow on the surface. On the screen before him though, the image had been coloured to signify the temperatures, the seas displayed in a soft orange hue. Gerry knew this to be around a healthy ten degrees Celsius.

The Supervisor spoke. 'The reason the images are so high quality is thanks to the starlight and heat from the tidal movement on the moon. We're picking up that tiny bit of radiation from the moons surface. From our perspective, headed toward the moon as quickly as we are, we're collecting a lot of it. That's what it looked like over a hundred years ago. The light from the beacon hasn't got anywhere near this far yet. We won't see it until we're about ten light-years from it. It would be like a moonlit night for hundreds of kilometres around the light source when it comes on. The beam of light never strikes the moon's surface directly, but the reflection from the clouds of adenine in the solar system would cast a little light back.'

It was Darren's turn to speak. 'There's not much light down there. Only starlight. We've amplified that tiny bit of light thousands of times to get a topographical image of the surface.'

'Nicely done.' Gerry was impressed with the result. The image was very old though, and he knew the moon would look much the same today, but what really interested him was that which he couldn't see here. On the moon today there was a huge torch amidst a churning sea, shining out into space, an interstellar lighthouse. Lighthouses were warnings of danger though, Gerry thought to himself, but everyone involved in this mission felt it to be more alike a beckoning. Whether natural or unnatural, at this stage of the journey it captivated them, each crew-member thinking only of what lay ahead, in awe of that which they didn't yet know. Even if the beacon turned out to be the result of a natural phenomenon on the moon's surface, they were conscious that they would soon be temporary residents of a very different kind of solar system than any one of them had ever visited.

Everyone went to work at their keyboards, updating their reports with their new observations and data. Gerry ensured the data link with Earth was working error-free, even having a brief chat with one of the mission organisers. Using entangled particles, manufactured back on Earth, the crew could communicate instantaneously with anyone on the planet. Change the state of the one of the entangled particle here on the ship, and the particle it is tied to back on Earth will change its state as well. Once it had been discovered how to make them, manufacturing a screen and some circuitry out of the particles was relatively easy. Now, what showed on one screen would show on the other, and when a signal went through a wire here, it would also go through its twin wire on Earth, proven to work at distances as far as man had ever been from Earth.

Personal calls were rarely placed though, as there were many procedures that needed to be followed before the call could be made. It would be closely monitored and analysed. The process was so involved because there was some concern that the data gained at huge expense by investors may be fed to a rival back on Earth, either encoded in the speech or hidden in the transmitted signals. A few sentences holding locations and available resources could be worth trillions of dollars.

He had just finished his conversation and severed the link when Gerry felt a faint brush of something soft against his arm. And suddenly it was as though cold air swirled violently about his left hand. He looked directly at the hand, but the source of the sensation wasn't visible.

'Hey everyone, any of you notice anything unusual?' He tapped a few keys on the keyboard with his right hand without looking, quickly setting the computer to carry out a status check of the ship.

'Nothing, what is it?' Darren said, his hand too going quickly to a keypad, using it to bring the big viewing screen back to the ship's main system's screen. He was watching Gerry as he did this, noticing with sudden apprehension the way he was holding his arm out in front of him and looking hard at it.

'I can feel something wrapping around my arm. I hope it's only a side effect of the medication we're on, or some of my damaged nerves playing up, but I've never felt anything like this before,' Gerry said loud enough for everyone to hear.

The Supervisor rose quickly from his seat and stepped over to where Gerry was sitting. He placed his hand near Gerry's arm and grimaced as he said 'You're not imagining anything, there's definitely something there.'

'Not just an effect of the speed or any electromagnetic fields we're passing through?'

'Unlikely for the effect to be so localised.' He ran his hands further around the arm, a few centimetres above the skin. In fact, this was as close as he could get to touching Gerry's arm, the unseen force feeling cold and soft under his hands, squirming and writhing. He tried to force his fingers into the invisible substance, but it didn't yield altogether, only allowing a small amount of give. 'It feels like jelly, something semi-solid.'

'The computer shows everything to be as it should. There's been nothing unusual in the sensor readings inside or outside the ship.' Darren was clicking through many screens of data very quickly, and found no clue to what may be causing the phenomenon.

Gerry attempted to slip his fingers under the clinging substance, a fruitless attempt to peel it away. It was very tightly wrapped around his arm now. It had a powerful grip, and he wasn't blind to what a danger this thing could be. If it had encircled his neck instead, the situation would have been dire indeed.

And, as suddenly as it had appeared, it was gone. There was the odour of electrical energy left over, like the smell of lightning when it struck close by. For an instant it reminded Gerry of the violent storms he'd been amidst back home in Northern Australia where he'd grown up.

'Whatever it is, it's stopped now' Gerry advised them.

The Supervisor was quick to organise a response to the strange event. A scientific action plan, which heartened Gerry, made him feel grateful he was aboard a research vessel rather than military one.

'We'll need to scan the ship thoroughly. If, whatever that was, is still here we want to know where it is and also if it does anything to the ship that could put us in danger. I don't want any more effects like that going on unnoticed on board. Hopefully that's the last we'll see of it though. I'll get the multi-frequency camera from the storage room, you lot work on something that might be able to contain it if it happens again. And let Charmaine know what happened.' The Supervisor walked quickly from the cabin as the others turned to their keyboards.

'I'll scan outside the ship in case we can find a cause for it out there.' Darren was quickly on the job, 'I'm thinking an external source of radiation of some type could have caused the effect. Some sort of field the ship could have passed through might have something to do with it. I can't believe it would be anything more than a temporary effect.'

Gerry would normally be inclined to think the same, as some unusual phenomena were observed regularly on these long, high-speed flights. But he'd felt the thing against his flesh. There had been a semi-solid feel to the invisible entity, slick and powerful though viscous.

Suddenly everybody jumped up from his or her respective seats. There was a loud series of cracking sounds just after the Supervisor had turned down the corridor and out of sight. A cry of pain and the sickening crack of breaking bones, sounds that Gerry recognised with a start. Before he rounded the corner, he knew the Supervisor had been mortally wounded. He knew the sound of a man dying painfully and violently.

He was still standing in the corridor by the storeroom door when Gerry reached him. But the top half of his body had been twisted backwards so that his head touched the floor near his heels. He had been snapped in half, folded like a piece of cloth in the middle. The pool of blood grew rapidly, running freely from his mouth and nose as Gerry quickly assessed the scene. He was startled when the Supervisor turned his head toward him. He saw his eyes open, even trying to blink away the blood that covered his upturned face. With a moan, he began to topple over sideways, and Gerry caught him, lowering him gently to the floor on his side.

He heard the others step up behind him, Jennifer moaning softly at the ghastly scene and Darren cursing under his breath. The noise had attracted Charmaine's attention too, and she stepped out of her cabin, greeted by a sight that stopped her in her tracks.

There was nothing anyone could do for him. The small group looked down at the injured man with feelings of hopelessness overwhelming them.

'I'll get him a painkiller.' Jennifer stepped past them, over the twisted body of her Supervisor, and ran up the corridor toward the supply room where the medical kits were kept, leaving a trail of bloody footsteps. She was running back toward them within a few seconds, a vial of Biomorph and a syringe clutched in her hand. However, she did not make it in time for it to be of any use.

The Supervisor made a hoarse gurgling sound, which Gerry was sure would have been a scream if his lungs where intact. And then he died, the blood, which had been spraying from his torn abdomen slowing instantly to a trickle.

For a moment there was silence as everyone took a moment to take stock of the strange and unexpected event. Darren and Charmaine had not yet bloodied their feet, and were backing away from the slowly growing pool of it in an attempt to keep it that way.

'They should know about this back on Earth, right now.' Gerry slipped instantly into the role of Mission Supervisor. 'Darren, go give Control a run-down on what's been happening. They may want us to cancel the mission.'

'I should bloody well think so. How the hell can we function properly after what's happened, even if we do get to the planetary system alive?' Darren said this as he turned away from the grizzly scene, his short legs carrying him at surprising speed back to the flight control room.

'Did anyone see anything that might help explain this?' Gerry was sure no one had, but had to ask anyway.

Charmaine, who was in her room at the time, shook her head. 'Nothing.'

Jennifer hadn't seemed to hear his question, and was looking up and down the corridor they were in. 'It must still be here. Whatever did this must be on the ship with us. There's no way anything could get on or off this ship while we're at hyper-speed.'

'Maybe something found its way on board in a previous mission. They're discovering hundreds of new alien species every day. Maybe the thing in here is one that other researchers have had contact with, without them knowing it,' Charmaine added. 'It sounds like a vintage Hollywood movie but it's a possibility.'

'The maintenance crews are very thorough. I doubt anything could get past all those scans they carry out unnoticed. Even if it is invisible, it must have some mass, and the ship's computers would have recorded the inconsistency. We'd have used billions more megawatts of energy just carrying an extra apple on board over this distance. It couldn't go unnoticed.'

'You agree with Darren then, that it's an effect of something outside?' Jennifer sounded hopeful, though Gerry wasn't sure that it was any less likely to be a danger to them if it was.

'Yeah, there can't have been anything on the ship during acceleration, or it would have been recorded by the computer and we would have been advised. And as you said, nothing could get on or off while we're moving so quickly, even if it could get through the three foot thick hull. We may have passed through a stream of particles or some sort of electrical field.'

'But if a stream of unknown particles was solid enough to tear him apart like that, surely there would be some damage to the ship. But the computer stayed quiet, not sensing anything out of the ordinary.' Charmaine was quick with the logic, and Gerry had no answer. The forces he had felt moving over his arm sure didn't feel anything like what you'd expect from a burst of radiation passing through the ship.

'We should clean up here and get back to the flight deck, Darren may have found something, and I don't want anyone to be on their own.'

It took them longer than expected to get the Supervisor's body back to his cabin. The blood ended up everywhere, and they didn't carry much cleaning equipment, which made the job harder. But, half an hour later the hallway was clean, though the smell of blood hung in the air. Charmaine had a tiny vial of scent she'd bought with her, though god knows why, and she used it all in an attempt to cover the odour. The two smells just mixed together, the blood and the perfume combining to create a stench that made all of them feel faintly nauseous. It filled the ship, but Gerry wasn't too concerned. They'd be accustomed to the smell before long and wouldn't notice it.

It reminded him of some horrible events in his arduous life, but he kept his mind on the job at hand. He had rolled the Supervisor's body onto a stretcher and Jennifer helped him carry it to his sleeping quarters. There was some dignity given to the Supervisor's rent body now, lying on his bed covered in a sheet from head to toe, his frightened eyes now hidden from view.

Afterwards they assembled on the flight deck, hoping Darren had found some explanation for what had happened. He did not have one yet, though he had almost finished a full scan of the space nearly a light-years radius around the ship.

'Nothing unusual,' was all he said to them before turning back to the main screen, tapping furiously at his keyboard.

The others just sat and watched the computer's scan results progressively fill the big screen in front of them, and they'd still seen nothing noteworthy when the scan was complete.

Darren finally filled them in. 'Nothing out of the ordinary out there. The scanners can't tell us much about what's ahead

49

because the ship gets there almost as quickly as our search signals do, but we know a lot about the space we've just passed through, and it's empty. Not even a cloud of dust within half a light year of our trajectory so far.'

'Just as it should be on our flight path.' Gerry felt he should have been happy with the result, as it narrowed their search down to on-board the craft, but he had been hoping for some sort of clue to what had happened.

'We should set up some of our imaging equipment so we get a look at what we're dealing with if something happens again.' On saying this Jennifer turned and was already walking through the exit when Gerry decided he'd have to go give her some assistance. Darren was in communication with Earth and Charmaine was furiously typing an incident report on the keyboard attached to her chair.

'Wait, I'll give you a hand.'

As if only now remembering the danger they were in, she stopped and waited for him to catch up before turning into the main corridor. 'Yeah, thanks. These ships can be pretty creepy at the best of times, and after what we've seen, I'd be a whole lot more comfortable with someone watching my back.'

'I'm still hoping they were isolated instances. It may never happen again.' Gerry was ever the optimist. 'I've been on a few long flights like this, and saw some very strange things happen on-board. There was never any obvious danger to us though. Everyone assumed that they were hallucinating, which seems a likely possibility considering we are ripping though space at thousands of times the speed of light. Talk about people being out of their element.'

He continued, 'But I've never heard of a hallucination snapping someone in half before this. If I hadn't felt that damn thing wrapped around my arm I'd have assumed some sort of shock wave passed through the ship which killed him. Unusual that nothing else was damaged too. We get some pretty freaky quantum-effects at sustained hyper-speed.'

'Yeah, I've learned enough about sub-quantum physics to know there's always unpredictable and sometimes very unlikely things happening. What we've just experienced could simply be one of those events in the 'shit happens' category.'

Gerry smiled. 'True, I just hope it happens elsewhere next time.'

They picked up a large camera each and lugged them to the flight deck, where they set them up to cover the room. They would record everything in front of their lenses, including visible light, light in all known invisible spectrum's, even radiation as it streamed through the ship. The screen at the top of each camera displayed an image of the flight deck, overlaid with colours and lines, which were the invisible forces and particles in the room.

Gerry took the time to study each image minutely. On being certain there was nothing in the cabin with them that didn't belong, he left them alone to record the scene. Darren had just severed their voice link with Earth, so Gerry asked what their stance was.

'They want us to continue with the mission. There is no evidence that we are still in danger, so the mission goes as planned. You have command now Sir.' Darren was watching Gerry's face closely for a reaction as he spoke, but he gladly noted that he didn't even blink in surprise or seem at all concerned by the news.

'Did they know anything we don't, concerning what happened here?'

'Sorry Gerry, nothing else to add. We're to assume it was a freak accident that won't be repeated.'

'Easy for them to say back on Earth, but they're right. Altering our flight path now would be risky in itself, and we'd just have to fly the same route back again anyway. I don't know about you lot, but I'm not keen on travelling through the area of space where the accident happened so soon.'

Charmaine spoke up, trying to sound confident as she said 'Well, let's get back to work.'

FIVE

'And the last thing I saw was my heart, still beating,
Breaking out of my body and flying away…'
Meatloaf – Bat Out Of Hell

They went back to their usual tasks, readying the ship and all it's survey equipment, for they'd soon be orbiting the planet that lay ahead, alongside it's mysterious moon. The mission was now panning out as they had hoped, everything going smoothly.

As the solar system grew nearer the crew's apprehension was subsiding. Only seventeen hours from their destination and nothing unusual had happened. Besides, they were too busy to pay serious attention to any niggling fears.

Gerry had the unenviable job of carrying out an autopsy on their deceased Supervisor. He wanted to check the corpse thoroughly for marks or any left over material that could have been left upon him when he was killed.

He found no visible evidence of trauma to any area of body other than the obvious wounds around his torso where his skin had been torn and spine broken. On looking at these wounds carefully, Gerry discounted the scenario where an object struck the Supervisor. There was no sign of impact at high speed from behind, in fact any external injuries at all visible on his back. His spine was very deformed, the break very obvious, and on peeling back the skin to examine the muscle underneath he discovered something interesting. There were many tears in the tissue, and to Gerry it seemed as though it had happened by overexertion. On testing the lactic acid levels, he was certain. The Supervisor had tensed his muscles so hard he had broken his own back. But what had made him do it? Gerry could only think a massive electric shock being a possible cause, though damage this extreme seemed unlikely without burns being evident. Though there was that smell of electrical arcing at the time, Gerry remembered.

The front of his body was a mess. Pressure had forced organs through the torn skin on his abdomen as his body had been twisted backward, though yet again there was no evidence of

52

external force being applied. From sight, it looked as though a very strong person had stuck a foot in the middle of his back and forced his neck and shoulders back and down at the same time, though leaving no mark of the foot on his back or hands on his shoulders. He had literally been broken in half.

There were only two possible conclusions Gerry could reach, and with little confidence. The first was that a wave of stream of high-speed particles had struck his body. It was not unknown for particles to stray into the hyper-speed lane and to tear through a ship, but the damage to the ship's hull was always obvious and catastrophic. There was nothing damaged here other than the Supervisor's body. In addition, their ship like all of the hyper-speed craft travelled a path mapped to avoid a collision with matter. However, just as Jennifer had said, when people were travelling in the mode they currently were it wasn't rare that the unusual happened. The effects of momentum, friction and vibration were very different when travelling faster than light.

Another similar theory was that any one of the billions of streams of radiation and fields that the ship was passing through every second had made itself felt. Just like the effect of cooking the insides of an object first in a old microwave oven or in the newer exciter ovens, a wave travelling through the ship could conceivably have been the cause of this accident, imparting some of it's energy inside the unfortunate Supervisor and nowhere else. Again though, Gerry thought it unlikely, and expected other damage to be in evidence if this were so.

He could not believe the death of the Supervisor to be an unrelated incident to the sensation he had experienced of something wrapped around his arm. They had to be effects of the same phenomenon. Maybe what he had felt had only been his nerves stimulated by a stream of radiation that went undetected by the ship's sensors. Unlikely, and it hadn't felt like it, he mused. There was a very solid feel to it when he had tried to prise it off with his other hand.

There was actually a third possibility, but Gerry did not bother considering it. Charmaine was out of their site at the time, so she had the opportunity to kill the Supervisor. However, there were no known means of a person killing another in this manner aboard the vessel.

When satisfied he had been thorough, Gerry covered the body and returned to the flight deck with no real answers to offer the crew. An unfortunate side effect of hyper-speed journeys. That was as much as he could offer them.

'Sorry I can't give you anything else. I know it's all pretty irregular, but I think you'll all agree, where likely to be out of the danger zone now. There must have been something in the space we've passed through, possibly some form of radiation that isn't gentle on organic matter. Chances are it's the last we'll come across anything like it again in our entire long and successful careers.' He was trying to keep them positive so they could concentrate on their work, as any mission Supervisor would have, but he truly believed what he'd told them.

Jennifer apparently wasn't so easily convinced. 'I would like to examine the body myself if you don't mind.'

'Of course. My autopsy notes are on file in the event log if they would be of any use as well.' Gerry expected the others to be curious from a scientific standpoint, an unexplained death bringing out the Sherlock Holmes in any inquiring mind, doubly so for a scientist. But he wondered if Jennifer's desire to make here own conclusions showed distrust for him. He knew he seemed a shadowy figure to the crew, so wasn't really surprised that they wanted a second opinion. Someone with his past expected a little hesitance in people to believe that what you saw was what you got. In fact, there were many reasons he might want to withhold information from them, even if it was only for their own good.

'Thanks,' she continued, 'I hope you won't be offended. It's not that I think you've missed anything, but I just want to be thorough as possible where our lives are concerned. I'm afraid I didn't find any foreign material of note in the sample I took from the skin on your arm to give us any leads.'

'No problem, I'll appreciate the second opinion. I could have missed something anyway. It is my first day on the job you know.'

Jennifer smiled and turned to go, 'Hey, what's wrong with that? I'm on my first day too. We got straight into the thick of it, didn't we?'

Gerry checked the cameras again. The small screens showed the flight deck to be as it should. There were no tell-tale signs, none of the colourful representations of unwelcome energies amongst them.

Darren came to stand by his side as he peered into the screen. 'All clear so far, Sir. I've been watching them closely. I've set them to sound an alert if they detect any radiation, fields or particles in here that shouldn't be, and thankfully they've been quiet.'

'Good move Darren. How long before we have to strap in for deceleration?'

'Only twelve hours to go. Time to get real busy soon. The trips I do for scientists always seem to be more difficult than the military flights.'

'It's the opposite for me, but yeah, I know what you mean. We haven't even started earning our wages yet. Almost time to do what we've been paid for. It couldn't get any freakier a trip than it already has, it'll surely be back to normal now.'

'I think we're out of danger now too, but I'm going to feel pretty edgy on the return trip, passing through that part of our universe again.' Darren was smiling, and Gerry could see he was genuinely relaxed.

There were not many people more at ease in dangerous situations than experienced long distance space farer's, and Darren was one of them. They were always in danger. Every minute of their working lives, and they became accustomed to it. Humans could never be very safe in space in their flimsy present form. There were steps under-way back on Earth to remedy this with a little genetic manipulation, but it would surely take years before we were truly able to withstand the rigours of high-speed space travel. There was only so much a thick hull and warped gravitational fields could do to protect the interstellar traveller at present.

'Any news from Earth that'd interest me?' Gerry asked him.

'They might be sending another vessel out in a few days to do a proper survey of the part of space where we ran into trouble. They don't know much about the area. Other than that, nothing they wanted to tell us. I could get back to them for you if you like.'

'No, forget it Darren.'

Gerry knew he should be contacting mission control personally, but it could be tedious getting any worthwhile information from them. Everything had to be censored first. It was just too risky sending important information concerning their mission, even though the entangled particle communication terminals were a relatively secure way of transmitting data. Everything transmitted from Earth needed to be filtered on a 'need to know' basis. Even daily trivia in the papers back home would sometimes be withheld from them. News items that were deemed to possibly negatively affect the functioning or mental well-being of the crew were considered a risk and kept from them. They didn't want anyone on the crew discovering an earthquake or the like had flattened their hometown. Their minds should be on the job.

'I wouldn't have minded knowing if we beat Japan in the cricket, but it's so unlikely that I'll assume we didn't anyway' Gerry said.

Darren grimaced. 'Yeah. If they had their older, unaltered genes Australia would still be number one in the world. Mucking about with their people's genes like that might catch up with them one day.'

'Maybe. Then again, we could have made a mistake in being left behind. There's something very natural about striving to be the best you can be, looking for enlightenment on a physical as well as on a mental level. They've been trying to do that for thousands of years if you look at most of the Asian cultures. They're just using scientific methods to work towards their goal of perfection.' Gerry didn't bother mentioning the obvious fact that all those on board had their genes manipulated by the chemicals they ingested regularly. Visibly, they were the typical Earth person as they'd been for thousands of years, but a closer examination of their bodies would reveal dozens of ways that they were subtly different. It went with the job. They wouldn't, and couldn't, be here otherwise.

'True, and if it means getting back the cricket world cup, I reckon bring on the gene-splicers. And they could do something about my height while they're at it. My arse is way too close to the ground.'

Gerry laughed aloud at this and the sound instantly had the effect of lightened the mood of those within earshot. 'Get some sleep sometime soon Charmaine. You need to be ready and rested for deceleration in twelve hours. That goes for you too Darren.'

Jennifer would be on her own with the corpse, which could be unsettling for some people, and he still didn't like any of the crew being out of sight of the others too often, so Gerry left the flight deck and walked to the cabin where she was working.

'Very strange, wouldn't you say?' Gerry said on entering.

'I've just started. Looks almost like an explosive shell went off in his guts.' She didn't turn around when she said this, remaining hunched over the bloody bed where the Supervisor lay.

'Yeah, though without shredding his organs. I'm sure it was the pressure from the inside that made the internal organs burst through the skin on is stomach. You can see where the tear started at his navel.'

'You're right, the skin on his stomach wasn't cut open, it burst' she replied with a grimace.

'And you'll find when you have a look at his spine that it was bent to the point where it snapped, not hit or severed by something. There must have been a huge amount of force involved to do that kind of damage.'

'It does seem likely that some of the energy that exists outside the ship somehow leaked inside. The forces only millimetres from the skin of the ship, right now have the power to easily tear a star in halve, so the poor old Supervisor didn't stand much of a chance if some of that power somehow got to him.' Jennifer was agreeing with his observations so far, for which Gerry was glad.

'Could you help me turn him over?'

'Sure.' Gerry slipped on a pair of surgical gloves and together they turned the corpse over onto its front.

'My God. Look at that spine.' Jennifer was wide-eyed, tracing a line down his deformed backbone with a finger. Where the break was, the two broken ends of his spine were nearly twenty centimetres apart from each other.

'Seen enough?' Gerry asked.

'Yes, but I want to take a few more samples from his skin and organs. I know you've already done so and come up with nothing, but a few more samples from different areas of his body will raise our chances somewhat of finding a trace of something that might help explain his death. You can leave me to it if you like; I'll be back on the flight deck in a few minutes.'

'OK.' He turned and left the cabin, glad to be putting some distance between him and the stench in the small sleeping quarters. They'd better have some big plastic bags on board that they could put the body in, or he'd have to be ejected into space through the airlock sooner than Gerry had expected. They could open the airlock doors while at the velocity they were currently moving and jettison the body from the ship, but there was too much blood and gore. One drop leaking from the body-bag could spell disaster if it stayed in the hyper-speed lane and struck a vessel. They'd have to wait until they were at their destination. In only a matter of hours they'd be slowly orbiting the unnamed planet alongside its largest and most interesting moon, Clavus 3. Maybe the mission controllers would let them name the planet after their dead Supervisor. Gerry had to think hard for a moment, trying to recall his name. He'd only ever addressed him as 'Sir' or 'Supervisor'. After a moment Gerry remembered that it was Eric, which wouldn't be the most fitting name for a planet, but he liked it.

Smiling at this, Gerry walked back to the flight deck. Charmaine and Darren were peering into the small screens attached to their chairs, probably catching up on the procedures they'd been instructed to follow when they were at the survey site. There would be hundreds of tests to be carried out, all to be done within three days.

He let them work, and checked on the camera's that covered the room they were in. They obviously hadn't detected anything; otherwise their alarms would have alerted them. Gerry used the myriad controls to have a look at the settings. He flicked through the tiny on-screen menus till he found what he was looking for. He was presented with a list of the frequencies of radiation the camera was set to detect. Not all of the frequencies had a check next to them in the list, so he used the controls to turn them all on. No wonder they were turned off, they must have annoyed the last person to use it. To monitor the new frequencies Gerry had selected in the list the camera came to life. A soft beam of red light began to play over the room, and the thing made clicks and beeps.

This was obviously a more active way of monitoring that was needed to detect some particles or frequencies, but Gerry wasn't sure the others could work with the noise it made. Both

Charmaine and Darren had stopped what they were doing and were looking at him.

'Do you think we really need it doing the full scan?' Charmaine asked.

'Probably not, but no harm in letting it run for a few minutes just to be sure.'

She rose from her chair. 'If you don't mind, I'm going to finish off this in my cabin.'

As she turned to leave the room the camera that Gerry had adjusted began to make a louder, more earnest beeping sound.

'Hey, it's picked up something!' Darren was quickly by Gerry's side and they peered into the little screen. Charmaine had decided against leaving, and walked over to join them.

'What do you see?'

'Flashes of green. I think that colour signifies electromagnetic radiation,' Gerry answered.

'Yeah it does, but why would we be getting electromagnetic fields passing through here? Some equipment malfunctioning and building an electrical field in here?' Charmaine was straight onto the most likely cause.

'Could be' Gerry agreed. 'It's a very high voltage that would be needed to produce a field large enough to span the room. Darren, get Jennifer back in here right away, this could have something to do with the earlier event that killed the Supervisor.'

Darren rushed back to his flight seat and thumbed a switch, telling Jennifer she was needed on the flight deck. They heard Jennifer's voice crackling as she answered the call. 'Be right there.'

'If it's strong enough to affect the communicator signals, it's strong enough to cause problems with other devices on the ship,' Gerry told them.

He picked up the large noisy camera. 'If I walk this around the ship we should be able to pinpoint the source if it's on-board. It should show up like a bright image on this.'

Jennifer entered then, looking slightly perplexed. 'What's up?'

'I'll let the others fill you in. Everyone stays together in here, and keep your eyes open. Get that other camera scanning fully too. I'm going to see if I can find the source of the field. Maybe someone's just left an instrument on in the storeroom, or something electrical turned itself on by timer.'

Gerry walked slowly from the flight deck and into the narrow corridor. He was watching the screen closely as he walked, and noticed how large the electrical field was. Something electrical had to be arcing and emitting a very strong field.

Either that, or dare he think it, a breach in the hull. They'd almost certainly be dead by now if there were one though. Cracks in these crafts skin widened very quickly at faster-than-light speeds, and they would in all likelihood be a small cloud of interstellar dust within the blink of an eye if it were so.

Gerry noted the flux lines, normally invisible, but shining out at him in bright green from the camera's screen. They were concentrated toward one of the sleeping quarters. He opened the door to Jennifer's room and pointed the camera inside. The source wasn't in here, but he could tell he was getting closer. Shutting the door, he walked on to the next one. The Supervisor's room.

He knew before he looked inside the room that he'd found what he was looking for. Gerry felt his adrenaline surge when he heard a sound from within. Everyone was back on the flight deck. But now he'd heard something moving in the cabin. Gerry looked down at the camera's screen as he thumbed the door lock, watching for anything unusual as the door silently slid open.

Sure enough, he'd found the source of the electric field. But there wasn't any comfort held in the discovery for him. The electrical energy was coming from the Supervisor's body.

And the body was moving.

Knowing it was likely that whatever killed the Supervisor was still having an effect on his body Gerry had fought an urge to leave the room. He was not enjoying the sensation of the hairs on the back of his neck standing up, though he was sure it was just an effect of the electrical fields that pulsed through the room.

The crew would be no safer if he just locked the door to this room and went back to them. There was a chance the voltages induced by the field could damage vital components on the vessel. He had to try put a stop to it, quickly if possible.

When Gerry pulled the sheet from the corpse it twitched and writhed, as if having a seizure. He couldn't help but move a step back. Even for someone with a background such as Gerry's, someone who had encountered many strange events while hopping about the universe for a living, this was quit unusual.

The Supervisor's wounds were smouldering. Not slowly either. As Gerry watched, the flesh around the wound to his stomach was squeezing together again as tiny blue flames flickered briefly into life. There were tendrils of smoke rising from the places that the flesh was being seared together.

The stench of burning flesh was suddenly very strong in the room, mingling with the other smells of human remains. Gerry quickly stepped to a wall panel and switched off the gas detectors in the room so the noisy alarms wouldn't be set off in the cockpit. There was no reason to bring the crew to full alert just yet. He still wasn't sure they were in immediate danger.

It took only ten more seconds for the stomach wound to be sealed completely. The wound was in no way healed though, only seared together it seemed. The body twitched violently a few times and the wound opened again, more damaged and hideous than it ever was. Tendrils of stinking black smoke snaked upward from the gash. Then everything was still.

The camera display showed that the electric fields had dissipated completely. Gerry gladly noted that the camera had recorded the whole event, so he'd be able to relay the footage to the mission organisers on Earth for their opinion.

The crew wouldn't benefit from seeing it, Gerry decided. He'd quietly transmit it to Earth. Placing the heavy camera on the floor, he picked up the bloody sheet and re-covered the corpse. On leaving the room he reset the password on the door lock, ensuring no one could enter after him. If the crew discovered that the phenomenon was still making itself known they'd be nervous. Gerry was sure his shipmates had the presence of mind to accept unusual events such as this as a scientific curiosity and willingly put their lives on the line to learn more, but they would function better if they could concentrate on the job at hand. They were here to find the source of the beacon, not studying the strange effects of high-speed space travel, which could be done in a more organised manner on a later mission dedicated to observe just that. His priority at the moment was to him to keep the crew safe, but there was nothing himself or the others could do to control this enigma as yet.

He checked every room with the camera, and found nothing. All sign of it seemed to be gone. Maybe there was simply a residue in the Supervisor's wounds, something left over from the event that took his life. A chemical reaction of some type releasing so much electrical energy? Gerry knew this was unlikely, but every explanation for the strange events over the last 24 hours seemed just as improbable.

There was also the possibility that Jennifer had tampered with the body somehow. Hiding evidence maybe? He'd keep this in mind, but Gerry thought this doubtful. Every possibility had to be considered though.

Returning to the flight deck, Gerry gave the crew the all clear, but warned them to stay alert nevertheless. He felt like he was betraying them by keeping what he'd seen to himself, but his guilt would lessen somewhat after he'd sent the footage to Earth. Dozens, probably hundreds of people would analyse the images he had captured. They might be able to give them some idea finally of what had happened to the Supervisor.

'I've sealed up the Supervisors cabin for now, there's a bit of an odour, and of course a danger of disease, so I'd like everyone to stay out of there until we decide what to do with the body. We can't do much about it until we've decelerated anyway.'

They accepted this casually, for which he was grateful. After setting the camera back in position to cover the room along with the other on the opposite side of the room. At least if anything happened in here they should know of it within a few hundredths of a second. He was hopeful the early warning would be of some advantage to them, though the most effective means Gerry could think of that might keep them safe was to immediately use the camera's to pinpoint the source of the disturbance and then keep some distance from it.

The unusual effects had each time been localised, confined to various places on the craft. Not the sort of thing you would expect if the shell were damaged, allowing external forces into the ship, Gerry thought. Surely then the fields the ship passed through would be detectable in constant places, where the actual breach had occurred.

He sat in his flight seat and used the computer terminal there to check on the conditions in the Supervisors' room. Sensors in the room showed conditions in there to be close to normal, just tiny traces of smoke as would be expected after what had happened to the body. Gerry lowered the temperature in the room as far as possible in an attempt to stall the body's decomposition. There was more reason than ever now to keep the body with them for their return to Earth. He was sure the mission controllers would be saying the same once they learned of the new events. The experiences the Supervisor had been through before and after death needed to be studied more closely, in case there was a likelihood of it happening to somebody else, or they had stumbled inadvertently upon something previously undiscovered.

He typed the report quickly and sent it along with the footage he had taken, yet again very conscious of the fact that he was sending more information to earth than he was relaying to his crew. They were more equipped and had more time to make educated decisions from back home though, he reminded himself.

Thousands of scientists and other interested parties would be watching them closely now, and their collective knowledge, creativity and sheer computing power could be of a huge advantage to them all. Intelligence relayed to him from thousands of light years away had been indispensable on many a mission, in fact vital for his survival more than once.

He would never grow to fully rely on others to make his decisions for him, though he knew it was the way most people operated these days. Gone were the days of 'being your own man'. Community was everything, and Gerry knew it was the only way we could be so successful as a species, running rampant over the universe just as we had done with our home planet, and he didn't think very highly of it on a personal level. Even the huge collective human intelligence seemed to favour an aggressive expansion. The capitalist ideal was so ingrained in Western society on Earth it now seemed unnatural to even consider that there might be a better goal for a person to spend their lifetime chasing than the almighty dollar.

To Gerry's way of thinking we had become a truly dangerous pestilence, though most called it progress. Many had the same thoughts as Gerry throughout human history, but when we had left the home planet in huge numbers and impacted so many solar systems in a negative way, it was more than just an idle concern for many people. We had ensured our long-term survival as a species by 'spreading our spore' and exponentially increasing the power of our technology, but at what cost to the universe? Moreover, at what cost to ourselves?

A Mission Controller soon acknowledged receipt of the message, along with a promise he would hear back from them before deceleration via an encoded signal hidden within another innocuous message they would send. There was no way he could be sent a private message directly, all incoming transmissions being available to every crew-member. However, using a small bit of software, secretly stored in the ship computer's memory, he could filter out his message from another at his leisure without raising suspicion from the crew. Subversive actions like these were very much frowned upon, and actually, against the law, though his employers would never let minor legal technicalities jeopardise a mission's success.

A glance at the clock told Gerry they would be strapping in for deceleration in less than eight hours.

'OK, everyone get as much rest as you can before deceleration, it'll be your last chance for a while. Try to stay in this room. We'll even be sleeping in here for the time being. We haven't enough camera's to monitor any more rooms, and I still don't want us separated.'

With that, Gerry leaned back in the uncomfortable seat, and to the envy of the others in the cabin, fell asleep very easily. Within minutes he was softly snoring, appearing as relaxed as a person could be.

Jennifer and Darren did the same in time, though only after tossing and turning in their seats trying in vain to get comfortable. Charmaine continued working, seemingly inexhaustible.

SIX

'I stand tall with the unseen powers,
So why should I be scared of you?'
David Bromberg – Demon In Disguise

Upon waking, Gerry looked over the log of the cabin environment in which the Supervisor lay. He found nothing out of the ordinary picked up by the sensors while he'd slept. He noted that there were only two hours remaining until deceleration. The others still slept behind him, slumped in their seats.

Even Charmaine had succumbed to the inevitable, so he took the opportunity to check for messages. There was one non-urgent message that'd arrived twenty-five minutes ago. Gerry scanned it for an encoded message, and found none. It was as they had expected, the mission organisers back on earth wanted the body kept for them, and the mission was to continue as planned.

Gerry was disappointed, and a little worried, to find nothing new in the transmission that explained what had been happening on board. The most they could offer was that after analysis of the pictures he'd captured with the camera they were sure that the anomaly was electrical in origin. There had been thousands of volts surging through the Supervisors' body, along with a very high current, which would explain the burning Gerry had seen. The sources of the electrical energy, and where it flowed after ripping through the Supervisor's body, were still mysteries. The footage they had analysed back on Earth showed the power had been most concentrated around the wounds. The mission organisers had obviously been thorough, remotely checking the ships electrical systems for any power losses or surges and finding none.

To Gerry, the threat to himself and his crew seemed to loom suddenly larger. If it perplexed the scientist's back on Earth, they'd have real problems finding effective methods of defending themselves against it if a similar situation arose again.

The main screen was off, so he switched it on and went to the magnified view of the Clavus 3. The beacon seemed to be shining directly toward them. They were close enough now to have a very high-resolution scan of the surface, and some of the interior of the moon. There was enough amplified light reflecting from the surface for Gerry to make out an endless watery green expanse. He was surprised to see small flickers of light in the ocean around the beacon. It was possibly only interference with the sensors, but Gerry made a mental note to get Charmaine to have a closer look at the little green sparks of light. He would have her check the direction the main blast of light from the moon was aimed too, he decided. It really did look as if it shone directly toward them. Gerry was sure the light was too bright to be just the reflection from the cloud matter and surface of the moon now.

The screen went black suddenly, so Gerry checked the computer to see if the moon's natural rotation had shifted the main light source out of sight to the other side of the moon.

It had not. The beacon should still be visible from the ship. It must have switched off again. The flecks of green light were more obvious now, standing out starkly against the darker surrounds. They did not look anything like interference on the sensors now.

The viewing screen automatically brightened to compensate for the low light levels, and Gerry directed the computer to zoom in closer to the surface. It was a beautiful sight. Green flames shot through the endless oceans, wriggling and darting like luminescent tadpoles, hundreds of metres in length. It reminded him of the more remote areas of coastline in the Northern Territory back on Earth, where the fish would be visible under the surface on a dark night, the phosphorescence of the tiny creatures they swam amongst covering them in a green halo when they were disturbed.

There seemed to be no clear source or purpose for these undersea flames. Gerry watched them, transfixed by what he was witnessing. They appeared spontaneously and in random locations, some disappearing in less than a second without moving, while others would streak off and circle about crazily in an awesome display of power. Most likely chemical reactions, Gerry would be sure to have another look at Charmaine's data from the spectrum scan to see what chemicals may be available in the oceans to set off such a reaction.

A chime sounded, and a note flashed up on the bottom of the screen advising Gerry that a message from Earth had been received. He heard Darren shift in his chair, obviously awakened by the sound. Gerry tapped the keyboard, bringing the message into view on the screen.

'ANOMALIES FOUND IN CRAFT COORDINATE AND/OR VELOCITY DATA. TESTS HAVE BEEN RUN ON YOUR SENSORS AND COMPUTER SYSTEMS AND FOUND FAULTLESS. THE POSITIONAL DIFFERENCE OF THE SHIPS EXPECTED COORDINATES AND ACTUAL COORDINATES IS MINOR. CONTINUE AS PER PREVIOUS INSTRUCTION. YOUR COMPUTER SYSTEMS HAVE BEEN UPDATED TO ALLOW FOR YOUR CURRENT POSITION.'

'We're not where we are supposed to be?' Darren was wide-awake, staring intently into the small screen in his chair by his side, fingers rapping at the keyboard.

'We've overshot our expected position by a few hundred thousand kilometres. Not much in the bigger scheme of things, but it's unheard of for these navigation systems to be at all inaccurate. These ship computers can direct the craft on trips thousands of light years and always pull up within millimetres of the target destination. This is pretty fucking freaky.'

Gerry was thinking aloud. 'The cause must be external. I could understand falling short of the target, maybe due to a collision with matter or forces of some kind, but where could the extra energy come from that could accelerate the ship?'

'Why would you be so sure it's not a problem with the variable mass engine?' It was Charmaine who spoke, also studying her screen. Jennifer was awake too, rubbing the sleep from her eyes and yawning at the same time as she flicked up her own computer terminal.

'That almost certainly would have been detected. There's enough data coming from the engine to monitor it very closely. If the computers had picked up any change at all in its power output we would have been alerted. The timing of the position anomaly meant we were all asleep when we accelerated. It would have been so slight though that we could not have felt the push even if we

67

were awake. The synthetic gravitational field would have compensated for almost all of the extra acceleration forces. The computer would have detected the increase in g-forces, but the change may have been slight enough to be processed as just normal activity on board. We can be sure it wasn't designed to detect and adjust its flight-plan in the unforeseen and unlikely event that energy from somewhere was to accelerate the ship.'

Gerry looked quickly down at his screen. 'It definitely looks as though environmental systems blindly compensated for it, if we can believe the event log. Our gravitational field adjusted automatically a couple of hours ago to keep natural gravity, and went back to their original settings twenty-five minutes ago.'

Darren had confidence in the ship. 'Yeah, something out there gave us a push. If enough extra power came from the engine to give us a two hundred thousand kilometre shove, it would be glaringly obvious to the sensors attached to it. The alarms would have woken us immediately. The thing was humming along nicely.'

Gerry nodded. 'I agree. Darren, keep an eye on our speed, using the stars to check for error if you have to. I'm sure there's an old bit of star navigation software on the computer. Do you know if we're back to our planned speed for sure now?'

'Yeah, they're doing most of the navigation work for us back on Earth. I've got screens full of data. They're being very thorough. Everything is as it should be again.'

Jennifer found a message of interest in her urgent mail. It was from a friend at a university on Kamma, a planet even further from them now than Earth was. He had been looking over the ships up-to-date data feed at their Internet site. She relayed what she had read to the others.

'A friend of mine has pointed out something rather obvious, but interesting. The extra energy we gained could only have come from the direction we are headed. There's nothing natural known in the universe fast enough to catch us from behind and impart enough energy to give us that kind of push. It was more of a pull from something in front.'

'Maybe whatever is operating that beacon is getting impatient.' Darren was smiling as he said it, belying the serious nature of his statement.

'I saw something peculiar on the moon just before the message from Earth came in. Bring it up on-screen again.' Gerry hoped one of them would know what was happening down there when they had seen the latest images of the moon, but was disappointed. They were rewarded with the extra-terrestrial light show as soon as the image appeared before them, though no one could give a firm explanation of what they were seeing.

Scanning the distant sea for the next hour, surmising and exploring the possibilities while watching the light-display, they nevertheless learned nothing substantial from their observations. Everyone agreed that there had to be some sort of chemical reaction happening, but data showed the seas didn't hold any substances likely to account for the flashes of light.

Everybody sat bolt upright in their flight seats all of a sudden. Something was happening. Those that weren't already buckled in quickly clicked their harness's on. It was as if a wave of static electricity passed through them all. It quickly increased to a powerful buzzing over their skin. Gerry was watching the computer screen as Darren flicked through pages of sensor readings, looking for signs of any effect in the ships systems. The cameras in the room started beeping noisily, obviously picking up something noteworthy. Though there were thousands of other sensors both inside and outside the ship, none of them were picking up anything.

He looked over the crew, all of who seemed fine. Their hair standing on end was the only visual clue to the energies passing through their bodies, though it was apparent in their expressions that they were a little concerned about the turn of events.

They had things under control, so Gerry decided to have a look at the cameras. Even the one nearest him was out of reach, so he had to undo his harness to climb from his seat to get it. The buzzing through his body was so strong that he found he could barely stand upright. His legs shook violently, as though he was having an epileptic fit. He grabbed the camera and quickly sat back down before he fell.

His heart beat harder when he looked into the camera's viewer. The cabin was awash with swirling energies. Two colours stood out most of all. A bright green signifying extremely high frequency electromagnetic energy, probably what he'd seen affecting the Supervisors' body, and an aqua colour he understood to signify multiple radiation types. Using the camera's controls, he attempted to discern which frequencies of radiation the forces in the ship around them were emitting. He was annoyed to discover that the individual radiation types couldn't be distinguished.

Looking upward, away from the camera screen, Gerry noted that the phenomenon was now also creating visual effects. The cabin ceiling writhed and shimmered slightly, as if seen through a heat haze.

'There's no indication of dangerous radiation in here,' he called to the crew, 'though there's some sort of low-level mixed radiation types. The camera can't seem to separate them to determine what they are.'

They nodded to show they had heard him, but obviously weren't overly reassured. It wasn't the most comfortable of working environments, but they scanned the information they had available to them unerringly, looking for anything that might point them to the cause of the energies unleashed in the ship. They're hand's shook over their keyboards, making it almost impossible to type, so they each slipped their wrists under the restraints that were built into the arms of their flight-seats. Though placed to enable the crew to continue working at their keyboards during hard acceleration, they worked to control their muscle spasms too.

A message was received from Earth advising them that they were aware of their problems, and were on full alert looking for solutions. They were to continue, beginning deceleration only at the prearranged time.

There was nothing saying for sure that deceleration would stop the effects they were experiencing at the moment, Gerry thought to himself. If there was some fault with the ship it could actually make things far worst. He approved of their decision, though didn't like the idea of having to make his crew endure this stress for so long. He looked back into the viewing screen of the camera in his lap. As the colours swirled toward him in the camera's screen he felt the bands of light as they brushed against his skin.

There was an occasional pinching sensation as well now, Gerry noted with concern. And while he sat adjusting the camera's filters it progressed to a rather violent squeezing of their skin in places. His exposed face and forearms copped the worst of it, and the frequency of the painful twinges seemed to be becoming more regular. The little yelps of surprised pain from the others told him that they were getting the same treatment.

'Everyone alright?' he called, without looking over at them, busy trying to get more information from his camera.

'Yes' Charmaine and Jennifer called in unison.

'Yeah boss,' Darren called, stuttering and twitching as he spoke. 'I've paid for massages like this. It's good for the circulation. Most invigorating.'

Gerry called out again, 'Only ninety-five minutes till deceleration, so if this shit doesn't stop till then, the change in our velocity might have some effect.'

'We could move to one of the other rooms and operate the ship from the terminal there.' It was Jennifer.

'You mean this effect isn't the same throughout the ship?' Gerry asked, surprised and somewhat annoyed with himself for not noticing it earlier.

'No, this is the only room where the sensors are going around the bend. I don't know about the room the Supervisor's body is in though, the sensor readings have been blocked by someone.'

Gerry felt a twinge of guilt, but didn't bother explaining himself. He could do that later. 'Everybody stay here, I'll have a look.'

He stood on wobbly legs and somehow made his way out of the cabin. He grimaced as he passed over the spot where the Supervisor had met his violent end, continuing only a few steps more down the hallway and the uncomfortable sensation was suddenly gone. The effect truly was very much localised. He took a step backward and copped a hundred jolts and pinches on his body. He quickly stepped forward again but this time the sensations didn't leave him. He could feel the churning forces on his back; feel the pinching tendrils of invisible force curling their way around him again. It was as if the forces were clutching out at him, sending him into a new frenzy of twitching.

He leapt forward two steps hoping to get out of reach again, but it enveloped him completely again within a second. Clumsily opening a doorway, Gerry found himself entering Darren's room. The twitching of his body didn't cease.

71

It was the same in all of the other sleeping quarters. The camera showed the swirling streaks of light churning through every room. He had a look in the Supervisor's room, finding it alive with energies like the others, and switched the environment sensors back on while he was there. It was no different from the other rooms, other than the overpowering stench of the decomposing body. It would have to go. Gerry would ask for special health considerations from the mission controllers. The invisible forces were truly unavoidable now, encompassing the whole ship. He walked back to the flight deck still twitching.

'The sensors readings from all over the ship went wild when you left, we might as well stay put' Jennifer said.

'Yeah, I know, it felt as though the fields were followed me around the ship. Doubtful though, but that is what it felt like.'

'It looked much the same from here. Sensors went wild the very moment you stepped into each room. It could be attracted to our body mass, sort of sticking around us.'

Gerry had been thinking the same thing. 'Yeah, any electrical fields passing through the ship would likely find a path through our bodies. Far less resistance to it flowing through us, rather than through the empty spaces in the ship.'

Darren looked up from his screen. 'I'm sure the strongest sensations we're feeling aren't electrical. Have a closer look at your skin.'

They did, peering at the skin on their arms as they were pinched and slapped.

'Well I'll be...' Gerry said in surprise. He could see physical, though faint impressions from the invisible forces on his skin as they brushed and sometimes grabbed at it, with painful enthusiasm at times. Whatever was in the ship with them had substance, a palpable mass. Like the substance that had wrapped around his arm earlier, there was a tangible solidity to it.

'There is a very obvious physical effect,' he continued, 'I noticed everyone's clothes and hair rippling, but I assumed that to be an effect of the static electricity in here. It seems though it could be a more solid, physical force that we can feel.'

'It probably had something to do with accelerating our ship earlier. Something that feels as solid as this must affect the total mass of the craft in some way. It could have been what killed the Super' as well,' Darren added.

72

'There was probably an electrical charge involved which made his muscles spasm like they did, but it wasn't likely there'd be enough of a reaction from his body alone to break his spine. Extra force would be needed. And at a guess, I'd say that's what we're seeing on the cameras as the unknown energy' Jennifer said.

'He may have walked into a concentrated pocket of these energies. A good reason to stay put. I don't want anyone moving about the ship unless it's absolutely necessary.' Gerry jumped slightly as he finished, surprised by a spirited slap on the side of his head by something soft but heavy that no one had seen.

Each of the crew turned back to their computer terminals. Darren was busiest of all, readying the ship for deceleration. There wasn't actually much left to be done that couldn't be handled by the computer, but every pilot who took his job seriously would check over everything manually. The computer systems had always been amongst the most unreliable component in interstellar craft, and someone of Darren's calibre wasn't going to be caught out by a glitch.

They endured their freakish environment while they worked. They were buffeted and pinched mercilessly, and even received some scratches that were deep enough to draw blood. Time crawled under the conditions, but finally Darren signalled time to decelerate and reversed the ship so that they were facing back in Earth's direction as they sat in their flight seats. He fired the engines.

They were in luck. Everything went back to normal the very moment the engines fired to begin the lengthy deceleration of the ship. There were smiles all round.

'Out of the frying pan and into the fire' Darren said cheerily, though the g-forces would have made every word painful and difficult to utter.

At least they were slightly more accustomed to the effects of hyper-speed travel than the electric shocks and beating they'd been receiving. The cabin warped around them, one of the normal visual effects of the deceleration process. Now their bodies appeared stretched, knees sticking out two metres in front of the hips.

'Less than half an hour's time we'll be at the exit point of this hyper-speed lane,' Darren informed them, the strain on his body evident in his voice.

Gerry had just relaxed back into his seat and closed his eyes, when a woman's scream jolted him back fully alert. He released his harness and spun around in his seat in one lightning fast, fluid motion. Not many men could have made such a move against the thrust of the ships engines. He'd been trained to move about a vessel under hard acceleration or deceleration, and he'd found it useful on a number of jobs. Being the only person aboard who could freely move about in these conditions could have its advantages.

What he saw couldn't have been more unexpected.

The Supervisor was entering the flight deck. His blackened arms dragged him slowly across the floor, the sticky rubber surface giving his arms purchase even in their slimy state, though his progress was slow. He was firmly pressed against the wall by the g-forces, face-down and not looking where he was going, trail of wet gore smeared behind him.

Charmaine, Darren and Jennifer unbuckled their harnesses when they'd seen what was happening, though not able to rise from their seats, just prepared to if the need arose. It was unlikely they would have been able to do so anyway without injuring themselves. It was the most they could do to simply lift their hands to cover their noses from the rancid stench that the body had bought into the cabin with it.

There was moment of confusion, where everybody looked at each other wondering what he or she was supposed to do to handle this eventuality. Even Gerry was dumbfounded for a few seconds. His first reaction was to move to help his ex-boss, but risking his own life to help someone who was obviously long dead struck him as pointless. When one of the dead arms reached up to a console on the wall and began thumping hard at it, breaking some of the switches, Gerry found a purpose.

'Keep us going as we are Darren. Don't change our rate of deceleration unless we really have too.' With that Gerry swung his legs up and over his head, gripping the arms of the flight seat tightly as he threw himself out of it, weighing close to ten times his normal weight. He swung around to the back of the seat. If he let go where he was he would have crashed into the back of the cabin and probably broken his legs, maybe his back. He would have to use the Supervisor's body as a cushion.

Gerry swung himself left and right a couple of times, which took a lot of strength at these g-forces. When he let go the others were shocked by the amount of force he hit the Supervisor with, smashing the animated corpse away from the control panel like a rag-doll. Red and black liquid spattered the rear of the flight deck. The crash was deafening as Gerry hit the wall, sending a shudder through the ship, such was the force. The ships computer even beeped an alert, sensors detecting the violent collision.

He was getting what felt like a soft electric shock from the body. Only the hands still moved, flapping about uselessly against the wall where the body had been flattened. Kneeling on the solid part of the wall, crouched in the stinking mess, Gerry felt his throat constricting, and had some difficulty controlling the retching.

Extricating himself from the fetid refuse involved phenomenal effort. Many times his normal weight, Gerry found the gore to be incredibly slippery. The Supervisor's body had done it the easy way, falling effortlessly most of the way to the flight deck from his room under the deceleration forces. Gerry wasn't looking forward to seeing the mess out there. But now he had no way to get back to his flight seat against the thrust of the ship. It looked very close to him, as though he could almost reach it if he stretched, but he knew it would be in vain, only a trick of the visual distortion in the room.

Shifting himself away from the stinking refuse, Gerry called to Darren. 'I'll stay here till we've come to a halt. Only twenty minutes so it won't be too much of a problem for me.'

'Sure you don't want me to back off the deceleration rate a little, or altogether to give you time to get back to your seat? The body's not going anywhere now.'

'No, just watch out for new messages. They'd know what's happened back on Earth, and if they wanted us to change plans they'll tell us. It'll throw the rest of the mission timing out if we did, and that means big money losses for them, so I'm sure they'd want us to continue as planned. To tell you the truth, I'm in a bit of a hurry to get this mission over with too. You might want to get final authorisation to eject these remains when we've arrived too.' Gerry placed a hand between his head and the wall to stop his skull from pressing painfully into the hard surface and closed

75

his eyes to wait out the deceleration period while he pondered what had happened.

Jennifer was the most shaken of the crew after the incident. Her trembling was made more obvious by the visual effects of the ship's deceleration, and her horrified countenance was amplified by the stretching of her facial features. She had been the first to see the Supervisor crawl in and for a moment she'd thought he was coming toward her. He'd been a close acquaintance when alive, and it wasn't easy seeing him in his current state.

Charmaine had her own way of dealing with the stressful situation. Eyes closed, ignoring the tortuous pressures on her organs, she visualised steps involved in the mission ahead. She mentally mapped out the coming days, where they would be carrying out some very interesting research. There had been too many things going wrong lately that were out of her control, and she wasn't going to let anything that she could have an influence on go bad. With all the silly events on the flight here, things could surely only get better, she thought.

Darren was working through screens of data that would advise him of even the most minor problems with the ship. The Supervisor didn't appear to have damaged the control panel in any way or altered any important settings. He typed out a quick text message, asking them to verify that they had received video of the incident with the Supervisors body, and also requested permission to send the corpse out of an airlock as soon as they were able.

Seconds later he received the reply. Darren was fully expecting to have his request approved to dump the body, but it had been refused. They were now going to have to keep their long-dead crew-mate with them for the remainder of the mission. They had analysed the video footage back on Earth and decided keeping it was more important than ever now. The message said there was little reason to assume the body was any danger to them, as long as it was properly restrained under acceleration and deceleration to stop it falling about the ship. They'd decided that their employee needed a more thorough autopsy back on Earth.

Darren realised they were implying that they should ignore the fact that the body had moved under it's own power. He knew better. There was no way the body could have moved from the cabin to the flight deck under the effect of g-forces alone. The body would have simply rolled against the wall in his cabin when

76

they began deceleration, which was cushioned by the same mattress he would have been laying on. The beds were designed this way so that injured passengers could stay where they were when the ship altered its speed, simply rolling up the side of the curved bed when the gravitational centre of the ship moved.

Even now Darren could see the Supervisors black swollen fingers moving slightly, hear them thump softly against the wall panel. They should be pinned immobile to the wall under these g-forces, but they were moving under their own considerable power, as if exploring the surface they lay on. Whatever it was that impelled them had been having an effect on the ship for most of the journey now. There was nothing in evidence that made Darren think things would be getting back to normal any time soon. The effects on board were caused by something in the solar system they were about to enter, he was sure.

They were the lead story in news bulletins all over the universe he'd been informed. Billions were waiting on the outcome of this mission now. They must be expecting some more excitement as well, he though wryly.

In the time he had remaining until arrival, Darren checked some of the data they had received concerning the beacon. A mathematician back on Earth had calculated that the beacon was aimed at their ship, or more specifically, at the Earth behind it. Something seemed to know where their planet was in space. It must have been aimed in their direction over ten years ago.

'One minute to the hyper-speed lane exit point,' he called finally, 'And whether by chance or design, the beacon's aimed right at us.'

SEVEN

'I'm not alone because the TV's on...'
Jimmy Eat World – Bleed American

They exited the hyper-speed corridor and taxied relatively slowly the remaining distance to the moon. They cleaned up the fluids, spread over the ship by the Supervisors' body, while waiting to arrive. The smell was overpowering throughout the ship. Thankfully someone found an airtight body bag amongst the medical supplies in which they stowed the decomposing body, which was still twitching when it was zipped up inside. Gerry and Darren exchanged a look of concern after they had placed the body inside. They'd both felt the muscles in their arms twitching as they'd touched the corpse, and felt the pinpricks as tiny sparks of what looked and felt like static electricity jumped to their hands.

'We'll strap the body down this time, so it's ready for acceleration when we leave. I hope that our poor old Supervisor will be able to sleep in peace, and so will we. Whatever has contaminated Eric and making his body react like it is might be dangerous to all of us, so we need to get everything as close to sterile as we can.'

They quickly cleaned up the gore that was spread the length of the ship, so they could get back to their research. They had arrived, and they could finally do what they had come to do.

They assembled back at the flight deck afterwards, everyone showered and feeling quite well despite their circumstances. Gerry motioned for Darren to click on the viewing screen, and immediately they had the most incredibly detailed view of the moon before them. This would likely be on billions of screens all over the universe right now, if deemed suitable to release to the public. Humanity on the brink of yet another discovery, another special part of the universe we could call our own.

The beacon was still pointing right at the Earth; though it was due to pass around to the opposite side of the moon from them in an hour due to the natural motion of the moon in relation to them. They would be orbiting the dead planet alongside the large moon, only fifty kilometres from its surface.

They could see the glowing green trails of fire under the alien sea, flashing through the oceans at many hundreds of kilometres per hour, and amongst them floated the powerful beacon, piercingly bright in the inky, green-tinged darkness.

'The light source must have been moving to keep the light trained toward the Earth, actively compensating for the moons rotation.' Gerry wasn't surprised by this fact now. Enough had happened on board recently to give him the impression than an external force had some sort of semi-intelligent motive behind its actions. Something on the moon having an effect on their vessel from light years away seemed a ridiculous idea, but Gerry felt there was more than just coincidence involved. With the peculiar events on a strange moon, along with the unusual phenomena aboard their ship, Gerry thought it likely they were related.

'Whatever's moving that light around, began doing so years ago, and obviously humans have been in space far longer than that. And it's still moving it now. I wonder if there were any vessels lost out here ten to fifteen year's ago' Darren thought aloud.

'Yeah, though I suppose the chances aren't good that there's still people alive down there' Charmaine added. 'Anyway, even temporary survival down there would be difficult. The stranded ship theory still doesn't look too likely, nor does it help explain everything else unusual that's been happening here.'

'The light from the main source is thousand of times brighter than it looks on the screen,' Jennifer pointed out, 'the filters are working over-time to give us a decent picture. I can't wait to find out what it's using as a power source.'

'Well, let's find out right this minute. The first probe we're sending will circumnavigate the moon a couple of times, giving us a birds-eye-view of the surface.' Gerry was keen to get started, and he knew billions of people back on Earth would be waiting for their next move. He had earlier checked his computer terminal for the latest news on Earth, but found they had little to mention of importance other than this very mission. Their situation had taken over the media; page one all over the universe. The public had not been given the details of the mission, but they knew a mystery was about to be solved.

Not being much of a showman, Gerry would never change the way he operated because he was being observed, and probably judged, by many others. It was a routine part of space travel, people being able to look in on your lives whenever they found reason. No, there were safety reasons for Gerry wanting this mission moving. The longer they were here the more chance something untoward would eventuate, he was sure. There were far too many unexplained events so far on this trip, and he'd want scientists to have a very close look at the ship, the space they had flown through, and the Supervisor's body for some explanation before he would travel this part of space ever again. Maybe they would find the cause themselves soon, down there somewhere.

'Darren, fire the first probe.'

'Yes Sir… Fired.' There was a hollow thumping sound as the probe fired from underneath the ship, flying in a pre-programmed path to the moon's surface, where it levelled out to follow the surface, only metres above the churning sea. There were no waves, but the chemical soup was far from still. They saw whirlpool's kilometres across, bubbles broke all over the surface, and in places there were rivers of darker fluid moving across the top of the sea, somehow separated from the rest and flowing within it's own invisible boundaries, without mixing.

'Mostly tidal and thermal activity we're seeing,' Jennifer said.

'OK, here goes, only a few more seconds and the source of the beacon should be visible.' Gerry, along with billions of people all over the universe, was holding his breath. This is what they'd come for.

The beam of light could be seen on the horizon, stretching up through thin bands of chemical clouds. And in the beam they could see the polished metallic gleam of their own ship. The incredible picture bought to mind of all those on board how far away from home they were. Here they were thousands of light years from their birthplace, bathed in a searing alien light, looking both too small and too vulnerable.

As the probe neared the light source, they could see that it came from beneath the sea, the churning fluid that the camera flew over lightening to a deep green, lit by the underwater light. One of the darting green objects suddenly came into view. It outran the probe, shooting out from beneath it and wriggled its way toward the beacon, leaving a fiery green trail behind it.

80

There was a collective gasp as it suddenly shot upward in front of the probe, clearing the surface and flying in a long curve that must have been hundreds of metres above the surface of the sea. They could see the cause of the underwater light show clearly now, the phosphorescent tail disappearing as the solid entity within broke the surface. Over ten metres long, this thing was more than gas or a chemical reaction of some kind. There was a solid entity at the head of the flaming trail. It resembled a fish, though its skin was smoother and softer looking, more akin to the flesh of a jellyfish than the scales of a fish. The flaming gasses that had enveloped it were quickly shed as it streaked through the vacuum of space. Almost no atmosphere and little gravity should have meant it continued its journey outward, into a long orbit around the moon, but it used some form of locomotion that enabled it to change direction and manoeuvre back toward the ocean. It plummeted through the surface, sending a spray upward for hundreds of metres as it regained its fiery trail, blazing brighter than ever now. Downward it went, headed straight for the source of the beacon that shone so bright from the depths.

Their view could not have been better. The crew stood before their seats now, wide eyes focussed on the viewing screen, entranced by what they were witnessing. The alien creature hit the base of the light source at what looked to them like a very high speed, when there was a flash of bright white light. Jennifer quickly sat down in her flight seat, studying the new data on her computer terminal.

'The main beam of light just got three percent brighter for a moment.'

'It could have mindlessly swum into the light, like a moth to a flame.' Gerry observed.

'Yeah, and it must have died doing so.' Charmaine added, stating the obvious.

Darren had an interesting question. 'Do you think the beam is produced by those creatures alone, a natural phenomenon?'

As he said it two more of the fish-like entities shot into view, them too propelling themselves into the inferno deep under the ocean surface.

'Again, the beam's increased power by another seven percent. They do seem to be playing a part in powering it.' Jennifer

81

pointed out. 'Darren could be right. The beacon might be freak of nature, a natural occurrence.'

The probe passed close to the beacon, and they could see that where it exited the water, the beam of light over twenty metres in diameter was causing steam to billow from the surface of the churning chemical sea.

'Go with probe number two Darren' Gerry ordered. 'We'll have a look at that light source from close up. If the beam is a product of the creatures energy we would expect to find an ignition source, or some type of chemical reactant down there.'

The probe that now shot from the ship would dive into the ocean and gather data from the alien sea floor. The view before them went from the camera in the first probe, which would continue flying over the moon collecting data for them for a few more minutes before plunging into the sea, to the camera in the underwater probe. It descended quickly, the lighting equipment it carried not switching on as it broke the ocean surface. It was not required here, as it powered toward the ocean floor alongside the massive beam of light, which shone far out into space. As it neared the bottom, they could clearly see a perfectly circular hole in the sea floor, from which the light was emanating.

'Use some stronger filters Darren; let's see if we can find out what's producing this light.' The screen suddenly dimmed, and they could make out the rocky sides of the circular trench, going down as far as they could see, the bottom too far down to make out.

'That better?'

'Yeah, thanks Darren' Gerry answered. Just then another one of the fish-like creatures plunged toward the trench, and before they could even blink it had shot down the hole and violently exploded. A shock wave sent the probe backward, but it automatically moved back into position and continued slowly circling the trench, camera trained inward at it. A dark-green cloud was all that was left of the creature, which dispersed quickly in the turbulent seas, the shimmering beam of white light brightening visibly.

On board the research craft, sitting in the middle of the light beam, there was a collective shiver. All onboard felt something wash over their skin, something akin to goose bumps running over their bodies. The computer beeped, a message popping up at the bottom of the screen. The content was just garbled text, so Gerry cleared it by touching a key on the keyboard on the arm of his seat.

'Strange' he muttered, and clicked through a menu on the screen until they were seeing the computer's status screen.

Charmaine noticed the anomaly immediately, as did Gerry. 'The processors running at one hundred percent, but we hardly have the computer doing anything' she said.

Gerry touched another key, bringing up a list of jobs the computer was carrying out. 'There's an unknown process running, and it's keeping our computers real busy. I could stop it, but I'm not sure if it'd be a good idea. Darren, get a message back to base advising them of the situation. We could have a virus affecting the system or a hardware problem that they could diagnose for us.'

'It feels as though there's enough static electricity running through the ship to effect the electronics' Jennifer said. 'The hull is hardy enough to cope with surges from solar flares only kilometres away, but somehow the energy from the beam's getting through.'

'Yeah, have a look at the temperature outside too. That light is dumping a lot of heat on us and a few other types of radiation as well. The hull's not able to stop all of the microwave energy. The sensors are picking up strong readings throughout the ship.'

'Thank god for those little pills we pop every night. I don't think we'd be too healthy right now without them. I can almost feel my DNA coming to bits' Jennifer said only half jokingly.

'We'll know about it immediately if the radiation reaches dangerous levels anyway, the interior sensors are all working fine' Gerry said, reminding the crew and himself that their environment was being monitored minutely and, for the moment at least, they were in no danger.

The computer sounded a tone, signifying a message received. Darren bought it onto screen.

'UNKNOWN COMPUTER PROCESS HALTED BY MISSION CONTROL. CODE ANALYSED AND FOUND UNSTRUCTURED. ELECTRICAL/RADIATION SURGE LIKELY CAUSE. CONTINUE AS PER INSTRUCTION.'

'We'll move out of the light as soon as probe number two's finished it's run. I don't want it producing any more glitches with the computers. Then we'll also find out for sure whether the light can actively follow our position or is simply aimed in Earth's direction and we just happened to be travelling the same path' Gerry said, clearing the message from the screen.

The probe was still circling the undersea trench, but now it's camera looked upward, and they could see the turbulent motions of the chemical laden waters in the brilliant light from below.

'There's a lensing effect created by the atmosphere somehow,' Charmaine said, 'it's refracting the light beam. That's how it's kept trained on us for so long. The rotation of the moon should have pointed the beam of light elsewhere, but it seems it's been pointing our direction for an hour, maybe longer.'

'God knows how anything could regulate the densities of the clouds above the light source to aim a beam of light so precisely and so constantly though,' Jennifer added.

'But it couldn't be just by chance that it's been facing our direction. It must be tracking Earth's location, somehow' Gerry said.

'No sign of human involvement yet though,' Jennifer observed.

The view on the screen changed again as the camera swung downward, focusing on the impossibly bright hole in the sea floor.

Another message from mission control flashed up on the screen.

'PROBE NUMBER 2 ROUTE ALTERED BY MISSION CONTROL. CONTINUE TO MONITOR.'

Gerry smiled when he saw that the probe had began a descent into the trench. 'They've sent it in for a closer look. This should be interesting.'

'Probe number one just dumped into the sea, flight program completed successfully' Darren told them.

The filters on probe number two's cameras were turned up to maximum in an attempt to see through the glare from the trench, and other types of sensors used non-visible forms of radiation to make up a picture of the tunnel it was traversing. The walls seemed naturally formed, rocks sometimes protruding from the edges, no sign of mechanical cutting through the rock, only the signs of slow erosion.

84

'This could be an old lava vent, from a time when the moon was volcanically active...' Jennifer began, but was stopped mid-sentence by what she saw. There was part of a spacecraft protruding from the rock at the end of the tunnel. They recognised the shape of the main drive outlets instantly. An early model hyper-speed craft.

The screen went blank suddenly, and simultaneously they felt what seemed like a wave of static electricity washed over them.

'There goes our probe I think. Darren, what happened?' Gerry said quickly.

'The probe's ceased transmission of any data, including its heartbeat signal. It must be badly damaged, maybe destroyed' Darren said, fingers working furiously over the little keyboard at his side.

'The mass of those creatures was converted to a radiant energy, and our probe seems to have gone the same way,' Gerry observed. 'The main drive must still be switched on. But the radiation is different than what you'd normally get from a hyper-drive. The fact that we're still alive attests to that.'

The air seemed alive, the sensors showing high levels of radiation passing through the ship. However, there was something more, something the crew could not see that would brush against them, bumping them rather firmly as it moved about the room. Everyone on board had a firm sense that they were not the only occupants, though none of them found reason to voice their concerns. They were experiencing something that they were ill prepared for. There would surely be later missions that would be equipped to study the new phenomenon, dedicated to just this task, but for this crew there was a timetable to follow. Gerry was now sure that the moon they were surveying was linked to the strange actions of the Supervisor's body and the palpable forces that now swirled about the flight deck. Down there they might find some of the answers to the strange events on board, he thought.

'Time to move us out of this beam, Darren' he said.

'Firing port side thrusters.' With that, Darren touched the keyboard and they felt a slight push as the ship slipped slowly sideways, out of the light that shone from the moon. The screen before them soon showed the beam stretching up into space beside them, shining like a solid pillar of light as it passed through

85

the chemical clouds that enveloped much of this solar system. When clear, Darren fired the small ion thrusters on the opposite side of the ship, bringing it to a standstill. The strange sensations experienced by the crew could still be felt.

Charmaine noticed something unusual. 'The clouds seem to be moving.'

She was right. As they watched, the wispy chemical cloud was condensing around the ship. It was thickening rapidly.

'It shouldn't be attracted to us for any obvious reason, should it Darren?' Gerry asked, ignoring the sensation that a cold, viscous liquid was running over his scalp and down the back of his neck.

'Not that I know of. Never heard of it happening before. The opposite if anything. Sometimes hyper-speed craft build up a huge electrical potential, but it has the effect of repelling matter near the ship, not attracting it.' He worked at the keyboard for a few seconds. 'The sensors show us to be neutral, that the ship hasn't built up an electrical charge. The clouds have a varying electrical potential though. Much the same as the readings we're getting in here right now.'

'You mean the electrical activity that we can feel in here is related to the activity in the adenine clouds somehow?' Gerry asked.

'Looks like it. Unusual though. We're well insulated from environmental stuff like that' Darren replied.

'Obviously not well enough, if this mission's anything to go by' Gerry said, glancing at the ceiling, which was shimmering ever so slightly.

A message from Earth flashed onto the screen. 'MESSAGE CORRUPT. RETRANSMIT.'

'But we didn't send a message. Tell them Darren.'

Darren typed the message and sent it, and another from Earth immediately popped up on the screen. 'THIRTY-THREE MESSAGES RECEIVED. ONLY ONE LEGIBLE. POSSIBLE SHIP COMPUTER MALFUNCTION. DIAGNOSING. STAND BY.'

'It looks as though our computer's been sending garbled messages to Earth without us knowing of it. There's no other problem with our communication though, thankfully' Darren said.

Everybody suddenly turned to look at each other. They had all heard it. A thruster had fired.

Darren was quick to find out why. 'The ships somehow moved out of position, the computers just putting us back where we should be.'

'Any idea what moved us in the first place?' Gerry inquired.

'Sensors show some irregular vibration through the hull while we've been here. We could have been bumped by something. It doesn't seem too unlikely; I'm getting a little knocked about myself.' Darren's hair was standing on end, and waving softly left and right, an unusual effect of the unseen forces about them. He was rocking backward and forwards a little, something soft and invisible repeatedly slapping against his chest.

There was the sound of thrusters firing on the opposite side of the ship now, bringing it to a standstill.

'At least the light hasn't moved to follow us; it's still pointing straight at Earth. It'll be out of sight, on the other side of the moon in a few minutes.' Jennifer informed them. 'It is definitely actively tracking the Earth. For some reason something is keeping the light trained on our planet. Very strange.'

Gerry felt as though he had someone's knuckles pushing firmly against his forehead now. He could not help himself but to try brushing them away with his hand but, just as he'd expected, it passed through the invisible object and the sensation continued unabated.

'Send probe number three now, Darren. The seafloor looks pretty dead, but this'll be the first time people have analysed it fully.'

'Done' Darren said, as there was a bang from beneath them. He changed the screen's display to the view from their ships external camera, so it was as though they looked out of a window upon the alien scene. They wouldn't even be able to see the moon if not for the light-intensifiers in their cameras, which amplified the tiny amount of starlight that struck it. The tiny ion jet on the probe could be seen glowing white hot as it headed toward the surface. This one was of the high-speed penetration types of probe, which was very small, and fired deep into the target to take underground readings and transmit them back to the ship.

'It'll only take thirty seconds for the probe to reach the moon.' Gerry told them, just as he received what felt like a punch in the stomach. He covered his abdomen with his arms, and they successfully blocked the blows that mindlessly hammered at his midriff. 'This bloody thing's getting a little too enthusiastic at times.'

'Yeah, it's touched me in places I didn't even know I had.' Jennifer said, smiling. They all laughed, glad to be able to alleviate some of the tension. No one sat still in their seats; each kept busy dodging slaps and bumps that they couldn't see coming.

'The mass we have aboard is three percent higher than it should be. And it's slowly increasing,' Darren said.

'Just how much extra weight do we have on board?' Gerry asked.

'One hundred and twenty seven kilograms.'

'The light on the moon's just gone out. It's passing to the other side of the moon now. It might be switched off to save energy when there is no means of it keeping aimed at the Earth. I'm assuming the thermal layers in the seas or the atmosphere are somehow bending the light an amazing amount, as we've seen, but the beam can't be refracted round from the other side of the moon.'

'It looks as though those entities we saw in the sea calm down where the light isn't visible' Gerry observed.

'CANCEL CANCEL NO' appeared on the screen, flashing in a red box that was reserved for urgent alerts from the computer system. This did not look like your average message from the software running on the ship's computer system though, thought Gerry.

'Darren, tell mission control that our computers throwing up spurious system messages now.' Gerry ordered.

Darren's fingers flew at the keypad, and he had just barely finished typing the outgoing message when they received one from Earth.

'COMPUTER SYSTEMS HAVE BEEN ANALYSED AND FOUND FAULTLESS. IGNORE DUBIOUS MESSAGES AND DOUBLE-CHECK SHIP SYSTEMS DATA MANUALLY. EXTERNAL INTERFERENCE WITH SYSTEM SUSPECTED. SOURCE YET TO BE DETERMINED.'

'Something's messing with our ship and they're not even sure what it is back on Earth. Must be a real mystery, if the thousands of egghead's watching this from back home are stumped. I'm glad at least they seem certain that there's nothing wrong with our computers.' Darren sounded as confused as the rest of them felt.

'The probe has reached the moon. It's burying itself now.' Charmaine told them.

Suddenly all hell broke loose. It was as though a massive tentacle thrashed about the flight deck. They were all struck heavily and repeatedly. Everyone except Darren was lucky enough to be able to make it from his or her flight seats and take cover on the floor. He was buckled in and suffered worst than any of them. He was severely pounded by the invisible objects that lashed the room, and Gerry could see that he'd almost lost consciousness already.

Disregarding his own well-being for the few seconds it took to scramble on all fours to where Darren sat, Gerry was knocked over twice and winded before he could get Darren's buckle to release. He just needed to tap a key on the keyboard, but that was easier said than done. His arms were beaten wildly as he reached out, making it difficult to be sure he was hitting the right key. He dare not miss; it wouldn't do to hit the wrong keys on a hyper-speed craft, so he waited till he was sure he had his finger on the correct one before pressing. As soon as he'd done so he heard the restraints click open and he tore aside the harness and dragged Darren, by the front of his flight suit, out of the chair.

'Thanks boss. I'm all right now, just glad to get my head a little closer to the ground, both to stop myself passing out and avoid any more whacks like that in the head. I copped a couple of good ones there,' Darren said jovially, despite a thin line of blood trickling from one of his nostrils.

'Charmaine, Jennifer, you OK?' Gerry called. He couldn't see them from where he was.

'Yeah' they called in unison.

'Don't you think it's time we got out of here?' Charmaine added.

'Mission control should be seeing all of this. They can move the ship for us if they think it'd help. Best we just wait it out, it could be temporary, like the other times.' Gerry called back to her.

'Let's just hope it doesn't damage anything vital.' Darren said. If anything though, it was getting worst, the sound of the insides of the ship being battered was deafening.

'Mission Control… If there's anything you can do from there, now would be a good time.' Gerry called loudly, hoping the microphones were picking up his voice. Company policy stated that mission control could only accept typed entries from the computer terminal as legitimate messages normally, but under these circumstances he hoped they would respond to his suggestion nevertheless.

Suddenly everything was quiet. Each of the crew stood slowly, wary of a fresh onslaught. Whatever the substance was in the ship with them, it was subdued now. Darren checked the on-board mass, finding it to still be above the expected level.

'We've still got the extra weight on board.' he told the others. 'A message has just arrived too.'

'MULTIPLE MESSAGES RECEIVED. SHIPS COMPUTER AFFECTED BY UNKNOWN ENTITY/S. PROCESSORS RUNNING AT 100% DUE TO UNKNOWN INSTRUCTION SETS. ENTITY OF UNKNOWN ORIGIN HAS CONTACTED US. CONTINUE AS PER SCHEDULE.'

'Looks like we've stumbled onto more than one new life-form. If those suicidal fish weren't strange enough, we've got one hundred and twenty kilos of invisible cargo on board, and someone that's decided to check out our computers and send messages behind our back to our bosses.'

'Can we see what the messages were?' Gerry asked.

'Yeah, just a sec,' Darren said, and tapped at is keyboard until a list of old messages came onto the screen before them.

'It's sent about a hundred messages to base from our computer. The later ones are more structured. You could only guess at a meaning for some of the messages.' Gerry said. 'They're mostly combinations of the words PROBE, CANCEL, and TALK with seemingly random words scattered through there. It simply looks like a computer glitch to me, I can't see how they came to the conclusion that they were from an intelligent entity with so much certainty.'

'A lot's been happening on-board, after factoring those events into the equation we could well come to that conclusion. And something is aiming that beam of light at Earth, or at least built it to do so.' Jennifer said. 'There is a vessel down there, and possibly its crew as well.'

A new message popped up onto the list on the screen. 'PROBE DAMAGE PROBE' was the new message sent from their ship.

'How is probe three going?' Gerry asked Darren.

'Probe three has reached its target. Data's being transmitted. Everything is looking fine. We're getting a scan of the moons interior. Want to take a look?'

'Yeah, bring it on-screen.' Gerry answered.

'My god...' Charmaine exclaimed when the image came into view, 'what have we found?'

'I tend to agree with mission control all of a sudden. That can't be naturally formed.' Gerry said. The probe had buried itself in the rock five kilometres below the surface. It was sending various waves of energy through its surroundings, while receivers both inside the probe and also on the ship picked up the stray energy and analysed it to find what it had passed through, and bounced off. The result was a detailed x-ray view of the moon.

It had been hollowed out. Millions of tunnels ran throughout the moons solid core, giving the appearance of veins as fluid moved through them, colour-coded by the computer to signify their composition. The pattern they made as they interlaced the moon was too organised, to the eye seemingly geometrically perfect. The manner in which most of them wound their way toward the source of the light beam, which was off now, gave it an ordered appearance. The tunnels seemed to emanate from the remains of the hyper-speed craft that was down there.

'Do you think that whatever did that to the moon is the same entity that's been messing with us here on the ship?' Darren asked nobody in particular.

Gerry gave his opinion. 'Very likely. The technology required to modify the moon like this, and muck about with the systems of a hyper-speed craft while it's at thousands of times the speed of light is necessarily very high.'

'They've made the alterations that humans have made to the Earth over the last few thousand years seem like child-play. Whatever lives, or lived, here must have been here a very long time' Charmaine observed. 'There are signs of life all through those tunnels too. Look at all those red dots, there must be thousands of them.'

'The fish things we saw in the seas do you think?' Gerry asked her.

'Probably. Their mass is about the same, with some smaller life forms scattered throughout the population, possibly the young, though its possible we could be looking at a few different species. One thing that's become evident after many discoveries of places with alien life is that where there's one species you're sure to find thousands of others nearby. The seas are sure to be full of microscopic life considering the copious amounts of useful chemicals available. We'll soon know for sure, but those fish creatures have to live on something, so we have to assume that they're not the only form of life on this moon.'

A new message from Earth appeared on the screen. 'COMPUTER SYSTEM SECURITY BREACH. CONFIDENTIAL INFORMATION SYSTEMS HAVE BEEN COMPROMISED BY UNKNOWN ENTITY. BREAKING COMMUNICATION LINK. WILL RECONNECT ASAP. CONTINUE AS PER SCHEDULE.'

'They've cut off communication. We're on our own now.' Darren told them.

'It'll probably only be until they can make the system a little more secure. They've just been taken by surprise I think. I bet they weren't expecting an attempt to hack their system from space, using one of their own dated vessels computer terminals' Gerry said.

'It must be important, they're not getting any information at all from us now the data links closed, which must be concerning them.' Jennifer said. 'They won't like the idea of shelling out all that money for a blank screen back home.'

'We're recording everything that's happening here anyway. They can catch up when they get the data link running again,' Gerry added.

'Maybe they've seen enough' Charmaine said cryptically.

'Could you clarify that?' Gerry asked her.

'Why didn't they just sever the link for the downloaded data, and keep uploading information to us' she said.

She was onto something, Gerry thought. 'Yeah. Why couldn't Mission Control keep talking to us without accepting data coming from us, Darren? At least they would have been able to keep us up-to-date on analysis of the new data. Right now they probably know a whole lot more about what we've discovered here than we do.'

'No idea I'm afraid. It doesn't make much sense.'

Another message appeared on the screen. This was a local message, the type you would normally send from your sleeping quarters to the flight deck or vice versa. However, everybody was in the same room. Nobody would have needed to send a message, only speak it.

'NEED COMS. OPEN DATA LINK. RECONNECT. LINK CLOSED FROM CLAVUS 3. NEEDS OPEN.' It read.

Gerry was the first to speak. 'I think the reason we've been ostracised by Earth is trying to talk to us.'

'They must be messaging us from the ship down there. The crew is still alive. Do you think they can hear us?' Darren asked quietly.

Gerry shrugged his shoulders. 'Who knows? The microphones that normally relay our audio back to Earth constantly are still on. We cannot be sure if they are monitoring them, and I agree that it's likely that we've got people down there. That's if the person we're talking to here via our messaging system is actually down on the moon. We can't even be sure of that yet.

'Can you hear us?' Gerry called loudly, ensuring that the microphones would pick up his voice clearly.

Everyone held his or her breath waiting, watching the screen for some response. None came.

'Type a message Darren, sending it to all of the local terminals. Try telling them that our computer security was breached' Gerry instructed.

Darren entered the message and had it sent to all seven of the computer terminals on board the ship.

'Done Sir' he said in a few seconds time.

To their surprise a reply appeared on the screen immediately. 'WE DO NOT UNDERSTAND. WE NEED TO MAKE CONTACT. ARE YOU HERE TO RESCUE US OR ATTACK US?'

'Ask who we're talking to.' Gerry told Darren. He had to know whom he was communicating with. Nothing seemed to make much sense.

Darren tapped quickly at the keys. 'Done.' He said. His message appeared on the screen as soon as he entered it, and underneath a new one appeared.

'SURVIVORS HERE' it said.

'I think we've got a partial explanation there,' Gerry said. 'Ask their location.'

'WHAT IS YOUR LOCATION?' appeared on the screen as Darren did as instructed, and a reply came back instantly.

'ON MOON. CRASH SITE. OUR SHELTER IS OUR VESSEL. THE LIGHT' it said.

'YOUR LOCATION IS WITHIN THE CRASHED VESSEL ON CLAVUS 3?' Darren typed without having to wait for Gerry to ask him to do so.

'YES. MOON. STRANDED SURVIVORS OF RESEARCH MISSION.' The peculiarity of the reply made Gerry hesitate a moment before continuing the conversation. How could anyone possibly survive down there for more than ten years?

'Ask him if it's they who've been affecting our ship.' Gerry said. Darren entered the message and the reply made everyone's heart beat a little faster.

'YES. WE HAVE INFLUENCE ON SHIP. OUTSIDE SHIP TOO. AND AROUND MOON. OUTSIDE MOON' he had written.

'HOW IS THIS POSSIBLE? PLEASE EXPLAIN' Darren asked.

'WE HAVE CHANGED. SURVIVORS NOW. DIFFERENT. SYMBIOSIS BETWEEN OURSELVES AND THIS ENVIRONMENT.'

'BUT YOU ARE IN GOOD HEALTH?' Darren typed next, conscious of the peculiarity of the question. There was a long pause before they received a reply.

'YES. CHANGED HUMAN. ENVIRONMENT ALTERED US. WE ARE PART OF THE RADIATION IN THIS SYSTEM. IT IS THE RADIATION THAT JOINS US ALL HERE. YOU ARE PART OF IT NOW TOO.'

'This is getting hard to believe, though I must admit that it sort of loosely explains a few things,' Gerry said to his crew. 'There's been all sorts of weird electrical and other forces playing havoc with the ship and especially the death of the poor old

94

Supervisor. I wonder if they know the radiation they're talking about may have killed him. Ask how many of them are down there Darren.'

'2 SURVIVORS' was the reply. Darren typed another message quickly, asking how many of them there were altogether on their doomed flight.

'2 SURVIVORS. 1 DEAD. YOU SURELY KNOW THAT.' was the reply he received.

'How long have they been stranded there?' Gerry instructed Darren to enter next, more than a little confused.

'11 YEARS 4 MONTHS. A LIFETIME TO US' came back, not much help in the way of explanation to the frightened crew, but Gerry was expecting as much. One of the Mission Directors had had a quiet word in his ear before departure, advising him to expect some human involvement concerning the beacon.

'YOU HAVE BEEN LIVING AMONGST AT LEAST ONE NATIVE SPECIES ON THE MOON' Darren typed.

'YES. THEY COME TO US. TO OUR LIGHT.'

'There is at least one type of organism they know about down there by the sounds of it. They must be talking about those fish-type entities we saw,' Gerry noted aloud to the crew.

'That would explain their food source, but I wonder where these people lived on the moon though. The underground structures don't hold any trapped air, and they're ship couldn't have kept them alive more that a year or so. And what does he mean they're changed humans?' Charmaine inquired, hoping one of the other sharp minds aboard could clarify things for her.

'He might not be perceiving things properly at the moment. If they really have been stranded there for years you'd have to expect some mental damage. I'd really like to know how it is that he's communicating with us through our local messaging system. We could be way off track too if we try making too many assumptions. Also, it may be that he's not quite saying what he thinks he is; his communication skills may have deteriorated after all this time. We'll have to talk to him a little more before we'll know for sure if he's communicating effectively' Jennifer said.

'Remember the unexplained movement of the chemical cloud around the ship?' Gerry said, 'It's been concentrating around us since we've been here. It could be thousands, even millions of kilometres across. These gas clouds cover most of the planetary

95

system. God knows how they can be shifting about so much in a strong vacuum though.'

Gerry paused for a moment, worked his way through a few menus using the computer keyboard at his side, quickly finding what he was looking for. The small screen attached to his chair displayed details about the messages they were receiving. They weren't coming from any of the terminals on board the ship. They weren't coming from any of the computer-input devices aboard. The computer seemed to be sending them out on its own.

'I can see why they were more than a little concerned about the security risk to their computer systems back on Earth. These people are controlling our local messaging system from within. They've somehow got the software sending messages for them. If they've got that much control over the system, they could conceivably have similar command over any of the ships other components' Gerry said.

'I hope they don't decide they need to send us somewhere. As long as they keep away from the engine controls and the environmental systems I don't really mind them snooping about' Darren added.

'WE ARE READY FOR RESCUE. AWAITING YOUR INSTRUCTIONS. THANK YOU. WE HAVE WAITED TOO LONG' appeared on the screen, a new message from their mysterious contacts.

'These stressed-out people surely couldn't know their actions would be taken as a sign of aggression' Jennifer said. 'They simply taught themselves how to navigate our computer system, and considering they only seem to have limited communication skills remaining, they must have had some difficulty. I'm sure they were just trying to get our attention, and somewhere down there they found some way of doing so.'

'It also pays to know your enemy. Nothing at the moment is pointing to the fact that this new discovery of ours is going to turn on us, but I can see Mission Controls point of view. We can't let anyone access to too much of our information, let alone people like these, who seem to have stumbled across something very strange, and possibly aren't in a stable frame of mind. If I can't see any of our classified info without a concrete reason to do so, I'd be a little annoyed if these people could, and I assume so would many other people' Gerry added.

Charmaine nodded. 'Mmm, whatever the threat may be, this must be creating a real stir back on Earth. Do you think Mission Control knows who these people are?'

'Very likely someone will, but they won't know we've even found anyone until they reconnect our data link.'

Darren switched the view on the large screen before them back to the visual of the moon. There was an unexpected change. The space around themselves and the moon was glowing a deep blood red. Everyone knew the signs; a hyper-speed craft of some type was approaching.

'They're sending another ship' Jennifer said. 'About time, this is surely the most important mission in years, you'd think they'd be sending dozens of people to have a look at what we've found here.'

But before anybody could feel any relief that they were soon to have a helping hand in this hazardous part of space, Gerry set her straight. 'That's not an effect of a run-of-the-mill hyper-speed craft I'm afraid. Have a look at the energy levels out there, whatever is coming our direction is going a hundred times faster than any ship like ours could move.'

'What sort of ship do you think it is then?' Charmaine inquired.

'It's not a ship. It's a missile.'

EIGHT

'... Sick of the treason, sick of your lies, fuck no we won't
listen, we're gonna' open your eye's...'
Pennywise – Fuck Authority

'What!' the crew exclaimed in unison.

'How could you know that already?' Darren added.

'The high strength of its infra-red signature. Look how bright
the infra-red light is showing up on our screens. The only thing
that can move that fast is the newer hyper-speed missile. They've
never been used in anger before, as far as I know' Gerry
explained.

'So, they're going to destroy the moon. If we stay where we
are, we'll be killed too' Jennifer said quietly from her seat behind
them.

'Or we could be the target; they could assume something is on
board our ship. The battering we copped earlier tends to make
me believe that there's still something here with us. I know those
people trapped down there are most likely responsible for playing
with the computers, it doesn't explain the objects we felt knocking
us about in here.' Then Darren added fatalistically, 'They
wouldn't want something like that coming back to Earth with us.'

'Even if one of the smaller warheads is fitted, the energy it
imparts as it hits an object in this planetary system will be enough
to take out us, the moon, and most likely the planet we're orbiting
as well.' Gerry explained. 'Thanks to the extra data and
manpower they've got back on Earth and elsewhere, they know a
lot more about this thing that's been messing with our ship with
than we do at the moment.'

'It's all very routine for them. They can do what the like with
us now, the world knows our communication links have been
severed, so if anything happens to us it'll be a case of nobody
knows anything.' Gerry had involuntarily acquired a keen insight
into the politician's mind during his career.

The United Nations should be in charge of the mission now.
This was far too important to be considered just another

company-run research mission. Gerry knew this mission had important implications for the future, whether positive or negative no one could yet know. Maybe their suddenly aggressive stance was the right one for future benefit to the human race, but he felt it was plainly and obviously *wrong* on any scale of humanity or morals, therefore a fatally flawed action in Gerry's way of thinking.

There were many precedents, Gerry knew, and the underhanded way their countries had, for 100's of years, placed sanctions on their destitute enemies to kill their women and children was an example, as was using assassination to topple democratically elected governments to their own end. Foul forms of terrorism, arrogantly justified by their perpetrators every time.

He knew logically that there were no rules, no set universal definition of what was right or what was wrong. Any intelligent being had to follow its own path, decide what actions would make it happy, would give itself and its family the highest quality of life. For some, following their society's rules would give them what they wanted or needed, for others, life wasn't so simple. Politicians were one such type, whom operated on an ends-justifies-the-means basis. Gerry knew this was what he was contending with.

'They've been very quick in deciding to neutralise the threat. They're either being frighteningly reactionary, or they know something we don't.' Jennifer said quietly, obviously deep in thought.

'I had the misfortune of seeing it first-hand not too long ago. Our government seems to have taken on an aggressive stance when it comes to discoveries of any off-planet threat' Gerry told them.

'Politicians are the one people I'd want to keep away from military power, but in the western world they're the only ones who wield it' Charmaine said, venom in the tone of her voice.

Obviously not willing to get into a philosophical argument, Darren turned to Gerry. 'How long do you think we've got before it gets here? The sensors have been picking up the energy for two minutes.'

'It'd take fifteen to twenty minutes to cover the same distance we did in two days. It's much faster, can accelerate quicker than we did because it's not carrying any people, and of course it doesn't have to waste time decelerating.' Gerry told him. 'We could have as little as seven minutes. And that's assuming it's coming from Earth, though that's pretty much a certainty.'

'Shit.'

'Well, we won't be here when it arrives.' Gerry said.

'But Mission Control said to continue our research, they won't be happy when they find out we're on our way back.' Darren reminded him.

'Try sending them another message. There isn't any chance of them getting it if they've switched off the receivers at their end, but they'll get it as soon as they switch everything back on. I doubt they will though. I think they are past the talking stage. They've perceived a threat, and will want to neutralise it before any complications can arise. They're good at this.'

'What should I tell them?' Darren asked.

'Hyper-speed missile from unknown launch site is on a heading for our location.' Gerry dictated. 'Returning to Earth now. Please respond ASAP.'

'Should we really be heading back to Earth? What makes you think they won't eliminate us on the way back or just wait till we get all the way back and put us under military controlled quarantine? They could get rid of us at their leisure then.' Charmaine said to Gerry, while Darren entered the message.

'I agree, they're sure to put us in quarantine for a while, and there is a good chance that they won't take any risks with this life form we may have on-board and just get rid of us, but as I see it we've no option. We couldn't go to any of the other off-planet settlements, they would just have to report us to base and we'd gain nothing.' Gerry replied.

'Message sent.' Darren said. 'As I see it, they can't blame us for saving our own skin. We're not even sure what the hell they're up to back home. If Mission Control has real concerns about using the data link to contact us, they might have assumed we'd notice that the missile was on its way and head back to Earth as a matter of course without risking setting up the link to advise us.'

Charmaine nodded. 'True. And there is the chance that the communication equipment on board has been effected by our invisible friend, or friends, and Mission Control's been trying to contact us but can't.'

100

'Yeah. OK Darren let's go.' Gerry ordered.

Not another second was wasted. Buckling themselves quickly into their seats, the crew felt the g-forces change as Darren immediately spun the ship around and accelerated using just their ion jets, away from the strange planetary system. It only took 2 minutes to make their way back to the hyper-speed lane, but to the crew it seemed to take forever, the tension growing by the second.

When the ship was is position Gerry gave Darren a nod. 'Fifty percent thrust will be enough.'

'Here goes!' he said, tapping a key on his keyboard to begin the insane surge of power that enabled hyper-speed travel. He was plainly glad to be getting away from this strange place, though every one of the ship's occupants had one thought on their minds. The two survivors of an unknown mission, a mission that somehow went bad long ago. Two people, surviving against all odds, were now certain to meet their end by the hand of their own people. They simply had no time to pull them from the moon. They didn't even know for with any certainty where they were down there.

Just as they were smashed back into their flight seats a message appeared on-screen.

'MISSILE IS TARGETING US' was all it said. And as well as contending with the huge forces of acceleration, their unseen companion was back, churning with a renewed energy through the cabin. It seemed to have no problem overcoming the g-forces as it made itself felt. The crew-members were struck with what felt like huge, fleshy, cold arms.

Jennifer immediately gained a split lip that bled profusely, and Darren received a slap that was heard loudly by the others, who were more than a little concerned about the amount of force that was put into it. He would soon have one very black eye, Gerry thought, watching the side of Darren's face immediately begin to swell.

Another local message appeared on the screen after the last one. It simply said 'DO NOT LEAVE', and abruptly the battering ceased.

'Well, looks like we can be sure whatever it is that's knocking us about in here is connected to the two stranded people on the moon. You alright there Darren?' Gerry asked, speaking with

101

difficulty through lips that were stretched back tightly, and a tongue that was trying to disappear down his throat due to the g-forces.

'Yeah, no worries. Reminds me of back home actually, the last time I copped a whack like that the missus caught me looking at the young blonde next door.' Darren replied heartily.

'Try getting a fix on the position of that missile, Darren.'

'Will do.' he replied, fingers immediately flicking over the keyboard under his hand, which was strapped to the arm of the flight seat to keep it there.

'Found it,' he said shortly, 'it'll be going past us in just over five minutes.'

'There's a chance we'll collide, though small I know. Do we have a fine enough reading of its position to know how close well get?' Gerry asked.

'If these co-ordinates are accurate we'll be four hundred and seventy metres apart when we pass, give or take a hundred metres. Do you think it's enough?' Darren said.

'Unless it's been set to explode in our proximity, it should go straight past us without even registering our presence. I think you'll all agree, the target's almost certainly the moon, while we would have been the unfortunate *collateral damage.*'

Everyone subtly nodded, without speaking.

'STOP MISSILE' appeared in the list of messages, on a corner of the big viewing screen before them. It was another of the messages that came from an unknown source, somehow being generated by the computer, at the whim of the unseen being that seemed to have stayed with the ship throughout their massive turn of acceleration.

'Tell them we have no way of doing that.' Gerry instructed Darren.

'Sent' Darren said, and in the same instant a reply appeared.

'TELL EARTH TO STOP MISSILE'

'Tell our friends we have no possible way of doing that either.' Gerry said next. Darren complied.

'YOU STOP MISSILE' was the message that came back immediately.

'How?' Gerry asked. Darren entered the question and the response wasn't what the crew was looking for.

'STOP MISSILE WITH YOUR SHIP.'

'You mean collide?' Darren entered without being asked, though they already knew the answer.

'YES. SHIP MUST COLLIDE WITH MISSILE.'

'Tell them we don't want to sacrifice our vessel or ourselves. It's out of our hands now.' Gerry told Darren.

'NO' was the simple reply.

'Tell it that whatever entity it is they have on the ship is safe as long as it's on the ship with us.'

'WE ARE ON MOON. NOT SHIP. MUST SAVE MOON. WE DONT HAVE KNOWLEDGE OF ANY OTHER ENTITIES ON YOUR SHIP.'

'They do seem to have some link with something aboard. Are we communicating with them all, or is the thing in here with us just an effect that they've somehow created remotely?' Gerry said to no one in particular. Then as an afterthought, he said to Darren 'Let's see what more they've got to tell us. Ask them to describe the way they're affecting our ship in more detail.'

Darren entered the question and they were rewarded with an instant response.

'AM HUMAN BUT CHANGED. OUR ENVIRONMENT HELPED US LIVE. WE GREW STRONGER. BETTER THAN BEFORE. WE HAVE FOUND NEW WAYS. WE HAVE A LONGER REACH. WE SURVIVED.' It explained.

'That doesn't explain much. They've mentioned their environment a fair number of times. It must have enabled them to survive somehow, rather than hinder them. I can't imagine how. Ask them their names and how they got there,' Gerry instructed.

'I AM TRAVIS HOLMES. DAN GASTON IS HERE TOO. BARRY SCOTT WAS HERE. DIED LONG AGO. SCIENCE EXPEDITION. IT WAS SECRET.' was the answer.

'That might have something to do with the decision to eradicate anything alive in the planetary system. They might have reasons for keeping the mission secret even today. Also, they could have found something in the data they were getting from our probes that frightened them. They surely couldn't destroy a find like this without some very good reasons,' Gerry though aloud.

'Someone hundreds of years ago said that if the only tool you have is a hammer, you will treat everything like a nail,' Darren added. 'He probably had a government like ours in mind when he said that.'

'These research missions really have become just scouting trips for the military haven't they?' Jennifer said.

'Yeah, just the fact that I'm here attests to that.' Gerry said. He was going to continue when the g-forces changed suddenly, so that they were pressed downward into their seats now, as well as hard back.

'What's going on Darren?' he called with difficulty. Everything went back as it should be under hyper-speed acceleration as he finished speaking.

'The ship's moved position. Sure enough, we're now on a perfect collision course with the missile,' Darren explained. 'That was a very risky manoeuvre, we're lucky to still be in one piece after changing position at this speed.'

'Try moving back again Darren, very slowly this time though. You'll need to decelerate for a few minutes before starting the course adjustment.'

'Nothing's happening.' Trying a few more functions on the computer Darren continued, 'A whole lot of the ships control systems aren't responding. We're not piloting this any-more.'

'Darren, ask what some of our other options may be to stop the missile.' Gerry was guessing the occupants of Clavus 3 had something to do with their ship controls playing up.

'THIS IS THE BEST OPTION' was the reply that appeared next on the screen.

'OK Darren, I'll take over our side of the conversation now. They've taken full control of the ship now, so it looks like some hard bargaining is required.' Gerry said, beginning to enter the next message with the keyboard himself. 'Someone see if you can pull any information from the computers about these people.'

Everybody regularly checked the big screen for messages as they worked at their keypads, knowing there was only three minutes until they would collide with the missile at a combined speed many thousands of times faster than the speed of light, if something wasn't done.

Negotiating for your life with a strangely altered human intelligence that you know little about wasn't part of Gerry's expertise, but he felt there was little else they could do to help themselves in this predicament.

'THEY WILL SEND ANOTHER MISSILE IF YOU STOP THIS ONE' Gerry typed.

'PROBABLE. WE HAVE OPTIONS. TIME NEEDED TO PREPARE DEFENSES. MISSILE MUST BE STOPPED NOW. MUST SURVIVE.' came back.

'YOU ARE SCIENTISTS. SURELY THERE MUST BE MORAL REASONS TO TRY ANOTHER WAY.'

'GIVE US OPTIONS. WE WILL CONSIDER ALL.' The reply read.

'YOU HAVE CONTROL OF OUR SHIP. USE THE SAME METHOD TO TAKE CONTROL OF THE MISSILE. ABORT IT YOURSELVES.' Gerry suggested.

'NOT POSSIBLE. WE HAVE LIMITATIONS. THERE ARE ONLY 2 OF US.'

'WHY NOT TALK DIRECTLY TO EARTH?' Gerry entered, 'YOU MAY CONVINCE THEM TO ABORT THE ATTACK.'

'COMMUNICATION LINE CLOSED. WE CANNOT OPEN. EARTH MUST RECONNECT.'

'Darren, keep trying for control of the ship. We need to decelerate now if we want to be able to change course to avoid the collision. These people seem to be top-notch computer hackers. Jennifer, you see if you can find out how they're doing it.'

Two minutes remaining before impact. Gerry tapped on his keys, frantically exploring their options.

'WHAT ABOUT USING ONE OF OUR SPARE RESEARCH PROBES TO COLLIDE WITH THE MISSILE INSTEAD?' was his next idea.

'WE HAVE NO CONTROL OF YOUR PROBES' was the reply, and it gave Gerry a glimmer of hope. He turned, with difficulty under the forces produced by their acceleration, to speak to the others.

'We've still got control of the probes. Could we use the thrust of one of them to move us off this collision course? Sort of give us a shove from one side?'

Charmaine spoke. 'Sorry, not enough time left to programme the probe to carry out those manoeuvres.'

'What about just sending one or more of them out in front of us, on exactly the same trajectory? We might be able to destroy the missile before it gets to us.' Gerry tried next.

'Again, not enough time to programme it.' Charmaine said grimly.

Gerry turned back to his keyboard.

'WE COULD EJECT SOME OF THE EQUIPMENT WE HAVE ON BOARD THROUGH THE AIRLOCK. USE OUR EQUIPMENT INSTEAD OF OUR SHIP TO INTERCEPT THE WEAPON' he typed.

'YES. A VIABLE OPTION. WE HAVE GIVEN YOU CONTROL OF AIRLOCK DOORS' was the message Gerry got back.

'WE WILL ALSO NEED TO CANCEL OUR ACCELERATION TO ALLOW PHYSICAL MOVEMENT. WILL YOU ALSO RETURN CONTROL OF OUR COMPUTER SYSTEMS?' Gerry asked hopefully. The weight that crushed them into their flight-seats was suddenly lifted.

'ACCELERATION HAS BEEN CANCELLED. WE WILL MAINTAIN CONTROL OF SHIPS COMPUTER SYSTEM. EJECT EQUIPMENT NOW' appeared on the screen.

'One minute till impact' Darren advised them.

'OK, everyone grab whatever you can that's not tied down and assemble it near the airlock door.' Gerry ordered quickly. Within an instant he was alone on the flight deck, everyone else frantically collecting what was mostly scientific equipment from their cabins.

'CAN YOU OPEN THE INNER AIRLOCK DOOR NOW?' Gerry entered into the messaging system. He heard a thump and knew it had been opened.

'I hope they're damn careful which doors they're opening and closing' he muttered to himself.

He ran out of the flight deck and was glad to see what was already a considerable pile of scientific components. There was something else next to the equipment that caught his eye. It was the body bag that contained their Supervisor.

Darren noticed Gerry's questioning look as he was putting his office chair onto the pile. 'We need as many items out there we can if we want a decent chance of hitting the missile.'

106

Gerry nodded. 'I agree. Only 30 seconds left. Let's get this stuff out there.' With that they kicked and pushed the equipment through the airlocks inner door, Charmaine and Jennifer running back laden with more items, which were quickly thrown into the space between the airlock doors. Last of all went the Supervisor's body.

Sprinting back to the flight deck, knowing they only had about 15 or 20 seconds till impact, Gerry hammered a message into his keyboard.

'CLOSE THE INNER DOOR AND OPEN THE OUTER ONE NOW.' There was the sound of the airlock doors operating. The others were back in their seats in an instant.

'It looks like we've done it' Gerry said.

'10 seconds before impact Gerry, time to decelerate.' Darren advised.

'DECELERATE NOW' Gerry entered with the keyboard, as the others strapped themselves into their seats in preparation.

'NO.' That was all. It wasn't the reply any of them expected.

'You fuckers!' Gerry called out loud, the impotence of his gesture annoying him. There was little else he could do.

He was deciding whether or not he should message them one last time with the same phrase when he was flung upward so violently that he heard vertebrae grind loudly together in his neck.

It was such a severe pounding he wasn't sure whether or not he had been unconscious for a time as he turned to assess the condition of the others.

Jennifer was slumped in her seat. Darren looked dazed but was already working at his keyboard in an attempt to discover what had just happened. Charmaine seemed fine, even smiling.

'We're still here!' she exclaimed, sounding as surprised as Gerry felt. 'But Jennifer's been hurt.'

'Any idea what happened just then, Darren?' Gerry asked as he released his harness and rose to check on Jennifer.

'The missile's continued on its same course. I can't tell whether or not its been damaged. It had contact with either our ship or the stuff we ejected. There was an explosion.'

'Yeah, there was a hell of a bang back there. Just lucky we're moving fast enough to get away from there by the time any real damage was done I'd guess,' Gerry said, checking Jennifer's pulse and breathing. 'We probably outran the shock-wave.'

107

'Some of the equipment is gone' Darren added, still looking over the data. 'We missed the missile and it collided with some of the things we threw out there.'

Everyone's weight shifted a little, and all but Jennifer turned to look at Darren. He was smiling. 'We've got control of the vessel again too.'

'Make sure our flight-path co-ordinates are still set to get us back to Earth safely.' Gerry called to Darren, at the same time producing a tiny liquid-filled balloon from under Jennifer's seat, which he squeezed between his fingers while holding it under her nose. There was a little spray of vapour, and she stirred and opened her eyes instantly.

'What happened?' She said first, looking in surprise at the others.

'We were lucky. The missile must have contacted something we threw out. It would have missed us anyway. As it happens, throwing our equipment out almost got us killed.'

'Well why are we still here. Didn't the weapon explode?'

'No,' Gerry replied, 'it's still headed for the Clavus 3, though we've no way of knowing whether it's still armed. The explosion when it clipped something might have damaged its firing mechanisms. After it exits the hyper-speed corridor it's probably going to be too damaged to change course to complete the journey to the moon.'

A message came on-screen. 'LOSING COMMUNICATION SOON. YOU WILL SOON BE BEYOND OUR REACH. MISSILE IS NOT. WE CAN SURVIVE. WE ARE PREPARING DEFENCE. RESCUE US. RETURN.'

Gerry strode back to his seat and typed a reply. 'WE CANNOT. SHIP MAY BE DAMAGED. MUST RETURN TO EARTH.'

'BUT YOU CANNOT RETURN TO EARTH. YOU ARE INFECTED.'

'CLARIFY.' Gerry typed.

'RADIATION IS POWERFUL. IT HAS REACHED OUT TO YOU. IT HAS LEFT ITS SPORE. YOU MAY HAVE BEEN CHANGED AS WE HAVE'

'WE HAVE HAD NO PHYSICAL CONTACT WITH THE ENVIRONMENT YOU ARE STRANDED IN. WE

CANNOT BE INFECTED' Gerry stated, though not as sure of this as he would have liked.

'YOU HAVE FELT THEIR ENERGIES IN YOUR VESSEL. THE SPORES ARE NOT MATTER. THEY WILL ASSIST YOU AS YOU WILL ASSIST THEM. SYMBIOTIC. YOU ARE LIKE US NOW.'

'OUR SUPERVISOR DIED BY UNKNOWN CAUSES. WAS HE INFECTED?' Gerry asked.

'OF COURSE. ALL WILL BE INFECTED. CREWMEMBER BARRY SCOTT ALSO DIED STRANGELY WHEN WE ARRIVED. SOME MAY HAVE A BAD REACTION TO THE SPORE. COMMUNICATION DISTANCE IS BEING EXCEEDED. RESCUE US.'

'WE WILL GET INSTRUCTION FROM EARTH. ARE YOU STILL THERE?' Gerry inquired. He sat for a few seconds looking at the screen, waiting on a response. There was none.

A series of beeps could be heard coming from Darren's console at his side, and before he had even glanced down to see what was happening they knew what it meant.

'Mission Control are back on-line again.' Charmaine said.

A new message on the screen read 'MOST COMPUTER SYSTEMS ON EARTH HAVE BEEN DISABLED BY UNKNOWN SOFTWARE. NETWORKS IN MOST REMOTE COLONIES ALSO AFFECTED. SOURCE OF MALICIOUS SOFTWARE TRACED TO YOUR ON-BOARD COMPUTER NETWORK. CONFIRM RECEIPT OF THIS MESSAGE.'

'MESSAGE RECEIVED.' Gerry typed. 'WE HAVE FULL CONTROL OF SHIPS SYSTEMS NOW.'

A new message appeared. 'DATA WE HAVE RECEIVED FROM YOUR SHIPS COMPUTER INDICATES LOOSE CARGO ON A PROBABLY HEADING FOR EARTH. CAN YOU CONFIRM?'

'YES. WE WERE FORCED TO EJECT EQUIPMENT AND SUPERVISORS BODY THROUGH AIRLOCK WHEN THE STRANDED HUMANS ON CLAUS 3 SOMEHOW AFFECTED SHIPS SYSTEMS.' Gerry informed them. There was a long pause before the next message appeared.

'THE SITUATION HAS BEEN MONITORED AND GOVERNMENT HAS BEEN ADVISED. THE ACTIONS

ARE TO BE CONSIDERED AN ACT OF HOSTILITY. ENEMY IS LIKELY STILL ONBOARD AND/OR COMPROMISING THE SHIPS CONTROL SYSTEMS. YOU WILL BE PLACED UNDER MILITARY QUARANTINE UPON RETURNING TO EARTH. USE THE REMAINING PROBE TO CHANGE TRAJECTORY OF LOOSE CARGO IMMEDIATELY.'

'MESSAGE RECEIVED AND UNDERSTOOD.' Gerry typed in return.

He turned to Charmaine. 'OK, this is your department. I need you to launch the research probe we have left. Try giving that loose equipment a nudge to a safer trajectory. You have ten minutes maximum till we'll need to launch.'

He spun in his flight seat to face Darren. 'Get the exact position of the flotsam. We need to know which direction we'll be sending the probe.'

'Will do' Darren replied, fingers already flying over his keyboard as he turned back to face the small screen by his side that he was working from.

'It's not the most ideal probe we could be using for something like this.' Charmaine said. 'The one we have left is for travelling overland. We'll be using the same thrusters that would normally take it from the ship to a planet's surface. It'll be impossible to do any fine steering after it's been fired.'

'We might be able to position our ship in a way that allows the probe to hit all of the objects even though we fire it in a straight path. It'll be a little like ten-pin-bowling. We'll wait till Darren gets an exact position for us.' Gerry told her, though he understood their chances of success were not very high.

The large screen before them went to a view of a three-dimensional grid, a cube that showed their own position as a bright red triangle, it's point signifying their direction of travel. Alongside could be seen their stray cargo, displayed as smaller orange triangles. Darren clicked a pointer over one of these and a list of co-ordinates popped up at one side of the screen.

'There's your trajectory to programme the probe with,' Darren said to Charmaine.

After a moments deliberation she said, 'It wouldn't do any good firing it from here. We'd only hit one, maybe two of the objects.'

110

'I agree,' Gerry said, 'We need to send every tiny piece of that stuff out of it's current trajectory. I'm sure you realise that even if we leave something as tiny as a nut or bolt on it's current path at this velocity we can possibly say goodbye to the Earth, and that includes the space-stations and other satellites around it, if there is a collision.

'Jennifer, we need a plan B, some other way of stopping the objects if this doesn't pay off. Maybe moving our ship alongside and someone going out and pulling the cargo back in would have to be considered. Look into some alternatives. I'm sure they've got one final alternative mapped out for us back on Earth, and I don't think it's one we'd like.'

Jennifer nodded, understanding the seriousness of the situation. They might be commanded to ram their ship into the objects if all else failed.

Gerry turned to Charmaine. 'Is the probe ready for firing?'

'Yes, it's just waiting for co-ordinates.' The gridded view of the space they flew in was changing it's perspective, constantly moving and the magnification changing as Darren looked for the most effective trajectory the probe could be sent. After a pause that felt to Gerry like an hour, but would only have been 30 seconds in reality, Darren spoke.

'This is as good as we're going to get. If we move there we'll have a decent chance of hitting all of the objects. We'll be relying on them ricocheting into each other if we want to send all of them astray though. It's a long shot.'

'Let's give it a try.' Gerry said. 'Move us to position Darren.'

Everybody ensured they were securely strapped in, and they barely had time to take a breath before they were wrenched backward and downwards into their seats, their bodies sustaining forces that would have permanently crippled people who were without medical enhancement.

'Enter the co-ordinates of the objects Charmaine, and get ready to fire the probe when we've reached position.' Gerry called with difficulty.

'Done. It's ready to fire,' she said shortly.

Everybody sat silent while the ship moved to its new position, all forced to consider the unthinkable; what to do if this failed. The next few critical moments would decide their fate, and possibly that of their entire home planet. The actual likelihood

111

that any of the equipment would strike the Earth or its satellites was very low, but the act of sending any object at greater-than-light speed through an inhabited solar system was criminal in the extreme. Sentences were harsh for a deed of this type, no matter what the reason may be. Self-defence wasn't an excuse for placing people's home planet in immediate danger.

'We're in position' Darren said, and at the same moment the weight felt to lift from their bodies.

'Give us an outside view Darren.' Gerry instructed. Instantly the large screen before them switched to a show their equipment floating beside their ship.

'Fire the probe' he ordered next.

'Fired.' Charmaine said, the crew exchanging glances as they heard the thump from beneath their feet as the probe shot off into space.

The articles they had left spinning lazily in space next to their vessel were only metres away from their hull, and the probe slammed into them almost immediately. Its trajectory had been calculated well, and everyone aboard felt a strong sense of relief as the probe, along with almost all the lethal items was slammed away from the ship. Almost all of them. The Supervisors' body seemed to keep its trajectory unchanged, only sent into a wild spin when something had stuck it.

'Darren, have we altered the corpse's trajectory enough to avoid it hitting the Earth?' Gerry asked.

'We'll know for sure in a few seconds.' Darren replied, looking intently at the small screen by his side. The others were looking at the main viewing screen as they waited for the results.

'No, there's been no change. He's still on a heading that takes him straight through our solar system. We managed to send everything else out of this flight-path though. None of the other items should go anywhere near our system now.'

'REMAINING MASS ON A TRAJECTORY ENDANGERING EARTH. COURT-MARTIAL PROCEEDINGS WILL COMMENCE UPON YOUR RETURN.' Mission control had been watching their progress and messaged them with instructions. 'YOU HAVE THE OPTION TO ATTEMPT A HYPER-SPEED SPACE WALK TO REMOVE THIS OBJECT. ANOTHER OPTION IS TO ATTEMPT A COLLISION BETWEEN YOUR VESSEL AND

112

THE DEBRIS. FINAL OPTION IS TO FIRE A HYPER-SPEED MISSILE FROM EARTH TO REMOVE THE DEBRIS. THIS OPTION IS UNDESIRABLE AS IT MAY POLLUTE THE LIGHT-SPEED HIGHWAY YOU ARE USING. ADVISE US OF YOUR DECISION ASAP. SUCCESSFUL REMOVAL OF THE DEBRIS WILL BE LOOKED UPON FAVORABLY AND MAY RESULT IN LEGAL PROCEEDINGS AGAINST THE CREW BEING CANCELLED.'

'It seems we're in trouble when we get back.' Gerry noted.

'What for!' Jennifer exclaimed, obviously shocked to discover officials on Earth considered them criminals.

'We ejected items from our ship at faster-than-light speed. Just because we did it to save the ship and our lives doesn't make it any less illegal. The law states that it shouldn't be done under any circumstances. We've broken one of the oldest laws of space travel.' Gerry explained.

'Arseholes,' Darren cursed, instantly wishing he hadn't when he noticed on his screen that the transmitter was on, relaying the audio on the flight deck back to Earth, where his body would be listening.

'Only one thing for it, we've got to finish cleaning up our mess. They want a volunteer to go out and push the super's body out of the hyper-speed lane.' Gerry said to the crew. 'I'll go out right away.'

'But the risks of a space walk at this speed are very high. Maybe the safest option for everyone is to just let them use a missile to destroy the body.' Charmaine said.

'Like they said though, there'll be a chance it leaves some garbage in our clear hyper-speed lane and ruin it for decades. They'd won't be able to use it again until it's been cleared, just on the chance that there was still some matter floating around out there that could destroy their ship if they struck a piece of it. That'd mean thousands of people on the outlying planets would be stranded without supplies, because any vessel heading out there won't be able to use this return lane to get back to Earth. We'd could be stuck out here too.'

Darren spoke next. 'Also, colliding with the body would be too risky. Changing course now to strike the body with enough force to send it out of the hyper-speed lane wouldn't be possible without breaking our necks. We just can't manoeuvre gently enough on manual control at these speeds. And if we decelerated to try approaching the body at a gentler angle we may lose track of it. A soft object that size won't be picked up by our sensors at all while we're at greater than light speed, if it gets more than a few kilometres away. Then even Earth won't be able to track it, because they're relying on the information from our sensors. I'd guess they wouldn't even be able to target it with a hyper-speed missile if that happened.'

'I agree,' Gerry said. 'The issue of our own safety can't be our main consideration in a situation like this. If we fail, the consequences could mean devastation for our home planet, possibly even lead to its total destruction. We have to be sure this works. Tell them I'm on my way out there, Darren. I'll go get suited up.'

'Yes Sir.'

With that, Gerry walked from the flight deck, leaving the others to prepare for his space-walk. He found a suit in one of the storage rooms. Thankfully it hadn't been thrown out of the ship with the rest of the equipment they'd attempted to stop the missile with.

He was in his suit in less than a minute, the hundreds of emergency drills he had been forced to endure during his career paying off. He clipped an ion thruster unit to the back of the suit, and another smaller one on the front, which would propel him to the Supervisor's body and back again. He kept his helmet off for the moment, holding it under his arm as he walked to another storage space where the medication was kept. He'd need a few chemicals to protect his body against the effects caused by the radiation that would rip through his body during the hyper-speed space-walk.

Next stop was his cabin, where he swallowed the pills with a cup of water. He sat on the edge of his bunk for a moment, waiting for the medication he had just taken to show itself in the form of side effects. They did, and a wave of nausea came over him, along with a dizziness that would have made it impossible for him to stand. For a few seconds he was so disorientated that it was only with great fortitude that he kept himself sitting upright.

The sensations passed, far more quickly than the one and only other time he had taken such potent medication for this purpose.

Gerry was doubly surprised when the effects soon wore off altogether. The stomach cramps and shaking normally lasted for hours.

Walking back to the flight deck, feeling far healthier than he should have, Gerry surprised Darren with the bounce in his stride and the cheery look on his face. 'You're a tough bastard alright. It'd be hours before I could get up and walk after taking those pills' Darren said with a smile.

'Are you really sure you took the medication for radiation protection?' Jennifer inquired, also expecting his condition to be far worse.

'Yeah, but I'm feeling fine. The formula must have been improved since I last needed to take them. They made me sick for weeks last time I used them.'

'No, the pills have been unchanged in composition over the years. You're handling the side effects really well.'

'That's just it. The effects wore off completely in a couple of minutes.'

'Well, we're ready to go whenever you are,' Charmaine informed him.

'There's no big rush though,' Darren added. 'We've got nearly two days before we get close to home at our current speed.'

'No, now is as good a time as any. Let's do it.' Gerry told them.

'We've got the lights on outside. The body bag is shining brightly, 35 metres to our port side. You'll have no problem seeing it when you get out there,' Charmaine informed him.

'Open the inner door for me Darren,' Gerry said as he placed his helmet on. He gave it a twist and he heard it lock in place. At the same time a display lit up inside, giving Gerry a myriad of information about his environment.

He walked out of the flight deck alone, visually checking his suit while he went.

'Are you receiving audio?' Gerry said inside his helmet.

He heard Darren's voice come from speakers inside his helmet near each of his ears. 'Yes sir, receiving audio and data from all suit sensors.'

'Good.' Gerry said as he stepped into the space between the airlock doors. 'Close the outer door now.'

It slid quickly closed and Gerry was locked in the small cavity between space and the comfortable insides of the ship. He wasted no time, peering through the small window and locating the body immediately, Gerry told Darren to open the outer door.

Darren did so immediately and without comment. As soon as it began opening Gerry felt himself being sucked out as the air in the space with him shot out into the void. It wasn't unlike leaping from an aircraft, like skydiving on Earth.

Any nervousness he felt as he left the relative safety of the vessel was replaced by sheer exhilaration as he fired the tiny ion thrusters on his back. He was in control of his motion, and that gave Gerry all the confidence he needed.

Amidst the field of negative energy that extended a few hundred metres from the ships drive, his bodies momentum allowing him to sustain a velocity many times greater than the speed of light, Gerry was in his element. This was why he left Earth so often. The petty reason's used by politicians to kill and oppress back home that also controlled his own life seemed too distant and alien to concern him out here. He was suffused with a sense of contentment, though possibly only seconds from death. At least it would only come from a mistake of his own, instead of by the command of some arrogant men on Earth, that so many innocent people endured.

His thumb moving over a tiny control stick on his belt at his side, Gerry ensuring he wouldn't hit the body, changing his direction slightly as he neared the rapidly spinning body-bag to drift just past it. Inside the ship, Darren was wondering what his boss was doing.

'Why didn't you give him a shove from this side, Sir?' Gerry heard him say.

'I've decided to bring him in. There's too much of a risk leaving him out here, on any trajectory. It'll be just as easy as sending it off-course anyway.'

'Yes Sir, you're right of course. There's a fair chance he'd miss the Earth even if we left him where he is, though the hyperspeed lane we're in actually exits in a direction a few billion kilometres from the Earth at this time of year.'

'Yeah, the chances of it actually hitting the Earth are very low, but there are just too many space stations and other structures in our solar system, let alone the natural formations,' Gerry added.

116

'I could probably move it enough to make it miss our solar system altogether, but I'd rather be certain. It doesn't take much to be labelled a terrorist these days. I'd rather make sure that they know back on Earth that we don't have any ill-intent.'

'I remember looking at some calculations for the energy released by an object when it collides with another at thousands of times the speed of light' Charmaine said, knowing the familiar sound of their voices would help keep Gerry relaxed. 'If something as large as that corpse did hit anything there would be a major chunk of our solar system obliterated. And if by any tiny chance it hit our sun the whole system would obviously become uninhabitable outside of a spacecraft.'

'OK, I'm in place and going to try to cancel his spin' Gerry said, as he came to a halt as close as he could get without being struck. Rivulets and droplets of fluid had leaked from the body bag, and were trailing behind it. This was going to be more difficult than Gerry had imagined. The body was spinning so quickly that if he reached out to stop it he would in all likelihood be knocked away from their current position. He didn't know how far he might be tossed into the void before he could regain control using the tiny thrusters on his suit. He would have to attempt to grab hold of his dead boss to stop them bouncing away from each other.

Thinking on the same line, Darren said 'Careful, he's rotating real fast.'

'Right then, here goes' Gerry said. And with that he reached out and grabbed hold of what he hoped would be the feet end of the body. Instantly he was thrown into a mad spin, only retaining his grip on the body bag with difficulty. Turning about, with the legs clutched to his chest, Gerry was forced to let go with one of his arms and reach down to turn on the thruster on his back. He kept his thumb over the directional control, adjusting the direction of thrust slightly as needed, slowing their spin. It was working, and it only took about ten seconds for Gerry to cancel their spin completely.

'Well done. Come on in' he heard Charmaine say in his earpieces.

'On my way' Gerry said, firing the thruster on his back for a few seconds to start them moving back toward the ship's airlock.

He'd been winded slightly when the body's feet had struck his abdomen, but his breathing quickly returned to normal.

It took quite some time to get back alongside the vessel, and he was kept busy trying to contain the strings of fluid that leaked from the bag, deploying an occasional squirt from the ion jets in his suit to fine-tune his trajectory. The droplets of blood could destroy a planet at greater-than-light speed, and Gerry was doubly careful to collect as much of it as he could. There were a few droplets on his visor and his left arm was smeared with the red slime. The suit would need to be cleaned before he went back into the ship.

'Somebody put a bottle of cleaning fluid in the airlock. I'll need it to sterilise this suit before I can get out of it. And we'll need another body bag, or something else to wrap this up again too. It's been punctured. Open the outer door after you've done that.'

'Will do' Jennifer answered.

Drifting slowly back, Gerry floated lazily toward the doors. He could see Jennifer through the tiny window now, giving him a little wave after placing the items he needed on the floor within the airlock doors. She turned and disappeared on the other side, as the inner door closed behind her.

Then the door before Gerry slid open, and he again triggered the ion jets on his back, negating the shove from the usual blast of air that shot from the airlock when it was opened. He kept them firing for a couple of seconds longer, pushing him and his baggage into the small space within the ship.

Something went wrong with his suit when he fired the tiny thruster on the front in an attempt to bring himself to a stop. A massive pain shot into his chest and his helmet filled with smoke, making it difficult to see. He pulled his finger from the control and the pain instantly lessened. The thruster must have been damaged when he'd grabbed the Supervisor. It had burned his chest, very badly considering the amount of pain he was feeling, Gerry thought with some concern.

The ships artificial gravity started to affect his body as he began entered the airlock, and once inside the Supervisor's full weight could suddenly be felt. Gerry struggled to keep it from dropping from his arms, the bag being partially filled with fetid body fluids, making things more difficult as they flowed down to one end. He placed the body as gently as he could onto the floor, ensuring it was clear of the door. The pain in his chest was so intense, and he knew he was close to losing consciousness.

'Close the outer door,' he said into his helmet microphone. It immediately slid shut behind him.

'There are some problems with your suit. Your air supply is polluted and doesn't seem to be cleaning itself up, and there's even been a slight pressure loss' he heard Darren say.

Gerry realised with a jolt that his suit may have been breached and immediately barked an order to open the inner door, regardless of the threat of infection from the rotted corpse at his feet. He wanted to get back into the pressurised ship without delay. He was choking in his suit too, the smoke making the air inside too harsh to take a breath. Placing a hand over his chest in an attempt to slow any leakage, he felt a fresh wave of pain. A cold, clammy feeling washed over him, a sensation that Gerry was familiar with after injuring himself in dozens of motorcycle accidents back on Earth. He was going into shock already. It wasn't a good sign.

As the inner door slid open Gerry removed his helmet. A pillar of smoke billowed out from around his suit collar as he gasped for air. The burning in his chest worsened and he slumped against the wall inside the airlock and lost consciousness.

NINE

'I can't explain the pain you're going through...'
Morcheeba – Otherwise

'He's waking,' was the next thing Gerry heard, and he found himself in his cabin with the crew standing around his bed.

'How is everything? How long have I been out?' he asked, sitting up. He suddenly remembered his chest wound and was expecting a lot of pain, but there was only a dull ache.

'You've only been out for ten minutes. Do you need anything for the pain?' Jennifer said. Everyone seemed to be acting peculiar, Gerry noticed, seemingly a little alarmed.

'No, I'm feeling fine.' With that, Gerry looked down at his chest, steeling himself for the sight of a horrible wound. But there was none. Only a red circular scar and a smear of black powder that looked like soot, which brushed off easily with a wipe of his hand. Now the look of concern on his face matched theirs.

'It was a smoking wound when we got your suit off, but it healed in a matter of minutes. Has anything like that ever happened to you before?' Jennifer asked, taking a swab of the wound site for analysis. She had the most medical experience of anyone on board, but her hand shook as she took the sample.

'No, of course not.' There was a slight tingling sensation from the burn site as he sat fully upright and swung his legs off the edge of the bunk.

'I'm not sure you should be moving about. The damaged thruster burned you internally. Five minutes ago there was a gaping hole in your chest.' Darren advised.

'How's your breathing?' Jennifer asked next.

'Fine.'

'That was the freakiest thing I've seen for a long time,' Darren said. 'Well, since our dead Supervisor crawled out to join us in the flight deck that is.'

'Those two strange occurrences are almost certainly related.' Jennifer pointed out. 'It may have something to do with that infection the two stranded people mentioned.'

'Whatever it was, I'm glad it did whatever it did' Gerry said, neglecting to say that it also made him feel somewhat uncomfortable. 'Let's get back to the flight deck.'

'No you don't. We need to check you out a lot more closely.' Jennifer demanded. 'We should be able to find some explanation for what just happened. Either some outside influence we couldn't see patched you up or your body must be altered in some way to heal like it did. Look, there's not even a scar now.'

Glancing down, Gerry saw she was right. It was as if he'd never been burned.

'Alright then, you've already taken a swap of the wound site. Taking a blood sample might be a good idea. You other two get back to the flight deck though. I want to know what happened to that hyper-speed missile' he instructed.

As Charmaine and Darren left the cabin, Jennifer turned to the case of medical equipment, quickly finding what she needed. Pressing the device she'd found against Gerry's forearm, they watched the chamber begin to fill with blood. But before it was halfway full, the flow stopped, just as quickly as it had begun.

'What the hell?' Jennifer exclaimed, looking up at Gerry's face, half expecting him to suddenly drop dead. Blood wouldn't normally just stop pumping through the device like this. He was sitting there, obviously quite alive though.

'Try again,' he said calmly.

'I've never seen that happen before' Jennifer said, as she placed the instrument a little higher on his arm and gave it a slight push to activate it a second time. Again it began to fill, drawing a sample of his blood painlessly through the skin. But before the sample was complete it stopped again.

'That'll do for any tests you want to carry out anyway, Jennifer,' Gerry said as he stood. 'The thing must be faulty.'

'Not much can go wrong with an instrument as simple as this, but I guess it could happen. Wait just a second, there's something I want to try.'

'Just make it quick.'

'Will do' Jennifer said, at the same time producing a scalpel, which she flicked up quickly and nicked Gerry's arm.

'What was that in aid of?' Gerry demanded, a trickle of blood starting to flow from the cut.

'Bear with me for a second. Watch the wound closely' she answered. Gerry held back an angry response, and instead did as she instructed.

'Jesus' he muttered. Gerry was sure there had been a flash of blue light from inside the cut. And as he watched there was soon another one. 'What could be causing that?'

'No idea, but the stranded people's talk of radiation exposure could go some way toward an explanation,' Jennifer told him. 'Though it doesn't give us much to go on.'

There was a buzzing sensation around the wound now, and soon there were dozens of tiny blue sparks playing across it. He'd seen this before. Gerry remembered how the Supervisor's body had electrical energy playing across it. The others might as well know what he had seen now.

'I saw the same electrical effect on the Supervisor's body. It did seem as though something was trying to heal his wounds. Maybe he was just in too much of a mess to be fixed.'

'If this is an infection of some kind we've all been exposed to it' Jennifer said, at the same moment nicking her own forearm with a fresh blade. They both watched it closely, and it didn't take long for them to be rewarded with a reaction. Again the sparks appeared and the cut quickly healed. Wiping the tiny line of blood away with a tissue, Jennifer and Gerry could no longer even be sure exactly where the cut had been.

'So do you think it's the effect of something external, or somehow coming from our own bodies?' Gerry asked. It felt to him as though the healing blue sparks that they had seen were coming from within. He'd felt them moving toward the wound, his muscles twitching as they worked there way down his arm.

'It's too hard to say at the moment. We might have something on our skin that's reacting with our wounds. We need to test the swabs I took and also have a close look at your blood sample. Everyone on board will need to be checked for symptoms.'

'You do the tests right away,' Gerry instructed. 'I'll get back to the flight deck. I want to know what happened to that hyper-speed missile.'

'Should only take me about 20 minutes' Jennifer said, gathering the medical equipment she'd assembled in Gerry's cabin while he'd been unconscious.

122

Gerry strode back to the flight deck and found Charmaine and Darren busy at their workstations. 'What's new?'

'Clavus 3 is still there. The missile never changed course. We would have expected it to exit the hyper-speed lane when it neared the planetary system, but instead it just stayed in the lane. It'll be out of range of our sensors in a few minutes. It's still going, and it'll keep doing so unless they destroy it remotely from back on Earth,' Darren informed him.

'They'll probably wait until it reaches the end of the hyper-speed corridor before they do that. They might not be able to steer it out of the corridor to destroy it at the moment because of the damage it sustained.'

'Very likely' Darren said, 'We've been in contact with Mission Control too.'

'What did they have to say?' Gerry asked.

'They commended us for removing the stuff we jettisoned and bringing in the Supervisor's body for full examination. There'll still be a military investigation into why we pushed everything out in the first place though,' Darren informed him.

'That's to be expected. It should make for an interesting report. I guess you told them of my miraculous recovery.'

'Yeah, but they knew most of the story anyway. They've been monitoring the audio transmission from our ship again. They'll have a medical ship meet us when we near Earth. We might be in quarantine for quite a while. It could take some time for them to piece together what's been happening here.'

'It worse than you know' Gerry told them grimly. 'Whatever it is that healed my wound is affecting Jennifer too. Her cuts are healing in seconds. I'd guess it might be the same with you two.'

'And the Supervisor was infected as well. It could have been what killed him too,' Charmaine said in sudden realisation.

'Very likely' Gerry concurred. 'How long have we got before we need to strap in for deceleration?'

'Just under 44 hours.' Darren replied.

'If anybody's tired, now would be a good time to head for your cabin for a few hours sleep' Gerry advised.

'No thanks, there's too much to think about to get any sleep' Charmaine said.

'Yeah, I'm feeling pretty wired,' Darren added. 'I'd rather stay here and check on some of the data we collected from Clavus 3.'

123

'Fine, you'll have to see Jennifer after she's finished her preliminary tests. We want to know for sure whether or not everyone on board is being affected by whatever it was that fixed my wound, and maybe killed our Supervisor.'

Darren and Charmaine both nodded, turning in unison to look down at the computer screens under their right arms. As they got back to work checking on the reams of data they had collected so far on this mission, Gerry went back to his cabin.

He sat at his desk and flipped up the computer screen. And for the next four hours he checked over the ships systems, manually scanning thousands of screens. After feeling satisfied that he'd covered all of the ship in his status checks, making adjustments where necessary, Gerry messaged the others to say he was going to lie down for a few hours, and to wake him if anything changed.

But as he lay in his bunk, expecting to quickly drift off after the eventful last few hours, Gerry found he couldn't sleep. In fact he found it impossible to lay still. His mind was full of the figures he'd seen when checking the ship with his computer. He couldn't clear his mind. It seemed to swim with calculations and interpretations of the data he'd seen. He lay there for an hour, tossing and turning, until he realised it futile, that sleep just wouldn't come.

Leaving his cabin, Gerry walked back to the flight deck. The others were working there as he entered.

'Come up with anything from those tests yet Jennifer?' he said first.

'Not much to go on. Charmaine and Darren's skin has the same reaction as ours does to a wound.'

'The blood-test produce any helpful results?'

'Nothing. It's normal. The swabs we took of your skin were a little unusual though. There wasn't anything foreign I could see under the microscope, but it's emitting some sort of radiation that the instruments can't identify. There were tiny flashes of electrical energy too. So faint though, I only picked them up by accident while I was using the spectral analysis machine.'

'Could it just be residue from the thruster that burned me?' Gerry asked.

'No, I've taken swabs from everyone on board now, and it seems to be the same all over our bodies. We seem to be emitting some unusual type of radiation that we can't see and can barely pick up with our instruments. It only makes itself visible when we've sustained a wound, when it somehow helps it heal. I can't even find a single molecule of any substance that doesn't belong, yet something on our skin is charged with a small amount of electrical energy.'

'Has anyone noticed any other possible symptoms?' Gerry asked them.

'Yes,' they said in unison.

Charmaine explained, 'I don't seem to be getting as tired as I should be, but that might be a normal reaction to the stress we're under.'

Jennifer and Darren nodded their agreement.

'I had the same problem,' Gerry replied, 'I should have been out like a light but instead I'm feeling quite lively. You're right though, it could be normal under the circumstances, though I must say I don't remember losing much sleep during the quiet moments of an eventful mission before.'

'No, it's our only escape sometimes. To be awake is to be stressed' Charmaine added.

'Jennifer, have you sent a medical report to Mission Control?' Gerry asked. 'They can hear everything that's going on in here, but as you know, it's got to be typed to be official, before it's acted upon.'

'I submitted the report, they can pull it from the computer whenever they like. They've got the data from all of my scans. Hopefully they can come up with more of an explanation from their labs on Earth than I could out here,' Jennifer answered.

'Whatever happens, we won't be setting foot back on Earth for a long time. We'll be in quarantine for a few weeks at least. Longer, if it takes them some time to discover why these things have been happening on-board,' Gerry advised them. 'So we'd be doing ourselves a favour if we can help them analyse our condition.'

'Great, there goes my wondrous physique,' Darren said jokingly. 'Just what I need. To be stuck on this ship for another month. My arse couldn't get much flatter than it already is, sitting about for weeks on end.'

Gerry barely heard him. He suddenly found his mind rapidly flipping through their options, his brain seemingly out of his control as thoughts and decisions sped through. He snatched a sharp intake of breath, the barrage of calculations and assessments felt like a physical assault, giving him a frightening sense of losing his sanity.

'Are you alright Sir?' Jennifer inquired, noticing something unusual was going on with their boss, the sudden change in his facial expression and the slight tensing of his body. She was relieved when he focussed on her voice and lifted his head to look at her.

'My head seems to be doing some strange things,' Gerry answered, losing the strange mental activity as quickly as it had begun.

'I've been having something like those so-called 'moments of clarity'. I didn't think it worth mentioning before, though I admit it's a pretty scary feeling' Jennifer said. 'Was it anything like that?'

Gerry wiped the back of his hand across his forehead, finding it damp with perspiration. 'Yeah, pretty much the same, though I don't know if clarity is quite the right word for it. It's like my mind was racing out of control. Not a nice feeling.'

'I haven't noticed anything like that yet,' Charmaine said. 'Only the complete lack of any weariness. I should be dead tired after everything I have been doing over the last few days but sleep is the last thing on my mind. I'm not complaining but it's unusual.'

'I must admit I've had the feeling I've been slightly drugged, or something, for the past hour or so. I don't quite feel myself at times, though it's nothing I can put my finger on,' Darren told them.

'We've got to try getting ourselves clean.' Gerry advised. 'As Jennifer said, we've likely been infected by something previously unknown. Let's hope we can rid ourselves of it before we get back to Earth. We won't be welcomed back with open arms while we're like this, I'm afraid.'

'We should simply try the showers before anything else,' Jennifer suggested. 'If we're lucky the substance will just run off our bodies in the sonic blast.'

'It's worth a shot' Gerry replied. 'You go first, Jennifer. Turn the jets up to full power and stay in there for the maximum allowed time.'

'OK,' Jennifer said as she stood, 'I'll test myself again afterwards to see if it's made any difference.'

Gerry nodded, and as she left for the showers he turned in his flight seat as far as he was able, to face the others. 'You two should take a break, grab something to eat. I'll keep an eye on things here for a while.'

They both stepped from their flight seats and headed for the door.

'I don't think I'd be able to keep anything down, but I'll try,' Charmaine said over her shoulder.

They left Gerry alone on the flight deck, and he didn't waste a second. Recalling the last message received from Mission Control from the computer's memory, he checked the file's size. It was too big to account for the tiny message it contained. He'd been sent an encrypted message, hidden within it.

Running the software immediately, Gerry brought the resulting message up on the screen by his side. He read it quickly, fingers poised over the keyboard to clear the screen if any of the crew-members walked in.

'CREW PHYSICAL MEDICAL TESTS SHOW POSSIBLE RADIATION EXPOSURE. SOURCE UNKNOWN. RADIATION TYPE UNKNOWN. POSSIBLE HOSTILE ACTION FROM CLAVUS MOON RESIDENTS. THE TWO SCIENTISTS ARE CONSIDERED A MILITARY THREAT. THEY HAVE GRIEVANCES. ATTACK MAY BE BIOLOGICAL/CHEMICAL/NUCLEAR USING YOUR SHIP AS A CARRIER. OUR HYPER-SPEED MISSILE MALFUNCTIONED CAUSING NO DAMAGE TO THE SYSTEM. AUSTRALIAN GOVERNMENT IS CONSIDERING NEXT COURSE OF ACTION.

'PROCEED TO PROGRAMMED WAYPOINT. NO PHYSICAL CONTACT WILL BE MADE WITH YOUR VESSEL UNTIL CIRCUMSTANCES BECOME CLEARER. PREPARE FOR MINIMUM 2-WEEK QUARANTINE PERIOD. YOUR COMPUTER SYSTEMS HAVE BEEN ISOLATED FROM THE NETWORK DUE TO DESTRUCTIVE CODE ORIGINATING FROM IT PREVIOUSLY. COMPUTER SYSTEMS ON EARTH AND SOME COLONIES HAVE BEEN SEVERELY EFFECTED. THIS IS CLASSIFIED INFORMATION. KEEP THE CREW

CALM. HAVE THEM TEST THE VESSEL/LOCAL COMPUTER SYSTEMS/MEDICAL DATA THOROUGHLY. THEIR DATA IS VITAL. MAJOR MILITARY STRATEGIES WILL BE FORMED BASED HEAVILY UPON THEIR FINDINGS. YOUR ONBOARD AUDIO AND VIDEO ARE BEING MONITORED.'

Gerry deleted the message and sat for a moment, letting the implications of what he'd read sink in. They'd said that the two scientists they had contacted while visiting Clavus 3 *had grievances*. They obviously had more information than they were letting on, Gerry knew, but that was always the way. Had they always known they were stranded there? Or was it a form of exile, ostracised from their home planet for some unknown reason.

And what did they mean by forming military strategy around their findings on this ship. Surely they had more to go on than that, Gerry thought hopefully. If they found the effects they were experiencing aboard the ship as well as those effecting their bodies were a potential risk to people on Earth, would they retaliate by sending another powerful missile at the moon and it's two abandoned occupants?

'They couldn't be sure it's the work of the stranded scientists. They could just be victims like us, trapped on the moon by the same forces that we've felt on this ship' Gerry muttered to himself. Charmaine interrupted his reverie when she came back onto the flight deck with handfuls of the concentrated food trays.

'What was that you were saying?' she asked as she handed him a package filled with a yellow slime. He glanced at the label and saw that it was macaroni cheese, though he wasn't convinced.

'Nothing, just babbling to myself' he answered casually. 'Surely I don't have to eat this.'

'I know what you mean. And it's not only the quality of the food. I've had a tiny spoonful and I'm ready to bring it right back up again.'

'You do look a little pale. I hope the food hasn't been contaminated.' Gerry said, opening his own tray and taking a tentative sniff. 'Smells alright.'

He took a spoonful into his mouth, but as he swallowed he felt a tremendous retching sensation grip him. The macaroni cheese was ejected straight back into the tray as he heaved. There was nothing else in his stomach to regurgitate, and the cramps in his stomach soon subsided.

'We're either ill in some way that makes it impossible to eat or this food has been contaminated by the radiation or whatever the hell it was that's been effecting us.'

'Only one way to find out,' Gerry said, 'We'll test the food right away.'

Just then Jennifer walked in looking refreshed after her shower. 'I'm going to head straight back to my cabin now to test my skin swabs after the sonic shower, to see if it did any good. You two aren't looking too healthy,' she added. 'I'd advise one of you to go for a clean-up right now.'

'Charmaine, you go next' he ordered.

Jennifer handed her a fresh skin swab. 'Give the skin on your wrist a quick wipe with this when you're done.'

'Here's something else I'd like you to check for contaminants,' Gerry said as Charmaine left for the showers, handing Jennifer his unpalatable meal. 'The food seems to be making us ill.'

'That's all we need' she replied, immediately heading out the door, keen to get to work.

Gerry wasn't hungry, and neither was anyone else it seemed, so he wasn't too concerned about the lack of food. They would be exiting the hyper-speed corridor in less than 40 hours, so they weren't going to starve. From there they could be delivered new supplies from Earth as they sat out their quarantine period.

Pondering their situation, Gerry was startled by a burst of activity in his mind. It was as though a light had been switched on in his head, his thoughts and interpretations of what he had witnessed over the last few days flicking so rapidly through his conscious mind. It was as though he was considering dozens of points of interest at once, seemingly without any effort on his part. It frightened him, and knowing that it was likely a strange external influence that was causing it to happen made it more ominous.

He was suddenly convinced that Jennifer wouldn't find any change when checking their skin samples after the sonic showers. Same with the food, he was sure now. It wasn't contaminates that made it unpalatable, rather a reaction to it by their infected bodies. Whatever type of radiation they had been in contact with was making them ill, unable to eat. Gerry felt certain now that it had been some form of radiation that the ship had passed through that had brought on the unusual effects they'd experienced on this mission. Once the sensation ceased he wasn't sure how he'd deduced these things, only that he had.

It lasted only a few seconds before his myriad thoughts stopped churning, but it felt to him like a prolonged physical assault. By the time things went back to normal he'd slumped forward in his flight-seat, so far that he had almost fallen out of it and onto the floor face-first.

Sitting back into his seat again, Gerry heard the chime of the intercom being used, and Jennifer's voice rang out from the speakers above.

'Some-thing's happened to Darren. We're in his cabin. He was lying unconscious on the floor when I came in.'

Gerry thumbed the intercom button on the keyboard at his side and spoke quickly. 'I'll be right there.'

Darren was sitting on the floor near his bed, looking dazed, as Gerry entered. He was relieved to find him already conscious.

'He just came to. I don't think he could have been out for very long.' Jennifer told him. 'He seems to have had some sort of seizure.'

'I'm alright now' Darren said, wiping his pale face with the back of a trembling hand. 'Just had a bit of a dizzy spell. Something seems to be doing some sort of freaky shit to my brain.'

'I just had a bit of a moment myself.' Gerry told him. 'You're right, our radiation exposure, if that's what it is, has made us a little sick. Have you had anything to eat?'

'No, I'm not hungry. Even just the thought of food makes me feel ill.'

'What about you Jennifer, had anything to eat?' Gerry asked next.

'No, I feel the same as Darren. I should be starving by now, but instead I'm not interested in having anything to eat at all. I don't think I could keep anything down, though I don't really feel sick at the moment,' she replied.

'We need more thorough tests done. We need to know what's happening to us. They're not going to be much help to us when we're back near Earth in quarantine. They'll be able to bring us some more sophisticated medical equipment, but we'll be doing all the tests ourselves. The nature of our illness means no-one will be coming near the ship.'

'You're right. I'd guess they'll be using automated vessels to bring us supplies,' Jennifer added. 'The most likely cause for our illness is radiation exposure, and since it's having such a peculiar effect on us and the ship they're not going to expose any more people to it before they know exactly what we're dealing with and they have made it safe.'

'They wouldn't risk exposing anyone to whatever it is. Remember what happened to our old Supervisor. We need to find out, and quickly, what we've been exposed to' Gerry told them.

Charmaine had obviously heard the message on the intercom and finished her shower early. She had entered the tiny cabin quietly behind them and was looking down at Darren with a look of strong concern on her face.

'We're all starting to get sick, aren't we?' she said, as Gerry and Jennifer helped Darren up from the floor. He sat on the edge of his bunk immediately, obviously having trouble standing.

'I'm alright.' Darren said, in a vain attempt to allay their fears. 'It's probably just the lack of food.'

'How are you feeling now?' Gerry asked him, Jennifer handing him a cup.

'Better every second. I'll be right as rain in a moment,' Darren replied, then taking a long swig of water from the cup. 'At least this'll stay down.'

'You stay here for a while Darren, till you're feeling well enough to come to the flight deck. Get some sleep if you can,' Gerry instructed.

'I'll try. I'm way overdue for a decent sleep' Darren said, and rolled back into his bunk, where he closed his eyes. Gerry turned to Jennifer as they left the cabin.

'Run the tests on the skin samples and the food. Our illness seems to be progressing. I don't know about you, but my brain's doing some pretty strange things.'

'Yeah, mine's playing up too. It seems to be buzzing with activity, even while I'm not consciously trying to think about anything,' Jennifer replied as she turned to leave for her own cabin where her medical equipment was kept. 'In a strange way it's actually made my thinking a little clearer. It really is like being under the effects of some type of performance enhancing drug.'

'I don't like the idea of anything messing with my mind like this.' Charmaine added. 'It's just too important to have your head together out here.'

'I'd say they'd be working round-the-clock on the problem back on Earth. Hopefully we'll get some sort of solution from them soon,' Gerry said optimistically to Charmaine as the two of them headed back to the flight deck.

As he sat down in his flight seat, another wave of dizziness overcame him. In an unusual moment of clarity Gerry knew the truth of their situation. It wasn't all that it seemed. He felt certain now that their predicament was fully understood by some people back on Earth, that someone there knew what was afflicting them, though he knew not how he came to this conclusion. Gerry was convinced that his judgement wasn't flawed though his certainty made him uneasy. It was too much like paranoia.

That's why they've ostracised the scientists on Clavus 3, he thought to himself. They weren't letting the infected individuals anywhere near the planet. That's why they were so quick to attempt destruction of the moon and it's inhabitants. They had again become a threat, and this time those in power had decided to rid them of it permanently, even if it meant killing their former employees. The scientists on Clavus 3 were innocent victims, only their unwitting exposure to the radiation making them enemies.

'So now, we're likely the enemy too,' Gerry muttered unconsciously.

'What was that you said Gerry,' Charmaine queried, also noticing a strange look on his face. 'You're looking a little off-colour.'

'Nothing, just thinking out loud. I did have another one of those uncomfortable moments though, but I'm all right now. Just a little light-headed.'

Charmaine nodded solemnly and went back to work at her keyboard. Gerry couldn't fail to notice that she was looking decidedly pale herself. Their sickness was progressing, and there seemed nothing he could do about it. Nothing but sit about watching the effect on his crew from the radiation exposure grow worse as they waited to end their journey near Earth, where they could hopefully get some explanation, and possibly a remedy. He was beginning to have concerns that they might not all make it in time. The sickness seemed to be progressing quickly, symptoms notably worsening by the hour.

Gerry tapped on his keyboard, bringing up the messaging screen that he used to covertly contact Mission Control. He'd not been sent any new messages. After ensuring Charmaine couldn't see what he was doing he dispatched a quick note to Earth, hoping to gain some more information from them.

'EFFECTS OF RADIATION EXPOSURE WORSENING. THIS IS LIKELY AN UNKNOWN NATURAL EFFECT. NOT LIKELY A DELIBERATE HOSTILE ACTION. THE SCIENTISTS ON CLAVUS 3 MAY BE SIMILAR VICTIMS. THEY MAY HAVE INFORMATION THAT WILL ASSIST US. THEY HAVE SURVIVED ON AN INHOSPITABLE MOON FOR 10 YEARS WHILE PROBABLY UNDER THE EFFECTS OF SAME RADIATION POISONING. AN UPDATE ON THE SITUATION FROM YOUR PERSPECTIVE WOULD BE BENEFICIAL. I ALSO REQUIRE MORE MEDICAL INFORMATION CONCERNING OUR CONDITION. PLEASE REPLY ASAP.'

Hopeful that it wouldn't be a fruitless exercise, Gerry clicked *send*. Next, he flicked over to the screen showing incoming documents, of which there were none as yet. As he sat watching the screen, counting on a quick response, Gerry pondered their situation with his strangely altered frame of mind. Resolutions to the complex set of circumstances that had affected them and there ship seemed to come clearly to mind without effort, and it was as if he had previously explored endless possibilities without consciously being aware of doing so. Any subject he turned his mind to would be crystal clear, as though he had considered everything before, without actually having done so.

A soft beep could be heard issuing from his computer terminal, signifying a new message had just been received. Opening the new document, Gerry saw by the size of the file that the message he'd been waiting upon had arrived invisibly attached to the cover document, which was nothing more than a detailed status sheet of their ships systems. Gerry knew the ship was running fine, it was the message attached that he was most interested in.

Executing the small computer programme he had on file, Gerry decoded the hidden message, having it flick instantly on to his computer screen. As he began to read, Gerry felt his head spin again, though the feeling left again quickly. As though his mind had slipped into top gear, it was as though he already knew what they were going to say. He knew these people, and he now had a good understanding of what their true situation was. In spite of all the unusual and unexplained occurrences over the past few days, Gerry felt he finally had a grasp on what had been happening, though he didn't know how or why. He didn't want to rely too much on his new-found powers of deduction though. In his experience it had been only unstable minds that would come to far-fetched conclusions based on too little information. The sense of clarity his mind possessed at times felt too much like madness. He felt he was jumping to conclusions in the extreme. He read the message, and wasn't surprised to find the contents to be exactly as he'd expected, though a quiet part of him told him that it wasn't a good thing, that the way he was thinking wasn't natural, so therefore should be feared and controlled.

'NETWORKED COMPUTER SYSTEMS ON EARTH AND COLONIES HAVE BECOME INOPERABLE. ONLY REASONABLE CONCLUSION IS THAT IT WAS A HOSTILE ACTION BY SCIENTISTS ON CLAVUS 3. WE HAVE ANALYSED THE MESSAGES YOUR SHIP RECEIVED FROM THEM AND FIND IT LIKELY THEY WANT TO RETURN TO EARTH. THIS IS NOT POSSIBLE. THEY ARE A DANGER TO US. THEY HAVE BEEN UNDER FORCED QUARANTINE. THEY HAVE SINCE CARRIED OUT CRIMINAL ACTS. THEY MUST NOT RETURN UNDER ANY CIRCUMSTANCES. NEGOTIATIONS ATTEMPTED OVER PREVIOUS YEARS WITH THEM WERE UNSUCCESSFUL.

'THE SCIENTISTS WERE INDEED EXPOSED TO THE SAME RADIATION YOUR SHIP WAS. THEY WERE LIKELY EXPOSED TO FAR HIGHER LEVELS AND FOR A LONGER PERIOD OF TIME THAN YOU AND YOUR CREW. THEY ARE IRRATIONAL AND UNPREDICTABLE.

'MEDICAL DATA FROM YOUR SHIP IS CURRENTLY BEING ANALYSED. WE WILL HAVE MORE INFORMATION CONCERNING YOUR CONDITION WHEN YOU HAVE ENTERED QUARANTINE NEAR EARTH. YOU ARE SUFFERING FROM A RARE AND LITTLE RESEARCHED FORM OF RADIATION EXPOSURE. DRINK PLENTY OF FLUIDS AND SHOWER OFTEN. THAT'S ALL WE CAN TELL YOU AS OF YET. WILL ADVISE YOU OF ANY INFORMATION PERTAINING TO YOUR CONDITION AS THE SITUATION BECOMES CLEARER.'

Gerry cursed quietly under his breath. So they had known that they would find people on Clavus 3 before they'd even embarked on this mission, he thought bitterly. They'd had contact with them as well, yet they hadn't advised anyone, even him, of the fact. And it even seemed likely that they had known they would be exposed to the radiation. This so-called research mission wasn't what it seemed. He and his crew were the lab rats this time. Mission control had sent the Supervisor to his death, and who knows what would happen to the remaining crew. Gerry hoped he wasn't getting paranoid, a side effect of the radiation poisoning, but he couldn't come to any other viable conclusion.

Clearing the message from the screen, Gerry sat back in his seat and closed his eyes, pondering his next move. His head was still spinning a little, and when his eyes were closed it felt as though his body were spinning quickly around. As he sat in his flight seat, considering their future, his head began to churn again. His myriad thoughts seemed to pick up their tempo, flitting so quickly through his mind that he hadn't enough time to consciously consider them.

He took a deep breath and tried to relax as his senses spun wildly. It seemed to help, and gradually the feeling subsided. He opened his eyes and suddenly had another amazing moment of clarity. They were going to their deaths. He was sure of it. The scientists on Clavus 3 were considered expendable, as were they. This was all part of their mission. Even their radiation exposure had been foreseen. They were returning to a position near Earth where their condition could be safely studied, and they could then easily eliminated if the radiation-tainted ship, or its crew, became a threat, as the scientists supposedly had. Either that or exiled to the same moon the scientists were located, though how anyone could survive in such an uninhabitable alien environment was impossible to imagine. If they couldn't find a cure for their radiation poisoning what would be the next move from Earth? It wasn't something Gerry was prepared to think about just yet, and realising for the first time with so much clarity of mind what their true position was, he felt the full weight of their hopeless situation.

He turned his head to look over at Charmaine, who was typing furiously at her keypad, a stern look of concentration on her face. She noticed Gerry's glance and responded by simply pointing to the large screen in front of them and saying, 'Have a look at this.'

The scientific reports she was working on appeared on-screen, and she continued to enter data and flick through different screens at an amazing rate. Gerry couldn't help but hold his breath as he watched. She was working impossibly fast. He'd watched for as little as thirty seconds, and in that time she completed what would have taken a normal person at least an hour. He watched carefully for a while longer, trying to keep up with her just enough to see if she was making any errors. He couldn't see any, and within a few minutes she had created reams of reports and data analysis. Finally she stopped to look at him. There was a look of satisfaction on her face, though also a hint of fear. She was obviously happy with what she'd just done, but frightened at what it might mean. Her voice trembled slightly when she spoke to him.

'Not bad, hey?'

'Incredible. I'd guess you've discovered a new talent.' Gerry replied.

'If this radiation poisoning does kill us eventually, at least I'll get a lot of work done before I go', she said, though Gerry couldn't tell if it was simply optimism or black humour.

'How can you be so sure it's radiation poisoning we're suffering?' Gerry asked her, knowing she was correct, but wondering how she had come to the conclusion.

'I don't know for sure. I do, but I just can't remember exactly how I came to be so certain. It's as though my conscious mind can't keep up with my unconscious sometimes. I've thought it through without actually being able to get a proper grasp on what I was thinking about.'

'I know what you mean. My brain's been redlining too. It actually seems to be working better, though I'll admit it's a little disconcerting,' Gerry told her.

'Do you think the scientists on the moon are affected in the same way we are?' Charmaine asked next.

'It does seem likely, doesn't it?'

Gerry was careful to not say too much. He knew Mission Control would be listening to their conversation, and wanted them to know he was respecting the confidentiality of the information he'd been secretly given, otherwise he wouldn't be getting any more important classified information from them. 'That doesn't explain why the ship was being affected by it far before we got anywhere near the moon.'

'I was thinking about that,' she replied instantly. 'The adenine clouds around the moon seemed to have some peculiar properties. They could have been the source of the radiation. What if some of the radioactive material was blasted near, or even into, the hyper-speed corridor by a high speed drive like the one we're using.'

'I guess it's possible,' Gerry conceded, suitably surprised by the theory she had put forward. 'We could have passed right through it. Other visitors to the moon would have taken exactly the same trajectory to get there that we did. The blast from their vessels' drives could have been firing the cloud material, or even just a stream of the unknown radiation type, straight back into the hyper-speed corridor.'

'Yeah that makes sense,' Charmaine added, 'If we'd struck any of the cloud material at high speed the ship would have been obliterated. A stream of the radiation coming from it and passing through the ship, though, could account for our radiation poisoning, and would have left the ship intact.'

Jennifer entered the flight deck, Gerry noticing she was a little unsteady on her feet. She sat down with a sigh and closed her eyes.

'You alright there, Jennifer?' Gerry inquired.

'I'm just feeling a little off. It feels as though I'm seasick. It's getting worse very quickly isn't it?'

'Yeah, but the unsettling feeling seems to pass quickly,' Gerry replied.

'It just comes in waves,' she added. 'It's going away again now though.'

'How did you go with analysing those samples?' Gerry asked her as she looked up and straightened herself in her flight seat.

'I couldn't find anything unusual about the food. It's untainted,' she explained. 'The skin samples were a different matter. They were sending some of the test instruments haywire. I could actually see the constant electrical discharges under the microscope around our skin cells.'

'It doesn't sound like it's the sort of thing we're simply going to be able to wash off.' Charmaine noted.

'No,' Jennifer agreed, 'but the regular treatments for radiation exposure might be what we need. We'll want to start the treatment as soon as we're back near Earth, so we'll need to tell Mission Control to have the necessary medication ready for transport to us.'

'I'll do that now if you like Sir,' Darren said to Gerry as he walked in and sat down. He was looking relatively healthy now.

'Looks like the sleep did you good. Hold off messaging them for the moment Darren. I might want to request a few other things of them.'

'OK. I didn't get any sleep though. Just tossed and turned. I don't feel the least bit tired though,' Darren replied

'Jennifer believes we need radiation treatment as soon as possible. We seem to be coming to a common conclusion that we are suffering from an unusual type of radiation exposure,' Gerry said to them all. 'So we may want to ask Mission Control for permission to accelerate the ship.'

Darren spoke first. 'It's definitely a good idea. I've never been so keen to get back to Earth. The extra rate of deceleration will be rough on us though.'

'So does everyone agree we should give it a go?' Gerry asked, looking over a row of concerned faces.

Jennifer and Charmaine nodded in unison.

'Formally message them the request Darren, and ask them to get some radiation specialists and some appropriate medical supplies ready for our arrival,' Gerry instructed.

'No problem Sir,' Darren said as he flicked up the screen beside his seat. 'Anything else you'd like to tell them?'

'That'll do' Gerry replied. 'They've got their audio and video link open so they know what's been happening here. They'd be using the data from Jennifer's medical reports to formulate some sort of plan too.'

'But I thought their computers were down. How are they going to analyse any of our data or receive our messages?' Charmaine asked, as Darren went about sending their requests to Mission Control.

'Not all of them, it seems.' Gerry answered. 'Keeping some computers separate from any external networks is part of normal computer security. Viruses or hackers can't harm them if there's no outside connection to them. They'd have isolated networks like that available to process our data.'

'Message sent.' Darren said. Everyone glanced at each other. Darren had sent the message in seconds.

'That was quick.' Gerry observed. 'Charmaine's been doing the same thing. It seems the radiation exposure is causing our minds to be a little hyperactive.'

'Yeah, I seem to be doing things rather quickly and easily. I'm thinking a bit differently as well. Our sickness is making me feel a little out of sorts, though I'm feeling healthy enough.'

'It looks like we're all experiencing the same effect,' Jennifer added. 'I put together dozens of medical reports earlier, if you're interested. They only took me a few seconds each. I was worried I was just churning out garbage, but I double-checked and they seem to be as close to flawless as I've been able to get any medical reports I've produced in the past.'

'Also, no-ones been able to sleep. That can't be good. Do you think we should be using sedatives to slow us down, maybe get some sleep?' Gerry asked her.

'No, I don't think that's necessary just yet. Our performance doesn't seem to be lacking anything due to tiredness, exactly the opposite in fact. Also, having the chemicals in out system when we get to Earth will effect the results of some of the medical tests. We don't want anything holding up their analysis.'

Just then the computer beeped, signifying a message received. Darren bought it on-screen immediately.

'PERMISSION GRANTED TO INCREASE ACCELERATION. SPECIALIST MEDICAL STAFF HERE WOULD LIKE TO ASSESS YOUR CONDITION IN THE EARLIEST POSSIBLE STAGE. FULLY EQUIPPED MEDICAL TEAM IS STANDING BY.'

'OK then, lets put the pedal to the metal.' Gerry ordered. 'Strap yourselves in, and give us ninety percent thrust Darren.'

'Yes Sir, thrusters fired in five seconds.' Darren replied as the others made sure they were properly positioned in their flight seats and their harnesses secure. Charmaine and Jennifer stole a worried glance at each other. Twenty-five percent more thrust than they usually used meant twenty-five percent more force on their bodies. Neither of them had ever been in a ship that could accelerate so rapidly.

'Two... One...' Darren advised, and then his voice was cut off as all hell broke loose, the ship unleashing an insane surge of power.

There they sat for the next seven hours, forced mercilessly into their flight seats by the massive forces of acceleration. Then there was a few minutes respite, as the ship cancelled acceleration and spin around automatically so that it was travelling backward, still travelling at tens-of-thousands of times the speed of light.

As soon as they had reached the appropriate position the hyper-speed drive fired again, smashing them back into their seats for the next nine hours as they decelerated. It was a tortuous journey for each of them. Their radiation-affected brains churned at times so badly that both Charmaine and Darren vomited over themselves. Combined with the forces but upon their bodies as the ship decelerated, the crew had a terrible time of it. None of them, not even Gerry slept. So too, none of them had gained the respite of losing consciousness, not even for a moment. Each of them realised that this was unusual. They felt every painful second as they smashed through space at speeds rarely attained by hyper-speed vessels carrying people.

TEN

'Satan, laughing, spreads his wings...'
Black Sabbath – War Pigs

They were still awake, and strangely more alert than they had ever been as they watched Earth loom on the screen before them. They were positioned a long way from the planet, a space station a few hundred kilometres away from them was their nearest neighbour. Darren changed the view on the large screen before them, bringing an image of the station on-screen. It was a welcoming image, and as they watched there was a flash from tiny ion drives and they saw a vessel departing, headed in their direction. A message tone sounded and Darren bought it onto the main screen for all of them to see.

'TREATMENT FOR RADIATION EXPOSURE ABOARD SHUTTLE. QUARANTINE MEASURES APPLY. NO CONTACT WILL BE MADE WITH YOUR SHIP. OPEN AIRLOCK TO RECEIVE SUPPLIES. YOU WILL BE ADVISED FURTHER ASAP.'

Darren closed the message and the view turned back to the approaching transport vessel. They sat and watched without speaking, while what could possibly be a cure quickly bridged the distance between them and pulled alongside. Darren opened the outer airlock door.

A panel slid open and a robotic arm emerged, a package in its grasp. It extended silently toward them, startling more than one of them when it knocked loudly against the floor in the airlock and released their supplies. They were surprised to see another robotic arm emerge from the vessel, which grasped the first arm and with a twist it, disconnected it. It then smoothly flung the detached arm into space; something very much frowned upon in any situation. Their Mission Supervisors on Earth obviously weren't going to accept any risk of contamination, but Gerry was surprised that their concern was so great that they were worried that the delivery vessel's loading arm could have been tainted by the radiation, after such slight contact with their vessel. Surprised

141

that they would disregard international law and leave another hazardous object floating in space so near Earth.

'Close the outer door Darren, and open the inner. We'll go have a look at what they've given us' Gerry instructed, as the vessel promptly departed.

They all rose to the sound of the doors thumping open and closed. They reached the airlock; Gerry stepping inside to pick up a large chest that had been left for them. Putting it down in the corridor he quickly tore open the packaging. They'd sent some fresh food, real food. And hot. Gerry hoped maybe that it would help them get their appetites back. Alongside were dozens of boxes of pills and vials. He pulled them out and handed them to Jennifer, saying, 'Let's start the treatment as soon as possible.'

He lifted the trays of steaming food out of the box and passed them to Darren, leaving only a small plastic device with wheels, which he recognised to be a remote-controlled sensing device. It was a type of probe that was often used in dangerous situations on Earth to assess an environment by distance via a remote control. He pulled it from the box and switched it on as he placed it on the floor. It immediately rolled off down the corridor, clicking and beeping as it scanned their ship. Hopefully it would pass enough data back to Mission Control to give them more of an idea as to what had been happening to them and their ship.

'Job done, let's go eat' Gerry said, with more cheer in his voice than he was actually feeling.

Back on the flight deck they found they were still having problems with food. It smelt great, and they all wanted to eat, but on taking a mouthful they would bring the food straight back up. Their bodies weren't even letting it reach their stomach before they began retching. After repeated attempts they gave up and just sipped the water instead. None of them were hungry anyway.

Jennifer passed them each a few pills, which they tried to swallow with water. It was no use. Before they could finish swallowing they could only cough the pill back up. Their bodies just weren't accepting anything other than water. On messaging Mission Control they were instructed to try another drug intravenously.

They'd have to test just a tiny amount on someone first though, to ensure that their bodies wouldn't react adversely to it, as they seemed to with food. Gerry decided he would be the test subject.

'This is only one-hundredth the normal dosage,' Jennifer said as she pressed a small device against his forearm and gave him the shot.

Within an instant of the device's click, which meant the dosage had been administered, Gerry's arm started to burn around the injection site. It was incredibly painful, but there was nothing he could do but watch as a large part of his arm began turning a purple colour. Tiny blue sparks flickered along the length of his arm, his skin alive with some sort of electrical energy.

'This isn't looking too promising.' Gerry said through clenched teeth. He held his arm as still as he could while everybody watched in horror as a lump grew on his forearm. Within seconds it looked like a severe abscess. It wasn't long before the skin broke open, releasing a spray of blood that the others had to step back to avoid.

There was a puff of smoke as a blue flame sprayed briefly into life, seeming to jet from the wound. The pain began to ease thereafter, and in less than a minute, other than the spinning sensation in his head, Gerry was feeling fine. There was soon no sign of the smoking abscess, and even the dark purple patches along his arm were fading as they watched.

'Thank god we only used a small amount.' Charmaine said, breaking their stunned silence.

'Looks like we need some other options' Gerry said as he rose from where he was sitting on his bunk, a little unsteadily thanks to the churning sensation in his head. 'Let's go see if Mission Control has any other ideas.'

Jennifer typed a medical report when they got back to the flight deck, in record time, and sent it to the mission controllers, along with a message asking if they want their skin samples to test for themselves.

They replied immediately, stating 'UNDER NO CIRCUMSTANCES WILL SAMPLES OF THE RADIOACTIVE MATERIAL BE REMOVED FROM YOUR VESSEL. WE ARE USING THE DATA YOU COLLECTED, AND THAT WHICH THE PROBE IS CURRENTLY GATHERING, TO FORMULATE A PLAN OF ACTION.'

143

The last line caught their attention most of all. 'WE HAVE PREVIOUSLY HAD ACCESS TO SAMPLES OF IRRADIATED MATERIAL OF THIS RADIATION TYPE. IT IS DIFFICULT TO CONTAIN.'

'They know about the radiation' Jennifer stated with a tone of surprise in her voice. 'They've seen some samples already. But how would that be possible? They haven't removed anything from the ship, inside or out.'

'They've known about the strange form of radiation for a long time now I think,' Gerry told them. It was obvious from the message that they weren't bothering to keep the fact hidden from the crew any more. 'They'd have more data on it than you'd have realised. They've probably been studying it for years. It is peculiar that they kept such an important discovery so quiet though.'

'Damn it,' Charmaine complained. 'I knew we were being kept in the dark. We're scientists. We should have been given all the data to work with. And how long have you known about this?' she said, looking at Gerry.

Gerry couldn't tell them about his personal messaging system he had with some important people back on Earth. He knew it could become vital at some stage before they resolved the situation. 'I realised it yesterday after looking over some of the computer data. They seemed to know what they were looking for. Most of the probes have been modified, equipped with extra radiation sensing capabilities.' He said, inwardly cringing at the deception. He wasn't lying, he consoled himself, simply wasn't giving her a full answer to her question. He couldn't give them the whole truth.

Before Charmaine could speak again, Jennifer closed her eyes, gasping, pressing her face into her open hands. 'I feel real sick all of a sudden.'

They couldn't do anything but sit and watch her agony, each of them knowing all too well what she was feeling. Ten seconds lapsed before she opened her eyes and pushed her body upright again in the flight seat.

'I just had another one of those weird moments,' she said. 'Something dawned on me when it was happening. They were pretty sure we would be exposed to the radiation. In fact, I think they were counting on it.'

144

'How so?' Charmaine asked her.

'I'm not really sure. I thought of lots of reasons when I was spinning out, but I can't remember what they were now. I'm certain about it though. We were used like unwitting lab rats.'

'Don't base too many conclusions on what goes through your head while you're feeling sick. It could well be just delusion caused by the radiation exposure. I'm having the same thoughts, but we can't trust them to be logical conclusions,' Charmaine reminded her.

'I agree,' Jennifer answered, 'but my thinking is clearer than it's ever been, by a long shot. I won't be certain of anything though until we're given some more information.'

Darren was quiet, and when Gerry looked over at him he was staring blankly in front of him, his face tinged a pale green. 'She's right you know. This is all just part of our real mission. Now they've got us under the microscope.'

Gerry was getting concerned about the crew. It was difficult enough to function properly while they felt so ill, but the strange thought processes they were experiencing could make their predicament more dangerous than it already was. He didn't want to have to worry about the actions of the crew while they were possibly suffering delusions.

Mission Control would have logged every word they had spoken. He was considering the implications of what they had just discussed when a message arrived with a beep. Darren, recovered slightly though still looking very unwell, bought it on-screen.

'CONCERNS HAVE BEEN RAISED OVER YOUR MENTAL HEALTH UNDER THESE UNUSUAL CIRCUMSTANCES. MEDICAL OFFICER IS ADVISED TO ADMINISTER INHALED TRANQUILISERS TO ALL CREW. ACTING SUPERVISOR IS INSTRUCTED TO KEEP ALL ABOARD AWAY FROM SHIPS CONTROLS. EVERYONE IS INSTRUCTED TO USE COMPUTER SYSTEM FOR DATA PROCESSING ONLY. PLEASE NOTE YOU ARE UNDER MILITARY QUARANTINE.'

'Why'd they bother telling us to keep away from the ship's controls. It's not like we're going anywhere.' Darren said after reading the message. 'And that last line sounds like a threat to me.'

'I'd say they're just having some concerns that we're not thinking straight in our condition, and they're a little worried we might do something rash or illogical. Just trying to head off a problem before it becomes one, I suppose,' Gerry replied.

'Maybe. They definitely sound like they mean business. They're always strict when it comes to quarantine matters though, and who could blame them. I certainly wouldn't want to pass this illness onto anybody else. Who knows how far the radiation extends from our bodies, or how much it will taint our environment,' Charmaine added.

'They're probably checking on that now.' Gerry observed, pointing down at the robotic sensor that was slowly travelling the length of the wall, obviously scanning for traces of something. 'We'll know how much radiation the ship has absorbed pretty soon I'd say. It was unusual that the food was untainted. Though the specialised instrumentation they'll be using now might come up with a different set of results.'

'So should I go get us that tranquillising gas they want us to take?' Jennifer asked. 'It's not a bad idea actually. I'd prescribe it myself if a patient was suffering from insomnia like we are and I wasn't able to use tablets or injections.'

'Yeah, go get it,' Gerry answered. 'I doubt we'll be able to use it though. Anything but water has been rejected so far.'

'We can only try. We really should be getting some sleep. Another day or two of this and we will really have some concerns over our mental fitness.' Jennifer advised as she rose to leave.

'Yeah, I'm having some crazy thoughts already' Darren said. 'I seem to be able to think more clearly than ever sometimes, but it's different than normal thought processes. I'm not sure if I'm smarter than I've ever been or just delusional.'

Gerry was checking some of the ship's sensor readings when he noticed something unusual. 'Darren, have a look at our radar screen. There's something blocking part of the signal. Either that or it's been damaged.'

Darren tapped his keyboard to bring the radar screen up where they could get a better look at it, on the main viewing monitor in front of them. At a glance he could see what Gerry meant. 'You're right; part of the radar's scan is being blocked by something.'

146

'I don't think we have an external view that'll let us see what it is either' Gerry added.

'No, and the only suit we had on board was ruined on your last space-walk. We can't find out what it is' Darren said.

Charmaine had an idea instantly. 'We could use one of the spare probe sensors I've got in my cabin. We could use one to scan through the hull and give us a picture of what's there.'

'Nice one,' Gerry said smiling. 'Let's get right on it. It'll be good for us to have something useful to do instead of sitting about worrying about things.'

With that, Charmaine, Gerry and Darren left the flight deck for Charmaine's cabin. Jennifer joined them later as they were considering which sensors would best suit their requirements.

'There's no point trying to use the tranquilliser. I tested a little and got the same response as when we tried the radiation medication. We can't breathe the stuff. It just made me feel a bit sick and I had a coughing fit,' she advised them. 'What are we looking for here?'

'Something we can scan through the hull with. Something is messing with our radar signal. It may be damaged,' Gerry informed her.

'This one will do the trick,' Charmaine called to them, lifting a complicated-looking mass of electronics encased by a sphere of clear plastic. 'Someone will need to be on the flight deck to record the pictures this picks up.'

'I'll go get things ready' Darren said immediately. As he made his way back to the flight deck the others moved the scanning equipment into one of the storage rooms, which they were sure was closest to where the radar sensors were situated outside the ship.

Gerry helped Charmaine lift it to a position where it was directed at the hull, as close as they could work out the radar component would be located. They heard Darren's voice over the intercom system. 'Ready to receive data.'

With that, Charmaine flicked a switch and the machine whirred into life.

'We've got a picture here,' Darren's voice called immediately from the speakers above. 'Try moving a little to the right.'

They did as advised and heard his surprised tone of voice over the intercom. 'There is something on the hull. Come check it out. God knows what it is.'

Placing the instrument back on the floor, the three went back to the flight deck, where Gerry made an alarming discovery. Darren had placed an image of the object that was stuck to their hull on the large viewing screen. Gerry recognised the shape as soon as he entered the room and glanced at the screen.

'That's a magnetic charge. Now what would that be doing there?' he said to the crew. But as he asked the question, the obvious answer came to him.

'It must have been placed there when they dropped off supplies,' Darren surmised, backing up what Gerry was thinking. Everyone already knew the answer. The hyped-up state their minds were now in helped give them the answer immediately. Gerry's memory had a quality of clarity about it that amazed him. He even now remembered an extra thump when the automated supply ship had met them. He'd thought nothing of it at the time. He mentally kicked himself for being so careless. He should have known something was amiss. Then again, he thought to himself, he wasn't thinking quite as sharply then as he was now.

Jennifer spoke next. 'That'd be an insurance policy against us going haywire and doing something silly. They've been concerned over our mental state, and I guess it's their way of keeping things under their control.'

'Well, it hasn't helped my mental state any' Darren said. 'This was just supposed to be a job, a means of income. This mission's turned real sour.'

'Yeah,' Gerry agreed, 'we'll probably get an explanation soon. They're receiving our audio, so they know we've found it.'

'Let's hope they don't just set it off now. Do you think it's on a timer or operated by remote control?' Jennifer inquired of Gerry.

'Could be either. Or both. It might be set to detonate if we try moving the ship, too.'

Their attention was bought back to the big screen before them when the computer sounded the chime indicating an incoming message.

'REQUESTING VIDEO LINK' appeared on the screen. Darren pressed some keys to bring up the video-messaging

148

screen. They were expecting to be talking with one of the mission controllers, but instead were suddenly part of a large meeting. Gerry counted seventeen people seated before them. Some he recognised, most he did not.

'Hello crew,' spoke an elderly man seated at the front of the group, 'I guess you'd appreciate some explanations.'

'We certainly would' Gerry answered instantly.

'Frankly, so would we,' he continued. 'But I think we can clarify the situation a little for you. I'm James Reardon, head of Australian Security and Intelligence Organisation. We've been given command of your mission. It's our job to sort this mess out and bring you home safely.'

'Was the magnetic charge really necessary?' Gerry asked next.

'From our perspective it was. You're in control of a powerful vessel, and we have been given reason to be wary of your mental state due to the radiation exposure. It's only there in case your condition gets far worst, and you aren't responsible for your actions.'

'We have billions of people to protect, and that is the reason for this meeting' said a younger man, seated to the left of the screen. He needed no introduction. Everyone on board knew they were speaking to the Prime Minister of Australia. Seated alongside him was the English Prime Minister. This was certainly a high-powered meeting.

'Understood Sir,' Gerry replied.

'The radiation exposure you are suffering from was not unknown to us before this mission,' the Prime Minister continued. 'Doctor Hepworth will fill you in.'

A nervous-looking man stood up from his seat at the rear of the group. He nodded to the crew politely before speaking.

'We first found evidence of the radiation about twelve years ago, on a previous mission to the moon you just visited. As far as we knew, the crew had perished after our last contact with them. They had become mentally unstable and had made certain threats. We assumed they had died in circumstances related to their condition.'

'So the people we found there are from that mission?' Gerry inquired. 'What happened to them?'

149

'We know as little as you do on that score,' Hepworth replied. 'Somehow they took their vessel down to the moons surface and have been living there since.'

'They're unstable. They used your ship computer to link with ours back here on Earth, and damaged our systems. It seems they altered their ship somehow, to make it habitable for a long period. They must have modified their main drive to work as a rescue beacon. There's no way they could have left the moon using the drive, for two reasons. One, it was too badly damaged, and two, the vessel was submerged.'

'Do you think they crashed there or landed deliberately on the moon?' Gerry interrupted.

'It could only have been a deliberate act' the scientist explained. 'From the data we gained from your probes we know the ship was carefully positioned at the end of a natural tunnel in the moons surface. It couldn't have got in such a position by mistake.'

'But why would they do such a thing?' Charmaine asked them. 'They must have known they'd be stranded there.'

'Who knows? Remember that they were mentally unbalanced. There may have been no logical reason behind their actions,' Doctor Hepworth answered.

Something else was playing on Darren's mind. 'Why did you send the hyper-speed missile at us?'

'The Intelligence and Security official cleared his throat and stood. 'That would be my department. The scientist returned to his seat as the ASIO man gave his reasons for their actions.

'We apologise for the close call. We knew you'd have a visual warning of the incoming device and have time to distance your vessel from the target. There was no chance we could risk connecting our computers to yours again to give you warning. We're still having problems with the majority of our systems down here.'

'Was it a virus?' Gerry asked.

'Not that we can tell. It was more a single destructive programme. It ran once on your computers and damaged every computer connected to it, which included millions that were connected to it via the Internet.'

'Any idea why they did it?' Gerry asked next.

150

'Yes. They wanted to return to Earth. It wasn't possible, and we told them as much. They responded with the malicious software and threatened further retaliation.'

'And they had some control over our ship, which they could have used as a weapon, so you decided you had to neutralise the threat as soon as possible,' Gerry finished for him.

'That's correct' the security man said simply.

Gerry continued. 'And now we've been poisoned by the same radiation, which was probably ejected into our flight path by the stranded scientists ship when is entered the planetary system and crash-landed on the moon.'

'Yes, that seems likely.'

'So we are as unwelcome back on Earth as they are, I can understand that. But we haven't turned feral like they have. We don't need a bomb attached to our vessel' Gerry told them. He couldn't feel comfortable talking with these people while they had their finger on the trigger.

'I'm afraid it must stay until we've found some solutions. Don't let it worry you. There's no harm it can do to you unless the effect on your brain from the radiation exposure impels you to do something that is a danger to others.'

'I feel as clear-headed and as sane as I ever have, just a little hyperactive' Darren said, the others nodding their heads in agreement.

'We're thinking and working better than ever' Charmaine added. The Security and Intelligence man paused for a moment before speaking.

'There's the problem,' he said finally, and sat back slowly into his seat.

'Is that how the people on that mission twelve years ago survived? Does this radiation exposure change people so much?' Gerry asked no one in particular.

Doctor Hepworth spoke from his seat. 'It seems the only logical way we could find it possible, especially after observing your own medical condition. They have been living in the vessel for more than a decade. The old hyper-speed vessels were very cramped inside. They could not be alive after such a long period if they were still operating with normal human body function. They may have altered the vessel to assist their survival, but it surely couldn't account for more than 10 years without food.'

Jennifer spoke next sounding decidedly dejected. 'And now we're going to go the same way. You couldn't let us back onto Earth even if our radiation exposure couldn't effect anyone else, could you?'

'No.' the ASIO officer replied. 'You may have been affected in a similar way. They became a danger, and evidence suggests you may do the same.'

'Are we going to have to sit here in this ship until a cure is found for our condition? It might take years' Charmaine interjected.

'Maybe,' Doctor Hepworth replied, 'but we could gain much by studying your condition over the next few months. The data we collect could go a long way toward finding a cure for your condition.'

'What do we do in the meantime?' Gerry asked next.

'Stay here and wait things out. There's no alternative' the Security and Intelligence official advised.

'Do we have a choice?' Jennifer asked.

'Yes, you can go anywhere you like, as long as you stay within your vessel and keep it some distance from other ships. We believe you are functioning well enough to carry out another mission while waiting for our test results. We could give you a shuttle if required to help you carry out your research, but you mustn't exit it under any circumstances. We will always have access to your data via the entangled-particle communicator link,' the ASIO man stated. 'We can still help you wherever you are.'

Or set off a magnetic charge from any distance, Gerry thought to himself, knowing that it wouldn't help their cause if he'd said it aloud.

'What are you doing with the two scientists on Clavus 3?' Gerry inquired next. 'Do you still need to eliminate them?'

'Yes, there's no way we can leave them there. Any passing ship could come under their control, just as yours did. They've altered their communications equipment in some way. One of them was once a computer scientist. We suspect it was him that made a mess of our computer systems here on Earth. We consider it an act of terrorism. Any of our enemies could strike while our systems security is compromised. Not to mention the articles they forced you to dump from your ship in a trajectory that would take them through our solar system.'

152

'Yeah, sorry about that.' Gerry apologised. 'There wasn't any other viable option though. They were going to use our ship to block the missile.'

'We realise that. The incident will be investigated, but it's not likely you'll have charges laid against you,' the security official advised.

For the radiation-sick crew, it was of little comfort. There were far more pressing issues than legal proceedings being bought against them back on Earth. It could be years, it now seemed, before their condition might be properly assessed and their normal health restored, allowing them to return home. Gerry thought even this to be an optimistic outcome. Reversing their condition may not even be possible.

'So what's our next move?' Gerry asked.

'Nothing, just sit tight and wait for medical results. You are still on the payroll, and we could give you some more work if that's what you want. There's a backlog of jobs. You're effectively quarantined as long as you stay within the ship. We could give you a simple mission or two to keep you busy while you are waiting.'

Gerry felt that it was just a means of getting them away from Earth yet keeping them under close surveillance. If he was right about them being exposed deliberately to the radiation then this was all just part of the experiment. Deducing whether or not the radiation poisoning was a great danger to the human race would be relatively easy for them if they could watch them work as the effects of their contamination showed themselves.

'Thanks, we'll consider it,' Gerry told them. 'None of us are feeling very confident at the moment that we'll still be functioning effectively in a few days time. It has been quite a while since our last meal.'

The intelligence official looked hard and serious into the camera. 'Those scientists on Clavus 3 have survived for more than a decade without food. Chances are, you'll be OK.'

'Our minds seem to be working especially well lately. We're all sure we were knowingly sent through the radiation streams by the mission planners. It isn't just paranoia, is it?' Gerry asked bluntly.

'As we said earlier,' the intelligence man answered, 'we've known the two scientists were under the effect of something they'd been exposed to while carrying out a mission there twelve years ago. One of them had gone down to the surface of the moon. We'd assumed that's where they were irradiated, not while still aboard the vessel. We were confident we hadn't exposed you to undue risk. The possibility was there, but we couldn't say for certain that we were sending you into danger.'

Their heads swimming and minds churning with activity, the crew glanced at each other quickly, all sharing the same thought. They were guinea pigs, their bodies used by Mission Control to sample the radiation from somewhere on or near Clavus 3. And it seemed the experiment had only just begun.

'Any idea what may have caused the physical effects we experienced on route for Clavus 3?' Gerry asked next. 'Probably the same phenomenon that killed Eric, our Supervisor.'

'We assume it was the effects caused by a malfunctioning hyper-drive. The scientists were messing with your onboard computer systems at the time. We believe it was a result of their tampering with your engine-controls' the Intelligence officer informed them.

'I think it's obvious what we need to do. We've got to go back to Clavus 3 and get some more information from the scientists there' Gerry said, and his companions nodded their agreement. The idea didn't go down too well with the representative's back on Earth though.

'That won't be possible. We can't risk them gaining control of your vessel,' the military official told them sternly. 'We're keeping all vessels and probes away from that solar system indefinitely.'

'I suppose we have some spare time if nothing else.' Gerry said. 'Send us some mission plans and we'll consider our options.'

'Will do,' their Mission Supervisor acceded, speaking for the first time. He looked distinctively uncomfortable amidst the high-profile people in the room.

'If that's all, we'll leave it there,' the Intelligence and Security man said. 'We'll be in contact with you as soon as we get some results from the data we're collecting from your vessel concerning your blood and tissue samples, and also the vessels structural contamination if there is any.'

Gerry nodded affirmation and the screen instantly went blank. Each of the crew-members felt the full weight of their situation in the sudden quiet upon the flight deck. The silence remained

154

unbroken for a few minutes, the crew in deep thought, considering all that had happened to them on this ill-fated mission. The strange way their minds were working now had the effect of making them feel powerfully depressed, and a sense of hopelessness overcame each of them. They could see their future clearly. Too clearly.

ELEVEN

'If you're causing no harm you're alright with me...'
Ben Harper – Burn One Down

The next few days passed uneventfully other than their symptoms worsening slightly. Still without sleep, they worked tirelessly through the data they had collected during the mission. It didn't take them long to exhaust their supply of information without any breakthroughs, without discovering anything that might have helped them better understand their condition.

The effect of the radiation poisoning upon their mental processes was becoming more pronounced. There was firm logic behind each of their thoughts, and no one had done anything that could be considered irrational, though the hyper-activity of their minds certainly wasn't anything like normal. Thoughts seemed to enter their consciousness and were thoroughly considered, with seemingly no oversight, within milliseconds. Things they had often pondered in the past were resolved now. And as quickly as the thought had entered their minds it was gone again. Another would come to mind immediately, and would be considered just as efficiently.

The crew seemed to have improved mentally and physically in a profound way, though none took pride in their newfound abilities. They felt only fear and awe.

While Darren worked furiously at his computer terminal on his flight seat Jennifer was in her cabin laying on her bunk trying to get her thoughts in order, trying to get reign over her over-active mind. She wasn't succeeding.

Charmaine was still working hard at her computer re-analysing the data they'd collected from Clavus 3. She was tireless in her exertions, making the most of her unusual mental state. Gerry was on the flight deck too, looking over plans for five missions that he'd been sent. None of them were very interesting to him at the moment. He felt their circumstances weren't conducive to a safe or stable work environment. Anyway, simply mapping the surface of some of the more recently discovered planets and

156

releasing a few research probes didn't help their personal circumstances, or cure the crew's strange condition.

After a few hours of near silence aboard the ship, only the tap of keyboards to be heard, Gerry was surprised to see his small computer screen by his side suddenly change views, and he was looking at a message. It was from Darren, who was sitting only metres away from Gerry. The content of the message explained why he didn't simply speak to him.

'THIS IS FROM DARREN. WE NEEDED A PRIVATE MEANS OF COMMUNICATIONS. THERE IS SOME THINGS WE NEED TO TALK ABOUT WITHOUT EVERYONE ON EARTH KNOWING ABOUT IT. I HAVE ALTERED THE SOFTWARE THAT LETS US MESSAGE EACH OTHER. AS FAR AS THEY KNOW ON EARTH I AM READING SOME MISSION PLANS. THEY DON'T KNOW WE ARE TALKING WITH EACH OTHER.'

Gerry looked over at Darren when he'd finished reading the secret message. He was a little shocked. If he were to do his job properly he'd arrest Darren immediately and inform those on Earth that he was carrying out subversive action. But he considered the repercussions of both action and inaction, and his new-found clarity of though gave him the answer quickly. He'd keep quiet about it.

Gerry wrote back. 'I HOPE YOU WERE DAMN CAREFUL. THEY WILL BE WATCHING FOR ANY UNUSUAL USAGE OF THE COMPUTERS. IF YOU ARE CAUGHT AT IT YOU'LL RUIN YOUR CAREER AND MINE.'

Darren's reply came immediately. 'I KNOW THE RISK, I WOULD PROBABLY BE LOCKED UP FOR YEARS. I WAS VERY CAREFUL. I HAVE DISCOVERED SOME COMPUTER PROGRAMMING SKILLS I NEVER KNEW I HAD. IT SEEMED VERY STRAIGHT-FORWARD.'

'MESSAGE CHARMAINE TELLING HER A PRIVATE MESSAGING CHANNEL HAS BEEN SET UP. SEND ONE TO JENNIFER WHEN SHE GETS BACK TO HER TERMINAL AS WELL' Gerry typed.

The did need to discuss their options without being restricted by orders from Earth. They weren't going back there any time soon. It was likely that they'd be exiled like the scientists on

Clavus 3, Gerry decided. It wasn't that he and the crew were going to do anything damaging against Mission Control and their military advisors, but they needed to discuss *all* their options, some of which topics may not make the officials on Earth feel too comfortable. Gerry didn't want to give them reason, or an excuse, to set off the mine they'd attached to the hull of their vessel.

Charmaine looked up wide-eyed when she received Darren's message. But she quickly regained her composure to keep those who were watching from seeing anything unusual. She was going to keep their secret, and Gerry's tension eased somewhat. She had just broken the law though, taking part in subversive action, and she didn't look too happy about the fact. It probably wasn't often that she had done anything illegal, Gerry thought, if ever. If Darren had been as thorough as he said, there shouldn't be much chance of being discovered anyway. As far as they knew back on Earth they were busy working. Their computer screens would be seen to be displaying a mission plan or scientific report, and the cameras and microphones on-board would show them to simply be working as normal at their terminals.

Another message appeared on Gerry's screen. It was Charmaine.

'I WOULDN'T NORMALLY GO ALONG WITH SOMETHING LIKE THIS BUT I DO NEED TO TALK WITH YOU ALL PRIVATELY. I THINK THERE IS A WAY TO GET RID OF THAT BOMB.'

She'd obviously been working as hard as Darren had. And, both of them upon questionable projects, Gerry noted. He hoped officials on Earth weren't justified in their mistrust for the ill researchers aboard. He trusted his own state of mind. It just seemed in top gear. Hopefully the others were as alert and mentally fit as he was, and to Gerry it seemed to be so.

'WE CAN'T DO SOMETHING LIKE THAT WITHOUT MISSION CONTROL KNOWING ABOUT IT.' Gerry typed in reply to Charmaine's message. 'THE CAMERAS ARE ON US WHEREVER WE ARE ABOARD THIS SHIP.'

'I REALISE THAT. WE WOULD HAVE TO CUT COMMUNICATIONS BEFORE WE DID IT' Charmaine replied.

Gerry was more than a little concerned about the way things were going. After so much work over the last few days in an attempt to reverse their condition caused by the radiation exposure, the crew was obviously looking at other ways they could help themselves. It worried him, these signs of desperation, though he knew they should investigate every possibility. But the crew seemed to assume their biggest threat to be the explosive charge attached to their vessel. They perceived the threat from fellow humans to be even direr than that of their radiation exposure. What worried Gerry most was that he agreed with them. It seemed obvious to him, there being little doubt in his mind. Their radiation poisoning may be a threat to their well being, but the decisions made by security officials on Earth were a more immediate issue. If they decided that their best option was to eliminate the risk, they would be atomised in the blink of an eye.

He could imagine them now, feeding misinformation to the media, setting them up to disappear. Being killed on one of these missions wasn't unusual. It would be as simple as releasing to the newspapers an account of their death on duty caused by radiation exposure in a barely known solar system many light-years from Earth.

Gerry was all for individuality, but his crew were risking all of their lives by taking subversive action. Mission Control and the security officials on Earth were supposed to be making their decisions for them, but the crew didn't seem to want to leave their future up to their superiors. They seemed to think that they knew better. This concerned Gerry, mainly because he agreed with them.

Attempting to get more of a grip on their situation, Gerry forced himself to relax, did his utmost to clear his mind of the thoughts that were racing through at an amazing rate. It worked to a minor extent, and he considered their immediate circumstances. It took all of two seconds, never mind it's complexity. He could not stop his mind rushing with activity, bursting with ideas as soon as he began to consider something.

They couldn't leave things as they were. He and the crew were not handling their inaction very well. Having nothing to keep themselves occupied, they'd resorted to illegal activity. Gerry didn't feel they were misguided acts. They all simply

159

understood the danger they were in if they did nothing to help themselves. They were exploring every option and following those that held the most promise.

Mission Control had suggested they go on a simple mission while their condition was assessed, but this held no interest for Gerry. Their futures were in the balance at the moment, and they might not be alive in a few days time, for all anyone knew. He wasn't going to spend what could be the final days of his life taking images of barren planets and checking through hundreds of pages of data from the probes. He needed to be pro-active in finding a cure for their condition, or at least try to discover what their future may hold as the effects of the radiation exposure ran their course. Those on Earth might not be too concerned that the ill crew may never return home, but Gerry was.

The only information they could obtain here was filtered and so censored by the military to be almost useless. If there were people on Earth that knew something about their condition they weren't in evidence.

Gerry knew what they needed to do to give them any real chance of a recovery from the radiation exposure. Staying where they were wasn't an option, he felt. Sitting idle while being studied by people on Earth did not hold much hope for them, he feared.

They had to go back to Clavus 3. The two scientists stranded there would know more about their affliction than anyone else would. In addition, it was their duty to return, Gerry felt. Mission Control had ignored the fact that they had failed to rescue a couple of stranded space farer's who had signalled them for help. This was breaking one of the oldest and most fundamental rules of space travel.

'OK. HOW DO WE GET RID OF THAT BOMB CHARMAINE?' Gerry typed.

'IT'S A MAGNETIC CHARGE. WE HAVE LARGE ELECTROMAGNETS IN SOME OF THE SURVEY EQUIPMENT. WE COULD POWER ONE OF THOSE UP TO PUSH IT OFF THE SIDE OF THE SHIP' was Charmaine's reply.

The next message appearing on their small screens at their sides was from Darren. 'THAT SOUNDS RISKY. THE

160

ELECTROMAGNET WOULD PLAY HAVOC WITH THE ELECTRONICS IN THE MINE. IT MIGHT SET IT OFF.'

'IT'S A POSSIBILITY' Gerry entered next. 'DEVICES LIKE THAT TYPE OF MINE ARE WELL SHIELDED FROM EXTERNAL FORCES THOUGH. THEY CANNOT BE GOING OFF AT THE WRONG TIME AND THEY NEED TO BE ABLE TO BE DEPLOYED ANYWHERE. CHANCES ARE CHARMAINES PLAN WILL WORK.'

'WILL THEY KNOW IT'S GONE THOUGH?' Charmaine messaged them next.

'NOT UNLESS THEY VISUALLY NOTICE THAT ITS BEEN REMOVED' Gerry advised, knowing enough about the type of weapon attached to their ship to be confident of the fact. There most likely weren't any electronic locators in the mine.

Jennifer came onto the flight deck, noticing how intense everyone's focus was on his or her computers.

'Has something happened? Any news about our radiation poisoning?' she asked them as she sat down.

'No,' Gerry lied. 'Just looking over the mission plans we've been offered.'

'That doesn't really interest me...' she started, when she noticed the message on her little computer screen.

It read, 'THIS IS GERRY. DON'T SHOW YOUR SURPRISE. THIS IS A PRIVATE MESSAGING SYSTEM SET UP BY DARREN. WE CAN TALK WITHOUT ANYONE ON EARTH KNOWING ABOUT IT. IT IS ILLEGAL, BUT I HOPE YOU DON'T MIND'

Gerry looked over at Jennifer, hoping she would not condemn them by alerting the Mission Supervisor's on Earth. She didn't. She kept quiet.

'DARREN WILL FILL YOU IN ON WHAT WE'VE BEEN DISCUSSING' Gerry typed next. And aloud he said 'Come on Charmaine, lets go have a look at some of the equipment we've still got onboard. Some of those survey instruments might be useful.'

'OK' she said simply as they both stood and left for her cabin, hoping those back on Earth that were monitoring their movements and the audio in the ship hadn't noticed anything amiss.

Charmaine knew what she was looking for. As soon as they'd entered her cabin she walked over to a large device and began looking it over. Their Supervisor's would be watching them, but would only see them checking their equipment. They were expected to do their part in studying the phenomenon they were experiencing. The equipment they had on board was perfectly suited to studying strange environments, such as their radiation-tainted vessel. If they'd realised they were going to use it to dislodge the explosive charge attached to the hull of their ship, Gerry guessed they would have already detonated it. The official's back at home weren't about to play gentle when there was a vessel with enough power to destroy a solar system positioned near Earth, with four mentally affected individuals at the controls.

Without a word, Charmaine pulled some tools from a rack against the wall and began removing parts of the machine.

'Do you need a hand?' Gerry asked.

'No, this'll only take a moment' Charmaine replied without looking up from her bench. Large coils of fine wire were revealed as the device was disassembled and Charmaine removed the largest one.

'This is what we're looking for' she said, having problems trying to keep her eyes averted from the overhead cameras. Knowing there were at least dozens of important people watching them as they took subversive action was making her nervous.

'Let's get back to the flight deck' Gerry told her.

Back in their seats, Charmaine and Gerry read the conversation Darren and Jennifer had been having in their absence. It seemed Jennifer approved of their actions too. Her last message read 'WE HAVE GOT NO HOPE IF WE JUST SIT HERE AND BE STUDIED. BY THE TIME THEY HAVE OBSERVED THE EFFECTS ON US THE POISONING WILL HAVE RUN ITS COURSE. IT MAY HELP PEOPLE IN THE FUTURE BUT DOESN'T LEAVE US MUCH HOPE. LET'S DO IT. LETS GET BACK TO HELP THE STRANDED RESEARCHERS.'

Gerry again felt surprise that everyone was so willingly turning to illegal activity in order to save themselves. He knew his crews background and had no doubt that they would follow Mission Control's instructions to the letter if their circumstances weren't so unusual. Officials on Earth hadn't proven to be of any help,

162

and if they had any information that might help them understand their condition they weren't offering it.

Gerry felt strongly, though he knew his decisions were being affected by his mental processes after the radiation exposure, that their most promising hope for a cure and safe return to Earth, was in their own hands. The scientists on Clavus 3, Gaston and Holmes, had survived for over a decade after their exposure to the radiation. They knew what Gerry's future held, and that of his crew, better than anyone did. If they returned to Earth decontaminated, it was likely they could go back to a normal life there. Though they may have broken the law repeatedly already, and could expect a jail-term upon their return, at least they would have some hope of returning home to a regular existence after it was over. Gerry felt it to be their best option, and so did everyone else onboard, it seemed.

Gerry sent a message to Darren immediately. 'ARE YOU ABLE TO SHUT OFF COMMUNICATIONS FOR A MINUTE OR SO?'

'YES. WHENEVER YOU ARE READY. I PREPARED THINGS WHILE YOU WERE AWAY' Darren typed.

Gerry was amazed by the efficiency of his crew. Without sleep for a few days now, they were working brilliantly.

'WELL DONE' Gerry typed. 'WE SHOULD HAVE ENOUGH TIME. THEY WILL THINK THE GLITCH IN OUR COMMUNICATIONS IS DUE TO THE DAMAGE INFLICTED BY THE STRANDED SCIENTIST EARLIER. THEY SHOULDN'T SUSPECT WE'RE UP TO ANYTHING UNTIL WE FIRE THE HYPER-DRIVE. WE'LL BE HUNDREDS OF KILOMETRES AWAY BEFORE THEY HAVE TIME REACT.'

'THEY'LL KILL OUR DRIVE BEFORE WE CAN FIRE IT' Jennifer entered into her computer for them all to see.

'NO THEY WON'T' Gerry replied, tapping at his keyboard faster than he'd have thought possible before this mission. 'I'VE GOT MANUAL CONTROL STATUS. SPECIAL PRIVILEGES. I CAN OVER-RIDE ANY REMOTE COMMANDS SENT BY MISSION CONTROL TO OUR SHIP.'

'JESUS. THEY MUST HAVE TRUST IN YOU' popped up on-screen from Darren. 'THERE CAN'T BE MANY PEOPLE WITH THAT AUTHORITY.'

'LESS THAN FIVE OF US AT ANY ONE TIME. IT'S TO ALLOW FOR EXTREME CIRCUMSTANCES,' Gerry explained.

'SO IF SOMETHING HAPPENS ON EARTH, WHERE THEY LOSE CONTROL, THEY'LL STILL HAVE YOU OUT HERE AS A WILDCARD,' Darren typed.

'YES. SOMETHING LIKE THAT,' Gerry answered. He felt no reason to be dishonest with them, but the revelation of the power he held seemed to worry them. He couldn't help but notice the sideways looks they gave him. Jennifer's head dropped and her eyes closed, Gerry realising her mind had clicked into top gear, probably making some sense of the new information. Their condition wasn't improving, and the moments of hyperactive brain activity were in fact increasing in their regularity. She was pale and shaking when she eventually looked up.

'THEY'LL SEND ANOTHER HYPER-SPEED MISSILE AFTER US' she entered into her computer.

'YES,' Gerry agreed, 'WE'LL RECEIVE THE SAME TREATMENT AS THE TWO SCIENTISTS ON CLAVUS 3'

'WE WILL BE SEEN AS AN EVEN MORE IMMEDIATE THREAT THAN THOSE TWO' appeared on their screens with Darren's name showing as the sender.

'WHAT DO YOU MEAN?' Charmaine typed next. Gerry replied for Darren, entering his answer at lightning speed.

'HE MEANS THAT IF WE ARE CONSIDERED MENTALLY UNSTABLE DUE TO OUR RADIATION EXPOSURE WE WILL BE AN IMMEDIATE THREAT BECAUSE WE HAVE FULL CONTROL OF THE SHIP'S SYSTEMS. AN IRRATIONAL ACT ON OUR PART COULD RESULT IN THE DEATH OF BILLIONS OF PEOPLE.'

'YES' Darren entered after he'd read Gerry's message. 'A BUNCH OF MANIACS WITH AS MUCH POWER AT THEIR DISPOSAL AS ANY COUNTRY ON EARTH. WE'RE EVEN MORE DANGEROUS THAN THE UNITED STATES GOVERNMENT TO MOST PEOPLE ON EARTH NOW.'

'WE COULD STILL FOLLOW ORDERS FROM MISSION CONTROL IF YOU WANT. WE COULD SIT HERE WAITING FOR THEIR MIRACLE CURE FOR THE RADIATION EXPOSURE.' Gerry told them.

'I'D RATHER NOT GIVE UP HOPE' Charmaine messaged next.

'ME EITHER. IF ANY ONE OF US DOESN'T WANT TO MAKE A RUN FOR IT WE SHOULDN'T GO THOUGH' Gerry typed.

'WE HAVE TO GIVE IT A GO. IF WE CAN GET SOME MORE INFORMATION FROM THOSE SCIENTISTS ABOUT OUR ILLNESS WE MIGHT BE ABLE TO RETURN TO EARTH WITH A CURE' Darren typed next.

'YES. WE'D HAVE TO DO A LOT OF APOLOGISING, BUT IF WE SEND BACK SOME MORE SCIENTIFIC DATA THEY WOULD HAVE TO LISTEN TO US. THEY WANT TO KNOW ABOUT THE EFFECTS OF THE RADIATION EXPOSURE AS MUCH AS WE DO' Gerry added quickly, fingers blurring over the keyboard. It was not only his mind that was hyperactive.

Jennifer typed her agreement. 'LET'S GO BACK AND SEE WHAT WE CAN FIND OUT. WE ARE SUPPOSEDLY TOP-NOTCH SCIENTISTS AFTER ALL, JUST DOING WHAT SHOULD HAVE BEEN DONE ON THIS MISSION. LET'S GET BACK AND FINISH OUR ANALYSIS AND RESCUE THOSE PEOPLE WHILE WE ARE THERE.'

'ITS DECIDED THEN' Gerry advised. 'FIRST WE NEED MORE PROBES. AS MUCH EQUIPMENT AS WE CAN USE. DARREN, MESSAGE MISSION CONTROL REQUESTING SUPPLIES AND EQUIPMENT FOR ONE OF THE MISSION PLANS THEY SENT US. IF THEY THINK WE'RE GOING TO CARRY OUT ONE OF THEIR ROUTINE SURVEY MISSIONS WHILE WE'RE QUARANTINED ABOARD THIS VESSEL THEY'LL GIVE US EVERYTHING WE NEED TO GET BACK AND CARRY OUT A RESCUE ON CLAVUS 3.'

Darren did as instructed, sending a request for equipment to Mission Control. They immediately received a reply.

'REQUEST GRANTED. ALLOW 20 MINUTES LOADING TIME.'

'WE'LL WAIT UNTIL WE'RE LOADED AND GET RID OF THAT MINE WHEN THE SUPPLY SHUTTLE HAS LEFT' Gerry told them. His mind swam with thoughts, considerations concerning their situation, and he leaned back into his flight seat and tried to relax.

Meanwhile, the others watched the large screen before them. It seemed an eternity before they saw a flash of light on the nearby space station, signifying the launch of the supply ship. Darren looked over the itinerary for the mission briefly while he kept an eye on the approaching ship. They would be receiving six new probes and a 2-person shuttle-craft for the job, he saw. Food and medication was on the list, though Darren considered it unlikely they would be able to make any use of it.

There was silence aboard their vessel, everyone preparing themselves for what they would be doing of the next half an hour. Going against orders from both Mission Control and military leaders wasn't something any of them had ever done before. They didn't want to now, but they knew there were no other viable options.

When the supply vessel came alongside, an audio message was received from Mission Control.

'Open outer airlock door' was the simple instruction. Darren did so, and they heard items thumping onto the floor in the airlock.

When the noises stopped they received another message. 'Prepare for loading of probes and survey craft.'

Darren checked that all clamps and bays were open under their ship so they could receive the new probes and their little 2-person craft. The thumps and clangs of metal could be heard for the next two minutes as the attachments their vessel required were put in place.

First they received one last message from Mission Control. 'Loading complete. You will be advised shortly of departure time.'

Gerry opened his eyes upon hearing this. He watched with the crew in silence as the supply ship quickly covered the distance back to its home space station.

It was time. Gerry sent a private message to his crew.

'THE LONGER WE SIT HERE THE HIGHER THE CHANCE THEY'LL FIND OUT WE ARE UP TO

SOMETHING. WE'LL DO IT RIGHT NOW' he instructed. 'CHARMAINE AND I WILL GO GET RID OF THAT EXPLOSIVE.'

'WHEN SHOULD I CUT COMMUNICATION?' Darren typed.

'WHEN WE GET TO CHARMAINES CABIN. WE CAN'T HAVE THEM SEE US SETTING UP THE ELECTROMAGNET' Gerry entered into his keyboard.

'READY WHEN YOU ARE' Darren replied.

'OK CHARMAINE. LET'S GO.' With that, Gerry and Charmaine rose from their seats. There were expressions of concern on their faces, each of them feeling the weight of their betrayal.

On entering Charmaine's cabin they heard Darren's voice on the intercom system. 'Communications have been severed. We're on our own.'

A surge of adrenaline hit the bodies of all on-board, hearts hammering in chests as they half-expected the explosive charge attached to their ship to be detonated. Feeling every step could be his last, Gerry lifted the massive coil from the table and they made their way quickly out again. They rushed the device to the place where the explosive was attached to the hull, and Charmaine didn't waste a second plugging it into a power source on a panel on the wall.

'Hold it by the frame and get it as close to the hull as you can without touching it. Make sure you don't touch the coils either, you'd get a hell of a zap' Charmaine advised.

Gerry lifted it to a place on the wall he knew the explosive charge to be attached.

'Ready' he called.

With that, Charmaine flicked a switch and the device hummed into life. It shoved Gerry away from the wall, the electromagnetic force acting upon the device he held as well as the mine attached outside, but he stood his ground, though almost losing his grip on the coil. Darren's voice could be heard from the intercom speakers instantly.

'It came off. It's floated off into space!'

'Let's get back to the flight deck as quick as we can' Gerry instructed, placing it on the floor when Charmaine had switched it off. He pulled an acceleration strap from the wall and placed it

167

around the device, in order to prevent it moving around the ship as they accelerated.

They returned to the flight deck and took their seats, using the harnesses needed for hyper-speed acceleration. Darren and Jennifer were already strapped in, and were looking at Gerry with expressions that betrayed their fear, waiting for him to make the next move.

'Just sit tight and relax,' Gerry said. 'I'll get us out of here.'

The ship's ion thrusters fired into life, tiny engines used to make adjustments to the ship's position. Gerry watched the navigation screen on the large monitor at the front of the flight deck. When it showed the vessel was pointed in the right direction, as close as he could tell to the clear hyper-speed lane, he fired the main drive.

'We made it!' they heard Darren call from his seat, which he had been slammed back into. As the seconds ticked by the others began to feel the same sense of relief, knowing they were already thousands of kilometres from Earth, and from the magnetic mine.

'SHALL I RESUME COMMUNICATIONS WITH MISSION CONTROL?' appeared on the big screen before them. It was a message from Darren, now unable to speak to them due to the massive g-forces dragging at his body.

'NOT YET' Gerry typed in reply. 'LET'S ENJOY THE SILENCE FOR A WHILE. IT FEELS GOOD TO BE FREE.'

'YES SIR. I WOULD LIKE TO ENJOY IT WHILE WE CAN' Darren agreed. He was smiling, obviously relieved to be out of immediate danger. The visual distortions created by hyper-speed travel had made Darren's smile seem huge, literally stretching from ear to ear. Gerry couldn't help but smile also, seeing Darren look so much like a cheery cartoon character.

Each of them was overcome by mixed feelings. A sense of horror for what they had done combined with a gladness that they were no longer obligated to spend their foreseeable future in quarantine near Earth while their condition was studied. They were truly free now, in control of their own future. They barely noticed the usually painful effects of hyper-speed acceleration as they sat lost in their thoughts. They were envisaging their futures, which now seemed much more positive. There was nothing like a faster-than-light journey that bought on such a strong sense of freedom. Total escape. Literally escaping their very universe for a time.

Gerry used his new-found mental abilities to consider their possible destinies. They were now surely Earth's most wanted, but it was a far better situation than being held as lab rats by people who had knowingly sent them into grave danger without warning. He held them responsible for their situation, though he felt the majority on Earth would disagree. They would have been fed just enough facts to give them the opinion that they were dangerous rogues. They would almost certainly have gained *terrorist* status, he decided. Everyone who was deemed a threat to Westerners without having the backing of a powerful military seemed to get that label nowadays. Terrorism wasn't violence for political gain any more. It was any action that put the US, the UK, or Australia in perceived risk. Not only the physical risk of violence toward them, sometimes just economic risk.

As the vessel's velocity increased, their sense of self-determination grew along with the distance between the Earth and themselves. They wouldn't be truly safe until they returned to Earth with some good news and lots of data on their medical condition. Though Gerry knew that even this might not placate them.

Turning about as much as he could in his flight seat, Gerry looked over the crew. The fear was gone, replaced by a calm acceptance. They knew what had to be done, and they were doing just that. They had a purpose now, an outlet for their restlessness. Their hyperactive minds would surely drive them to insanity if they'd sat in quarantine for the next few months. Their mental activity was too urgent, too demanding of action.

With these thoughts, along with thousands of others whipping through their minds every minute, the four rogue researchers fired across the galaxy, on a mission like none other before it.

TWELVE

'Sometimes it makes me wonder,
How I keep from going under...'
Grandmaster Flash – The Message

When Darren cancelled acceleration as they neared the halfway point of their journey, Gerry immediately focussed the ship's sensors on the moon ahead. They were seeing it as it was nearly a decade ago. The beacon was shining out at them, the light and other forms of radiation it emitted taking many years to reach this part of space. For all Gerry knew, the moon might no longer exist.

'It's time to switch communications back on,' Gerry said to Darren.

'Will do. I'm not looking forward to it though' Darren replied as he tapped a few keys on the keyboard at his side. A message came on-screen. It was from Mission Control.

'RETURN TO EARTH IMMEDIATELY. CRIMINAL CHARGES HAVE BEEN FILED AGAINST ALL ON BOARD. DO NOT MAKE THIS SITUATION WORSE THAN IT ALREADY IS.'

The last thing Gerry wanted to do was talk with these single-minded people, but he had no option. He might be able to placate them enough to avoid having military force sent against him and his crew. Surely there was a chance he could get his superiors to see his point of view. He knew he was doing the right thing by everybody, but that wasn't enough. He needed the support of those on Earth if he was ever to return safely.

'WE WILL RETURN ASAP' Gerry typed. 'WE NEED MORE INFORMATION FROM THE STRANDED SCIENTISTS. THEY'VE LIVED WITH OUR CONDITION FOR A VERY LONG TIME. WE WILL SEND ALL DATA COLLECTED TO MISSION CONTROL.'

'NO. VESSEL MUST RETURN IMMEDIATELY. NO CONTACT MUST BE MADE WITH THE TERRORISTS ON CLAVUS 3' was the blunt reply they received.

170

'WE WILL NOT RETURN WITHOUT ATTEMPTING TO COLLECT MORE INFORMATION. IT NEEDS TO BE DONE. WE ARE THE ONLY PEOPLE WHO HAVE LITTLE TO LOSE. WE HAVE BEEN EXPOSED TO THE RADIATION ALREADY AND MAY BE THE ONLY PEOPLE THE SCIENTISTS WILL SPEAK WITH. THEY WANTED US TO RETURN. OUR VESSEL'S COMMUNICATION SYSTEM CAN BE USED BY YOU TO NEGOTIATE WITH STRANDED SCIENTISTS IF THAT IS YOUR WISH' Gerry typed in reply.

'NO. RETURN TO EARTH NOW. CLAVUS 3 IS A MILITARY TARGET. IF YOU CONTACT THEM YOUR CREW AND YOUR VESSEL WILL GAIN SAME STATUS.'

'OUR APOLOGIES BUT WE HAVE LITTLE ALTERNATIVE. WE RECEIVED NO DATA ON OUR MEDICAL CONDITION FROM EARTH. WE ARE EQUIPPED TO STUDY CLAVUS 3 ENVIRONMENT AND COLLECT TISSUE SAMPLES FROM SCIENTISTS FOR MEDICAL TESTS. WE MUST CONTINUE FOR THE SAKE OF US ALL. THIS IS THE BEST OPTION.' Gerry advised Mission Control.

'NEVERTHELESS, YOUR MENTAL CONDITION IS NOW UNDER SERIOUS SUSPICION. YOU CANNOT BE ALLOWED TO KEEP CONTROL OF YOUR VESSEL IN THESE CIRCUMSTANCES. THE TERRORISTS HAVE GAINED CONTROL OF YOUR VESSEL PREVIOUSLY AND MAY DO SO AGAIN. RETURN,' was the message they received in reply.

'THE SCIENTISTS ONLY DID SO TO DEFEND THEMSELVES. EVERY PERSON HAS THIS NATURAL RIGHT. I BELIEVE THE CREW AND I ARE MENTALLY FIT. WE ARE SEVERING NORMAL COMMUNICATIONS NOW. WE WILL HOWEVER SEND ALL DATA WE COLLECT BACK TO YOU AS SOON AS IT COMES IN. WE WILL TALK AGAIN WHEN ENOUGH INFORMATION IS GATHERED TO MAKE CURING OUR CONDITION A POSSIBILITY' Gerry typed finally. He turned and nodded to Darren, who cut communication with Mission Control.

They were on their own again.

171

'Keep an eye on our long distance sensors everyone.' Gerry warned. 'There's a possibility they'll send another hyper-speed missile.'

Darren and Gerry then took the opportunity to check that the equipment in the airlock had not shifted about too much, moving it against the wall ready for deceleration. After doing this, they returned to the flight deck and sat down.

They sat silent in their seats for the remainder, cruising through the galaxy at trillions of kilometres an hour, until it was time to cancel some of their velocity.

'Time to decelerate' Darren called. Everyone checked their harnesses and found the most comfortable position in their flight seats. When the ship spun around and the g-forces hit them they were ready.

Everything went smoothly for the first ten minutes, after which they noticed a soft blue light suffuse the flight control room. Their own skin was effected most of all. It shone a sparkling iridescent blue.

Gerry couldn't stop his body twitching occasionally, as though he was receiving electric shocks. He felt something solid but unseen slap against his neck. It was happening again.

'I guess we're passing through the field of radiation again.' Jennifer yelled with great difficult from behind them. 'I hope this doesn't make our symptoms too much worse.'

Gerry used his computer to enable sensor data to be sent to Mission Control. They were now receiving visual and audio from their vessel back on Earth, along with all detectable radiation levels. Is should appease them somewhat, Gerry thought, allowing them to be part of their unauthorised mission. It would be easier for them to target the ship and send weaponry after it, but Gerry decided the risk was worth it. They could sever the data link at any sign of aggression from Mission Control or their military advisors.

A text message appeared on the main screen before them. Where the senders user-name was usually displayed there was only a blank line. This told Gerry immediately where it was from. The stranded scientists on Clavus 3. Alive, and obviously relieved to have them return.

'WE ARE GLAD YOU HAVE RETURNED SAFELY. WE KNEW YOU WOULD RESCUE US IF YOU LIVED.'

'RESCUE MAY NOT BE POSSIBLE. MISSION CONTROL HAS FORBIDDEN CONTACT. EVEN TALKING WITH YOU NOW IS A CRIMINAL ACT ON OUR PART' Gerry typed quickly.

'WILL YOU ATTEMPT TO HELP US?' was the instant reply.

'WE WILL DO WHAT WE CAN. IF IT IS WITHIN OUR MEANS TO SAFELY ASSIST YOU WE WILL DO SO.' Gerry told them.

'THANK YOU' was the simple reply.

'YOU MUST NOT THREATEN THE SAFETY OF OUR CREW OR THAT OF PEOPLE BACK ON EARTH. MISSION CONTROL IS RECEIVING OUR SENSOR DATA AND WILL PROBABLY RETALIATE AT ANY SIGN OF AGGRESSION. WE WOULD ALL BE IN DANGER OF A MILITARY ASSAULT. THEY MAY EVEN BE PLANNING AN ATTACK NOW. WE DON'T KNOW,' Gerry added as an afterthought.

'WE WILL FOLLOW YOUR ORDERS. WE WANT THE SAME AS YOU. ONLY SAFETY AND RESCUE' the scientists messaging them from Clavus 3 conceded.

'THERE ARE MANY QUESTIONS WE WOULD LIKE TO ASK YOU. WE NEED TO KNOW MORE ABOUT OUR MEDICAL CONDITION. WE MAY BE ABLE TO FIND A CURE FOR OUR RADIATION EXPOSURE IF WE KNOW MORE ABOUT IT' Gerry explained.

'WE WILL HELP. DECONTAMINATION IS THE ONLY WAY WE WILL BE ALLOWED TO RETURN TO EARTH' was the typed response. They seemed to understand the situation, which gave Gerry new hope.

'YOU ARE CONSIDERED TERRORISTS ON EARTH. WE MUST WORK QUICKLY TO FIND A SOLUTION' Gerry typed. 'WE WILL BE ARRIVING WITHIN HALF AN HOUR. DO YOU HAVE MEANS OF RETRIEVING MEDICAL TEST EQUIPMENT IF WE DROP IT AT YOUR LOCATION?'

'YES,' was the reply, 'PLACE IT CLOSE TO OUR SHIP AND WE WILL BRING IT INSIDE.'

Gerry didn't know how they were going to do so, but he didn't have time to explore their methods.

'WE WILL WATERPROOF EVERYTHING FOR THE TRANSFER. I WILL PILOT THE SHUTTLE.' Gerry explained, surprising his crew with the message he'd sent. Charmaine was the first to contest his plan, straining to speak under the constriction of her body while under deceleration.

'It's hundreds of metres under the sea, and the shuttle doesn't have an airlock. You'll actually have to open the cabin to release the equipment.'

'I'll be in a pressurised suit' Gerry explained, surprised by how quickly he'd arrived at a workable plan of action. 'I will probably need to swim out and place the test equipment in their airlock. I can't see how they could retrieve the stuff any other way.'

'Unless they have a suit that still functions on board' Darren noted. 'One of them could come to the shuttle themselves to get the gear. We could attach it to the exterior of the shuttle, so you don't need to open the hatch. The electronics in the shuttle are only water-resistant; they can't handle being fully immersed.'

'It's an exploration shuttle though,' Gerry explained, 'it's made to cope with that kind of treatment. They can almost as easily be piloted using manual controls as they can by using fly-by-wire.'

'Still, can we check with them? It could make things much easier.' Darren asked.

'That would be preferable, but it's unlikely they would still have a suit on board. They've proven to be amazingly resourceful up till now though. If they say they can retrieve the equipment them I'm sure they have something in mind. Message them again if you like though, asking them how they plan to get the items into their ship.

Darren did so immediately, typing quickly at his keyboard. 'HOW DO YOU PLAN TO RETRIEVE OUR MEDICAL TEST EQUIPMENT?'

'WE WILL LEAVE THE SHIP AND PHYSICALLY TRANSPORT THE CARGO' was the simple reply.

'Looks like they do have suits aboard. That helps us. We'll take the shuttle somewhere near their ship, as close as we can get. Their suit's can't be in very good condition after more than a decade down there, so we'll need to ensure they don't need to be outside too long.' Gerry instructed, at the same time working through their inventory, deciding what equipment should be taken to them. They would need as much medical data as they could

174

possibly get if they were to show Mission Control that their unauthorised research was of value and give them a chance to find a cure for their radiation exposure.

There they sat in silence for the remainder of the deceleration period, each working on the details involved in collecting useful data. Their work was flawless and fast, even though they were being pressed hard into their seats by the g-forces. They also were receiving the electrical jolts that intermittently shook their bodies, a sign they assumed meant they were again being irradiated, though Mission Control had blamed it on the stranded researchers messing with their computers.

Each was also receiving physical blows from something invisible but solid that seemed to be flailing about the flight deck. The physical manifestation of the field of radiation they had entered was of deep concern to Gerry and his crew. It was so alien, so unusual, they knew it would be difficult to find a way of ridding their bodies and minds of the radiation. Even with thousands of scientists on Earth studying their data and medical samples it could take many years to find the means to reverse their condition. They had stumbled into something almost unknown; something that as yet was a mystery to the educated people that might assist them from their laboratories on Earth and elsewhere. They had so much to learn before they could hope to return to a normal life, whatever or wherever that might be.

The stranded scientists they would soon be meeting must surely have more knowledge of their condition than anyone else. Gerry was relying on receiving useful information, and he was hoping they had it to give. At least they seemed mentally stable, Gerry thought, which should enable him to get a detailed list of symptoms, along with the medical samples and test readings from their bodies.

With these thoughts churning through their minds as they worked, Darren finally signalled that they had completed deceleration. Gerry was the only person who could pilot their vessel via manual control, and it was he who used his keypad to shut down the main drive.

The g-forces lifted instantly from their bodies, and Gerry gently changed trajectory for the final leg to Clavus 3. They were outside the hyper-speed lane now, in uncleared space travelling at a more sedate speed. There was a much higher chance of striking some debris out here, though it hadn't happened very often in the history of interstellar travel. They could relax for the moment, freed from the torturous effects of hyper-speed deceleration as together via their computer terminals they formulated a detailed mission plan.

Their concentration was so intense that they were barely aware of the time it took to reach the moon. But here they were, the crew's sense of foreboding growing stronger. Their boss was going to go down there. Gerry was about to meet these strange people face-to-face, separated only by a centimetre-thick windshield. He and his crew now felt those same emotions that people on Earth must have felt when encountering themselves. An animated corpse and strangely healing wounds didn't help to instil a sense of empathy. Neither did taking control of a ship's computer system and trying to cause a collision between the vessel and a hyper-speed missile. Not to mention corrupting a planet's computer networks from many light years away. There was plenty reason for everyone to be wary.

When the vessel came to a complete halt they rose to ready the equipment that they would be delivering to the dark moon. Jennifer had already organised what they needed to take and it didn't take long to get it together near the airlock, where they packed the easily damaged equipment in pressure-bags. After clearing the airlock of items they'd been given when near Earth which didn't need to be sent down, they carried in the remainder of the cargo.

'I'll get suited up and go out and attach the cargo to the shuttle. You lot go back to the flight deck and keep an eye on things. Tell the scientists we'll be down there within thirty minutes.' Gerry ordered, picking up one of the packages from the floor that held a new suit he'd use for his space-walk.

'Yes Sir,' Darren nodded as he spoke. 'Mission Control has an opportunity to kill two birds with one stone while we are here. They might be tempted to send another hyper-speed missile.'

'It is a possibility.' Gerry said as he turned to go back to the supply room. 'Keep a close eye on the long range sensors.'

While the crew was preparing for his space-walk and ensuing journey to the undersea world that imprisoned two fellow scientists, Gerry got into his suit. Once he had it fitting correctly he spent longer than usual ensuring it had no defects. He was conscious of the fact that he'd almost died, actually, should have died, the last time he'd worn one of these.

Once Gerry was happy with the way it fit and functioned he grabbed a large roll of carbon fibre tape from a shelf above him, which he would be using to secure the cargo to the exterior of the shuttle he'd be piloting.

Speaking into the microphone in his helmet, Gerry heard his voice loud and clear from the ships intercom system. 'I'm ready to go.'

Up front, Darren, Charmaine and Jennifer heard his voice booming from the overhead speakers.

'We're receiving your audio and suit data. We're ready up here.' Darren told him.

'Received. Close the inner door' Gerry instructed after he'd entered the airlock, standing amongst the silvery bags of test equipment.

The door closed behind him and after slipping the roll of tape over his arm and picking up as many of the packages as he could carry, Gerry ordered 'Open the outer door, I'm ready to go.'

The door slipped quickly open and Gerry stepped out without hesitation. He ignored the uneasy feeling as his innards suddenly lost their weight and his sense of balance disappeared when he left the gravitational field that engulfed the ship. The effect of gravity produced by the variable-mass engine in the vessel only extended to a few centimetres outside the hull.

With a free hand, Gerry thumbed a switch on the sleeve of his suit; the ion jets pushed him gently away from the ship when they fired. Using the controls to spin him around and send him moving toward the underneath of their ship, where the small shuttle craft was clamped.

'I'm strapping on the cargo now' he told the crew when he reached the tail of the aircraft, where he would attach the equipment.

'Yes Sir' he heard Darren say in his helmet speakers.

Once all the packages he'd brought with him were held securely with the high-strength tape, Gerry went back and retrieved the final few items from the airlock and soon had them attached as well.

177

'I'm done here. I'm coming back inside' Gerry told the others. On entering the airlock he had Darren close its outer door and pressurise it. He left his helmet on when this had been carried out so that he could keep communication with his crew and strode back into the ship as soon as the inner door opened.

'I'm going straight down into the shuttle. There's no time to waste. If Earth sends anything against us while I'm down there, don't hang around to pick me up if you don't have time. Just get out of here. I've left my computer logged on so you will have manual control of the ship, Darren, if you need it.'

'Heard and understood. We should have plenty of warning though. You should have time to get back here if anything comes our way' Darren replied.

Gerry leapt down a small flight of steps to a tiny room underneath the ship, where he would enter the shuttle. He could see into the craft when he pressed a switch on the wall and the door slid back. He would have to be wary. There weren't any explosive charges attached to the hull of the shuttle, he'd made sure of that, but he was careful to look thoroughly around the inside before he entered. He didn't want any more surprises from Mission Control and the politicians that were directing them.

Going leg-first down through the shuttle door, Gerry again felt the gravitational pull release his body, leaving him weightless as he used rungs on the wall to lower himself to his flight seat.

'I'm in the shuttle' he told the others as he pressed a switch on the control panel before him to close the shuttle hatch.

'Ready when you are' he heard Darren's reply from his helmet speakers.

'Switch to communication from my suit to the shuttles transceiver, Darren' he instructed, finally finding a spare moment to remove his helmet. The shuttle life-support system was working fine.

Darren's voice rang out from the intercom speakers. 'Do you copy?'

'Received' Gerry answered, his voice sounding harsh and loud in the relative silence of the cramped shuttle interior.

His crew had already programmed the shuttle's trajectory, so there was little for Gerry to do other than clip his seat restraints in place and enter one command with the keyboard before him to initiate the launch.

178

He heard thrusters fire above as the shuttle separated from the main vessel.

'You're on your way' Darren said.

'Good luck' he heard Charmaine and Jennifer add. The tiny craft Gerry sat in took a few seconds adjusting its position, aligning itself in readiness for a pre-programmed trajectory.

When the main thrusters fired, they did so gently, carefully calculated to give the utmost acceleration without tearing loose the equipment that was strapped to the hull of the shuttle.

After a few minutes accelerating, the vessel was finally approaching the moon's surface at a reasonable rate.

'Tell them I will be there in eight minutes' Gerry instructed his crew. 'Tell them they'll need something to cut the packages from their restraints too.'

'Will do' Darren replied.

On nearing the moon's extremely thin atmosphere the shuttle reversed thrust, slowing enough to ensure their cargo would neither be burned nor stripped from its tethers as they hit the thin gasses that enveloped the surface of the moon.

He felt a jar when the craft hit the atmosphere and the shuttle began to vibrate slightly. Glancing through the translucent plate at the rear of the shuttle, Gerry saw that the cargo he'd strapped to the tail-section was still in place.

Gerry was pushed forward hard into his seat restraints as the shuttle slowed. The front of the craft began to pull up as it neared the churning surface of the dark sea, slowing to a controlled glide. The thermal activity in the ocean below him was shown as swirling patterns of red amongst the colder orange colour on his main viewing panel before him, placed in such a way to look as though it was a clear windscreen he was looking through. It was only the filters that controlled his view which were applying the colours to signify different temperatures; in fact, it was pitch-black down there. Even the light-intensification filters could not be of any use, there being so little light striking the moon surface.

But in an instant the view changed dramatically. The sea lit up a phosphorescent green, and a powerful beam of light appeared, a fiery white pillar stretching off into space. The beacon was back on.

179

'Looks like they're making sure we know where they are. We don't need the help, but it sure makes for a nice view' Gerry told the others.

'It looks great from up here too.' It was Charmaine. 'We've got a visual of your shuttle, when the adenine clouds aren't in the way. Very nice.'

'Yeah, I wouldn't like to be stuck here for ten years though.' Gerry added. 'I sure wish we could pick these guys up.'

'Same here,' Darren said. 'But we all know that would be too risky. Mission Control would probably react immediately. They'd want to get rid of us before we had the chance to expose anyone or anything else to the radiation we're most likely giving off.'

'For sure Darren, only a thought. If we can get enough data from the stuff we give them we'll have a chance at saving all of us,' Gerry agreed.

The shuttle slowed gradually, almost coming to a stall, before plunging into the green-tinged ocean. Gerry barely felt the transition, the small vessel designed just for such purposes. It shot through the water toward the base of the pillar of light. He heard a motor switch on from behind him, the craft automatically keeping his speed up, feeding in power, as it was required.

'This is the most comfortable trip I've ever had. Great flight programme you put together' Gerry said to his crew, amazed by the perfection of his flight so far, especially considering their lack of sleep over the past weeks. The cargo still appeared firmly in place when he turned to check on it.

When Gerry was a few hundred metres from the light source he instructed Darren to tell the men down there to switch off the beacon. The life-forms they'd seen on their first mission had seemed to explode as they neared the altered hyper-drive on the scientist's ship, as did one of their own probes. It had been altered into the equivalent of an emergency flare, a flare that atomised anything that neared it. Gerry didn't want the shuttle he was in going the same way.

'Yes Sir' he heard Darren say, and seconds later Gerry's world turned dark again. Other sensors on the shuttle took over, compensating for the lack of light and the screen before him changed colour, signifying temperature variations and a realistic simulation of his surroundings was produced using radar imagery. He could see where he was going still, though Gerry knew that it

180

wasn't important. His journey was plotted out by a huge set of computer commands and it would carry out these instructions flawlessly, no matter how little light or other sensor data was available.

Gerry held his breath as the vessel reached the vent, half expecting the drive below to switch on again and fry him. He couldn't trust the people down there, and probably never would after they'd tried slamming his ship into a hyper-speed missile in an effort to protect themselves.

The powerful beam stayed off though, and in no time Gerry could see the bottom half of an old hyper-speed research vessel. His craft slowed its descent automatically as it neared their destination, the front of the vessel swinging upward to level it out in readiness for landing.

When he felt the rubbery landing struts hit solid ground Gerry switched on an external light source and was able to see around him using natural light instead of the simulated images. Through a small, clear panel by his left side, Gerry could see the wreck of the hyper-speed vehicle that held two lonely survivors.

'I'm down. Are you getting these pictures?' Gerry asked his crew via the radio link.

'Congratulations,' Darren replied. 'We're receiving your data. We can see everything you can. Camera four is getting a perfect image of their vessel.'

Gerry switched the view on the main screen before him to that from the camera Darren was using. He was right. They were able to study it in minute detail. 'Make sure they're getting these pictures back on Earth, Darren. This should keep them off our backs for a while, as long as we're collecting such valuable data for them.

'The entangled-particle transmitters are switched on. They should be getting everything from us. It's just that they can't transmit anything to us' he heard Darren answer. Gerry could see the airlock door protruding from the rocky hole the front of the vessel was squeezed into. There wasn't much room for occupants to escape the vessel, but as long as they could open the airlock door they should be able to get out to collect the instrumentation attached to the rear-end of his craft.

'Ask them what's keeping them Darren' Gerry said, in a hurry to get out of here after only a minute since landing. The sense of

181

entrapment the two scientists must have experienced for the past decade was contagious. This was surely the highest security prison imaginable. Though he'd never been claustrophobic, Gerry had to fight the urge to grab the controls and fire his vessel away from this place.

'I sent the message, but they haven't answered yet. They might be busy getting prepared,' Darren replied after a moment. Just as he spoke, a shaft of light appeared as the airlock door opened.

Gerry was shocked by what he saw. He heard his crew out in orbit utter their surprise over the radio.

'What the fuck are they doing?' Darren yelled.

Gerry had no answer for him. The fools had opened the airlock door without wearing pressure suits. They peered into the spotlight from the doorway with blood streaming from everywhere it could escape their bodies, wearing only their torn and tattered uniforms. Their clothing was very similar to today's flight suits, and Gerry noted that the insignia over the right breast was the logo of the very space-research organisation he was now working for.

Though they were still some distance from him, Gerry could see the pained look in their eyes, eyes that were focussed on him. Through the streams of blood that were being squeezed from their faces under the tremendous pressure, Gerry could still see life in those eyes. It was amazing that they hadn't died instantly. It couldn't be much longer. But, as they all watched in horror, one of them dragged himself out onto the rocky sea-floor. And as he began making his way on all fours toward Gerry's vessel, his companion exited in the same way. Soon they were both crawling toward him.

'Jesus, they're determined.' Gerry said to the others. 'Why didn't they just let one of us take the equipment into their ship?'

'This doesn't look good, Gerry.' Charmaine said through the radio. 'There's only one obvious reason. They don't want the test equipment; they want to get away from there right now.'

'I think Charmaine's right,' he heard Darren say. 'They've put you in a dilemma. If you don't help them get out of there they are going to die.'

'They're going to die anyway' Gerry replied. They had made it half the distance but their progress was slowing. The chest of one

182

of the men had caved in under the pressure, and they could clearly see the bruising spread across his torso. Still he inched his way toward Gerry's vessel, though barely moving. His companion had collapsed though and lay twitching on the rocky sea-floor, obviously close to death.

The sea had turned red with blood; crimson fog as far as the light on his ship could penetrate. It was a hopeless situation, and as Gerry considered his options, his mind began to swim with activity.

Shaking his head in a vain attempt to dispel the sense of disorientation, Gerry suddenly knew what he had to do. In the strange state of mind that overcame him for a few moments, he'd decided on his best option.

'I'm going to bring them in. Use my pressure suit's radio to speak with me' Gerry instructed his crew back on the main vessel. To their cries of disbelief as they watched him on their screens, Gerry lifted his helmet from the floor and placed it over his head.

'You can't do that. They're going to die anyway, if they're not dead already, so why contaminate our ship with their bodies?' he heard Jennifer say via the microphone in his helmet, which he'd quickly latched into place.

'We haven't got anything to lose,' Gerry explained. 'We might receive an extra dose of radiation from their bodies, but the information we could get from an autopsy would go further toward finding a cure for our infection than the data we could get while we're here.'

'You're right there,' Jennifer agreed, 'as long as you're able to make it back here after you've drowned the electric's in the shuttle by opening the hatch.'

'I'll be able to handle this on manual control. It won't be the first time. I'll just need you lot to guide me back' Gerry explained to her, at the same time instructing the computer to open the shuttle's hatch on the roof above him.

As the door slid open, Gerry was slammed down into his seat as the alien sea burst its way into the shuttle. The electrical system instantly shut down, circuit breakers making a thump as they triggered. Gerry could hear the motor still humming at the back of the ship, something he was very glad for.

It was dark for a few seconds, only a little light entering the vessel from small windows. The external spotlight was still shining brightly, running on its own sealed power source. Switching on the light on his suit helmet and releasing his seats harness, Gerry wasted no time in jumping upward through the shuttle's hatch.

Emerging to stand on the roof of the shuttle, Gerry glanced about him. Looking into the darkness around the ship, away from where its light was directed, Gerry could only see where his helmet's beam was pointing. He spun slowly around, letting it play across the walls of the cavern he was in. The rocky walls held no visible sign of life, and nothing moved in the sea around him, though the sense that something could be approaching from behind was far stronger than one would feel if one was immersed in one of Earth's more familiar seas.

Shrugging off the uneasy feeling, Gerry jumped from the shuttle, landing very softly on the rocky sea-floor. The two bodies lay only metres from him. Travis Holmes and Dan Gaston, he did not know which was which. Once brave researchers, roving the universe at great danger for the benefit of science and humankind, now disfigured corpses of maligned terrorists. In the depths of an alien sea, they had succumbed at their own hand, something that the might of Earth's military had failed to achieve on their last attempt. Gerry felt a pang of sorrow for their plight.

Wading through the depths would have been difficult enough in his only slightly weighted suit, but the lack of gravity on the moon made it even more difficult. Gerry used his arms to propel himself to the closer of the two scientists, the one that was still twitching softly as he lay face-down on the ocean floor.

In a blood-tinged sea, Gerry effortlessly lifted the pale body and carried it back to the shuttle. He lowered it into the cabin and placed it in one of the seats, putting the harness in place to prevent it floating about. The frightened eyes were open, seemed to be focussed on him. He used his fingers to close them, relieved when they stayed shut as they should.

Retrieving the second body and carrying it back to the shuttle, Gerry was forced to use straps fitted into the walls to restrain it, there being no remaining seats other than his own flight seat.

Gerry was reminded of the way that his own chest had healed, within minutes of being horribly burned by a damaged ion-drive in his suit. He thought it probable that it was a side effect of their radiation exposure. The corpse he had harnessed to the wall glowed a soft electric blue. He could see patches of light playing over the bruised and deformed chest even under the bright light produced by his helmet lamp.

Within his suit, and immersed in the alien sea, Gerry could do nothing to help them medically. He couldn't even check their vital signs. Their radiation exposure may somehow assist their healing, but there had to be limitations. These people were barely recognisable as human, such was the damage to their bodies.

Pulling a knife from a rack on the wall, Gerry exited the shuttle one last time and quickly cut the cords holding the supplies that he'd strapped to the exterior. He would be forced to leave them here, as the added weight of the scientist's bodies would take the shuttle up to it's maximum payload. After moving the equipment away from the shuttle to ensure it wouldn't get in the way of his departure, Gerry hastily climbed aboard.

He didn't want to waste any time getting back to the main vessel. The advanced medical equipment they had on board could seemingly work miracles. Knowing the chances were extremely minimal that anything could be done to help these two, nevertheless, Gerry made his way back to his seat quickly as he could.

Pulling on his harness with one hand and using a winder to close the hatch with the other, Gerry told his crew he was on his way back.

'I'm all done here. You can start guiding me back whenever you're ready' he said into his helmet microphone.

'Alright then,' Gerry heard Darren say. 'First we go vertical three hundred metres. Take it slowly.'

'That should be no problem. This sea is clear enough for me to be able to see the tunnel walls in the ship spotlight' Gerry answered.

The shuttles controls felt heavy and wooden as Gerry fired thrusters to lift the ship from the sea-floor and position it so it was pointing upward, ready to climb out of the tunnel. He heard an electric pump whir into life automatically somewhere in the floor, and he could see bubbles rising to the front of the ship, as air was being forced back into the shuttle's interior. It was at such a slow rate though that it would be of little assistance to Gerry's

185

unsuited passengers, though he thought that little could be done to help them now anyway.

Feeding power to the main drive, Gerry began the ascent with utmost care, taking into consideration the tons of seawater that sloshed about within the vehicle. Though designed to be useful and safe in almost any environment, and surely the most versatile and sturdy transport vehicle ever made, the shuttle Gerry was piloting had its limitations.

The climb out of the ravine went smoothly, Gerry making only slight alterations to their direction when needed. Darren had a thermal image of the shuttle in front of him aboard the main vessel, and he used it to guide Gerry back to the surface, in a position ready for launch.

Following the same trajectory as his entry, Gerry gained the ocean surface only after a painfully slow ascendancy from the depths.

'I'll need about fifteen minutes to let the shuttle's pumps get rid of this water.' Gerry radioed to Darren.

'No problem...' Darren began, when everything on his viewing panels turned a shade of red.

THIRTEEN

'Trust in my self-righteous suicide,
I cry when angels deserve to die...'
System of a Down – Chop Suey

'Are you seeing what I'm seeing?' Gerry asked his crew.

'Yes. They've sent something, or someone, after us. Should I cut our data link to Earth?' Darren replied.

'Yeah, honesty has got us nowhere. I'm guessing the light frequency shows it's too fast to be a manned ship' Gerry answered.

Though he had spent most of his life making decisions after weighing up the odds of success, and then trusting those odds to get him through, he had an innate aversion toward making plain assumptions. Jumping to conclusions was something Gerry was loath to ever do, but he seemed to have been making decisions upon little information regularly over the past week or so. He'd usually regard this behaviour as illogical and something to be reviled, but lately he'd been using it as a means of survival. He wasn't surprised by Darren's reply.

'Right first time,' Darren said. 'It's not as fast as that hyper-speed missile they sent after us, but no-one could be aboard something travelling that fast.'

'I'm fairly sure they haven't sent something to help us in our mission. Every-thing's going quite smoothly. They'd know exactly what we're up to, and they've decided to get rid of both their problems at once,' Gerry explained. 'We've got about 20 minutes, at most, to get out of here. We're at the mercy of the quarantine laws. They'll cancel the risk of us infecting others using whatever means available now.'

'So you think that they've sent some sort of military hardware after us?' Charmaine asked.

'Very likely' Gerry advised. 'Probably one of the automated gun-ships. Once it's locked on to our position it will be able to track us anywhere, and easily exceed our speed to follow us until it's done its job.'

'I've heard about that thing,' Darren said. 'A gunship designed to take out spacecraft. What the hell would they need something like that for? Everyone I talked to just thought it was just another bullshit rumour.'

'They did manage to keep any evidence from the general public somehow, knowing they'd have a lot of resistance to them building their military stance in space even further,' Gerry explained. 'Not many people want to see the US government trying to take control of the known universe like they tried on Earth before the war. If self-declared World Police was too much for everyone to stomach you could imagine how people will react when they learn that purpose-built US military vehicles were steadily amassing in space.'

'Maybe we should re-establish our communications link with Mission Control and negotiate,' Jennifer suggested. 'If it is what you say then we have to try something. This is a perfect chance for the government to test its new weapon. They probably haven't had the chance to use it before, so they'll be just itching to give it a go.'

'I can't see how talking with them will do any good now.' Gerry answered. 'Every-thing's been said, and they've been getting enough data from us to know what we're doing. Attempting to bring these two people closer to home isn't something they're going to negotiate with us about. Our condition is obviously considered just too dangerous to them.'

'You mean they'd rather study the phenomenon at their leisure than be forced to interact with us to find a cure. I'll admit, based upon our earlier actions, we are a wild card. But surely they're not going to treat us so severely. Nobody could just leave them there to die. We had to help them,' Jennifer said.

'The same establishment has been doing this for hundreds of years Jennifer. You should have realised before anyone else that their reaction would be to eliminate us. Being in the medical profession for so long, you must know how they treat people who attempt to escape forced quarantine.'

'I know. I agree with the hard-line stance. One infectious person with a rare disease could cause a natural disaster if people's immune systems haven't had to cope with it before. But we must accept that there will be risk involved in keeping any infected species alive. I'd expect them to give us a chance, time to study our radiation exposure further.'

'They can do that without us complicating things' Gerry replied as he waited for his vehicle to be pumped free of the alien waters. The sky was a deep red above him, and knowing it was the energy released by something destructive coming their way made him impatient, forced to resist the stress brought on by their predicament. The seawater was at his shoulder level, and dropping excruciatingly slowly.

Darren, who obviously had some knowledge of the myriad powerful military devices that were at their assailant's disposal, one of which had likely been sent against them, was impatient to leave.

'We've got to get out of here Gerry. If we've any chance of getting away before their scanner locks on to our position we've got to take it. Their engine and tracking equipment will be far better than ours is.'

'I know Darren,' Gerry replied through his helmet microphone. 'Once it's locked on we'll be tracked wherever we go, by something way faster than we are. But we've got what we came for. We've two bodies to analyse that have been exposed to the radiation for over ten years. Our chances of finding a cure have increased a hundred-fold.'

'Great.' Jennifer said over the radio, bitterness evident in her voice. 'We can find out all we need from the corpses we have, but in any likelihood we're soon to end up that way ourselves.'

'We'll be out of here in fifteen minutes,' Gerry said. 'Position the ship for a quick departure.'

'Will do. But where to?' Darren asked.

'Anywhere in a direction away from Earth. We need to keep some distance between our ship and whatever it is they've sent after us. We need time to work out some sort of plan of action, and maybe discuss our position with Mission Control. I don't hold much hope that we can convince them that our intentions aren't a risk to them, but I'd like to try getting them on-side again.'

'Understood,' Darren said over the radio. 'I'll find the nearest hyper-speed lane and aim us in that direction. Wherever it is we go, we don't want to be out in uncleared space for too long.'

'Yeah, go to it Darren.' Gerry instructed. The seawater was down to his waist now, dropping slowly but surely. A glance behind him made him even more impatient to leave this strange moon. The corpse in the rear seat was clearing the surface, head dropped on its right shoulder at an impossible angle. Blood-covered and emaciated, the pale corpse was a shocking sight to behold. It was a mental leap for Gerry to comprehend that it was a living human being only a matter of minutes ago.

Without being able to use the monitors to view his surroundings, Gerry instead peered through the tiny window on his right side, using a lever on the wall panel to move the spotlight mounted outside.

The surface of an incredibly calm sea was revealed, stretching as far as the powerful beam could penetrate. He couldn't feel any movement, though the shuttle he was in was certainly being gently swirled across the moon's surface by the powerful tidal currents they'd seen when they'd sent their probes down.

Gerry was scanning the ocean surface, as expected, finding it barren and lifeless, until something caught his eye. A glimmer of light flickering into existence deep under the sea to starboard.

As Gerry watched it grew larger, and he realised it was coming in his direction. Within seconds he could clearly see a green trail streaking out from behind it. It was one of those creatures they had seen earlier, when first surveying the moon.

Gerry began to be concerned when it didn't slow or change its trajectory, instead continuing straight for him at blinding speed. Its size was becoming apparent, and Gerry guessed it to be about the same size as the shuttle he was in.

Hoping to avoid a collision, Gerry switched off the spotlight. They seemed to be attracted by the light of the beacon that had bought them here, like a moth to a flame, and Gerry thought that the spotlight might be having the same effect on them.

It worked, the green light slowing immediately, and moved instead to the left in a wide arc.

'Gerry, there's something moving near your ship,' he heard Darren say over the radio.

'I know, I can see it' Gerry answered. 'It's one of those glowing, fish-like creatures.'

In fact, Gerry was given a perfect view of it as it passed beneath his vessel. He could make out the complete profile of the creature. It was much like a fish, though with a longer and thinner tail, like that of an eel. A huge black eye, the size of a

190

dartboard, bulged from the side of its head. Considering the almost complete darkness of the moon, Gerry was surprised it used vision to operate. Maybe they could see light-frequencies invisible to humans, or possibly used the light from their own bodies that seemed to be generated as they moved, Gerry thought. If so, it would probably be able to see the shuttle right now, which was a little disconcerting from Gerry's point of view.

'You should be safe' Jennifer advised, as if picking up on his thoughts. 'The sea's loaded with micro-organisms, which must be what it lives on. There's no sign of any other species down there it could be feeding upon.'

'Yeah,' Gerry agreed, 'I doubt its tastes will extend to include the shuttle, but it could do some damage if it struck us. I'll keep the lights off, I think it may have been attracting them.'

'They are probably the reason the light from the hyper-drive of their ship would pulse randomly. Gaston and Holmes might have known that it was having an effect on the wildlife down there and were switching it off intermittently,' Jennifer noted.

'Or they just had problems keeping the hyper-drive running. They were submerged. Not the best place to run a faster-than-light engine' Darren added.

'You're probably both right. I was just thinking the same thing. They would have felt the explosions as the animals were being vaporised by their engine' Gerry replied, his mind working feverishly, his thoughts having an almost painful clarity. To Gerry, the way his mind was giving him such strong insight was the strangest and most pertinent side effect of the radiation poisoning they'd received. No longer wanting or needing food, and wounds that healed in minutes, paled in comparison to the effect on his thought-processes. He still had confidence in his own mental state, but the very sharpness and efficiency in the way his brain now functioned was disconcerting. He was concerned that if he and the crew were thinking straight they never would have absconded from quarantine in the first place, their peculiar new mental state possibly to blame.

The thing outside moved away from the shuttle, and Gerry watched its phosphorescent trail stretching off into the distance as it moved away from him. He kept the camera aimed at its leading end, where the alien creature flailed its way through the sea,

191

gaining a velocity that was amazing for something so large. With a start, Gerry realised where it was headed.

'It's going for the wrecked ship' Gerry told his crew.

'Yeah. We can see it. It'll reach it in a few seconds' Gerry heard Darren say. Sure enough, moments after he finished speaking there was a flash of light in Gerry's viewing panels.

'It hit the ship at disappeared from our sensors,' Darren explained. 'I can't be sure, but I think it destroyed the ship. It looks like it's in more than one piece now.'

Gerry saw pinpricks of light begin to appear in every direction.

'There's hundreds more of those things on their way,' Gerry heard Darren say. 'It looks like they're swarming toward the ravine where the old vessel is.'

Gerry watched as they quickly approached and for a moment he felt a little alarmed, concerned that they might be coming for him and not the old ship. Darren was right though. As they neared Gerry saw them dive, headed toward the abandoned vessel in the depths below.

They kept coming in huge numbers, Gerry feeling the turbulence as they passed, the shuttle rocking softly upon gentle waves.

'These one's aren't trying to ram the wreckage. They seem to be congregating around it. The ravine is full of the creatures,' Charmaine said via the radio. 'I wish we could see what's happening down there instead of just looking at radar scans.'

'We might never know' Gerry said. 'At least we can be sure of one thing. They were using the hyper-speed drive on their vessel to protect themselves from those things. Once they stopped operating it, the ship didn't survive for long.'

For the remaining ten minutes it took for the shuttle to be pumped free of seawater Gerry sat silent, listening to the soft hum of the vessels motors, his thoughts interrupted only once when Darren radioed to advise him that the main vessel was in position for a quick departure.

When the last of the liquid gurgled out through the pumps Gerry fired the thrusters, which lifted the shuttle slightly from the sea's surface. And with a deft hand he accelerated the vessel, manually piloting the ship which normally used hundred of sensors and a computer to operate. The stubby wings along with the tiny ion-jets underneath the shuttle only created enough lift to gain altitude when he'd reached huge speed, howling across the surface of the sea, the main engine roaring behind him. Large moons such as this one made things difficult for shuttle pilots, with gravity too high to leave the surface vertically, and too low an air density to easily fly in the conventional manner.

Lifting from the surface of the sea, relying only on the limited view from the tiny windows, and without any instruments, Gerry was effectively flying blind. He considered switching the power back on, but decided against it in the circumstances. It was still very wet inside the shuttle, and it would most likely just short-circuit and trip the circuit breaker again. Anyway, the vessels navigation system might not react well to being powered-up mid-flight, he decided. These were the most versatile and reliable vehicles people had yet designed, but they still had their occasional faults when the limits of their capabilities were tested.

'Everything looking alright from up there?' Gerry asked the crew.

'Yes, we have a clear visual of you. The light caused by the vessel coming from Earth is making it real easy to see you. Keep climbing at your current rate and I'll let you know when you've reached the correct altitude' Darren advised.

Gerry could hear the veiled impatience in his crew's voices as they conversed with him over the radio for the remaining minutes that he steered the shuttle in a wide, climbing arc toward them. He wished he could hasten his arrival, though there was nothing else he could do. Idly chatting while one of the US government's weapons of mass destruction was tearing its way through space toward them wasn't good for the nerves.

Nearing the parent vessel, Gerry had just reversed thrust when he heard a thump from the radio and then Charmaine's frightened voice, 'Darren and Jennifer just fell unconscious. They're slumped in their seats. What do I do?'

'Don't be too worried about it Charmaine. It seems that every time we get stressed it's happening. I'm alongside now. Just hang tight. Do you know how to ready the hatch for docking?'

'Yes, I think so. I haven't needed to do it before, but I know where the settings are on the computer' Charmaine replied.

'Go to it then. If you have any problems just tell me and I'll walk you through the procedure' Gerry told her. 'Just relax; we don't want you collapsing as well.'

193

Relieved when he found he didn't have to wait any longer than twenty seconds for Charmaine to do what he'd requested, Gerry saw the hatch connections moving into position while as he watched through the tiny side window. Gerry was conscious of the fact that if the shuttle had electrical power, the docking would have been carried out automatically and would have taken less time; and time was something that was running out for them. He could not allow any more such delays to their departure.

They were on the run now, pursued by a killing machine that moved twice as quickly as they could. There was no way they could outrun it, but they needed the time to form and implement a plan of escape. He hoped that their altered brain function would be an advantage, the radiation exposure still having an effect on his thought processes. Indeed, his mind was swimming with the quick-fire thoughts that churned through it. He had already thought of dozens of options to attempt escape from the military vehicle, though none of them struck him as truly workable. Most of his ideas involved sacrificing one or more of his crew, or himself, and that wasn't a viable option. They needed each other more than ever now, with their home planet turning its back on them.

'Thanks, Charmaine, I'm on my way in. I'll be with you in less than a minute' Gerry said as he moved the shuttle directly under the main vessel, and with rare skill he gently docked. The shuttle's hatch didn't open automatically because of the lack of electrical power, and he was forced to open it manually using an old-fashion winder on the ceiling.

Looking down at the two bodies he considered taking them out of the shuttle and moving them into the main vessel, but quickly decided against it due to the lack of time. If they were alive they wouldn't have been able to stay in the shuttle when the main ship accelerated. The lack of proper protection from both radiation and the ships thrust, would quickly kill anybody down there. But these two people were very dead. The radiation may have saved his life once, when burned by the suit thruster, but his injury paled in comparison to those sustained by Gaston and Holmes. Crushed and disfigured, the strange blue glow wasn't evident on either of their bodies now. Gerry quickly removed his helmet and then one of his gloves, then using his bare fingers to check them both for a pulse. Neither had one, as he'd expected, though some very unusual things had happened over the past few days, so he had felt the need to double-check.

Leaping up through the hatch, Gerry sprinted to the flight deck, where he found Jennifer still slumped in her seat, mumbling something to herself. Darren was sitting upright now, wide-awake, with consternation written all over his face. Charmaine was looking equally concerned.

'Darren's just had one of those bursts of hyperactive mental activity. When he came to he said there's no need to leave here. We're not going to be able to escape the attack vessel. And we have no defence against it at all,' she told him.

'I agree that we're in a bind,' Gerry told them. 'But we might be able to use the extra time we gain to formulate some kind of escape plan. I'm sure you'll both agree, the mental condition we're in gives us a better chance than ever of achieving the near impossible. Get us to the hyper-speed lane Darren.'

Charmaine continued to speak as they felt the ship move under Darren's control, taxiing under the low power of regular thrusters toward the point where they would fire the main engine. 'This radiation poisoning does seem to have its advantages. I've never been overly intelligent, and still aren't, but what my mind can sometimes do lately is incredible by anyone's standards. Especially when I fall unconscious, it seems.'

'Yeah, it's the same for me when that happens' Darren added as he worked at his keyboard. 'When the body goes to sleep my brain comes alive. My thought processes are constantly a bit hyperactive now, though.'

'Our condition might very well be our means to get out of this situation,' Gerry told them as he removed his suit. 'Let's just get the hell out of here so we've got some more time to think.'

Jennifer finally woke completely and sat up as Gerry finished extricating himself from his pressure suit. She looking dishevelled and stressed, and didn't speak a word, simply looked down at her computer screen and continued working. On what, Gerry had no idea. Their research mission was over now, and their only goal was survival. Maybe she just wanted to keep busy, Gerry decided. He had done the same on the few occasions he thought he might not have long to live. Keeping your mind occupied was far less stressful than sitting around pondering the end.

'How long till we reach the hyper-speed lane Darren?' he asked.

'Nine minutes.'

'That's too long' Gerry said with sudden consternation. 'The damn ship will reach us before we even get there.'

'Our hyper-speed drive will still function outside the hyper-speed lane now, even without your top-level operator status. We're not connected to any computers. We've been isolated, so the remote fail-safe mechanisms aren't stopping us,' Darren advised. 'All we can do to give ourselves more time would be to start hyper-speed acceleration now, in uncleared space. There's a good chance we'll make it without colliding with any matter.'

'All right then Darren, let's go,' Gerry instructed after he'd placed his suit in a storage space and moved to his flight seat. 'Plot a trajectory that will take us to the hyper-speed lane without us needing to decelerate too much or need to make too hard a turn into it when we get there.'

'Will do...' Darren replied, and seconds later, 'I'm done.'

As soon as Gerry's harness clicked into place the variable mass engine fired, and their universe turned to the violent madness bought on by modern hyper-speed travel. It was worse than usual, this time Darren had obviously opted to accelerate under full power. Right to the limiter. Gerry could tell, by the way he could feel the skin on his body being stretched almost to the point of tearing under the incredible thrust. He hoped the two women would be all right. This level of force could break bones. Though the engine itself extended its protective field throughout the ship, it could not insulate them completely from the forces generated. Only barely enough to allow them to survive.

There wasn't any conversation happening and talking was, in fact, impossible. It was the most they could all do just to take an occasional small breath. After only five seconds of hyper-speed acceleration Darren used his keyboard under his hand to type a message, which appeared on the large screen before them, where they could easily read it.

'WE HAVE REACHED THE HYPER-SPEED LANE. HOLD ON. I NEED TO TURN NOW TO ALIGN US WITHIN IT'

196

Everyone was thrown violently sideways in his or her seat. Gerry knew what a dangerous manoeuvre this was. Vessels travelling so quickly were not, and could not be built to safely make such a turn. To do so at faster-than-light speed had a frighteningly low success rate under test conditions. If their computer had still been connected to any other functioning network in the universe it would not have even be possible to attempt it. The engine was firing a trail of lethal radiation behind the ship, and if directed toward any life for thousands of light years behind them would kill it instantly. There were mechanisms to stop anybody firing a drive in any direction outside of a hyper-speed lane, but they had stopped functioning when the two scientists had sent some sort of virus to Earth, which corrupted their computer systems. Also, their vessels flight computer had been deliberately disconnected from any others. It had set them free to use the drive whenever they felt it necessary. Now they really were a danger to humanity, Gerry surmised. It was of no surprise to him now that everyone would want them either quickly caught or killed. Though they had not fired the drives exhaust in the direction of Earth, there were other settlements, in other solar systems, that would surely not appreciate having a hyper-drive fired haphazardly in their vicinity.

'DO WHAT YOU CAN TO KEEP OUR EXHAUST AWAY FROM THE DIRECTION OF EARTH OR ANY OTHER COLONIES DARREN' Gerry typed. It was probably a moot point, Darren knew what he was doing, but Gerry felt he had an obligation to mention it. By their escape attempt, they were risking the lives of 20 billion people back on Earth, and millions of others on the settlements.

'I'M TRYING. BUT I CAN'T GUARANTEE THAT WE AREN'T EXHAUSTING INTO SOLAR SYSTEMS THAT CONTAIN PEOPLE OR OTHER LIFE. WE ARE NEARLY THERE THOUGH' Darren typed in reply.

And suddenly they were shoved back into the middle of their flight seats, and another message from Darren appeared onscreen. 'WE MADE IT. ACCELERATION TO CONTINUE FOR 48 MINS.'

Gerry could see Darren's huge smile from the corner of his eye. He was obviously pleased he had pulled it off successfully.

197

'WHERE ARE WE HEADED DARREN?' Gerry inquired via his keyboard.

'TO THE MOST DISTANT NORTH-WESTERN SECTION OF THE GALAXY. THERE ARE SOME NEWLY DISCOVERED PLANETS WHERE WE CAN HIDE OUT.'

Gerry knew the area well. It was where he had been sent to help cull a small, semi-intelligent species of mammal little more than a year previously. Christian cultists, who had decided that life was not to their liking on Earth, had also already begun to colonise the planets in the area, demanding they be given the opportunity to follow their own self-righteous destiny. Governments all over had organised, and even paid for the trip for them, Gerry had read, and most saw it as an expensive though effective way of stopping them messing dangerously with politics on Earth. He had been amused to read that some of them had already decided that God had taken a full two weeks to create their new planet, such were its new inhabitants importance to Him.

Jennifer was the next person to send a message. 'WHY DON'T WE USE THE BLAST FROM THE MAIN DRIVE TO STOP THE SHIP THAT'S COMING AFTER US?'

Gerry had considered it already, and had his answer ready. 'IT WOULDN'T WORK. THERE'S NOTHING ALIVE ABOARD THAT VESSEL. THE INSTRUMENTS IT USES WOULD HAVE BEEN DESIGNED TO WITHSTAND EXTREME CONDITIONS. PROLONGED EXPOSURE MIGHT HAVE SOME EFFECT BUT IT WOULD HAVE CAUGHT US LONG BEFORE IT MALFUNCTIONED'

'HOW ABOUT SENDING OUR SHUTTLE BACK AT IT TO TRY FOR A COLLISION. WE HAVE HAD A BIT OF PRACTISE AT THAT' Darren asked next. The ideas were coming forward quickly, as Gerry had hoped. They just needed to find the solution with the highest probability of paying off. Though, sadly, Gerry had considered this latest one from Darren also, and knew for certain that it would be a pointless exercise.

'NO GOOD DARREN. THE WEAPONRY THAT THING CARRIES WILL TAKE IT OUT BEFORE IT GOT WITHIN 10 LIGHT YEARS OF IT.'

'WHAT ABOUT SENDING OUT A PILE OF JUNK OUT AT LIKE WE DID AGAINST THE HYPER-SPEED

198

MISSILE? IF IT FAILS TO ATOMISE EVEN A TINY PIECE OF THE STUFF IT COULD DESTROY IT WHEN IT COLLIDES WITH IT' Charmaine entered next.

Gerry thought it to be their best plan of action so far, though it would only do as a last resort, if all else failed. He rated the chance of success as extremely low.

'IT DIDN'T WORK AGAINST THE MISSILE. THE VESSEL THAT IS AFTER US NOW CAN CLEAR ITS OWN PATH, AUTOMATICALLY DESTROYING ANYTHING THAT APPROACHES IT. AGAIN, THERE WILL BE LITTLE CHANCE OF SUCCESS. IT IS OUR BEST OPTION SO FAR THOUGH. ANY MORE IDEAS?' he typed.

'SORRY, NONE THAT HOLD ANY MORE HOPE THAN THOSE WE'VE MENTIONED ALREADY' Charmaine replied.

'ALRIGHT THEN HOW ABOUT WE TRY GETTING INTO CONTACT WITH MISSION CONTROL' Darren tapped out next. 'IT'S OUR ONLY DECENT CHANCE. THE GUNSHIP WILL BE WITHIN RANGE TO ATTACK BEFORE WE REACH OUR DESTINATION. WE DEFINITELY WON'T HAVE TIME TO ABANDON SHIP BEFORE IT IS FIRED UPON.'

'IT DOES SEEM AS THOUGH IT'S OUR ONLY REALISTIC OPTION LEFT. SEE IF YOU CAN GET THEM ONLINE DARREN' Gerry instructed, though not comfortable with the decision. They would instantly know their co-ordinates and could possible even take control of their ship's flight systems if they had their computer networks functioning properly again.

While Darren was working to get in contact with Mission Control, Gerry used his own computer terminal to activate the ships long-range scanners, and found the gunship immediately. It was still in the hyper-speed lane that led to the moon they head just left. The fact that it was already close enough to be picked up by their ship's sensors bought the urgency of the situation home to him. And as his heartbeat rose, the stress bought on by what the next 40 minutes could bring had a now-familiar effect. His mind started racing, and the fury of the onslaught of mental activity was too much for him. Though held in place by his harness and the thrust of the ship, Gerry was effectively unconscious in his seat. His body limp and useless, while multitude thoughts and ideas swirled like something physical within his skull, battering their way painfully through. An unusual scene appeared in his mind, its clarity making it remarkable.

Gerry imagined he was in the shuttle attached underneath, watching one of the scientists twitching within his restraints. His eyes were no longer closed, and his mouth was wide open in a silent scream. The panic and the pain that emanated from the vision startled Gerry back to normal consciousness. He used his keyboard to tap out a message to the others, which appeared on the big screen before them where they could easily read it.

'HAS ANYONE NOTICED ANYTHING UNUSUAL FROM THE SHUTTLES INTERIOR SENSORS?'

'NO. WHY?' Jennifer messaged first.

'PROBABLY JUST MY IMAGINATION. A STRONG FEELING ONE OF THEM IS ALIVE DOWN THERE.'

'DIDN'T YOU CHECK?' Jennifer asked.

'OF COURSE. THOUGH NOT AS THOROUGHLY AS I COULD HAVE. THEY BOTH LOOKED VERY DEAD. SURELY THEY MUST BE.'

'THE TEMPERATURE IS A LITTLE HIGHER INSIDE THE SHUTTLE THAN IT NORMALLY IS' Charmaine messaged next. 'I'LL BRING UP THE INTERNAL VIEW.'

'THAT'S PROBABLY JUST THE HEAT IT GAINED ON THE TRIP TO THE MOON'S SURFACE' messaged Darren.

When the view from a camera within the shuttle came on-screen everything was as Gerry had left it. The bodies lay as they were, on in the flight seat and the other on the floor, still harnessed to the wall.

But as Gerry was about to tell them to forget about it, that it was just a strangely vivid daydream he'd had, he noticed a band of blue light flicker across the neck of the body that was pressed back into the flight seat. And he though he even saw a hint of movement. He could not possibly be alive down there, but Gerry couldn't shake the feeling. He needed to be certain.

'IT'S PROBABLY NOTHING, BUT COULD YOU CANCEL ACCELERATION FOR A MOMENT DARREN. I WANT TO HAVE A LOOK' Gerry instructed. Darren wasn't happy about the idea, knowing their pursuer was closing fast, but he instantly did as he was asked.

The thrust that was keeping them pinned to their seats quickly dissipated, allowing Gerry to release his harness and stand, though initially a little unsteadily due to the lack of blood flowing to his limps, a normal effect of hyper-speed acceleration.

'I'll only be a moment. Get Mission Control on-line while I'm gone,' he said to the others, before rushing from the room. At a rate of speed that impressed even him, Gerry made his way along the corridor and down the stairs that would take him to the bowels of the ship. Reaching the place where the shuttles hatch was located Gerry found nothing amiss. There was utter silence down here.

Stooping to peer into the shuttle's interior, Gerry hoped, and expected, everything to be as it should. The startling vision that had assaulted him a moment ago would surely be only an effect caused by his radiation exposure. He was somehow not surprised by what he found though.

Dan, the dead and mangled scientist he had placed in the flight seat, was obviously very alive. He must have released himself as soon as they had cancelled acceleration, and was sitting slumped by the side of his dead co-worker, who was obviously not going to miraculously come back to life. His body had turned purple and black, and the stench that emanated from it left Gerry without doubt.

Though conscious of the fact that he was interrupting someone whom was grieving for his friend, who had died only minutes earlier, Gerry did not have the time to be polite, or even stop to assess the strange new situation.

'Welcome back Dan, I'm Gerry Handley, the acting Supervisor' he said to the shockingly injured scientist. 'Try to relax for a moment; I'll get you some medical treatment.'

Gerry waited for a few seconds, and there was no response, though he wasn't surprised. A pool of blood was forming beneath the retching figure, and there were the familiar flashes of blue light flickering across the back of his neck. Stepping over him, Gerry made his way to the shuttle's control panel. Thumbing the key that switched on the shuttle's radio, Gerry ordered Jenny down, telling her to bring a stretcher with her. Gerry didn't have to tell her to hurry. The fact that an automated gunship was bearing down on them gave them all quite enough of a sense of urgency.

'She's on her way' Darren advised, and as Gerry turned back to the injured man, he was met with a gut-wrenching sight. Dan Gaston was looking up at him, and for the first time Gerry truly saw the damage that his body had sustained. While one eye was focussed on him, the other had been forced back into the skull, so far back that Gerry knew it must be pressing against his brain. Still though, it peered out at him from deep within the darkness of his bloodied eye socket.

'Something is coming' Gerry heard him whisper. The effort bought on a fresh torrent of blood from his mouth and nose, and he slumped forward, face-first onto the floor.

'We know' Gerry said, not sure if the injured man could hear him. 'Once we've got you comfortable we'll get out of here.'

In the darkened shuttle interior Gerry couldn't help but notice the sparkling blue light that played across the visible parts of the scientist's inert body. When Jennifer arrived, she lowered a stretcher into the shuttle and then made her way down to Gerry and their motionless patient.

Seeing the blue light that flickered over the back of his neck, Jennifer gave Gerry a quick glance, her concern showing in her furrowed brow. 'Let's get him to one of the cabins. We'll have to wait until we escape the gunship before we can do anything for him.'

Jennifer lay the stretcher alongside the injured Gaston, and with Gerry's help, rolled him onto it. The researcher moaned with the pain that came from being moved.

Although awkward, they managed to get the stretcher through the shuttle hatch without causing undue strain to the man upon it. He was remarkably light so they didn't bother using the electric lift. Gerry estimating around 40 kilograms, mainly from the blood loss than malnutrition.

And he was extremely resilient it seemed. For when they began to carry him to the cabin, where he would stay until they managed to somehow evade their attacker, he opened his eyes and indeed began to lift himself upright. They were forced to put the stretcher down for a moment, in case he fell from it. Jennifer placed her hand on his shoulder to still him.

'Don't move. You're badly injured and you'll only make things worse.'

'We must get away from here. Now,' they heard Gaston say, a fresh trickle of blood oozing from his mouth.

'We know,' Gerry said to him. 'As soon as we have you in a cabin bunk ready for acceleration we'll be out of here.'

'No time. Take me to the flight controls' he rasped, blue flashes of light flickering across his face from beneath his skin, the strange effects of the radiation exposure clearly visible. Though its action seemed to help their wounds heal, indeed probably saving Gerry's life when the suit thruster burned him, there was a terrible side effect. Dan Gaston should be dead. If not from his wounds alone, the immense pain should be sending him into severe shock, where mercifully he would fall unconscious and probably die. Instead, he was awake and lucid, obviously feeling all the damage to his crushed body.

'Should we try a sedative or some painkillers?' Jennifer asked Gerry.

'Our bodies won't accept them now, so I think we can be sure it will be the same for Dan here.'

'Yeah, we'd more likely just hurt him more' Jennifer replied.

'Take me to the flight controls,' Gaston repeated, again trying to roll out of the stretcher.

'Let's do as he says' Gerry said to Jennifer, and instead of taking him to one of the cabins they carried him to the other end of the corridor and entered the flight deck.

'We only have 18 minutes before the gunship gets here,' Darren said to them immediately, rising to help Gerry and Jennifer lift the injured man into one of the spare flight seats. His broken ribs ground together loudly with the movement, sickening even Gerry and Jennifer, who had seen many injured people during their dangerous careers.

Though moaning and choking on the blood that rose into his mouth, Dan Gaston's hand moved to the computer keyboard beside him while they were strapping him in.

Gerry grabbed his arm.

'Just sit tight; we can't have you using the computer. It's what you did with them last time that helped get us in the trouble we are in now. We'll be accelerating in a few seconds, so just let us do what we need to do.'

Gaston nodded slightly. 'Yes. But I can help.'

203

'No' Gerry told him, flipping the keyboard down to where it clipped onto the seat in a closed position, where Gaston would have trouble reaching it. 'Leave this to us.'

Gaston closed his eyes and seemed to relax, Jennifer helping him push his hands under the straps on the flight seats arms. They were only used to keep limbs from flailing about during acceleration and deceleration, and Gerry considered restraining him more securely. He decided against it, that it would take too much time. The acceleration forces would keep him relatively still anyway.

Everyone quickly resumed his or her seat, and when Gerry had seen everyone was ready, and that the seemingly unconscious Dan Gaston was as comfortable as he was going to be, he nodded to Darren.

Instantly they were shoved back into their seats, and the g-forces bought a loud cry from Gaston in the seat beside Gerry. From the corner of his eye Gerry saw streams of blood burst from his body, spraying horizontally to the rear of the flight deck. Jennifer was seated in an unfortunate position, almost directly behind the bleeding man. Gerry knew there was no way for her to avoid the mess that would be spraying over her. The gore, combined with the visual distortion created by hyper-speed acceleration, made for a hellish scene.

'GASTON ISN'T GOING TO SURVIVE ACCELERATION AT THIS RATE. DO YOU WANT ME TO TAKE IT A LITTLE EASIER?' appeared on the screen before them. It was a message from Darren.

'WE CAN'T' Gerry typed in reply. 'THERE IS NO WAY WE CAN OUTRUN THE GUNSHIP BEHIND US BUT WE NEED TO GAIN AS MUCH TIME AS POSSIBLE.'

When Gerry was sure that he had read the message, he sent instructions to Charmaine and Jennifer to try establishing contact with Mission Control. He needed to know their terms back on Earth, whether or not they had any possibility of bargaining with them for their lives. He could see no other viable way out of their situation.

While they were busy, Gerry checked for any hidden messages from Mission Control, though found none. He had hoped that they might have wanted to deal directly with him, devise a solution without the knowledge of the crew, but was disappointed.

The cabin suddenly lit up, an iridescent blue, and Gerry could feel the crackling surge of power around him. Again, it was as though solid objects were knocking them about, invisible, though wielding palpable force.

Turning his head to the side, Gerry saw that Gaston was affected most of all. The radiance of blue light emanating from him was near blinding. Tendrils of smoke rose from some of the wounds on his ribcage where his bones had punctured the skin, yet still he seemed to Gerry to be awake and aware of what was happening. The deformed face turned to look at him, and Gerry only hid his repulsion with great difficulty. The sunken, staring eye, the streams of blood that flowed from his ears, nose and mouth made for a terrible sight to behold. This remnant of a human being could surely not still live. Gerry was astounded by the man's sheer will to live, and his tolerance for pain. After more than ten years stranded in a tiny research vessel, Gerry guessed that many people would cling to their new life of relative freedom with fervour, no matter how painful it might be.

Nevertheless, under the distorted and gore-plastered face, Gerry was sure he saw something that resembled a smile appear. And along with it came the urgent tones of warning messages from the ships computer.

Gerry felt the g-forces, that were already squeezing him painfully back into his seat, grow suddenly stronger, and with huge difficulty he turned his head to look at the screen before them. An 'over-speed' warning was flashing.

'DARREN, I GUESS THAT IT ISN'T YOU WHO IS GETTING THE SHIP TO ACCELERATE SO HARD' Gerry typed, though it was more an observation than a question.

'NO' appeared on-screen after a pause. Darren was obviously having difficulty using his keyboard. Gerry knew first-hand just why, his own fingers on the verge of being bent back and broken, each of them weighing a few kilograms under such rapid acceleration.

More alert messages began to fill the screen as they're rate of acceleration continued to increase. As Gerry entered commands into his keyboard in an attempt to bring the ship back into their control he hoped Darren was doing the same. There was no way their ship could withstand the demands being placed upon it. The flexing of the thin hull could be heard as a metallic whine, which would surely be frightening the crew, and Gerry gritted his teeth against the sound of a thousand blackboards being scratched by a thousand nails as he worked painfully at the computer keyboard.

His efforts proved fruitless. The commands he entered were seemingly ignored by the ship computer, and they're acceleration rate continued to increase.

The forces were too much now for Gerry to turn his head to look at his companions, though out of the corner of his eye he could see they're injured hitch-hiker squeezed into the flight-seat beside him, face still turned toward him. There was no smile evident now though. Gaston's eyes were rolled up into his head, mouth slack and lips stretched back across his face. The g-forces were killing him, but still the ship continued to accelerate harder, Gerry sure that this very person was in control of their vessel, in control of their very lives.

With his vessel in someone else's hands, under forces that a manned ship should never impart upon its passengers, Gerry felt himself slip to the verge of losing consciousness. Moreover, within moments, sure that he would never wake, Gerry blacked out, unaware that the crew had already done the same more than a minute earlier.

All but one was unconscious. Their passenger, Dan Gaston, was very much alert. And as the research vessel continued to accelerate, and the electric-blue light played over the occupants bodies, a short message appeared on the large screen at the fore of the flight deck. It appeared on the screens in Mission Control back on Earth too, the communication lines inexplicably opened for an instant.

'LEAVE US BE. WE WILL NOT RETURN'

FOURTEEN

'It has to start somewhere; it has to start sometime,
What better place than here, what better time than now?'
Rage Against The Machine – Guerrilla Radio

On regaining consciousness, Gerry was disorientated for a moment. The computers alarms had gone quiet, the ship was no longer accelerating, and there was total silence on the flight deck.

In some disbelief that he was still alive, Gerry turned his head to look over his crew and their hitch-hiker. Darren and Jennifer were stirring, probably having been unconscious for a time, while Charmaine was still slumped motionless in her flight seat.

Gerry rose from his seat, slowly and painfully, thinking he had better check her vital signs in case she was not only knocked out but badly hurt. As he went to her his eyes were drawn to where the man they had rescued was seated. He was awake, and feebly attempting to extricate his arms from the flight-seats restraints.

Checking Charmaine's pulse and breathing, Gerry pondered his next move. Should he arrest this man, lock him in a cabin for what he had done? Whatever it was that he had actually done, Gerry wasn't sure. He looked too pale and weak to be any sort of threat now. Evidence of the extent of his injuries was plain to see. The rear wall of the flight deck was shimmering red, painted with his blood. As was Jennifer, who didn't look at all happy about being showered with his gore.

Charmaine seemed to be in good health when Gerry checked, only blacked out from the g-forces like the rest of them had been. All but the new self-imposed pilot of their vessel, Dan Gaston.

Gerry stepped back to his flight seat and used the keyboard to bring a map of their location on-screen. He was shocked to find that they were in orbit of a known planet. Gaston had taken them to a planet Gerry knew something of. It was Clarkson, the very planet that Darren had spoken about taking them. A planet holding a relatively advanced ecosystem, a place where people from Earth had already staked their claim.

Christian extremists ran this place now. Their destructive self-righteousness was a threat to anyone or anything that crossed their path, or those who scorned their ancient ideals. Out of thousands of habitable planets, this was not one where he would choose to be. Military units knew this place too. Even if they had outrun the gunship somehow, Earth ships would surely scan for them here. Even routine research missions carried out in this area of space would likely discover their position. There would be many of those here too, Gerry assumed. There were more species of life in the solar systems in this area than any other section of space yet explored.

There was no sign of the gunship on the map for hundreds of light years. Somehow, they had outrun it.

'It looks as though I've missed something. Where the hell are we?' Jennifer asked, noticing the map, which was displayed before them.

'We're right where Darren wanted to take us. Clarkson, the Christian planet' Gerry told her, passing her a cleaning cloth from a storage cabinet in the wall so she could wipe Gaston's blood from her face. 'The gunship is out of our sensor range. It looks as though we've outrun it.'

'I guess he had something to do with that' Jennifer said, nodding toward the pale scientist seated before her.

'No doubt' Gerry replied.

Seating himself, Gerry began checking the ships systems for any problems caused by their strange journey, and Darren was the next to wake fully. He looked at the screen and smiled.

'Looks like we made it to Clarkson.' Then he noticed some of the figures on the screen that Gerry was checking. 'Could we really have been moving at those speeds?'

'Nothing man-made ever has before,' Gerry reminded him. 'But the timeline fits. We must have been moving at those speeds to get here so quickly.'

'Shit!' Jennifer exclaimed when she saw what they were talking about. 'Twenty-eight thousand times light speed. That just isn't possible. There must be some malfunction with the ships instruments.'

'No, no glitches,' Gerry told her. 'These figures are accurate. Our friend's found some way to feed more power to the main drive.'

'But we were accelerating three times as hard as a human body can sustain.' Jennifer added. 'Even if he did get all that extra speed from our ship, we couldn't be alive afterwards.'

'Normally, no' Gerry replied. 'But it gets even stranger. Look at all those hull-breach warnings. The ships hull was being ripped apart for seconds at a time, but would then reseal somehow. The breach warnings were triggered more than twenty times during the flight, but here we are in one piece.'

Darren was next to put his thoughts forward. 'I can understand us surviving the journey, the way we all have quick-healing injuries thanks to our radiation exposure, but rents in the ships hull that quickly repair themselves is another thing again. You don't think the ship is being patched by the radiation the same way our bodies have been, do you?'

'Who knows?' Gerry replied. 'But we can consider that later. We need to decide on our next course of action. The gunship will almost certainly still be headed to our position.'

'Well we won't be able to stay out here in space. It'll detect us for sure' Darren said.

'I agree' Gerry told them. 'We won't be able to hide this ship. We'll need to abandon it.'

'But do we have to disembark here?' Charmaine said from her flight seat, where she had just woken. 'Most of the planet hasn't been surveyed yet. We don't know for sure what we'll find down there.'

'It won't be so bad' Gerry said, turning in his seat to look at her. She still appeared a little dazed, but healthy enough considering what she had just been through. 'At least there are people living there. We'll be able to get help and supplies if we need it' he reassured her.

'They don't accept outsiders. Surely you've all heard about the people down there. Anyone not sharing their beliefs or values is something they call a heathen. They won't give us assistance unless they think they can convert us to their way of thinking, or more precisely, their lack of thinking.'

Gerry understood Charmaine's trepidation, but felt she overstated the negatives. 'They are in the same boat as us. None of us are welcome on Earth or any of the other colonies. We've probably found our only like-souls in the known universe. If we are welcomed anywhere, it will be here.'

'Great. Look at what our lives have come down to' Darren said dejectedly, but was ready to leave their vessel that was at the moment, a sitting duck. 'We'd better leave now if we want to avoid the gunship that's probably still on its way.'

'Everyone is to gather any equipment or supplies that we might need to set up camp' Gerry instructed. 'And I don't want anybody worrying about where we are going. They are just people like us down there, albeit with some strange beliefs. They may use the emotional and creative side of their brain more than the logical and analytical side like we do, but this doesn't make them monsters. They are still just people like us, trying to do what they can to survive.'

'We aren't going to be able to take much down' Darren reminded them. 'We'll be close to maximum payload with just our bodyweight.'

Gerry nodded. 'Yes, just get together a few things that you are sure we could use to get by while we're down there. We won't have time to do a second shuttle run before the gunship reaches us.'

Everyone left the flight deck, leaving their hitch-hiker fumbling about weakly in his seat, still unable to release himself from his harness. His breathing made a wet, gurgling sound, and everyone was relieved to get some distance between him and themselves.

Charmaine, Jennifer and Darren went to the cabins and storage rooms where they gathered the essentials, while Gerry had the gruesome task of removing the dead scientist's body from the shuttle where he'd been left.

By the time Gerry had heaved the body out through the shuttle hatch and wiped away some of the gore that was spread within, the others were gathering, ready to board with their arm-loads of supplies.

'We'll be lucky to get this much in' Darren noted.

'See what you can do' Gerry replied. 'Jennifer, could you come give me a hand bringing Gaston down?'

She placed the large box she was holding onto the floor. 'I guess we'll need the stretcher.'

'Yes' Gerry answered as they left for the flight deck where their injured passenger was seated. When they got to him he was still fumbling with the harness.

Gerry and Jennifer both grimaced as they released him from his seat and lifted him out onto the stretcher alongside. Though he was light, the blood that covered him made him slippery, difficult to hold, and they had to take care not to drop him.

On the walk down to the shuttle their job wasn't made any easier by Gaston's incessant attempts to lift himself upright. He was probably trying to speak too, but all Jennifer and Gerry could hear was gurgling and choking sounds.

Darren and Charmaine had already loaded the shuttle with their supplies by the time they arrived there, leaving just enough space for the five of them to be seated.

The shuttle was only designed to carry two people and a small amount of equipment to and from a planets surface, so three of them would be forced to sit on the floor, backs against a hard wall. They couldn't even restrain themselves, all of the harnesses in the wall used to secure their supplies. Gerry would need to make this a very delicate flight.

When everyone was in position and as comfortable as they could get, Gerry switched on the shuttles electric's, and to his relief the interior lights and control panels lit up. He doubted he'd have been able to pilot the shuttle with this size payload without the automated controls functioning.

When the shuttle hatch closed, the reek of fresh blood grew sickeningly stronger, Gaston's rasping breaths louder.

Gerry didn't delay, deftly undocking and accelerating their vessel planet-ward, careful to keep the thrust low enough to prevent his passengers and equipment being placed under too much stress. If a box of their equipment broke loose it could crush one of his crew-mates.

Though in reality the journey took less than twenty minutes, it seemed far longer to everyone on board. Their sense of relief was palpable when they were close enough to the surface to make out the landscape in detail.

'This place looks so much like Earth' Charmaine said in surprise. Dusty grass plains, one of which they were approaching to land, surrounded by a lush forest. The vibrant health of the alien planet buoyed their spirits some, the thought of being stranded here not so disheartening.

'I'll set us down here' Gerry told the others. 'We're about thirty kilometres from the main settlement. If we decide to pay them a visit it shouldn't be a problem. And they shouldn't have been able to see our arrival unless they were very lucky. We might decide to keep our distance from them anyway. We'll need to weigh up the risks of our radiation poisoning infecting the people here before we do anything.'

The others murmured their agreement, still staring at the screen at the fore of the cabin, which showed the huge trees and bushes that looked so much like those on Earth. Numerous small animals could be seen scurrying from the plain into the undergrowth amongst the surrounding forest. They looked like types of rodent, in various sizes, but it was impossible to make out any detail.

Gerry had prepared for the chance that their illness would diminish and their appetites return, leaving them with the need to hunt for their food. He had brought with him the one weapon that had been locked in the main ship, a small calibre handgun that was supplied just for this purpose. He was glad that he had, as he watched the animals bolt for cover.

As they neared the sandy ground, Gerry switched on the thrusters underneath and reduced speed, gently turning the shuttle's flight from a controlled glide to a vertical descent. He found he had to use full thrust to stop them plummeting from the air. The extra payload on board was making itself felt, the shuttle having only just enough power to bring them down at a reasonably slow rate. He was again piloting the vessel using manual controls, not trusting the still-wet electronics in the shuttle.

When they touched down, albeit a little roughly, Gerry was surprised to find himself smiling, and a glance around the cabin showed he wasn't the only one who was in some way pleased with their arrival.

Darren was the first upright, and immediately helped Jennifer to her feet. Charmaine and Gerry unharnessed themselves and when the shuttle hatch slid open, smiles broke out all-round.

'Let's go get some fresh air,' Darren exclaimed happily.

One-by-one they ascended the rungs, exiting from the top of the shuttle. Gerry was the last to disembark, leaving their injured passenger inside for the moment.

The wave of warm, scented air that washed across his face when his head cleared the hatch made him gasp. It was always good getting back to Earth after a mission and taking that first breath, but this was something special. Earth didn't have air as sweet or as crystal as this. So many years worth of human pollution may have taken its toll on the home planet, but indeed Gerry wondered whether Earth had ever had air this clean and nourishing.

Though it was midday here, the light was softer than on Earth. It had a faintly orange tinge, and the sun looked smaller and easier to look at with the naked eye. As they stood on the shuttle roof and looked about, Gerry noticed one major difference from Earth.

'There are no birds. On Earth we would have seen flocks of them by now.'

'They might be low in numbers or maybe they just haven't evolved here yet.' Charmaine replied. 'They are a common life form on other planets with ecosystems like this, but not a genetic line that's guaranteed to appear. Flight stems from animals needing to find extra speed to hunt or escape predators on the ground, but the species here might have found other ways to move more rapidly, or other ways to avoid predators.'

'There's sure to be heaps of other differences from Earth, but I've got to say, it's bloody good to be here' Darren said with a grin. 'If we have to be in quarantine, I'm glad its here that we're waiting it out.'

'If we do recover from this radiation poisoning do you think they'll forget everything we've done and let us return to Earth?' Charmaine asked nobody in particular.

'It's our best bet I'd say' Gerry answered. 'They'll most likely have a communications link with Earth of some kind at the settlement here. If our health improves we should be able to bring them here to check our condition.

'We'll need to set up camp before nightfall,' he continued. 'Let's get Dan out of there and find him somewhere more comfortable to recuperate.'

It took more than an hour for them to move Gaston and the equipment they'd bought to a breezy location at the edge of the dense forest, under the shade of a massive tree. Gerry thought it best to get some distance between themselves and the shuttle. Their pursuers would detect its location down here with ease. It was likely to be attacked, or at the very least it and its surroundings would be monitored closely.

His crew had packed four two-man tents, which Gerry quickly erected with help from Darren. Charmaine and Jennifer unpacked the equipment they would be using for the night, such as lighting and medical supplies for Gaston.

Gerry was a little amused to see that they hadn't even bothered packing any food. They'd obviously accepted the fact that they were unlikely to need it for some time. When they're radiation sickness would subside and the need for food return was anybody's guess. With so long between meals he'd expect to be bedridden, but instead felt healthy and hunger-free. They still seemed to need water, though rarely, and Gerry guessed their supply would last up to two weeks. He'd seen plenty of rivers and creeks on the flight down, so he was sure that they wouldn't have a problem finding more when they needed it.

Last of all, they lifted Gaston out of the shuttles stinking interior. He cried out when the sunshine struck his face, Jennifer covering his eyes with strips of bandage to make the walk to their camp more comfortable for him. His skin was a sickening grey colour, and it was difficult for them to believe that they carried anything but a corpse in the stretcher. His slight movements though, and the attempts to speak, belied this.

When they made it to the camp, Gerry and Darren began sliding Gaston, still on his stretcher, into one of the tents. He became extremely agitated, and even managed to sit upright.

'Leave me outside' he cried, bringing forth a fresh torrent of blood to stream down his chin. They did as he asked, placing him in the shade and removing the cloth from his eyes. Blinking furiously he looked briefly over his new surroundings, and collapsed back onto the stretcher and lay still.

No one was surprised that he would be so averse to confined spaces. He must have dreamed out being outdoors like this while trapped under the remote sea. Gerry could see his bruised ribs moving under his tattered shirt, constantly amazed, and relieved, to see he was still breathing.

He then spent a few minutes gathering some firewood, which was plentiful around their camp, and soon had a fire burning, around which everyone gathered as they finished setting up their respective sleeping places. It seemed strange to Gerry, sitting around a fire that they didn't need for cooking or even for boiling water for tea or coffee. It was comforting though, a moment of relative normality, outside the confines of the ship and no longer sitting ducks, an easy target for their pursuers. What was happening in space now seemed distant, somehow unreal.

Gerry knew it wasn't the case in truth, the gunship that was on its way would not stop simply because they had left the ship. It would be able to scan for them down here, and still launch an attack from orbit. They would have to get some distance between themselves and the shuttle before long, the surrounding area being the first place their attacker would look for them. They could spare a few hours though, Gerry decided. Time to get some perspective, to determine their best route of escape, and to get some rest.

The days were short here, and as the sun made its way quickly toward the horizon they sat in silence around the fire, each immersed in their own thoughts, their memories of better times. None of them collapsed during the afternoon, the radiations effect of rendering them unconscious for a time seeming to diminish along with their stress.

Gaston woke as the light began to fade, and to their amazement turned on his side to face them and began talking with them.

'Thank-you,' he said first.

'There was no way we could just leave you there,' Gerry told him. 'If it was within our capability we were left with little option but to try to rescue you. It was one of the first rules of interstellar travel that we were taught.'

'Anyway, it's you that we should be thanking,' Charmaine added. 'You kept us out of reach of the gunship. I don't know how you did it, but if not for you it would have caught us by now.'

'I only removed our engines power limiters. You and your ship did the rest' the sickly researcher muttered. They all had to lean in close to hear what he was saying. During sunset on a strange planet, talking with someone who should have died five times over, the scene was surreal, somehow distant from the reality that Gerry and his shipmates had previously known.

'You have been bathed in the same radiation I have,' he continued. 'You have survived what other humans could not.'

215

'What type of radiation have we all been effected by? You must have some idea after all this time.' Gerry asked.

'We have been observing our condition closely, but know little more than you,' Gaston murmured. He paused for a moment to take a few rattling breathes before continuing.

'The radiation was difficult to detect even though we had the most sophisticated testing equipment available. We could only observe its effects.'

'And did you come to any conclusions?' Gerry asked.

'It's not like any previously known form of radiation. It has more components. Its interaction with matter is very complex. It has evolved. It is self-replicating. Therefore it is alive.'

'What makes you say that?' Jennifer asked. 'That's a big leap considering how little we know about it.'

'As far as we could tell,' Gaston continued, 'without enough nutrient matter on the moon, nature had found it impossible to form solid, living entities, not even single-celled organisms. But the moon is floating in a cloud of adenine and various gases. It must have been enough to form something close to DNA. We believed that the radiation does the rest. The matter in the clouds around the moon, together with its radioactivity, has combined to form living organisms. A symbiosis between matter and radiation.'

'Nature does always seem to find a way to create life. Even if it's only remotely possible, it will happen if given enough time.' Jennifer added.

'The self-replicating particles have very little individual mass though weigh billions of tons as a colony. Not unlike an Algae bloom on other planets and moons. This life evolved in space though, rather than on the moon's surface as we would expect' Gaston added.

Charmaine spoke next, asking what they were all thinking. 'You say the moon's surface was without enough free nutrients to form these living particles, and our research of the moon points to the same thing, yet we saw large creatures that looked like fish down there, and the sea was full of micro-organisms.'

'We knew about them. Our cameras in our ship have been functioning continuously. They were attracted to the light emitted by our hyper-drive. They are nothing like fish. They evolved from our waste,' their strange passenger replied.

216

No one spoke for a moment, each pondering what he'd said. Gerry was tempted to get up and walk away, the strangeness of the scientist's reply almost laughable. But something kept him seated. There was a believable line of logic through everything the scientist had said.

'The nutrients needed to form the organisms came from your ships waste-removal system?' Charmaine asked.

'Yes' the crippled scientist replied. 'As I've said, the moon is rich with the building blocks of life, though not enough material to form even cell walls for single-cell organisms. The environmental system of our vessel had what was needed. The species you saw must have grown mostly from our dead skin cells and hair we've shed. We haven't eaten, or needed to eat, for over twelve years, so there was obviously not much waste being ejected from the ship, but it must have been enough. Again, a sign of the symbiosis between the moons radiation and matter. It helped them evolve quickly, as soon as the possibility of creating new life became available. We have discovered something truly amazing.'

'I guess that's why the creatures rammed your ship when we left. They were releasing the nutrients. If the radiation had that sort of effect on the ecosystem of a moon, what's it going to do to us?' Charmaine asked no one in particular.

'I would have died long ago if not for this radiation poisoning.' Gaston said softly. 'It's not all bad. It is an effective symbiosis. It assists us and we assist it.'

'How are we assisting it?' Jennifer asked him. The scientist shifted his head to look at her from where he lay. His expression showed contempt, obvious to them even though his face was so badly damaged.

'Have we not spread its spore?'

No-one had a reply, and as the last light of the day faded from the alien sky the stranded researchers sat in silence. Though they each wanted sleep, they knew they weren't going to get any. They now had little respite from their suddenly arduous lives. Those moments of peaceful sleep, so taken for granted in the past, now unattainable, leaving only a longing for the sense of freedom that sleep bought with it.

Nightfall here was much like on Earth, though some of the stars were much larger and brighter than any seen from Earth. Animals that sounded like crickets could be heard chirping from

217

the undergrowth ringing their camp, along with other sounds that Gerry was unfamiliar with.

Jennifer was concerned to see a tuft of grass flash a soft electric blue near Gaston's stretcher when the injured man moved. It was only a flicker, but she was sure she saw the light play quickly across the blades then go dark. They may already be infecting the flora and fauna with their radiation poisoning. She couldn't bear to think of the consequences yet.

'We were deliberately sent into that radiation, weren't we?' Darren said after a while. It sounded more like a statement of fact than a question.

'It seems likely' Gaston said softly from the stretcher. 'They've known for years that we had stumbled into something interesting. But the only way to find out exactly what it was we had found was to send someone else in to check us out and do some tests on the moon.'

'That's why they gave us the shuttle and supplies even after we had been placed under quarantine. I didn't understand why they would do something so silly till now. They wanted us out here' Gerry said.

'But why us?' Jennifer wondered out loud. 'I was doing some good work back on Earth.'

'Who knows?' Charmaine said. 'Maybe we were simply the best applicants for the job. There's nothing to say that we were considered expendable.'

'No. We probably just drew the short straw' Gerry added, though he knew there was a definite reason for the powers-that-be on Earth to keep him at a distance. He'd been part of a team that had completed a very sensitive mission less than a year ago. An act of violence toward a defenceless alien species, something that still plagued his mind. He had helped eradicate an entire species of intelligent beings. It was something that needed to be kept quiet. And now his silence was almost guaranteed.

He didn't feel there was any advantage to be gained by telling his companions that there was a good reason for mission officials to remove him from Earth for an indefinite period. He could see that they were thinking of their own reasons for being sent on such an ill-fated mission.

For the next hour they sat together, nobody speaking. There seemed little to say. Each absorbed in their own thoughts,

218

considering their new futures. Though there was a sense of sadness there was also hope. An optimism that was difficult to explain, but which they all felt.

They were startled when the sky lit up a bright red, for a moment night turning to day. They all knew what it meant. The gunship had found their ship and destroyed it. They had no way out of here. They had rescued one researcher only to be left stranded themselves.

Those on Earth would know the shuttle was missing, and would look for them down here. Gerry was thinking he'd soon need to get everyone packing and moving away from the shuttle as far as they could, when he noticed the fog rolling in. It was dense enough to block everything from sight, even under the bright starlight, and as it crept across the plain toward them Gerry was optimistic that it would help keep them hidden from the sensors on the gunship above. They would need to use infra-red sensors at night, Gerry knew, and fog like this, or even high humidity would render them useless. They had a reprieve, though probably only for a few more hours.

With no longer a need to move camp till morning, Gerry advised the others that they were safe for the night, and moved to his tent. As he lay down within, he couldn't help but smile. Beating odds that were normally insurmountable, here they were, still alive and even a little happy. The cheer in the voices of his crew outside was testament to the sense of relief everyone felt that they had made it to a place like this. A little more control over their own destinies had been returned to them. Whether they were considered terrorists or simply lost researchers by people on Earth seemed of little importance now. Their situation spoke for itself. They were on the outside now, and whatever they did tomorrow would be totally up to themselves to choose.

He closed his eyes, mimicking sleep, and he managed to relax to the point where he was just barely conscious. Still able to think, and remember, yet also gaining his mind and body a little of the rest and relaxation it craved.

As the dense fog enveloped the camp, obliterating the night sky and bringing dampness to the air, the others slid Gaston into his tent without any complaint from him, though he was still awake and looking healthier by the hour. Occasionally flashes of the blue light spread across his body, then flickering out of

219

existence as quickly as they had come. He would cry out in pain whenever it happened.

Charmaine and Jennifer went to the tent they shared and lay down, also resting without sleep. Feeling as though they needed to sleep, yet not given any, was a torment, yet they too finally relaxed to some extent. Darren stayed out by the small fire on his own, deep in reverie.

Gerry felt something crawling on his neck as he lay in his tent, and crushed the thing, which was the size of an ant, with his thumb in the darkness. He thought nothing of it as he got comfortable, but just as he was about to close his eyes he saw a tiny flicker of blue light beside him. It was the same insect-like creature he'd squashed. It was buzzing about on the ground, flashing electric blue, just as his wounds had done when they had quickly healed. It was the same coloured light that played across Gaston's injury-ridden body and seemed to be sustaining him.

And now this bug seemed to be infected by the same radiation, after coming into contact with his skin for only a moment. As Gerry watched, it regained its ability to fly, and buzzed effortlessly to the top of the tent where it alighted. The blue light it emitted died away, and he could no longer see it. The impact of what had just happened hit Gerry hard.

'You shouldn't be so healthy' he muttered as he stared up into the darkness. The tiny creature began chirping softly from above him.

'What have we done?'

FIFTEEN

'You've got to leave me alone,
Cos' I'm stranded on my own...'
The Saints – Stranded

Gerry was the first of the group to emerge from his tent. He had spent the night without sleep, an annoying effect brought on by his exposure to the radiation. The others would be suffering the same, Gerry knew, and he felt a pang of frustration. There was nothing any of them could do but wait for their illness to run its course.

Privately, Gerry held little hope for a good outcome. Their lives had taken a sharp turn for the worse, and he could see no sign of their circumstances improving any time soon.

Though without sleep, or food, for days, Gerry felt physically healthy. Quietly, so as not to disturb his crew mate's rest, Gerry used his feet to push sandy soil over the smouldering camp-fire. The morning fog was thick, but it would be lifting soon, and Gerry wanted to be sure that the semi-automated military ship, that would be in orbit searching for them, would have difficulty finding them.

Back on Earth, this had always been Gerry's favourite time of the day. Half an hour before sunrise; the soft light of the approaching dawn, the gentle breeze that cleansed and cooled his usually simmering North Australian home.

As he looked across the plain before him, Gerry felt the same sense of serenity here. He took a few deep breaths, feeling some of the mental stress dissipate as he slowly exhaled. He stood where he was for a few minutes more, listening to the grasses whispering in the slight breeze, and to the small creatures stirring in the undergrowth nearby.

A rattling cough from Dan Gaston in the tent beside him drew Gerry back from his peaceful reverie. The man was still alive, which astounded Gerry. He was glad for him, though also profoundly pitied him. Nobody so severely damaged should be forced to continue living, he felt. The ongoing pain the researcher

221

would be enduring was a cruel torture that Gerry would never wish upon anyone, or any living creature.

'You alright in there Dan?' Gerry inquired.

'Just wonderful' was the gurgling reply, the sarcasm painfully evident to Gerry.

'Sorry,' Gerry apologised. 'Anything I can get you?'

'No, unless you've got a new body for me,' was the whispered reply.

Gerry thought it best to leave him be. Just speaking sounded as though it was doing him more injury. His breaths were coming faster now and sounded more obstructed, and Gerry could even hear the sound of his broken ribs grating together.

Deciding to attempt to hide the shuttle that they had arrived in from the vessel that would be searching for them from orbit, Gerry walked a small way from camp and broke a few large branches from a tree with thick foliage. As he began to carry them across the plain to where he'd landed the shuttle he heard Darren's voice from behind.

'I'll give you a hand' he said, moving toward a nearby tree.

'Thanks,' Gerry called back. 'I think they'll find the shuttle anyway, but I'd like to try hiding it from them.'

Gerry walked on slowly while he waited for Darren to catch up with him.

'Do you think it's too risky to pilot it somewhere with more cover?' Darren asked him when he was alongside.

'Yeah I'm sure of it, and we're probably lucky we made it down as soon as we did and cut the engines,' Gerry explained. 'The attack craft must have been close, and it would have targeted the shuttle easily if we had it running. They'd be able to see us even through this fog if we started the engine now.'

'I guess you're right,' Darren said. 'Even our regular survey equipment would be able to instantly pick up a heat signature like that.'

They strode the remainder of the walk to the shuttle in silence, watching tiny alien mice emerge from tufts of grass as they began their daily routine.

Gerry dropped his load of branches when they had arrived and climbed into the shuttle. The odour of fetid body fluids struck him as soon as he was inside. The stench was overpowering, making him retch, and he quickly clicked on an

222

interior light, opened an equipment cabinet, and found what he was looking for. A shovel that he would use to partially bury the shuttle, and a box of painkillers for Gaston. While he was there, he decided to take everything in the shuttle with him, in case it was destroyed, and began throwing equipment out of the hatch. There wasn't much to gather and he was soon scrambling for the exit, desperate for a breath of fresh air.

Darren was already tossing shovel-loads of the sandy soil onto the top of the shuttle when Gerry emerged.

'We'd better hurry, the fog's lifting' Darren noted. Looking about, Gerry could see that he was right, and used his hands to help scoop as much soil onto the craft as they could. It took them about fifteen minutes, and finally they placed the branches they had gathered over the roof of the shuttle and stood back to assess their work.

It was still visible from the sides, but from above it would be completely hidden from view. Gerry hoped that the shuttle would heat to the same temperature as the sandy plain that surrounded it, making it difficult to detect by the sensors on the automated gunship somewhere above them.

'That's about the best we can do I think,' Gerry said, turning to Darren.

'It's not like we've got anywhere to go anyway. I wouldn't be too worried if they do blow it up,' Darren said.

Gerry nodded. 'Yeah, me either. But it would be nice to have the use of a vehicle here. Anyway, let's get back to the others.'

After they had collected the equipment Gerry had retrieved from the shuttle and walked back to camp, they found the others up and about. Even Gaston had been moved from his tent and was reclining on his stretcher, his head propped up on some clothing so he could see around him.

Charmaine and Jennifer had begun to pack up their equipment and tents. They all knew that it wouldn't be safe to stay here, so near to their landing site. If their pursuers found the shuttle, they would surely scan the surrounding countryside thoroughly. They weren't about to sit about and wait to be found.

Gerry felt sure that it would be too risky to make contact with any of the settlers on this planet. Their presence here was not likely to be appreciated in any circumstance, let alone the health risks they presented to the locals. Their radiation sickness seemed to contaminate they're environment somewhat. Gerry remembered the bug he'd crushed, remembered how it had glowed, and how it had regained its ability to fly within seconds. Not only would they need to avoid contact with other people, they would need to keep some distance between themselves and any wildlife that crossed their path.

Gerry realised that it wasn't going to be easy, glancing into the dense forest that bordered their camp. They needed the cover of the forest canopy to conceal themselves, but carrying Gaston's stretcher would be difficult in the dense undergrowth. The best they could hope for would be to find the source of water that fed this lush alien forest. They could camp there for as long as they needed to, until their strange illness ran its course. Only then would they have any chance of returning to Earth.

As Gerry disassembled Gaston's tent and then his own, he told the others of his plan. None of them were very happy that there wasn't anything more proactive that they could do to extricate themselves from the situation, but they understood it to be they're only safe option. They could stay hidden from their pursuers in the forest, and avoid being seen by any of the world's settlers, who would very likely report their location to off-planet authorities.

They only had two rather small hiking backpacks, so together they went through their equipment and packed only the most essential of items. Smaller items were forced into their pockets until they were bulging. Gerry and Darren would need to carry Gaston's stretcher, so Charmaine and Jennifer would be forced to carry most of the equipment.

Gerry had just lifted one of the backpacks to help Jennifer put it on when there was a deafening sound of rendering metal. He knew what it was before he had even turned to look.

Sure enough, out on the plain a plume of smoke was rising from where the shuttle was positioned. Even from this distance Gerry could see the damage that had been done. The rear of the shuttle, where the engine sat, had been ripped apart. The semi-automated gunship in orbit had disabled their craft. The fact that they had not obliterated the entire machine was a surprise to Gerry, though he didn't have time to consider the implications of this. They had to get under more cover before the gunship scanners could locate them.

'Let's move' Gerry told the others, quickly lifting Jennifer's backpack onto her shoulders and then doing the same for Charmaine. He passed Jennifer a machete he had retrieved from the shuttle, ready for the likelihood that they would at some stage need to cut their way through the undergrowth.

Together, Gerry and Darren lifted the stretcher that held the injured Dan Gaston, and Gerry led as they moved along the edge of the forest looking for an easier path by which to enter it. They stuck close to the trees, relying on the overhanging canopy for cover from the machine above.

Within a few minutes, Gerry was pleased to see a rocky, dry creek-bed that wound its way into the jungle. It would make walking easier, and still keep them under the cover of the trees.

Dan Gaston seemed distressed as they walked, probably in quite a lot of pain. Jennifer had given him a painkiller with a little water but it was coughed up seconds later. Like them, Gaston wasn't able to ingest anything but water. In addition, the jolting ride would be aggravating his horrific injuries.

As Gerry continued to lead them deeper into the dense rainforest, Gaston seemed to relax somewhat. Within walls of lush vegetation they were well concealed, which gave each of them a sense of security. There were only tiny points of sunlight above them, the thick canopy blocking most of the light, though leaving them with enough to easily see where they were going.

None of them had any previous knowledge of the wildlife here, so they needed to be on their guard. They had no idea what may or may not be a danger to them. So far they had only seen the occasional rat-like creature scurrying past, and tiny bugs that buzzed around them but which never seemed to bite.

The humidity rose as they worked their way deeper into the rainforest, and after an hour of walking Gerry became optimistic that they were nearing a source of water. The trees and the undergrowth on either side of the creek-bed in which they walked had become incredibly thick and lush.

The group reached an overgrown section that they would be forced to cut their way through, so they took a moment to rest. Each took a small sip of water, and though they had packed some preserved foods, nobody ate. Gaston surprised them when he managed to sit upright and take a swig from the bottle without assistance. Gerry could see subtle flashed of blue light playing across the injured man's neck and shoulders as he moved.

Gerry took the machete from Jennifer and used it to hack off some branches from a tree that had fallen across the creek-bed, while the others sat in silence. He had just finished clearing a path for them when there was a loud crashing noise in the forest nearby, the sound of breaking branches.

Everyone swung their heads to look to the direction of the sound but they could see nothing through the dense jungle before them. They waited for a few minutes without moving or speaking but no more sounds came. Only the insects that buzzed around them and the chirping of small creatures in the undergrowth could be heard.

'Probably just a tree or large branch falling. I wouldn't worry about it,' Gerry said to the others.

'Yeah, but I would rather move on now in any case,' Darren replied. 'It could take us all day to find a place to camp.'

The group stood and picked up their supplies, Darren and Gerry again carrying the stretcher upon which Gaston lay, seemingly asleep.

As they continued their journey and the day wore on their progress became slower and more difficult. Sections of the creek-bed were filled with water, which forced them to climb the steep bank to make their way around it. This was made more difficult because they were carrying the stretcher. Gaston withstood the lurching and bumping without complaint, laying silent throughout.

They saw new species of animals as they walked, most of them small and seemingly harmless, which scurried for cover when they approached. Only one seemed as though it might be a threat.

It lay flat on a sandy patch on the creek-bed, and the group was only metres from it when they first saw it. It looked like a lizard, though with a more elongated jaw and only a short, stumpy tail. Its bulging eyes made Gerry uneasy. They were bright blue and seemed to study each member of the group in turn. The strangeness of this creature reminded Gerry how far from home they were.

Gerry motioned to the others to move to the opposite side of the creek-bed, where they could get past the creature without getting any closer than they already were. When they began to move the animal seemed startled and rose onto its hind legs. Its size became more apparent, its height almost that of Gerry's. The stance seemed threatening, and Gerry was ready to put down his end of the stretcher and grab the machete that Jennifer held if the thing advanced. It didn't though, only standing and watching them as they continued down the winding creek-bed until it was out of sight.

'I hope they don't get much bigger than that' Darren said, breaking the nervous silence.

'Or come in big groups,' Jennifer added. 'I'd hate to stumble into a big colony of them. It certainly looked like a predator.'

'I think we're getting close to the source of this creek,' Gerry said to the others, noticing a running stream trickling over rocks ahead. 'We shouldn't need to go much further before we find a place to camp.'

They stopped for moment to test the water. It tasted good and clear, with no hint of contamination with other chemicals. Gaston even managed a smile when he tasted it, remarking upon how unlikely it was that he was alive, drinking the waters of an alien stream. Gerry knew how he felt.

It was slow going over the rocky creek bed and it was more than two hours before they reached a place where the creek was full and impassable. The water ran off into the forest in many small rivulets, leaving the ground swampy. Gerry could see what looked to be higher ground about fifty metres into the dank forest and led them that way.

They splashed their way to the place where Gerry hoped they would find a camp-site. As the ground level rose so did the density of the undergrowth. He passed his end of Gaston's stretcher to Jennifer and took the machete from her. He cut a path through, as the others followed, and he noticed something disconcerting as he did so. The scratches that he was getting on his arms as he hacked his way through the foliage would flash an electric blue, and he could wipe the thin line of blood and in seconds there was no evidence of any damage to his skin. The radiation sickness was still having a powerful effect on him, Gerry realised regretfully.

The closest thing to a clearing they could find was still fairly overgrown, and they spent some time cutting back some of the foliage and pulling out some small bushes. When done, Gerry stopped to have a closer look at their surroundings. They were under the thick cover of the canopy offered by the massive trees around them. He could see the creek from the camp, and walking out only a few paces from the tree line, their height gave them the added benefit of letting them see quite a distance over the forest that encircled them. They were hidden, but had the ability to see if anyone, or anything, approached.

Gerry felt unusually energetic for someone who had just walked thirty kilometres carrying a man on a stretcher. Turning back to his companions, he could see that they were just as sprightly as he was. Nobody seemed tired, and indeed, they appeared restless. He watched for a moment as they set up camp, marvelling at their endurance. No sleep or food for over a week, yet they carried out tasks with zeal, eyes and skin glowing with health and vitality. Their radiation sickness had saved their lives repeatedly, and now it also sustained them. Gerry was pleased to see that none of them had even lost any weight.

I guess it's too risky to light a camp-fire,' Darren said to Gerry as he walked over to where he stood.

'The ship that's searching for us might detect the smoke or heat. It would be safer for us to do without one. We can use our battery-powered lighting tonight. They'd be less likely to be seen from a distance,' Gerry replied.

'Yeah, I'd rather be on the safe side too,' Darren added. 'It's not as though we need the fire to cook food.'

The days were short here, and Gerry could see that they only had about two hours of sunlight remaining. There was little else that they could do now, only wait for their medical condition to improve. It might take months or even years for the effects of the radiation poisoning to pass. And none of them knew if it would ever pass. Waiting for their sickness to run its full course was all they could do, even though the final stages of their illness might kill them. They may be waiting in vain for the radiation to dissipate, but what else could they do?

'I'm going to go have a look around the area while we still have some daylight,' Gerry told his companions.

'Do you mind if I join you?' Charmaine asked.

'Not at all' Gerry replied, not surprised be her willingness to learn more about this stunningly Earth-like planet. She was still

228

one of Earth's top-rated researchers, and the biology of their new residence would of course hold strong interest to her.

Leaving Darren and Jennifer to tend to Gaston, Gerry and Charmaine pushed their way through the thick, leathery leaves of the bushes that surrounded their new camp.

Gerry was amazed by how similar the plant-life was to that on Earth. At a glance, almost all of the trees and shrubs looked just like those seen in a rainforest on Earth.

Occasionally as they walked they would find one that Gerry had never seen the likes of before. There were some that looked like palms, but the fronds hung in thick sheets that almost touched the ground, some of them thirty metres tall. Other plants were only as thick as Gerry's wrist, yet stretched the full height of the forest canopy, held upright by woody tether lines that stretched from the surrounding area up to where they were joined to the trunk.

Charmaine had the misfortune of stumbling into a spiny tuft of grass, only about the size of a tennis ball, but with a nasty sting. The spines penetrated her boot and pierced her ankle.

'Careful, I think it left some splinters in there' Charmaine said to Gerry when they sat down and he began to remove her boot. She was obviously in pain, her face flushed red and voice strained.

'Don't worry, I'll have them out in a no time,' Gerry told her, pressing and then twisting a switch on the top of the boot to release the clasps, and then slowly slipping it from her foot. He could immediately see where the spikes had broken the skin in three places. She was right, the spiny ends of the grass had broken off and been left beneath the skin of her foot.

'This shouldn't be too difficult. They're hanging out just enough for me to get a grip on them,' Gerry told her, retrieving his utility tool from his pocket and flicking open the tweezers.

'Quickly,' Charmaine said, 'I think they're poisonous. It's hurting way too much for them to be just plain wooden spikes.'

Gerry did as she had asked, and while he removed them, he could see a ring of skin quickly going red around the puncture sites.

'They're all out, but I think you're right, there was some sort of toxin on the spikes. Do you think you're OK to walk?' Gerry asked her.

229

'Yes, but we should hurry I think,' Charmaine answered. 'If the pain gets any worse I might not be able to.'

'It's only a ten-minute walk back to camp from here. You'll be alright,' Gerry told her. However, as he spoke he noticed that familiar electric-blue sparkle around the wounds.

'Something's happening' Charmaine gasped, sitting forward so that she could see her wounded ankle.

In the soft evening light, they watched the blue flashes play over the ankle, the redness disappearing, and finally the puncture wounds healing over altogether, all within a few minutes.

Charmaine gave the ankle a rub with her hand and smiled. 'It's OK. I'm fine now.'

'I wonder sometimes whether our radiation exposure was beneficial,' Gerry said. 'It's kept us alive so many times, even if it has got us into all this trouble in the first place.'

'I've been thinking the same thing. Maybe everyone back on Earth and elsewhere *should* be exposed to this radiation. I'd be against it of course, in reality, but it could save a lot of suffering,' Charmaine added.

'We've only an hour or so of daylight,' Gerry observed. 'Would you like to head back to camp now, or keep going?'

'Let's keep going. It'd be useful to know a little more about the area we'll be sleeping in tonight,' Charmaine replied, pulling her boot back on.'

'I agree,' Gerry added. 'I'd be a lot happier if I had some better idea of what manner of wildlife we're amongst.'

They rose, continuing their walk around the camp. They stopped for a few minutes on the bank of the creek when they reached it. Flowing slowly and quietly, it looked quite deep in places. The water was clear but Gerry could not see the bottom in the dim light. There were tiny animals swimming in it, though too small and fast for Gerry to make out their shape. Types of fish or shrimp, Gerry assumed, just as would be found in a watercourse like this on Earth.

'We should be able to swim here in safety,' Gerry said to Charmaine. 'The water might even help remove the material that we've been infected with.'

'I hope so Gerry,' Charmaine replied. 'But this stuff washing off in water would be too good to be true.'

'Yeah, we can but hope,' Gerry said. 'It's too late to go in now. It's getting dark. We should get back to camp.'

'OK' Charmaine said, turning and beginning the short walk back. Gerry noticed that she had no limp as she walked, her ankle completely healed.

When they were within sight of the camp Charmaine pointed to the ground under some trees to their left. 'There's some more of those types of plants that hurt me. Hundreds of them.'

She was right, the ground was covered with the spiky plants. Gerry saw that one had caught a little furry animal, something that looked like a rat, in its spiny trap. He walked closer and could see that it was trying to wriggle free, but it was only making things worse for itself, as more spines pierced its side and belly with every movement.

Gerry could see some of the spikes sticking out of its skin, the toxic spines broken off and left inside the victim. It was what was happening around these wounds that got Gerry's attention. The skin was blistering, and the course hair falling out. He could actually see the skin bubbling, exuding a red-tinged slime.

Charmaine and Gerry watched in silence as the alien scene played out before them. The little animal stopped moving after a while, mercifully dead. Within a minute, the toxin in the spines had spread to cover the whole animal, the skin bubbling and swelling all over. The stench of a rotting carcass enveloped them, and Gerry realised what was happening.

'The plant is feeding itself,' he said to Charmaine. 'The toxin has sped up the decay process somehow. Look, the nutrients are already soaking into the soil.

Charmaine could see that Gerry was right, and took the opportunity to take some video of the feeding plant using her hand-held computer.

'That's amazing,' she said. 'The toxin has broken down the flesh in minutes. Nothing left for scavengers. The plant is getting all of it. The complete lack of direct sunlight under the canopy probably means those plants need to get their energy elsewhere.'

Gerry could hear the others in the camp talking, and it reminded him that they should be getting back. 'There's not much more to see here, Charmaine. Let's get back to the others.'

'Yeah. I'm just glad that didn't happen to my foot when I was spiked,' she said as she stood upright and pushed her computer into a pocket near her left shoulder.

When they walked back into camp, Darren, Jennifer and Gaston were in a circle in front of their tents. Gaston was lying on his stretcher, his head propped up on his arm. He was a disturbing sight in the soft torchlight. One of his eyes was sunken so far into his head that Gerry couldn't see it, only a gleam of light on an eyeball deep within the cavernous socket.

'Find anything that might concern us?' Jennifer asked when she saw them.

'Not really,' Gerry answered. 'Just watch your step when you're walking about. Some of those spiny plants are poisonous.'

'The creek looks safe to swim in,' Charmaine added. 'We'll be able to get clean tomorrow.'

'Sounds good,' Darren replied. 'Thing is though, I don't seem to have any body odour. Maybe it's another effect of our radiation exposure.'

'You could be right,' Gerry told him. 'It seems to be the same with me. A hike like the one we've been on would normally have me stinking up the insides of these overalls pretty badly, but I haven't noticed anything.'

'Nevertheless, it'll be great to wash off this dust and grime,' Jennifer added. 'It's been years since I've swam in a stream. I can't wait. All the waterways near where I live on Earth are too polluted to swim in.'

Gerry and Charmaine sat down with their companions on the bare earth, in a circle around the tiny torch that lit the area with a soft, white glow. The only sounds were Gaston's laboured breathing and the rustle of small animals on the leafy forest floor.

They sat and talked for hours, Gaston relating how he came to be trapped on the alien moon that had changed their lives so dramatically. Gerry was left with little doubt after he had finished his story that they were unwitting guinea pigs, part of a study on the strange properties of a radioactive adenine cloud that had been discovered there.

The realisation that they could have tracking equipment hidden in their supplies hit Gerry suddenly in the silence that followed Gaston's story. He immediately grabbed one of the supply bags and began searching it, checking every item for

232

tampering. He found nothing, but Darren found something in the bag he was searching.

'Have a look at this,' he said to Gerry. 'There's something small sewn into the lining of this bag.'

Gerry had a look and could see that he was right, and used his utility tool to cut back the stitching. He removed a strip of plastic from the tiny compartment and held it up to the torchlight. He could see the electronic components printed on it and knew by the shape of the circuit that it was a transmitter of some type, either a bug or a tracking device. He passed it to Darren, who nodded.

'That's a transmitter all right. Do you think they know where we are right now?' he asked Gerry.

'That thing hasn't got much range. They would need to send a repeater down here to pick up the signal from this and transmit the location back to the ship in orbit using a higher-powered transmitter. It would've taken some time to set up.'

'But it's been sixteen hours since we landed. They would have done that by now' Darren said.

'Yes, probably,' Gerry told him. 'Wreck the thing.' Darren did so, bending it back and forwards until it snapped in half.

They continued checking their equipment for another hour or so, finding only one more transmitter, which was also stitched into the lining of a supply bag. This too was destroyed and tossed aside.

'I guess that's why they didn't destroy the shuttle altogether, only its engine,' Gerry said to the others, the idea coming in a strange, momentary rush of mental activity that left him a little dizzy. 'They wanted to be sure we would take the equipment with us, so they could track us. It's as though they were expecting all of this.'

'They don't want to kill us do they?' Darren said, more a statement than a question. 'They just want to watch us, check on the effects of our radiation exposure.'

'That's probably about sum of it,' Gaston murmured. 'They knew from talking to us over the past decade that we were trapped on the moon that they had found something special. We were deliberately chased here. This planet is our quarantine area, probably for life.'

'But what of the people in the settlements here. Are they part of the experiment too? It's obvious we pose a health risk to them,' Jennifer said.

'Yeah,' Darren added. 'And also to the native wildlife. If they wanted all of this to happen then they've taken a huge risk.'

'They've decided the potential gains make the risk worth taking. I'd tend to agree with them,' Gaston said. 'In fact, though we were chased out here, I was the one who chose which planet we landed on. I quite like Clarkson.'

Gerry noticed that Charmaine did not look well. She was slumped forward with her head hanging. 'Charmaine, are you OK?'

'Yeah, just had a bit of a moment,' she answered, lifting her head. 'It's the first time it's happened since I got here.'

'It has been happening to us a lot less since we arrived,' Gerry realised. 'The seizures seem to be bought on by stress. I have been much more relaxed since we left the ship, which could explain why it only happened to me once a little while ago, and I was only effected for a few seconds.'

'Did you hear that?' Jennifer asked suddenly, looking upward at the leafy canopy far above.

'I didn't hear anything,' Gerry answered, following her gaze. 'Did it sound as though there was something moving up there?'

'Yes,' Jennifer whispered. 'It was probably just an animal moving around up there but it sounded big, like something came through the canopy.'

Gerry couldn't see anything up there, the darkness making it impossible. He could not even see any stars through the thick forest growth. He reached forward and picked up the utility tool they were using for light and switched it to its strongest beam.

Jennifer was right. When Gerry pointed the light into the treetops, he immediately saw a dark shape in the branches directly above them. It made a hissing sound when the light touched it, moving back into thicker foliage, seemingly trying to stay hidden.

'What is it?' Jennifer whispered.

'I don't know, I can't see it properly with so little light. Whatever it is, it's fairly large,' Gerry answered.

'Shouldn't we move camp?' Charmaine asked. 'It could be dangerous.'

'It's keeping its distance,' Gerry said. 'As long as it does we'll be safer here than walking around at night. Let's just keep an eye on it.'

'Well, at least we won't be losing any sleep worrying about that thing hanging around,' Darren said. 'We wouldn't be sleeping anyway, thanks to our sickness.'

'It's probably just one of the native tree-dwelling animals,' Gerry said, hoping to relieve some of their tension. 'Even if it is a carnivore, its natural prey certainly wouldn't look like us.'

Nevertheless, Gerry subtly moved his hand to where the gun he carried was strapped under his overalls, checking its position. He wanted to be prepared, just in case.

They sat and talked for a few hours more, each of them occasionally looking upward to ensure that the thing had not crept any closer. They could not see it though, only an inky black shape in the branches that would make a hissing sound sometimes.

They spoke of recent happenings, the strange set of events that led them to this planet. Gaston reminded them of the most powerful demonstration of the effects of the radiation yet. Gerry had asked him how the hull of their hyper-speed craft had withstood the velocity that Gaston had forced it to endure.

'There were pressure losses regularly during our flight here,' Gerry said to him. 'How did you get the ship to stay in one piece?'

'It wasn't my doing,' Gaston said, reaching into a pocket and producing a miniature screwdriver. 'Bend it' he said simply, holding it out for Gerry to take.

Gerry did as Gaston asked, and was so surprised by the effect that he dropped the tool. It lay on the ground glowing bright blue, sparkling around the bend that Gerry had made. The crew looked on, awestruck as the little metallic tool repaired itself, straightening itself out while they watched.

The show was over in less than a minute, and Gerry picked it up when the glow had vanished. Sure enough, the screwdriver was straight again. It gave off no heat, though it had been sparkling with energy only seconds earlier.

Gerry passed it back to Gaston. 'I see what you mean.'

'And maybe now you see how important the radioactive material we discovered is to people. Imagine what we could do with something as powerful as this,' Gaston replied, the effort of speaking obviously a strain. He turned to lay flat on his back, his breathing ragged.

'Mission control disregarded the safety of you and your crew as well as ours. There's no excuse for that, no matter how much they might gain,' Gerry said.

'Maybe so. But it's probably just a matter of perspective,' Gaston replied.

'I'm sure it is,' Gerry agreed, reaching behind and dragging his thin foam bed roll from his tent, leaning back on it and closing his eyes.

'They may not have even realised that when we crash-landed on the moon our drive would jettison the radioactive material on it far into space. Even into the hyper-speed lane you used to get here,' Gaston added softly.

'And that's what caused the strange effects on our ship,' Jennifer said in realisation.

'Of course,' Gaston murmured weakly.

'We were told by Mission Control that it was you messing with our flight systems that caused the effects, including the death of our Supervisor,' Gerry explained to him

'How convenient,' Gaston said. 'We hacked your messaging system using our computers, but that was to open a line of communication. They did not want to interface with our systems so we instead linked with yours. We had to do something to get some help, and it sure wasn't going to come from officials on Earth.'

Gaston was obviously now too tired to talk any more, and went silent, the others doing the same. The camp was quiet except for the rattling breaths from Gaston and the occasional hum from the thing in the treetops. None of them slept, all of them spending most of the night staring up into the darkness where their visitor perched, their hearts pounding a little harder every time it made a sound.

SIXTEEN

'...there's no release; no peace,
I toss and turn without cease...'
Faithless – Insomnia

As dawn neared and sky began to glow a soft blue, the camp was silent, all of them waiting for a glimpse of what might be sitting amongst the treetops above them. It was still there, they knew, having listened to its hissing and rustling in the foliage all night long.

With sudden realisation, as its silhouette started to become evident in the early morning light, Gerry was sure he knew what it was.

'It's a probe,' he said quietly to the others. 'Probably from the military ship that followed us here.'

'Is it dangerous?' Charmaine asked.

'Probably not by itself,' Gerry answered. 'Just a surveillance probe. The ship that is in orbit controlling it is the real threat.'

'They know exactly where we are. They can take us out any time they want,' Darren added.

'If they wanted that they would have done so long ago,' Gerry said, hoping to avoid any sense of panic in his companions. 'It's most likely just here to watch us, not kill us.'

'Until Mission Control decides that we have outlived our usefulness,' Jennifer replied, displaying the exactly the kind of pessimism that Gerry hoped to avoid.

'I guess they're listening to us as well,' Darren added. 'We'd better be careful about what we say.'

'We've got nothing to hide,' Gerry said. 'They probably just want to observe the effects of our radiation exposure. At least this way they'll know if our condition improves and they might let us go home.'

'Considering the way they've treated us all so far, I don't have much faith in them. Those bastards aren't going to do us any favours,' Darren said loudly, looking up to where the probe hovered as he spoke. He was angry, and Gerry knew he had every right to be, but it was doing little to help their cause.

Leaning forward to get closer to his companions in the circle, Gerry whispered to them, 'I've got the pistol from the shuttle. If the probe becomes a problem to us, I will take it out. They're constructed to be light in weight, not armoured. Relax and try to ignore it.'

'Why not just shoot it now?' Darren asked quietly.

'We wouldn't have time to get away from here before the ship above responded in some way, especially at night,' Gerry explained. 'They'd either kill us or send down a replacement probe. We'd gain nothing by destroying it.'

Darren nodded his understanding, Charmaine and Jennifer staying silent, considering their situation without speaking. Gaston was doing something that resembled laughing in his stretcher.

'Do you really think you have any choice in this matter,' he whispered. 'They and others have called all the shots up till now.'

'They may very well have us where they want us, but that doesn't necessarily mean we're beaten,' Gerry said, actually feeling a little more optimistic since seeing the probe. It made him feel a little closer to home somehow, even though it posed a threat. The video that the probe would be recording would be sent back to Earth via an entangled particle communicator. Scientists employed by the military would be watching their every move, Gerry knew, with probably less than a seconds delay caused by the huge transmission distance.

They sat and watched the probe for a while as the sun rose, letting them see it in detail. It was a sphere, and there was a strip of sensors across it that was facing toward them. The remainder of the surface was a smooth matte black. It hovered near the treetops under its own power, not suspended by anything. Gerry assumed that it would be built the same as their scientific research probes, using a gyroscope with a flywheel that spun at millions of revolutions per minute to control its movement. It could move in any direction using the mechanism, underwater, in the air, and even in space. At some stage, it would need to be recharged though, so Gerry knew it would need to return to the control ship in orbit periodically. That might give them some time to attempt to evade it, Gerry realised. He told the others of this but they were not consoled.

'That may simply mean that they'll kill us before it needs to leave for recharging,' Jennifer said. 'They won't want to give us any chance to escape.'

'Not necessarily,' Gerry replied. 'I agree with Dan here. If they wanted us dead, they would have acted by now. We're quarantined from Earth and under their observation, which is just how they planned it.'

'Maybe so,' Darren said. 'They probably learned as much as they could about the effects of the radiation exposure from Dan Gaston and his crew-mate while they were trapped in their ship on Clavus 3. They wanted to see how someone under its effects would function in the real world.'

'And here we are,' Charmaine added. 'Fulfilling our part in their plans just as they'd hoped.'

'Wonderful,' Darren said, while Jennifer stayed silent, bowing her head as if in deep thought, or in deep misery, Gerry couldn't tell.

Charmaine had an idea. 'We could split into two groups and go different directions. The probe could only follow one. At least some of us would be out of their sight.'

'We'll do that if we find that we need to,' Gerry said. 'But would you really want to be in a smaller group in a place like this?'

'No,' Charmaine replied. 'There's safety in numbers. There are too many unknowns here. We need all the eyes and ears we can get.'

The group sat and talked for a few more hours, there being little else they could do. Their lack of appetite and sleep had left them with so much time to spare. This made them restless, especially after having laid about all night without a second's sleep, only their thoughts to keep them occupied.

The inactivity was too much for Gerry after a while, and as the humidity and the heat had risen to uncomfortable levels, Gerry suggested they head down to the creek for a swim.

'Sounds good to me,' Charmaine said, getting to her feet immediately.

'Let's be careful though,' Jennifer said as she also rose. 'We don't know what might live in there.'

'Shush,' Charmaine replied good-naturedly. 'I don't need to be any more spooked than I already am. I'm going to enjoy this.'

Gerry and Darren lifted Gaston on his stretcher, to his protestations.

'I don't want to bathe. Leave me here,' he groaned.

'We can't leave you on your own,' Gerry told him. 'You can just relax on the bank where we can keep an eye on you. You aren't healthy enough to defend yourself yet.'

They walked down to the creek, sloshing through warm swampy water that covered the forest floor. Charmaine showed Darren and Jennifer the plant that had spiked her as they passed it, telling them to be wary of them.

The probe followed, hovering menacingly above them as they walked. It made a soft hissing sound as it moved, its camera and other sensors kept trained on the group.

The creek looked inviting when they reached its bank. Spots of sunlight penetrated the forest canopy and glistened on its surface, its waters sparkling clear.

They placed Gaston on a dry patch of ground near the bank and took a moment to look for any sign of danger in the gently glowing waters. There was none, and Darren was first to leap in, still fully dressed, having only emptied his pockets of anything that should not be in water. Gerry and Charmaine followed suit.

The water was colder than Gerry had expected and left him momentarily gasping. He turned to Jennifer, who was still on the bank, surveying the waters.

'Come on in,' he called to her. 'Just leave your boots and overalls on like we have if you like. They would stop anything small in here biting or stinging us. They need a clean anyway.'

'Alright then. I can only see tiny fish in there anyway,' she replied, emptying the contents of her pockets into a pile next to the others. She was more careful than the rest of them, preferring to clamber down the steep bank and lower herself into the water slowly, rather than leaping in.

'It's cold, but it's lovely' she said as she paddled out to join them in the middle.

'This is great. So much better than being stuck on that ship,' Darren added.

'Oh yeah,' Charmaine agreed, rubbing the sleeves of her overalls to remove the dirt. 'I'd like some soap, but I guess it wouldn't be right to pollute this water with something like that.'

'This is definitely a nice place for us to end up. Quarantine couldn't get much better than this,' Gerry said, while scraping away the mud that clung to his legs and feet. 'Under different circumstances I'd actually pay for a holiday in a place like this.'

Darren paddled to a shallow part of the creek to remove his boots, and seeing that they were clean, tossed them onto the bank. He glanced up at the surveillance device that clicked and hissed above. 'Yeah, but we don't need to look too far to see that this is no holiday.'

Gaston watched them bathe in silence, his disfigured face showing no hint of emotion. He didn't look well though, Gerry noticing that his legs and arms were twitching and his breaths coming in quick gasps.

After a while they decided that there was little sign of biting creatures in the water, and removed their boots and overalls, each of them left wearing only the standard issue white shirt and knee-length black shorts.

When Jennifer had finished washing the dried blood from her face and arms that had sprayed from Gaston's wounds on the trip to this planet, she climbed onto the bank and started doing the same for their injured companion. He lay silent on the stretcher while she used a wet piece of cloth to wipe away the gore that encrusted his face and neck. He made no complaint, even when she covered her fingers with the cloth and stuck it inside his sunken eye-socket and scraped away the blood and dead tissue within. It must have caused him a lot of pain but he showed no sign that it had.

'I hope this water is as pure as it seems,' she said. 'An infection would be a real problem because our bodies aren't accepting medication.'

'I doubt that will be a problem,' Gerry said, throwing his cleaned overalls over a low branch. 'If the radiation poisoning prevents us ingesting anything but water, I'd say our bodies won't accept foreign bacteria either.'

'I hope so,' Jennifer replied.

She continued to clean him, but when she got to his left hand she found in clenched tight into a fist, and she could not prise it open. 'Could you open your hand for me Dan?'

He did so, and she could see that he held something in it. A hint of a smile creased his face as his eyes focussed on her. 'Just testing a theory.'

Jennifer saw the thing move and realised that he held a small animal. It was the shape of a beetle but was partially covered in fine fur and had only four long legs. A large set of pincers protruded from its head, and Jennifer could see the fresh wounds on his hand where it must have been biting him. As expected, they flashed electric-blue, healing in seconds.

The creature leapt from Gaston's fingers to the ground and began to scurry away, but Jennifer was too quick for it. She reached for a boot and slammed the heel down onto the animal. It was sturdy though, and she hit it three more times before it stopped moving.

Gaston watched intently, obviously expecting something more to happen. When Jennifer saw what that was, she called her supervisor. 'Gerry, I think you should take a look at this.'

Having noticed that something was going on, Gerry was already half way up the bank. 'Is he alright?'

'Dan is fine, relatively speaking, but look at that animal,' Jennifer replied. 'I squashed it, but something strange is happening to it.'

Gerry saw what she meant. The little creature looked as though it had been almost squashed flat, with one of its front legs detached and twitching at its side, and flashes of blue light sparkled across its body. 'It's been exposed to the radiation.'

Charmaine and Darren realised that they might be missing out on something interesting, and climbed out to join the others. They watched in silence as the alien scene played out before them. As the blue light played across its damaged body the creature twitched and writhed, and seemed to become more animated with every second that passed.

After no more than a minute of this it righted itself and scurried away on its three remaining legs, the flashes of blue no longer to be seen. Gerry realised that he shouldn't let it escape, that it might infect its offspring, or other wildlife. He took the boot from Jennifer's hand and stooped to hit the creature with it, but before he could do so it had crawled under the thick roots of a tree alongside.

'That doesn't bode well for me,' Gaston said in a hoarse whisper.

'What do you mean?' Gerry asked. 'The radioactive material we've been infected with has kept us both alive when we would otherwise have certainly died, just like that bug.'

'But it was functioning fully again in a minute or so,' Gaston explained. 'I've been injured for three days now. I think the radiation has done as much as it is going to do to help me heal.'

'You may be right,' Gerry replied. 'How did that animal become infected anyway?'

'I kept it in my hand overnight,' Gaston explained. 'It crawled into my tent, and it wasn't hard to catch.'

'You probably shouldn't have done that. We don't want to be infecting the wildlife here,' Gerry advised.

'I agree, but that is exactly what they want,' Gaston whispered, turning his head to look up at the probe that hovered overhead. 'It is just such tests that they are most interested in, I believe.'

Gerry looked up too, and noticed that it was closer than usual; as though it had descended to take a closer look at what they were doing, listening in on their conversation. He knew that this was important information to those on Earth who studied their condition.

'Surely you don't think that they drove us here so that we could infect this planet with the radioactive material? There would be easier ways to do that, if that is what they wanted,' Jennifer said.

'But not without impunity,' Gerry said, realising what Gaston was getting at. 'We are the terrorists that are contaminating this planet, not them. As far as the public will know, any damage to this place, or harm done to the settlers here, will be our doing. They're hands are clean.'

'Bastards,' Darren said simply.

'Damn it,' Charmaine added. 'I should have realised it sooner. It certainly wouldn't be the first time the U.S. government has given a group of people dangerous power for their own ends, and then made them the scapegoat when the job was done.'

'Yeah, I wish the British or Australian governments had been running this mission,' Darren said. 'They wouldn't have been so self-righteous as to try something like this.'

Jennifer was holding her face in her hands, and when she looked up at the others finally, they could see that she was pale and shaking. 'I just got a little dizzy, but I think I know why we are really here. It just came to me.'

Gerry held out his hands and helped her to her feet. 'What are you thinking?'

'The U.S. government being full of closet Christians isn't just a silly conspiracy theory,' she explained. 'And here we are, infecting a planet that holds the only Christian settlements in the Universe. That is no coincidence.'

Gerry nodded. 'Go on.'

'They saw how the radioactive material helped Gaston and his friend survive something that no normal human beings could have. They want us to pass those abilities onto the Christian people here.'

'But it might kill them, like it did Eric, our Supervisor,' Darren said.

'That's why they are leaving it to us. We can absorb the blame if things turn out badly,' Jennifer explained. 'They're risking the lives of the people that live here in the hope that they will survive and become stronger. They've seen miracles happen, people healed and saved from otherwise certain death.'

'That sounds plausible,' Gerry said. 'Maybe this is the new garden of Eden.'

'Mankind has never tried an experiment so dangerous. This could be a turning point for the human race, for better or worse,' Jennifer added.

'The crazy fuckers...' was all Darren could say, shaking his head in disbelief.

'I think you're right,' Charmaine said quietly. 'But can we be sure that it is a bad thing?'

Gerry was conscious of the probe that hovered overhead, the very people that had engineered the situation they were in almost certainly listening in on their conversation. 'How about we go back to camp. And no more contact with the wildlife, Gaston.'

While they gathered their belongings, Gaston surprised them by managing to stand. He did so very slowly and carefully, holding onto a tree trunk to steady himself. He was stooped forward and his head hung down on his left shoulder, but everyone was amazed that he had made it onto his feet.

They waited while Gaston turned and began to shuffle back toward camp. The journey was excruciatingly slow, but he walked the full distance without assistance from anyone. Gerry found a stick on the way that Gaston could use as a cane and passed it to him, which he used to good effect. It doubled his rate of progress, though it was still very slow. The others followed patiently behind, Gerry at the rear carrying the folded stretcher that was no longer needed. Above him, near the treetops, the surveillance probe quietly shadowed them.

Gaston crawled immediately onto his tent when they were back at camp, panting and moaning after his exertions. The lack of sunlight under the canopy meant that it would take hours for their clothing to dry, so Gerry suggested they head to a small clearing that he and Charmaine had found the day before.

The others thought it a good idea, and although it wasn't cold in the humid forest they were keen to dry off. Gerry led them through the undergrowth, careful where he put his feet. They weren't wearing their sodden boots, and he wanted to avoid injuring their feet on spiny plants or being bitten by something.

The sunny clearing was not far however, and they reached it in only a few minutes. Gerry noticed something surprising as he threw his overalls over a shrub and placed his dripping boots upside down on a rock. The probe had not followed them. Unless it was hiding in the surrounding trees where he could not see it, Gerry assumed that it had stayed at the camp with Gaston, for some reason.

When their overalls and boots were in sunny spots the four walked around the area, looking at the plant-life and various little creatures that scurried about, letting the clothing they were wearing dry in the warm conditions.

They strolled about the alien garden for half an hour, careful to have as little contact with foliage as possible so as not to pass on any of the radioactive material that they invisibly carried.

By the end of this time the shirts and shorts they wore were mostly dry, so they left their boots and overalls where they were and trod carefully back to their camp.

Gerry was at the front, and was the first to step into the camping area where their tents were erected, and was shocked by what he saw. There was a gasp from one of the others as they too entered the camp.

'The probe was here alright. It had descended and had partially entered the tent in which Gaston lay. And they could hear talking. Not only Gaston's rasping voice, but also that of someone else.

Gerry was worried that it might be harming Gaston, and stepping forward he called loudly to the machine. 'What the hell's going on? Get away from him.'

The spherical device swung around as it backed quickly out of the tent, its panel of sensors trained on them. And within an instant it was back near the forest canopy, shooting up to there at an amazing rate.

Moving immediately to the tent, Gerry pulled the flap aside and looked in. Gaston seemed unharmed, lifting his head to look at him.

'It's OK. No harm done,' Gaston murmured.

'We heard talking,' Gerry said. 'What did they have to say to you?'

'Nothing' Gaston said simply, letting his head fall back onto the foam mattress.

Gerry had definitely heard a voice come from the probe, though he could not make out what it was saying. He was annoyed that Gaston had not told him exactly what was said, but he decided not to press the point.

The others had all seen what had happened and exchanged worried glances. They had seen something they should not have, and the idea that there was possibly more plotting behind the scenes made them uncomfortable. They had been pawns in the dangerous schemes of others throughout this ill-fated mission and it had brought them nothing but ruination.

Gerry could see that they were uneasy. 'They might have been simply checking on Gaston's condition.'

'I hope so,' Darren said. 'But why wait till we aren't around? If they have something to say why not say it now while we're all here?'

'Who knows?' Gerry replied. 'But we'll keep an eye on it and we won't leave anyone on their own from now on.'

Pulling their foam bedding from their tents, giving them something soft to sit on, the group sat in a circle and chatted for a few hours. The days here were short, and the way the forest canopy blocked the sunlight so thoroughly, made the day seem even shorter.

'Time to go get the rest of our clothing,' Gerry said as he stood. 'Anyone coming for the walk?'

'I will,' Charmaine said, also rising.

'We'll only be a few minutes,' Gerry said to Jennifer and Darren, turning to go. 'We'll leave you here to take care of Gaston.'

Moving quickly but carefully through the undergrowth, Gerry led as the pair made their way to the clearing where their clothes hung. There was a slight breeze that rattled the leaves of surrounding trees and swept away some of the cloying humidity that was characteristic of such a dense forest. The probe was nowhere to be seen, probably still back at the camp.

'This is nice,' Charmaine said as she pulled the sets of overalls from where they had been draped over the shrubs. 'Maybe we should move our camp to here. It's not as though we need to stay hidden anymore. They know exactly where we are.'

'We could do that,' Gerry replied. 'But the canopy is keeping the dew off of us during the night and will give us some shelter in case of rain. By the look of this place, I'd say it gets plenty of rain. The storms might be violent here. We'll just have to wait and see.'

'Have a look at this Gerry,' Charmaine called.

'What is it?' Gerry asked, walking to her with his arms loaded with boots.

'It's this bush. It's flashing blue in places,' she answered.

Gerry saw immediately what she meant. Where the clothing had been removed, the tips of the branches sparkled blue in the soft afternoon light.

'Do you think it's been infected with the radiation?' Charmaine asked.

'It does seem like it,' Gerry replied, dropping the boots he was carrying. Reaching forward and snapping a thin branch, Gerry was rewarded with an instant flash of blue light at the break. The flickering stopped after a few seconds, and they could see that the break in the twig had healed over. Though bent at a ninety degree

247

angle, the branch looked as though it would be capable of continued growth.

'This shows how important it is for us to avoid contact with the life here. This plant is showing the effects of the radiation exposure after only being in contact with our clean clothing for a few hours,' Gerry said.

'Yes, and who knows how its lifecycle has been affected?' Charmaine said. 'And what if it passes the radioactive material onto the next generation? The possibilities are pretty amazing.'

'They're the sort of problems we need to avoid. We don't know enough about the radioactive material to be able to contain it if it starts to spread through other life-forms on this planet,' Gerry said.

'Maybe we should cut this shrub out and burn it,' Charmaine suggested. 'It might help contain it.'

'We'd need to do so with at least four of them here that have been exposed to our clothing, and many more that we've brushed past while we've walked. It would be too big a job. We just need to avoid any further contact with the flora and fauna. It's the best we can do,' Gerry advised.

'Maybe the radiation dissipates after a while,' Charmaine added. 'If this bush returns to normal after some time, then probably so will we.'

'We'll just have to wait and see,' Gerry said, retrieving the boots he had dropped, while Charmaine collected the remainder of their clothing.

He could not help but admire her form as she moved. The tight shirt she wore showed off her lithe figure, and the soft orange light of late afternoon lent a sultry glow to her skin. She noticed his gaze and turned to him and smiled.

'I don't think your girl back on Earth would be impressed if she knew you were looking at other women,' she said light-heartedly.

'Point taken. It's only been a few weeks since I last saw her but it seems like forever,' Gerry replied, not bothering to tell her that he had never actually been in an exclusive relationship with Janet, his part-time girlfriend back on Earth.

'Should we go then?' she asked.

'Yeah' Gerry answered. 'It'll be dark soon.'

They walked slowly and carefully back to camp, Gerry leading the way. All was quiet upon their return. Gaston was still in his tent recuperating, while Jennifer and Darren sat on their respective bedding, looking thoughtful as they stared at the little torch that shined from the ground between them. The shadows had deepened in the failing light but Gerry could still see the probe above, hovering amidst the foliage of the forest canopy.

Yet again, the group endured a sleepless night. Charmaine worked on her hand-held computer throughout, while the others sat in silence, feeling restless and frustrated by both their lack of sleep and lack of anything useful to do within the inky darkness of the forest at night.

Nothing to do but wait, though exactly what they waited for, and for how long they would be forced to wait for it, was anybody's guess.

SEVENTEEN

'Instead of saying all of your goodbyes,
Let them know you realise that life goes fast,
It's hard to make the good things last...'
The Flaming Lips – Do You Realise?

Over the ensuing week, the group did little but explore the surrounding forest, and have a daily swim in the creek. Charmaine had some respite from the boredom, logging any new discoveries on her hand-held computer, including photos and sound recordings of some of the wildlife. It kept her relatively busy, and she obviously wanted to make the most of her time here. Gerry worried every time she left the camp for her long walks but could not bring himself to stifle her curiosity. Anyway, restricting her to the camp seemed like overkill. They had not yet been in any serious threat from the wildlife on Clarkson, and the place seemed relatively safe.

Gaston had gained strength, and was now able to walk at a reasonable pace. Every time he found that he had the strength to do so, he would emerge from his tent and walk laps around the camp. The groaning and shuffling of feet through the leafy forest floor annoyed the rest of the group, but they endured it, glad to see that his condition was improving.

The probe still hovered overhead, disappearing for about half an hour every two days, Gerry assuming that it was returning to the ship in orbit for recharging. It would not give them enough time to move camp to evade the probe while it was gone, but Gerry could not see much point in avoiding it anyway. It was doing them no harm, and the fact that Mission Control was fully aware of their situation might be beneficial. At least they could see that they were no real threat; that they simply wanted to wait out their quarantine period in peace.

It was midday, the group relaxing at the camp, taking some refuge from the searing heat. Though the temperature was high, even under the cover of trees, it was the humidity that affected them most. The air seemed thick, every intake of breath requiring

250

extra effort. In a small way it gave them a sense of drowning, their bodies forced to work hard to get enough oxygen from the sodden, low-pressure atmosphere. Their clothing stuck to their skin, not doing its usual job of keeping them cool due to the complete lack of any breeze.

Gerry stood at the edge of the clearing, overlooking the expanse of forest and swamp that surrounded them. There was a complete absence of wildlife sounds, even the multitude of tiny insect-like creatures had sought refuge from the heat and lay silent. Though he had spent most of his life in the tropics of Northern Australia, Gerry felt drained of energy and very uncomfortable in the cloying atmosphere of this water-soaked country.

He was turning back to the camp, deciding to lay about for a few hours until the heat passed, like every other creature in this land, when he heard something. A distant murmuring, the sound of people talking a long way off, too quiet for Gerry to make out any words.

'There are people out there,' Gerry said quietly to the others. Each of them rose quickly to join him, only Gaston staying where he was.

'Where are they?' Charmaine asked.

'I'm not sure,' Gerry told her. 'They're a long way off, but I definitely heard people talking.'

'We should stay hidden,' Darren said. 'It could be that they are just passing by chance, people from the Christian settlements out hunting, but they could have been sent here by Mission Control to take us into custody.'

'Or worse' Jennifer added.

'Hopefully they'll go right past us,' Gerry said. 'We'd have to be lucky for them not to find any of our tracks though.'

The group stood and listened without speaking, each of them eventually hearing the distant conversation, though it was too muffled for them to discern any meaning. Gaston heard nothing from where he laid, his ruptured eardrums badly affecting his hearing.

'We'll let them pass, and then I'll follow them,' Gerry explained. 'We need to find out why they're here. For all we know, they might be here to help.'

'But how could they help us anyway?' Jennifer asked. 'All we can do is wait. There is nothing we want from them.'

'Approach them, but do so carefully. Don't let yourself be seen with them.' Gaston murmured from behind them. 'Earth's military will act if we are seen to be risking the infection of those people.'

'How can you be so sure?' Gerry asked, turning to face their injured companion.

'They told me as much. We are only safe if we maintain quarantine,' Gaston replied.

Gerry was going to ask him when it was that he had been told of this, but then remembered the voices coming from Gaston's tent when the probe had been down there with him. 'But why didn't they advise all of us of this?'

Something resembling a smile creased Gaston's deformed face. 'You've disregarded most of their orders of late. What would be the point?'

'Maybe so,' Gerry said, annoyed by the apparent subterfuge, though the hypocrisy of this was not lost on him. 'And I'll do the same now. I'm going down to take a look.'

Telling the others to stay quiet and wait for him, Gerry slipped from the camp through the dense shrubbery. He moved quickly and quietly toward the voices. They didn't seem to be getting further away, and Gerry was concerned that they had stopped down at their swimming place. Their footprints and other signs that they had been there would be seen easily.

A sound behind him made Gerry spin around, and he found himself looking at the probe. It had followed him, and now hovered at head-height, only metres from him. Though it had startled him a little, Gerry was not concerned. Back on Earth, they would be as interested in these people's motives as he was.

'Just try keeping a little quieter,' Gerry whispered to the machine, certain that those directing it were listening and watching from their offices billions of kilometres away.

It was not long before Gerry had crept as near as he was going to get to the strangers without them seeing him. He could make out four people at the edge of the creek where they usually swam. They were all male and each of them carried an old-style firearm, simple rifles that fired solid projectiles. He knew they worked in a similar way to the compact pistol he carried, and could be as dangerous as any regular ion gun in the right hands.

The men were dressed in simple throw-over coats of a coarse brown fabric with a cloth belt around the waist, similar to that worn by many cultists in Earth's nefarious past. Though he knew little history, Gerry had heard enough to know these people were dangerous, members of the Christian cult, without argument the most bloodthirsty in Earth's history. This combined with indomitable arrogance and a lust for power, and had brought about the destruction of whole countries and indeed brought humanity to near total destruction on more than one occasion. They were governed by a set of ten common-sense rules of decency, all of which were studiously ignored by the members.

Gerry kept this in mind as he lowered himself to the ground and lay on his front, inching forward to get a better view of the party. The surveillance probe was just as careful, hovering at Gerry's feet only a few centimetres from the ground, looking over his shoulder.

'There's been at least three different people coming here,' Gerry heard one of them say. 'There could have been a lot more of them than that though. It is difficult to know for sure. The area has been busy.'

Peering through the shrubs, Gerry saw that it was a young man who had spoken, no more than twenty years. The other three were older men, two seemingly in their forties and the other perhaps in his seventies.

'Do you know for sure that they aren't from our settlement?' one of the middle-aged men asked.

'Only we travel this far from town,' the young man replied as he studied the ground. It has to be someone we don't know.'

'Not necessarily' the old man said in a harsh, gravelled voice. 'Young Christopher has been exploring far outside the town limits. I caught him out on Black Hill three days ago.'

'What?' the two bearded, middle-aged men exclaimed together.

'He should have been punished,' one of them added.

'He was warned,' the old man said, Gerry having to listen very carefully to hear what he was saying because he was facing away from him.

'He should go before the council, entering sacred grounds as he did. In fact, so should you,' one of the men said angrily. 'What were you doing there? You had no more right to be there than he did. It's not surprising that you didn't report him.'

'Get off your high-horse Paul,' the old man yelled back, in his grating voice. 'With all that's been happening lately I decided it was warranted.'

'That's where the thing was seen, wasn't it? Coming down Black Hill?' the young man asked, rising to face the old man.

'Yes. I thought it best to have a closer look up there. I didn't find anything unusual however.'

'You are much braver than I gave you credit for,' one of the middle-aged men said, obviously surprised. 'There were some rumours going around about what that thing they saw was here for. I wouldn't have gone up there if you'd paid me.'

'It sounds as though it was just a man-made probe. The heathens on Earth have decided to meddle in our lives again. They probably had something to do with the explosion in orbit that we saw a few weeks ago,' the old man explained.

'But the Father said it was a sign from our Lord,' the youngest of the group said, still scanning the ground for evidence. 'This would be a time of miracles, he said. The people we have been waiting for are to arrive soon.'

'Maybe they are already here, like people have been saying. This could be their tracks,' one of the others said.

'Perhaps,' the old man replied. 'What we have found here shows we definitely have visitors from off-planet. No one in our settlement has boots like the ones these people wore. Nevertheless, we should not assume anything more from this. Our planets saviours may well be on their way, but I don't believe the rumours going around that they are already here.'

Gerry heard everything, stealing a glance behind him to where the surveillance probe hovered quietly. That was most likely what the settlers had seen moving around the outskirts of their village. The explosion in space the old man mentioned was almost certainly the destruction of the hyper-speed craft that had brought them here, which Gerry and his crew had also witnessed. Rendered unfit for human habitation due to their strange illness, it was an inevitable end to the tainted spacecraft.

Gerry turned his attention back to the settlers when he heard one of them yelp in surprise.

'Look at this!' the young man said, holding a tuft of grass in his hand. 'There's sparks.'

From his vantage point, Gerry came close to involuntarily calling out a warning. He caught himself before he did so, not wanting to give away his position. The young fool was exposing himself to the same radioactive substance that had turned Gerry's own life upside-down. There was nothing he could do to stop him, however. Gerry realised he could be witnessing the beginning of a catastrophic event, a community of thousands overcome by an alien sickness that no one understood.

Unbeknownst to Gerry, those on Earth who took it upon themselves to make all the important decisions on behalf of humanity were considering the implications of these new circumstances. The probe rose from its position at Gerry's feet and into the sky, in plain view of the hunters that Gerry was trying to stay hidden from. With a hum, it transmitted target location to its parent ship in orbit.

The first sign that something was wrong was when one of the settlers pointed in surprise at the probe that suddenly hovered above them. The others only had time to lift their heads to see what he was pointing at when it was too late for them.

Gerry saw that the probe had revealed itself, and in the same instant, he heard a loud popping, crackling sound. He was horrified by what he saw happening only thirty metres from him.

The group was in disarray. The young man in the group was on fire, arms flailing against his body as he staggered about the clearing. Gerry saw the tell-tale green flames shooting from the person's body and realised that he was being killed by the military ship in orbit, burnt by one of the many beam-weapons that the machine carried.

The kid was being cooked alive, such a weapon taking some time to affect vital organs. The stench of burning flesh enveloped Gerry, and combined with the screams of someone dying in horrific pain, he found himself standing, no longer able to bear the brutality of what was happening. He pulled the firearm he carried from its holster under the fabric of his coveralls, took aim at the probe, and fired twice in quick succession.

His aim was true, at least one of the projectiles damaging a vital component in the machine, and the probe dropped from the air like a stone. It did not stop the attack on the young man though, the beam trained on him until he finally stopped moving.

The others in the group were backing away from the crackling body, but they did not get far enough. Without targeting information from the probe the ship was having difficulty locating the other men, and the invisible beam swept about the clearing haphazardly. The strategy was effective however. Only the old man avoided injury, probably because he moved less, instruments having difficulty discerning him from other objects in the area.

His two remaining companions were not so lucky. They were cut down in one pass of the beam. Instantly their skin began crackling in the intense wave of heat and they fell to the ground, thrashing madly about, only adding to the injuries to their bubbling, steaming bodies.

'Don't move' Gerry called to the old man, who was obviously very bewildered by what was transpiring, and probably had not heard him. There was nothing else that Gerry could do to help. He stepped back, ensuring he was under the cover of the treetops, not a visible target to the ship in geo-stationary orbit over his head. He holstered the firearm, knowing it was useless against the unseen gun-ship and its long-range weapons.

As Gerry watched, the old, white-bearded man was lucky. The beam played about the bodies beside him, heating them until they stopped moving, continuing to cremate the corpses until they were unrecognisable, and just smoking piles of ash. It passed within centimetres of the frightened old man, evident by the burst of flame over the ground while the invisible beam played over the area, igniting everything it touched. However, its searching failed to harm him and eventually the hum of superheated air disappeared, the gunship unable to locate the single survivor.

Gerry knew that without the probe to send targeting data, they were relatively safe from the military ship. Their clothing made them difficult to visually discern from the environment, and they would have little of their body's heat signatures detectable by infrared, especially due to the extreme humidity of this area, as well as the high radiant heat from the swampy surrounds.

'Come over here, under the cover of the trees,' Gerry called to the old man, the lone survivor of the horrendous attack. He

256

heard Gerry's call and walked in his direction, but was obviously extremely agitated. He was spinning left to right, rifle held before him, wary of an unseen enemy.

Gerry checked the position of his hidden firearm, just in case the terrified settler did anything stupid. He appeared relaxed, but ready for trouble, as the old man approached.

'And what was that in aid of?' he yelled at Gerry as he neared. 'Just who are *you*?'

'I'm not with the people who tried to kill you,' Gerry replied, watching closely where the barrel of the man's gun was pointing. 'They tried to kill us too. That's why we are here.'

'We? There are more of you?' the man asked, glancing left and right, obviously on the edge of hysteria. 'Where are they?'

'Not here. At our camp nearby,' Gerry explained. 'I have three friends with me.'

'Why have you come here? Almost everyone here left Earth long ago to avoid this. What has just been done is an atrocity. An act of war.'

'We came here to escape the same people who killed your friends,' Gerry said in his defence. 'We're now under supervised quarantine here. You and your friends have walked into the quarantine area. That's why you were attacked.'

'How were we supposed to know?' the settler yelled, waving his gun around nervously. 'You shouldn't be here.'

'I know, believe me,' Gerry said calmly. 'How about coming with me, to meet my crew. They were chased here with me in our hyper-speed research vessel. They're not far away.'

Just as he had finished speaking, Gerry was startled by a commotion in the bushes behind him, and he spun around. He saw Darren's red and sweaty face emerge through the undergrowth first. Charmaine and Jennifer were next to materialise, and as they each in turn saw the armed, agitated settler for the first time, they stopped and quickly raised their arms in surrender.

'We heard the shots and ran down here. Are you alright?' Darren asked Gerry, his eyes not leaving the stranger with the gun.

'I'm fine,' Gerry answered. 'The people were attacked by the hyper-speed gunship that followed us here. This fellow is the only one to survive.'

'Why the hell would they do something like that?' Jennifer said, slowly lowering her arms.

'They exposed themselves to the radioactive material,' Gerry explained. 'We've been quarantined, and now we know the extremes they will go to keep our infection contained.'

'They couldn't let them return to the settlement and risk them infecting the others,' Darren said, nodding his understanding. 'But where's the probe that has been following us?'

Gerry pointed to an area of thick grasses. 'I shot it. It was targeting these people for its mother-ship. I wasn't left with any other option.'

'Shit, I'm sure you did the right thing, but we're digging the hole we're in deeper and deeper, aren't we?' Charmaine said, more an observation than a question.

'Well sir, I'm Darren, the pilot' Darren said to the visitor, holding his arm outstretched, offering a handshake. The rifle wasn't pointed at him so he took the side of cautious friendliness.

The old man hesitated a moment but complied with a nod of his head. 'I'm David Oaks, though the people here call be Adam. I had the privilege of being the first man born on Clarkson. I am the village electrician.'

Here was a sign that something was not right about these people. The first person they had spoken to on Clarkson thought he was the first person born on the planet. This was of course impossible. No one had ever been born after either of their parents had been on a hyper-speed flight. A hyper-speed journey was of course the only possible way for them to get here. Gerry knew there could never have been a human birth here, but thought it would be best to debate the point at another time.

'I'm Gerry Handley, acting Supervisor, and these two are researchers from our vessel, Charmaine and Jennifer,' Gerry said, stepping aside to allow the two women to step forward.

'I'd shake hands, but we've been infected by a radioactive substance,' Charmaine said to the man. 'Darren should have known better.'

'Damn. I'm sorry,' Darren apologised instantly. 'I completely forgot the risk. I just feel so healthy. It's easy to forget.'

'It's too late anyway,' Gerry explained. 'David is in quarantine too now. They will not let him return to the settlement. He has been in a contaminated area. They won't risk it. He'll be contaminated for sure, after a while at our camp, if he hasn't been already.'

'But I need to get back,' the scared old man said gruffly. 'People will come looking for us. Moreover, my wife is not well. She can't cope on her own.'

'I'm sorry David, but I think you're now in the same predicament we are,' Gerry said. 'If you are spotted trying to return to your village by the vessel in orbit you'll almost certainly be attacked and killed just as your three friends were.'

David simply stood without moving, a dejected look upon his hairy, sun-ravaged face.

'We should get back to the camp,' Gerry said. 'You can stay with us until we get all this sorted out.'

He nodded assent and they all turned to start back through the undergrowth when they were stopped by a crackling noise nearby. What they saw sickened every one of them.

The young man of the group, whom Gerry assumed dead, had risen to his feet and was shambling toward them from the clearing. The beam had found him again though, a burning object moving through a forty-degree swamp making an easy target. Clouds of smoke and steam billowed from his bubbling skin. His screams for help went unanswered though, there being nothing that anyone could do to help him.

He stumbled onward for further than Gerry thought possible. It was only when the lad was within a few metres from him that Gerry could see why it was so. As the burning figure fell forward face-first into the ground Gerry could see sparkling blue bands of light streaking over his charred body. Though probably less than fifteen minutes after contracting the infective radioactive material, he was already showing it effects.

And it didn't give in easily, for minutes the blue light continuing to flash over the twitching body while the beam seared it into the ground, until the corpse was totally unrecognisable as ever having been a person. Even much of the bones glowed red-hot then crumbled into a soft ash.

Gerry realised that the reason the destruction of the bodies was so thorough was probably due to an attempt to sterilise them, to destroy the radioactive substance completely. It had not worked though. Gerry could see a burnt tuft of grass near the corpse sparkling blue, healing with the aid of the peculiar radioactivity. The dying man had barely made contact with the plant, yet it was enough to cause it to become infected almost instantly.

'Let's get back to camp,' Gerry said quietly to the group. 'There's nothing we can do here.'

'Not even bury the remains?' Darren asked.

'It wouldn't be safe,' Gerry said, shaking his head. 'They might still be looking for David. Even if they don't want to kill us, one of us might be mistaken for him.'

Darren just nodded, and together the group wound their way back to the camp, careful to stay well under the protective forest canopy. The stench of burnt flesh did not leave them though, and as the group sat down in the clearing to rest, the old man was leaning against a tree, vomiting noisily.

Gaston crawled from his tent, sunken eyes showing no hint of surprise when he noticed the settler who had arrived with them. Not so for David though, who had just finished retching when met by the sight of the hideously deformed man. He did not hide his shock well though, but nodded a greeting, though he had to look deep down into the man's skull to meet his eyes, and all he saw were the faint glimmers of light within.

David ignored the piece of bedding foam that Jennifer had placed upon the ground for him to sit upon, and instead sat on the bare earth some distance from them. While he recovered a little from his ordeal, Jennifer informed Gaston of what had gone before. She spoke loudly so that he could hear her with his damaged ears, but he showed no sign of emotion throughout.

'Like I've been telling you, they want us to stay isolated,' Gaston muttered when she had finished. 'They want us alive just as much as we want to stay alive. They need to study our condition, but there is no way they will hesitate to kill us if we break quarantine again. I believe we'll need to, to get the settlement nearby, but we'll have to be careful.'

'And that applies to anybody who approaches this area too,' Jennifer added, glancing at their trembling, troubled guest. 'Do you think they'll still try to kill him if they discover he is here with us?'

'Maybe, maybe not' Gaston replied. 'But I think he is one of us now.'

There was a disturbance in the leafy canopy above, and the nervous outcasts instantly shot a look upward.

'I guess we are about to find out,' old David groaned, clutching his long grey beard in both hands.

A new surveillance probe hovered amidst the foliage.

EIGHTEEN

'It's hard to believe that there's nobody out there,
It's hard to believe that I'm all alone...'
Red Hot Chilli Peppers – Under The Bridge

Gerry felt his hand involuntarily reach for the pistol he had
strapped under his shirt. It was a reflex action, and probably not
the wisest of moves, Gerry thought, so he only held his hand
alongside it in readiness, not drawing the weapon. The various
Government agencies that would be overseeing their quarantine
would know that it was he who shot down the first probe. They
would not risk losing this one so easily, probably the only
remaining probe from the military ship that sat in orbit, invisible,
over their heads.

Old David did not possess such restraint. He lifted his rifle
with fumbling hands and pointed it in the direction of the
hovering machine. Gerry held his breath, waiting or a pillar of
heat to burst through the treetops and sear the main to a
screaming death. They would be able to target him with perfect
accuracy now that a probe was here to send data back to them.

Instead, a booming voice rang out through the forest,
speakers in the probe reproducing the voice of someone from
Earth. 'PUT THE WEAPON DOWN. YOU WILL NOT BE
HARMED.'

The gun flew from the old mans shaking hands instantly, and
it was obvious that he was too frightened to use the weapon
effectively anyway. Gerry pitied him. David, or Adam as his
neighbours in the settlement called him, would still not know how
badly his circumstances had become. His day had gone bad, but it
was only going to get worse once he discovered that a radioactive
material that made him an unclean outcast like themselves had
infected him.

'YOU ARE IN CONTROLLED QUARANTINE AND
UNDER UNITED WESTERN MILITARY COMMAND. DO
NOT LEAVE THE AREA,' the voice from the probe boomed at

them. David just nodded his head and stared dejectedly at the ground near his feet.

Jennifer could see his discomfort and tried to console him. 'I'm sorry about your friends. Nevertheless, you are safe here with us. Our exposure to a strange type of radiation meant we were forced into quarantine.'

'If our condition clears we'll all be allowed to return home,' Charmaine added.

'Your condition?' the old man asked quietly, lifting his head to look at them. 'Are you ill?'

'We aren't sick exactly,' Gerry said. 'But we are showing some strange effects due to the exposure. They are keeping us here until they can determine whether we are a danger to others. They don't want us contaminating the home planet.'

'What are the symptoms? Are they clearing up somewhat?'

'Not yet,' Gerry answered. 'But it's only been a few weeks. One of the symptoms is an inability to ingest food. We haven't eaten in weeks.'

'Good Lord,' the old man said, obviously surprised. Yet another threat to his life, all within an hour. 'You don't look starved though.'

'No. We actually feel very healthy, except for a few dizzy spells,' Charmaine said. 'None of us have lost weight.'

'We don't need sleep either,' Jennifer added. 'We've been awake since our exposure three weeks ago.'

'Praise the Lord,' the old man exclaimed, making the sign of the cross on his chest. 'And your wounds, they heal quickly?'

'Yes, but how did you know that?' Gerry said in surprise.

'You're not the first to come here with the touch of Gods essence upon you. I could not have been born otherwise,' Dave told them. In sudden realisation, he slapped his hand over his mouth, and looked up at the probe, which listened from above. 'I'm sorry. I have said too much. Some things are not for the ears of those people.'

Gerry was stunned. They knew about the radiation effects already. Moreover, something else still concerned him. How could David have been born on this planet as he said he had? Hyper-speed travel ruined any existing DNA. A daily pill was the only thing that kept them from being consumed by cancerous tumours.

Indeed, Gerry and his crew had not been able to take this medication since the onset of their infection. He expected to see the first signs of malignant growths in a few weeks, death for each of them in the following months. However, maybe the healing properties of the radioactive material they were infected with would stop their bodies from turning against themselves. Gerry could only hope this was so.

The group fell quiet; only the soft hum of the probe and Gaston's ragged breathing breaking the silence. David was running his hands through the broad-leafed grasses that covered much of the clearing. Blue sparks flickered over the small plants as he did so, but he did not seem concerned. He seemed to enjoy the strangeness that the radiation exposure had brought with it, revelling in it in fact. His eyes were wide as he played with the unusually altered vegetation, reflecting the sparkling blue lights.

Gerry wanted to find out more from this man. He appreciated his unwillingness to talk in front of the surveillance probe though, and would do the same himself if one of the devices had just been used to help murder three of his friends. Unsure himself whether the things David knew would result in a favourable response from the quarantine officials, Gerry was glad he had kept quiet. He would wait for some privacy before talking to the old man concerning their condition again.

Their military overseers were not as patient though. The probe made some clicking noises and dropped a few metres. It was not far from David's head, and he cringed beneath it. The voice from Earth startled them all as it spoke loudly and in a modified tone, designed to instil utmost authority. It was a military device, after all.

'WE REQUIRE INFORMATION. WHAT IS YOUR FULL NAME? WE WANT TO CORRECT OUR RECORDS. THERE IS NO-ONE FITTING YOUR VISUAL PROFILE IN OUR EMIGRATION FILES. YOU CURRENTLY HAVE THE STATUS OF ILLEGAL IMMIGRANT.'

'My name is David Oaks,' he answered, obviously fearful. Gerry was angry with the officials who were directing the probe. David had been traumatised enough, yet still they harassed him. He felt like shooting down this probe too, but he restrained himself, knowing the reaction from the gunship in orbit would probably be extreme indeed.

There was five seconds silence, and then the probe boomed 'THERE IS NO RECORD OF YOU JOINING A FLIGHT TO CLARKSON. EXPLAIN THIS.'

David looked at the others in a plea for help, but there was little they could do.

'Your records are obviously wrong' Gerry said to the probe, hoping to divert it from its interrogation of the old man. 'I think you've done enough. Leave him alone.'

'STAY QUIET HANDLEY. THIS MAN MAY HAVE IMPORTANT INFORMATION. NOW, MISTER OAKS, YOUR PLACE AND DATE OF BIRTH.'

David shook his head, looking down at the ground as he spoke. 'I have made an oath to not speak of such things to outsiders. I would be breaking our vows. You cannot force me to do such a thing.'

'YES, WE CAN. A WRITTEN AGREEMENT FOR OUR TWO PLANETS TO KEEP OUT OF EACH OTHERS AFFAIRS MEANS LITTLE WHEN WE ARE IMPLEMENTING A COVERT OPERATION SUCH AS THIS. CAREFUL WITHHOLDING INFORMATION. WITHOUT IT WE WILL BE ABLE TO DO LITTLE TO ASSIST YOU ALL.'

None of them responded to the thinly veiled threats, the people back on Earth gave up, for the moment, and the probe climbed slowly back to its position in the canopy and remained silent. The scheming military minds that controlled their quarantine surely had a lot to think about.

A soft breeze began to rattle through the trees after a while, bringing some relief to the cloying humidity. It was actually quite pleasant, and each of them was able to relax somewhat, some laid out on their bedding, others sitting.

Gerry sat and contemplated all he had learned today. His mind was occasionally spinning into a hyperactive state, the sheer volume of considerations and possible solutions making him dizzy, even a little nauseous.

The effect was even stranger now though. Along with the hyperactive thought processes, he was visualising scenes of strange places he had never seen before. Fleeting as they were, they felt somehow of importance, and held so much detail. Each of them was seared into his memory once he had seen them, in

265

amazing clarity. He worried somewhat about his state of mind, but he appreciated his clarity of thought.

One thing that still had him at wits-end though was the suggestion from David that he had heard of the strange radiation exposure before, and that it had something to do with his birth. He could not have been born here. No child was ever born after a hyper-speed journey had been undertaken by their prospective parents. The genetic materials in their bodies was completely destroyed, without hope of renewal. But the official speaking to them via the probe had said that there was no record of David Oaks leaving Earth for the planet Clarkson, and no visual recognition file at all.

It was all very unusual, but Gerry felt that each strange event that had befallen them on this ill-fated research mission was linked to the others somehow. He felt on the edge of a solution, but it would not quite come to him.

Gerry needed to find out what it was that David knew. He'd seemed happy when hearing of the effects of their illness, acting as though it was somehow good news. He noticed that David was plastered in mud after his journey.

'Would you like to go down to the creek and clean up a little?' he asked David. 'I can show you the way there. There are some questions I'd like to ask you.'

'No, but thank you. Too much has happened for me to be concerned about things like that right now,' he replied quietly.

'I'll come down with you,' Charmaine said, standing up. 'These overalls could stand up on their own.'

'Right,' Gerry said, rising also. 'Anyone else?'

The others shook their heads or mumbled no, so he and Charmaine slipped through the undergrowth. They had worn a track in the past few weeks, so the going was easy. The probe had not followed them, staying with the others at the camp.

'Do you really think that David was born here?' Charmaine asked him as they walked.

'Normally I'd say no way,' Gerry replied. 'There's never been a mammal conceived after hyper-speed travel as far as I know. But he seemed to recognise the symptoms of the radiation exposure. I guess it could be possible if his parents were infected. It seems to help us heal in other ways. Maybe it repairs our reproductive mechanisms as well. I doubt it though.'

266

'More likely a mix-up with their records on Earth?' Charmaine added.

'Yeah, that seems much more likely,' Gerry replied. They walked quietly the rest of the way, each of them deep in thought. It was a pleasant afternoon though, so Gerry was light-hearted, feeling quite cheerful, even though he had witnessed the horrible deaths of three innocent people. He'd always been amazed what a person could become accustomed to after being exposed to repeated trauma in a short space of time, but it was the strange moments of clarity he was experiencing occasionally that helped most of all. Though they only lasted for seconds each time they came on, his sense of time became vague after each incidence of the hyperactive state of mind. It was as though he had already considered each event thoroughly and felt it pointless to waste his time dwelling upon them further. He knew it was an unusual mental state, something that in normal circumstances would be feared, but he wasn't concerned. He was rational, and probably more so than ever before.

In the soft light of late afternoon the creek was a beautiful place to be. The crystal-clear waters lapped against the rocks with soft rhythmic slaps, and though there were freshly cremated corpses less than fifty metres from them, the stench of burnt flesh and hair had been swept away in the breeze, and Charmaine and Gerry could not help but enjoy the serenity. Talk about getting away from it all. Even the light from the large sun would never reach Earth, so distant were they from the home planet.

They each took a deep breath as they felt their tension ease somewhat, and sitting on the bank facing each other they removed each others boots, which was much easier than doing so oneself. The grasses they rested upon sparkled when they were brushed, waves of blue light passing through them, a surreal effect in the twilight shadows. In fact, much of the area was under the effects of the radioactive material they had introduced here. They stayed where they were for a few minutes, watching the tiny blue sparks flashing through the trees as they were ruffled by the cool breeze One of the reptilian creatures sauntered past, too intent on its own task at hand to pay them any heed. It was smaller than the others they had seen, only about five feet long, and seemed harmless, so Gerry and Charmaine weren't concerned for their safety. It was the fact that flashes of blue sparkled over its legs as it walked that worried them.

'Our being on this planet may be changing it forever,' Charmaine said quietly. 'But I believe it could be for the better.'

'I know, but we couldn't have known what effects our presence here would have. Besides, I agree with Gaston. We were driven here by people on Earth with their own agenda. We're just the pawns in some sort of game,' Gerry told her.

'I think he might be right too, partially so anyway,' Charmaine replied. 'My mind races sometimes, and things become clear to me. Sometimes I worry that I might be going insane. Nevertheless, I have a strong sense that we are here for a purpose. Nothing that has happened on this mission was accidental. We're here for a reason.'

'Whatever the reason we ended up here, we just have to make the most of it. When we get back to Earth there'll be plenty of questions to be answered,' Gerry replied.

'Yeah. Should we go in before it gets too dark?' Charmaine asked, looking at the clear water beside them.

'For sure,' Gerry answered, getting to his feet and helping Charmaine to hers.

They each peeled off the coveralls and waded in, and though it was relatively cold in the late afternoon, the waters revitalised them.

Charmaine let herself sink for a moment to let her head soak in the crystal-clear waters, and ran her fingers through her hair as she emerged; ensuring all dust and mud had been washed away.

Gerry could not help but gaze upon her beauty for a moment. Her long, jet-black hair hung around her neck and lay across one shoulder. All concern for their predicament left him, and for a while at least, he was happy in the moment. As she noticed his gaze and smiled at him, he felt there was no other place he would rather be.

Charmaine could sense the change in the atmosphere too, a feeling that this moment was special, somehow important, and swam smoothly to him.

Gerry was surprised when he realised that the closeness he felt to this woman was to be reciprocated, and as she swam into his arms, he marvelled at the sensation of her bare skin against his.

She wrapped her arms gently around him, her lips pressed against his shoulder as she clung to him.

They held each other for what only seemed a moment but was certainly longer. The shadows deepened around them as their hands began to roam over each other's bodies, and long-neglected urges were realised.

It was dark when they walked back into camp. Gerry and Charmaine had both been gifted with a stamina that they had never known before, their lovemaking urgent and forceful, yet sustained for more than an hour. For both of them it had been a powerful encounter and the slightly stunned look on their faces as they rejoined the group did not go unnoticed.

'We were getting worried about you,' Jennifer said with a smile. 'We were about to go down and check up on you. A good thing we didn't, it seems.'

Charmaine threw Jennifer a steely look of annoyance but sat down without speaking.

'The wildlife around our swimming spot is almost completely contaminated with the radioactivity we brought here,' Gerry said, keen to change the subject. 'It looks like we might be here for a while. Even if the radioactive substance we're carrying dissipates, we'll probably be re-exposed to it by the environment we've infected.'

'Unless we keep moving,' Darren suggested.

'Possibly,' Gerry replied. 'It's an option, but that could just make things worse.'

'That's if Mission Control allows it anyway,' Jennifer added. 'They might fry us if we leave the area.'

Gerry looked up to where the probe, and as if on cue its speaker activated.

'YOU CANNOT LEAVE THE AREA. YOU ARE UNDER MILITARY ENFORCED QUARANTINE' boomed the probe, the man back on Earth obviously using his most authoritative tone.

It did not have the desired effect though, and all of them but Gaston began to heatedly debate the logic of the demand. Their complaints were ignored though, the probe simply howling at them that they had been given their orders, and then remained silent. Their protests were falling upon deaf ears.

'There is something I need to tell you, but I'm not sure that it is safe to do so,' David, the elderly colonist said from where he sat cross-legged upon the leafy ground.

'They know a lot more about our condition back on Earth than we first realised,' Gerry said to him. 'Whatever it is you've got to say probably won't be news to them, but it might help ourselves to understand our circumstances a little more.'

'Maybe so,' David replied. 'But if not, it might give them reason to kill us all. My people in the village might also be put at risk.'

'It must be important. Come for a walk David. The probe can't be in two places at once,' Gerry said to him.

David nodded, and they both rose to their feet and made their way out of the camping area. However, Gerry watched the probe move to follow David, keeping close enough to pick up anything he said.

'There's no point David. They want to know what you have to say as much as we do,' Gerry told him, pointing to the probe hovering a few metres above his head.

Returning to their seating positions, Gerry was considering shooting this probe, then letting David speak, but he was hesitant. The response from the military ship in orbit might be more violent than the response they would get if David gave them the information. However, it was a mute point anyway, because he had already begun to divulge his secrets.

'This great man, Gaston, is known to us on this planet,' the old man told them. 'He came here and joined our settlement more than twenty years ago.'

'Quiet,' Gaston hissed. 'You silly old fool.'

'They mustn't be kept in the dark any longer,' David replied, acid in his tone. 'It is because of us that they are in this predicament. You are the saviour of our people. Be proud of that.'

'And you would put them in even greater danger? Keep quiet man,' Gaston answered. His crushed body did not allow him to speak above a whisper, but they all heard the annoyance, and the fear, in his voice.

270

'Careful Dan,' Jennifer told their crippled companion. 'Don't get too worked up. You'll aggravate your injuries.'

Gerry, Darren, Charmaine and Jennifer exchanged glances. David had barely begun to tell them what he knew, and their sense of reality had been stripped from them. David and Gaston knew each other. One, a man who had been stranded on a distant moon for more than a decade, the other a settler on this planet.

Gerry's mid tripped into a hyperactive state when it had absorbed the new information. As his thoughts raced, he saw the reason behind much that had happened to them on this ill-fated mission. He saw the reason why they were here in the first place; here on this planet in particular.

Dan Gaston had brought them here because it was his home. He had used them to get back here. He had saved their lives in the process though, and Gerry could never be anything but grateful for what he had done for himself and the crew. But he was very likely the person who had exposed them to all this danger in the first place. Indeed Mission Control and most of the officials back on Earth probably were not actually expecting most of the events that he and his companions had been through. It suddenly seemed that Gaston was the biggest player in this whole saga, Gerry realised.

As quickly as the strange mindset came upon Gerry, it left him. His clouded vision cleared and he lifted his head. As usual, reasons for their circumstances that had previously eluded him had become obvious to him after the seizure, and he would have appreciated some time to consider his new insights, but he was not allowed any.

'WHY DID GASTON LEAVE YOUR SETTLEMENT TO GO TO CLAVUS, OAKS?' the probe boomed at David, startling Gerry and the others. 'IT IS A DEAD PLANET, ONLY THE THIRD MOON SUSTAINS LIFE, AND IT'S NOT HABITABLE BY HUMANS. THE REASON WAS NOT TO START ANOTHER SETTLEMENT, SO WHAT WAS IT?'

David looked frightened, but seemed determined to set the record straight. 'It wasn't the planet we were interested in, or the moons There was something in space nearby. Radioactivity or something, coming from the chemical clouds. The very same substance that is affecting everyone here,' he answered, pointing to indicate Gerry and the others.

271

'WHY. WHAT DID YOU HOPE TO ACHIEVE?' boomed the probe. 'OUR EMPLOYEES HAVE BEEN ILL FOR WEEKS AND HAVE GONE WITHOUT FOOD OR SLEEP SINCE THEY WERE EXPOSED.'

'It repairs our genetic material. We can become fertile again,' David replied. 'No longer will our community slowly fade as the settlers die here without children. We could have new generations to continue our work here. It is a miracle like none other before it, the touch of God that will allow his people to survive and prosper.'

Gerry found that he was not surprised by anything David had said, having realised much of their motives already, but hearing it spoken aloud made him inwardly cringe. Gaston had been right. David had placed them in far greater danger with his short speech. He planned to help rebuild a civilisation based upon a cult that had killed billions on Earth over the past few centuries in the name of Christian freedom, whatever that might be; the freedom to control and kill with impunity seemed their only obvious historical goal as far as Gerry could make out.

Cult worship was outlawed in almost every country on Earth, and no one could say that the world was not a better place for it. War for religious and racial hatred had ceased to exist, and no government on Earth would allow it to return. Civilisation had passed from thousands of years of self-harm to an era of tolerance, logic and compassion, and all could appreciate the prosperity brought by a peaceful planet. They would not risk going back to the old ways of segregation and murderous arrogance brought on by religion, and David had just stated that this was in essence what he and his people risked. It had put Gerry and his crew in great danger, and indeed, everyone on this planet would be seen as a potential threat, and therefore a target.

It was quiet in the camp for a moment, only the crackle of wood in the fire and the soft hum of the probe above them. Gerry knew they would be considering the implications of what Oaks had told them, putting the pieces together. The atmosphere was tense, and Gerry had a feeling that the next few minutes would decide their fate for better or worse.

'YOU MUST NOT HAVE CONTACT WITH ANY PERSON ON THIS PLANET. YOU ARE UNDER MILITARY-ENFORCED QUARANTINE. TROOPS WILL

BE DISPATCHED FROM EARTH AND WILL REACH YOU IN TWO DAYS. THEY WILL KEEP YOU UNDER GUARD, NOTHING MORE' the probe instructed finally.

'But my friends from our settlement will come looking for us,' David exclaimed. 'They won't know they may be walking into danger.'

'EVERYONE AT THE SETTLEMENT WILL BE INFORMED OF THE SITUATION. IF THEY STAY OUT OF YOUR QUARANTINE AREA AS INSTRUCTED THEY WILL BE SAFE.'

'But this is their planet. They will almost certainly come anyway,' David replied.

'FURTHER COMPLICATIONS TO THIS SITUATION WON'T BE TOLERATED,' the probe boomed back at him. 'QUARANTINE WILL BE SUSTAINED USING WHATEVER FORCE IS REQUIRED, WITHOUT LIMITATION.'

'We cannot allow heathen interlopers to turn our miracle, our salvation, into tragedy.' And upon speaking such a defiant phrase, David Oaks did the unthinkable. He leapt to his feet and ran from the camp-site, crashing through the undergrowth as he went.

'Stop,' Gerry yelled, but it was ineffectual.

Oaks was on his way back to the settlement, single-minded in his desperation to get back to his people. He would not stop for any of them, and Gerry knew that this would almost certainly result in his death. Indeed, the probe had burst through the canopy above, and was following him, no longer visible as it flew over the dark forest.

Gerry leapt to his feet and gave chase, yelling to his companions to stay where they were until he returned.

As he ran, following the sounds of cracking twigs that told him where Oaks was, Gerry also heard a sound behind him, and risked a quick backward glance. It was Darren, who had ignored a direct order and was following him. Gerry did not mind as much as he probably should have though, and was grateful for his crewmate's loyalty, although it could result in the death of both of them.

'Careful Darren,' Gerry called to him as they ran. 'We'll be outside the quarantine zone in a moment. David might not be the only target they'll be aiming for.'

273

'I know the risks, sir,' Darren called in return. He was having trouble matching Gerry's pace, but was making an admirable attempt. Being short and stocky, he bulldozed his way through the undergrowth, while Gerry ducked and weaved his way through.

Scratches and cuts on their skin flickered blue light as they scrambled to reach Oaks. The lack of light made it impossible to avoid the thorny bushes that impeded their progress. Gerry could have reached into his pocket and found a torch, but the last think he wanted to do was make their presence known to those on Earth. The probe was somewhere above their heads, and any light he used would have been obvious to its sensors. He was in no hurry to let them know that they were leaving the quarantine area. They had only moments ago been warned about what would happen to them if they did so.

David moved amazingly quickly for someone his age, no doubt a result of healthy living on this fertile planet. However, Gerry wondered too whether David's recent radiation exposure had anything to do with his endurance. Gerry's own stamina seemed enhanced; he had noticed his breathing was slow and easy, as though he was relaxing rather than running.

They had just crossed a dried creek bed that Gerry knew to border their quarantine area when he caught a glimpse of David up ahead. In the starlight he saw the silhouette of his head and shoulders, hunched forward as he strove to lose the probe that trailed him somewhere above. There was a pinpoint of bright green light shining on the back of his head. The probe was painting its target; keeping track of the fleeing mans location for the gunship in orbit.

'David, stop,' Gerry called to him as loudly as he dared. He hoped those on Earth that controlled the probe had not heard him. David heard, though did not halt his mad dash for freedom.

'No chance. I won't be imprisoned by the invaders,' he called back without slowing. 'We're a sovereign people...'

His words were cut short as Gerry lunged forward and neatly tackled him to the ground, careful not to hurt him. 'Take it easy. They'll kill you before they'll let you re-enter the settlement.'

'I'd take my chance,' Oaks said as Gerry helped him to his feet. 'I can't stay in quarantine for god-only-knows how long. One of us needs to make it to the village. Gaston has brought us

274

the means to build a civilisation. The people will have children again. Or society can grow instead of slowly dying, withering away to nothing.'

'I don't think that was part of the agreement when the settlers were given this planet,' Gerry said, brushing himself off. 'You know as well as I do that governments on Earth don't want potential rivals springing up within striking distance of the home planet. They rely on the destruction of our genetic material after hyper-speed journeys to keep off-world populations small and manageable.'

'I understand the possible implications,' Oaks said quietly, unaware of the glowing green marker that was still trained upon the top of his head. 'What I don't understand is your willingness to help them. Let me go to the village. The survival of a new civilisation is at stake.'

Gerry sighed, annoyed by the man's willingness to die for his cause so needlessly. Reaching up with one hand, Gerry let the targeting laser that was aimed at the old man's head flicker over his fingers so that Oaks could see it. 'They could kill you in an instant. Don't give up your life so easily.'

Oaks saw the lights flickering over Gerry's fingers that were held above his head, his shoulders slumping, resignation that his life was in the hands of officials on the home planet. 'The military personnel are on their way. What are we going to do?'

'Nothing yet. Getting ourselves burnt down in some attempt to escape the inescapable does not make any sense to me after what we've all been through. The people they send here to enforce our quarantine will always be able to find you. It's just an unfortunate fact, we are all alive only by the mercy of people we don't know, back on Earth. Don't give them an even stronger reason to kill us.'

Oaks nodded. 'Burning us to the ground would solve the problem for them. Within a few minutes they could remove the risk of the radioactive material spreading.'

'Yeah, let's not give them reason to do just that. Let's get back into the quarantine zone,' Gerry replied.

Oaks acquiesced, and the two walked back to camp without incident. The soft hum of the probe could be heard behind them as they walked, though the targeting laser it carried had been switched off. Gerry had begun to relax, but he was met with another problem upon his return.

Charmaine had gone missing.

NINETEEN

'Fear is a weapon of mass destruction...'
Faithless – Mass Destruction

'Nobody saw her leave,' Jennifer told him, obviously very worried, 'but we noticed her gone only a minute or two after you left.'

'We didn't see her,' Gerry advised. 'I'm pretty sure she didn't follow Oaks and I.'

'It's only been fifteen minutes since she disappeared. She could have just gone for a walk. No need to get worried yet,' Darren added.

'Did she leave her computer here?' Gerry asked.

'No, I don't think so. She probably has it in her pocket,' Jennifer answered.

'I'll message her to see what's going on,' Gerry explained, retrieving his own hand-held PC from a pocket on the chest of his flight suit and sitting down near the camp-fire.

'CHARMAINE, WHERE ARE YOU? ARE YOU OK?' he typed quickly. The screen showed that she had received the message, and within moments, he had a reply.

'I'M FINE. GONE FOR A WALK. IT MAY HAVE BEEN MY ONLY CHANCE TO LEAVE. WHILE THE PROBE WAS FOLLOWING DAVID. I ASKED HIM TO LEAD IT AWAY FROM CAMP. DON'T BE ANGRY WITH HIM. HE WAS JUST TRYING TO HELP ME. AND THE PEOPLE THAT LIVE HERE.'

Gerry was alarmed by the new events. Charmaine and Oaks in collusion? To what end?

'Where is she going, Oaks?' Gerry demanded. He didn't get any answers from him though, the old man merely shaking his head and avoiding eye contact.

Gerry was certain that he knew where she was headed though. 'She's going to try getting to the settlement, isn't she?'

Again, he got no response. Such was Gerry's annoyance he had to fight the urge to grab the old man and shake the answers out of him.

Gerry's computer beeped, signalling another message received. It was Charmaine. 'I'LL HAVE TO SWITCH MY COMPUTER OFF NOW. THEY WILL PROBABLY BE TRACKING MY POSITION BY ITS SIGNAL.'

Gerry saw her listing in the available contacts disappear, showing that she had indeed switched it off. She was totally on her own out there now. But probably not for long. The probe made a burst of mechanical noise and fired upwards through the canopy, out of sight.

As leaves and broken twigs rained down upon the camp, Gerry realised what he would have to do. If the probe found her, she would almost certainly be killed. He could not sit here and wait for that to happen. 'I'm going out to find her,' Gerry told the others. 'I am fairly sure that I know where she is headed, so I shouldn't have too much of a problem catching up with her.'

'Maybe we should all go,' Jennifer suggested.

'No, we'd stand out like the proverbial dogs balls. The gunship's scanners would easily track us. I'll go alone, and I'll need to hurry. The probe moves fast. I'd hate to think what might happen if it finds her before I do.'

'They won't be sure which way she's gone. I think we can be sure she is headed toward the settlement. You'll have a fair chance of getting to her before the probe does,' Darren said optimistically.

'She is the one that is helping you, isn't she, Oaks?' Gerry asked the old man. 'The person from Earth who has been helping you lot bring the radioactive material to the people here?'

Oaks again refused to speak, but Gaston answered for him. 'Yes. She's the one Mission Control was looking for. Someone on the inside who has directed your mission. To help us, along with all of our people on this planet. Bless the girl.'

'She's probably just succeeded in getting herself killed. You should have told me about your plans. At least I could have given her the pistol to defend herself,' Gerry told Gaston and Oaks.

'We won't be in quarantine any longer, when she gets to the settlement,' Oaks muttered. 'Once the people are infected and restored to health there will be no point keeping us here. We'll be free to go where we like.'

'As long as it is on this planet,' Gerry answered, still annoyed at this turn of events. 'Anyway, I've got to go. Just take it easy till I get back.'

Scooping up one of the tiny but powerful torches as he hurried out of the camp, Gerry jogged as fast as he dared through the dark forest that ringed their camp. He unzipped a pocket and switched off his computer as he went, knowing they would be using its signal to track his location.

When he made it to the relatively sparse swampland below, he switched on his torch momentarily, not wanting to use it unless he really needed to. The probe would easily find him if he left it on. The stars shone brightly enough for him to see by. However, in the light of the beam, Gerry could now see small boot prints in the mud. They would have almost certainly been left by Charmaine.

Switching off the light, Gerry started in the same direction that her prints were going. He ran as quickly as he dared over the slippery layer of mud, finding it difficult to keep his footing.

It took fifteen minutes or so to clear the swamp and reach another dense copse of trees. Again, he flicked on the light, and took only a few seconds to find more of Charmaine's footprints, entering the forest right beside him. He killed the light and moved onto the higher ground that edged the swamp, and had begun to weave his way through the trees and the undergrowth when he heard a sound. Gerry dashed under the nearest bush, hoping it was Charmaine he had heard, but knew that it could not be. He listened while something he couldn't see approached him from behind. It would almost certainly be the probe that searched for her.

When he heard the soft hum of the motor, he knew it for sure, and pressed himself against the trunk of the bush he was hiding beneath. It passed directly over his head, but suddenly turned and headed back the way it had come at quite a rate. Though Gerry could not see it, the clamour it made as it burst through the vegetation made its progress obvious.

Gerry was worried that he would be under immediate attack if he were discovered out of the quarantine zone now. They would want to keep them under close guard until the troops arrived from

Earth, who would then effectively be able to enforce their quarantine. If they could keep them together for another forty hours or so, they would gain complete control of the situation.

Continuing on his way, Gerry realised that even Charmaine could be a danger to him now. If she really was the insider that had led them into this situation, she could conceivably get nasty if he tried to stop her completing her subversive mission. Gerry wasn't even sure if she was doing the wrong thing any-more. Exposing a population to a relatively unstudied radioactive material would normally be an abhorrent act of stupidity in Gerry's mind, but in these circumstances, he was not so sure. He hoped it wasn't only the intimacy he and Charmaine had shared only a few hours earlier that was clouding his judgement. He would not be the first man to be irrational when it came to the perceived righteousness of someone he had become close to.

As he forced his way through the dense undergrowth, trying to maintain an effective speed, Gerry considered his circumstances from a personal point of view. When a person was scrambling through thorny branches on sodden ground on an alien planet there were no easy decisions, no simple way out of the predicament. He was on his own, in a difficult situation, as was Charmaine. He needed to reach her, to do whatever he could to keep her safe. He decided there was no other comfortable option, nothing more important that he could do to help her, and picked up his pace somewhat.

Charmaine was doing what she could to keep this remote community alive. Could he say with any certainty that she was wrong? Of course, he could not. For all Gerry knew, Charmaine was on a mercy run that had the potential to give a future to a settlement that simply seemed to strived for survival. Though there may be negative consequences in the long term, who was he to decide whether or not her plan had positive value? Its very complexity made that impossible.

It was dark within the thick vegetation, the canopy blocking even the meagre starlight now, and Gerry could only push his way blindly forward. He rebounded off unseen branches and ran into spiky plants that tore into his skin, his progress slow and laborious. The cuts flashed blue as they quickly healed, and he was concerned that the effect would attract the attention of the probe that searched for Charmaine. Occasionally an animal would run from him as he approached. He couldn't see what they were, but some of them sounded quite large.

Losing track of time as he continued to force his way forward, Gerry began to realise the hopelessness of what he was attempting to do. Finding Charmaine at night in a place like this would be unlikely. There was no way he could follow her tracks in the dark, and he dare not use the torch or turn on his computer to check his own location. He had a general idea where the settlement lay, but the further he walked the less certain he was of the direction he should be travelling.

He would still be at least twenty kilometres from the settlement that Charmaine was headed toward, and at his present rate of progress, it would take all night to cover the distance. Moreover, if he did not find her on the way there he would have to search for her again as he walked back to camp.

He had set himself a momentous task, but he wasn't deterred. It impelled him to walk faster, battering his way through the undergrowth, determined to find her as soon as possible.

However, it was she who found him. 'Gerry.'

He had heard his name called. Somewhere to his left. He stopped instantly and listened closely.

'Over here.'

She was not far away, and Gerry found her sitting under the thick fronds of a palm-like plant. He could just barely see her silhouette, even after he had sat down directly before her. The soft scent of her perfume and her quiet breathing made her identity unmistakable though.

'Are you alright?' Gerry asked, concerned that she was immobile because she had been hurt.

'Yes, I'm fine. I should ask you the same thing. Are you crazy, running through a place like this in the dark?'

'I'm fine. I wanted to find you quickly. The surveillance probe is searching for you,' Gerry told her.

'I know. It's flown past me a few times. I guess they know where I'm going,' Charmaine said quietly.

'I think they have a good idea you're headed to the settlement. They do seem to be concentrating the search in this area. Do you realise that they will kill you if they find you out here?' Gerry inquired.

Charmaine was silent for a moment, but when she finally spoke, Gerry could sense the determination in her voice.

'I do realise that, but what I need to do is far more important than my own safety. The survival of a new peoples is at stake, a settlement that could one day become a thriving civilisation. These people deserve a future just as much as those on Earth do.'

'I understand that,' Gerry whispered back. 'But are you sure that is for you to decide? We saw what the radiation exposure did to our supervisor. Would you risk doing that to thousands of people?'

'Something needs to be done,' she answered gravely. 'The risks are huge, but every settler on this planet wanted us to try. We have permission from everyone here. In addition, there are no children, so there is no chance of hurting anybody who did not agree to be part of this.'

'There must be more than just that driving you to do this. I know you orchestrated our mission from the beginning. Mission Control knows it too, now,' Gerry added.

I am sorry that I have risked the lives of everyone on our mission, and ruined their careers at the very least, but I feel strongly that the cause justifies some sacrifice,' Charmaine answered.

'You sound like a politician. But why you? How did you get tied up in all this?' Gerry asked, incredulous that there had been so much plotting behind the scenes. He had never been in true command of their mission.

'My father was the researcher who died while he was marooned on Clavus three. He died in that ship we found there.'

'So he was a settler here too?' Gerry asked with surprise. 'He was on the same flight as Gaston. He must have come from here.'

'Yes,' Charmaine answered finally. 'My father died trying to bring the radioactive material back here. I decided to do what I could to finish the task.'

'Do Gaston or Oaks know who you are? They must have both known your father,' Gerry inquired.

'I don't think either of them knows. David probably thinks that I wanted to assist him to get someone to the settlement just out of a simple willingness to help. He couldn't know that I'm

282

the daughter of his old friend. They haven't even seen each other for more than a decade. I was young when my father died.'

Gerry nodded without speaking. What was there to say?

'Please don't try to stop me going, Gerry. I want to start walking to the settlement at first light. It's too dangerous here at night.'

'Troops will be here in two days. They'll find you easily if you are at the settlement,' Gerry advised.

'They won't even land here if everyone here is contaminated,' Charmaine explained. 'The whole planet will be quarantined. We'd be safe.'

Gerry nodded his head, unseen in the inky blackness. 'You could be right.'

'And there are other reasons to spread our condition to the people here,' Charmaine added. 'Supply of the post-hyper-speed medication has been under threat for years. Companies on Earth are holding these people to ransom.'

'In what way?' Gerry inquired. 'I'm not following you.'

'There is no room for negotiation when these people are forced to trade with businesses on Earth. Prices are set on the terms that if they don't pay the asking price, the supply ship won't make a run here. No run from the supply ship means no government-issued DNA meds.'

'So the people here have been paying too much for supplies. So what? Western businesses have been extorting from minorities for centuries. Your solution isn't the only one available to these people,' Gerry said, still hoping to dissuade her from her incredibly dangerous project.

'I know,' Charmaine replied, 'but these people came here to be free, not to become slaves to the rich on the home planet. If this radiation affects the people here as it has us, they will be able to cut all ties with Earth. They'll no longer need the DNA medication to survive.'

'Nor will they need to eat, I guess,' Gerry added. 'And they will be fertile again, able to have children to build their empire after they are gone. I know your reasons Charmaine, I just can't agree with your methods. It's too dangerous to everyone on this planet, too full of unknown implications.'

'I've considered all of that. I could wipe out a hundred-year-old settlement by infecting the people, or on the other hand, they

283

might flourish into another human civilisation. The only people outside of Earth's solar system that can have children,' Charmaine said quietly.

'But how will the children be affected by the radioactivity? They might not survive,' Gerry said. 'Like I said, there are too many unknowns.'

'We might never agree on what I am about to attempt, but I must try to finish what my father failed to complete,' Charmaine added. There was the sound of rustling leaves somewhere above them, and Charmaine and Gerry sat silent for a few minutes, listening to the surveillance probe's hum as it searched for them overhead.

Though they could not see the device in he darkness, its trajectory was easy to follow by the sound of the vegetation it disturbed as it moved. It surveyed the area quite thoroughly, but Charmaine had chosen their hiding place well. Underneath the huge leaves of the palm, which itself was growing under the branches of another larger tree, there was little chance that they would be detected if they kept quiet enough.

'Well, I'd suggest we sleep here till morning,' Gerry said when the probe had passed out of range. 'But thanks to this radiation exposure, we can't sleep. Do you really want the people here to suffer side-effects like that?'

'We've stayed healthy in spite of that,' Charmaine whispered back. 'It could be seen as advantageous.'

'In the short-term,' Gerry added. 'But we don't know what will happen to us in the months to come.'

'Gaston is still alive,' Charmaine pointed out. 'He's stayed alive so long in an environment that couldn't possibly sustain normal human life for such a long period. We would have a far better chance of staying healthy if we live here than he had in that marooned hyper-speed ship. And David Oaks is proof that the children of people infected by this radiation can live healthy lives. He doesn't even seem to be effected by it.'

'So you truly believe that he is the first human born outside of Earth's solar system? Born right here, on this planet?' Gerry asked.

'Yes, I do. It explains the absence of his records on Earth. They don't know where he came from. My father told me as much before he died. In one of his letters, he mentioned that a

284

baby had been born on Clarkson many years before he had arrived. They said it was something that had touched them at some stage on their journey to the settlement. Something that had healed their genetic material. He said it was the essence of god. The catalyst to creation.'

'And that's what Gaston and your father had gone to find…' Gerry began.

'Yes, and they succeeded. They just didn't manage to bring it home to the people here. That's where I came in,' Charmaine explained.

'You won't change your mind about this, will you?' Gerry said, an observation rather than a question.

'No. I'm sorry,' she answered.

Gerry pushed some of the drier leaves beside him into a pile and lay down on his side. 'We might as well relax. We've got at least four hours until sunrise.'

Charmaine didn't answer, and quietly lay down beside him on the soft bed of leaves.

There they lay silent for the remainder of the night, comfortable in the humid forest in spite of the rips in their clothing from the spiky plants that tore at them as they had run through the alien wilderness, and in spite of the thick layer of mud that caked most of their bodies.

When the sun finally began to send a soft glow into the dense rainforest, Gerry had made up his mind. He knew what he had to do.

'I'm coming with you,' he told Charmaine as he helped her to her feet.

'I'm glad,' Charmaine said, smiling. 'This will all turn out OK. You'll see.'

'I hope so. For the sake of the settlers here, especially. They might be getting what they want, but that doesn't always turn out well,' Gerry said to her. 'They're gambling with their lives.'

'That's up to them,' Charmaine replied, unperturbed.

'But you're a biologist,' Gerry added as they began to weave through the forest floor. 'Aren't you worried about what the radiation exposure will do to the native life on this planet?'

'Of course I'm worried about that. This is probably the most dangerous experiment a person has ever conducted,' Charmaine explained. 'But I've been watching the plants and animals around our camp. We've infected about five hundred square metres of bushland, at least, and I haven't seen any negative effects.'

'Again, that's short term. The effects of the radiation might not dissipate over time. We may have altered the balances of life here forever. The radioactive material, whatever it is, might continue to spread, infecting this entire planet. You could turn it into a diseased no-mans-land. Do you really want to risk that?' Gerry said.

'I thought you agreed with my decision,' Charmaine said. 'But if you have to know, I'm as nervous as you are about the outcomes. Nevertheless, it's just something I have to do. A future civilisation, or a temporary settlement, human existence is at a crossroads on this planet.'

'I do see your point of view, don't get me wrong, but I just can't be sure that your solution is the best one for the problems on this settlement. And I'm sure sending troops here isn't any better a solution. If Earth does not respect the sovereignty of Clarkson as was agreed, there will be all sorts of trouble. And we can be sure that the settlers here will be the worst effected,' Gerry explained. 'They're between a rock and a hard place.'

'I wasn't the only person on Earth who thought it best that we attempt this. Any chance we have of creating a second planet for people, another world where we can reproduce and be self-sustaining, needs to be considered. It would be the most powerful tool we have of raising the chance of humanities long-term survival. We've had our eggs all in one basket for too long, so to speak.'

'I understand that,' Gerry replied as he pushed his way through a particularly dense copse of undergrowth. 'Returning these peoples reproductive ability may almost double humanities chances of still being around in a few hundred years, but it will more likely create a new enemy for us, in my book. Your attempt to guarantee the survival of humanity risks the ruination of Earth, and this planet.'

'Quiet,' Charmaine whispered suddenly. 'The probe's coming.'

They scrambled under some bushes and lay still, listening to the devices hum as it passed slowly overhead. Gerry wondered if they knew he was out here. If the probe had returned to the camp during the night, its controllers would have found he was missing.

'Maybe we should split up,' Charmaine suggested when the probe had passed out of sight. 'If we head to the settlement from different directions one of us will almost definitely make it.'

'No chance. I'm only out here to help keep you safe. I've got the pistol,' Gerry told her, instinctively checking the position of the firearm.

'Could we shoot down that probe then?' Charmaine asked.

'Too risky,' Gerry explained. 'If I miss we'll be fried in seconds. And this thing only holds eight more shots. The gunship will have a fix on us the very second I start firing.'

Charmaine just nodded her head, and they continued through the dense vegetation. Their progress was very slow, impeded by leathery vines that seemed impossible to break, spiny branches that tore at them, and their need to be quiet and cautious.

The probe was almost silent when it travelled slowly, and they were both aware that it would be very sensitive to any sight or sound of movement. There was a chance it could creep up on them, so they did not talk at all during the remainder of their journey, and did their utmost to stay under cover.

Indeed, seven hours of torturous travel ensued. Their clothes were shredded and the sunlight was fading when they reached the edge of the rainforest. Their skin was remarkably unmarked though, the radioactive material which infected them was healing their cuts and scrapes almost as quickly as they were sustained.

From their position at the edge of the tree line, they had their first glimpse of some of the homes that made up part of this far-flung colony. They were of a type common to third-world countries back on Earth; walls and roofs that had been constructed by a machine that was fed only sand, water, and a little wood pulp, and a perfectly formed slab of wood-like material would come sliding from the other end. Indeed, Gerry could hear one of the machines running somewhere in the distance. Preparing themselves for their new families perhaps, Gerry found himself thinking.

'Do they know you are coming?' Gerry asked Charmaine quietly.

She hesitated a moment before answering, her face reddening slightly with guilt when she turned to look at him. 'Yes. I messaged them before we landed.'

Gerry could only nod. She had been a busy girl.

'We need to get to their administration building,' Charmaine explained. 'We'll be safest there.'

'What makes you say that?' Gerry asked.

'They wouldn't dare attack the government offices here. It'd be an act of war,' Charmaine replied. 'No right-minded politician on Earth wants to be the first in history to order an attack on one of the off-world settlements.'

'You're probably right,' Gerry replied, sounding more confident than he felt.

'The hardest part will be getting from here to some cover near the houses,' Charmaine said as they looked over the sparse farming land that surrounded the town. Much of it was bare earth, freshly tilled, while the existing crops would offer them little cover, being mostly potato, cabbage and carrots. The nearest cover was a house over two-hundred metres away, on the very edge of the township.

'The probe will be keeping a close watch on the settlements borders,' Gerry added. 'We'll be out in the open for almost a minute.'

'I know, feeling lucky?' Charmaine replied with a smile.

'Not really, of late,' Gerry answered. 'But let's give it a shot. The longer we sit around here the more likely it is we will be detected. We'll head for the trees by the nearest house.'

Gerry and Charmaine surveyed the sky as they stepped out of cover, but the probe was nowhere to be seen.

'Run,' Gerry said quietly, and together they sprinted over the uneven ground as quickly as they dared without risking a fall.

Though finding the pace a little easier to sustain than Charmaine was, Gerry stayed behind her, constantly scanning the sky for the probe that hunted them.

They had covered more than half of the distance when Gerry saw the black pinprick in the sky over the rainforest they had just traversed. Though he could not be certain, it appeared to be

288

moving toward them. 'Fast as you can, Charmaine. The probes on its way.'

'Will we make it?' she yelled back at him without turning around.

'Yeah, but only just,' Gerry answered, though in truth he did not think they would. He risked another glance behind and saw that without a doubt it had seen them, having closed most of the distance already. It moved so quickly that it left a contrail behind it, a bright streak of orange that pointed right at them from the reddening late-afternoon sky.

Suddenly there was a boom from somewhere ahead of them, from the very trees that they hoped to gain safety within. Charmaine was startled into slowing her pace, but Gerry yelled at her to keep running, while he reached for the pistol, which was strapped within a large pocket on the chest of his flight suit. If she had known she had a laser targeting the back of her head, Charmaine would not have slowed in the first place. Gerry knew he would also have a pinpoint of light shining onto the back of his own head.

Only twenty metres from safety, Gerry knew it was too late. Drawing the gun, he spun around and took aim, his feet kicking up a cloud of dust as he slid to a halt.

Gerry did not need to pull the trigger though. While he was still steadying his hand, there was another crackling boom from the nearby garden. Gerry saw pieces of debris burst from the probe, and it fell from the sky, hitting the ground with a solid thud that reverberated through his feet. The probe lay useless, upside down in the freshly turned soil.

Not sure whether they should approach the home they had been running for, or flee back the way they had come, Gerry stayed where he was. Charmaine didn't stop though, running into the lush garden without hesitation, probably not aware that the probe had been destroyed.

Gerry found himself in more immediate danger, as young plants began to crackle around him, bursting into flame. The gunship had his approximate location. The heat beam was sweeping the area in an attempt to burn him down.

'This way, now!' barked a male voice from within the garden where Charmaine had run. Though he could not see who had spoken, Gerry did as advised. And he almost made it to safety unscathed.

He felt the heat on his heels even through the sturdy boots he wore and dived headlong into the dense cover of the trees. He was seconds too late though, and he felt the searing pain across the back of his legs as the beam passed over them.

The pain was immense, and he couldn't focus his eyes as he sensed people around him. Someone poured a pitcher of water over his burning legs, and he passed out, swept under by an overwhelming tide of pain.

TWENTY

'Give me the sky right behind the grey,
And build this dream in a sunset…'
Skunkhour – Up To Our Necks In It

When Gerry woke, he found himself indoors, under a ceiling fan and upon a comfortable bed. His legs still ached, but the pain was bearable. Charmaine was sitting on the edge of his bed, and around her stood more than a dozen people that he had never seen before.

'Welcome back. You're safe here for now,' one of the strangers said to him.

'Safe? They'll burn this house down with us in it,' Gerry told them, lifting himself up onto his elbows so he could more easily see.

'The house you ran to was burned to the ground. We are at a neighbouring property. They don't know where you are,' the same man advised. The man seemed friendly, and the others in the room did not seem to be a threat, so Gerry relaxed somewhat.

'But how did we get here?' Gerry asked him. 'The gunship up there would have been able to track so many people easily.'

'Underground,' one of the others explained. 'We've foreseen problems with officials back on Earth. We just wish they hadn't arisen so soon.'

'But we are all very glad you are here. We've been waiting for you. Waiting for the cure for decades,' the first man who had spoken added.

'I'm not sure you'd really want to put yourselves in our predicament,' Gerry said, noticing that Charmaine dropped her head a little when he spoke, probably showing guilt over the situation she had put he and her crewmates in. 'We've had nothing but trouble since we were infected, but I understand the needs of your community.'

'It's too late for second-guessing though. Now we have been in your vicinity we will also be placed in quarantine. Our whole planet, God willing,' the man replied.

291

Gerry felt surprisingly at ease though sitting in a room full of religious fundamentalists, but he realised that as long as he was perceived as being on their side he would be safe from them. In some sense, he felt that their cause was just, but it was the conniving means they had used that perturbed him most. He did not appreciate being an unwitting pawn in somebody else's dangerous experiment, but he though it wise to hide his resentment.

'I guess my burns healed on their own,' Gerry said, brushing soot and burnt fabric from his calves. His skin seemed undamaged, only the missing hairs making it obvious where he had been burnt.

Charmaine nodded. 'Yes, we all saw it happen.' A murmur passed through the group, and there were smiles all-round.

'The effect is far stronger in you than it was in the first person who came here with it,' a swarthy middle-aged woman to his right said. 'I'm sorry that we deceived you, but we knew that you and your crew would never voluntarily be part of our plan.'

'You're right about that,' Gerry replied, trying not to convey the annoyance he felt in the tone of his voice, though not completely succeeding. 'Did Charmaine tell you what happened to the others that walked into our quarantine area?'

'Yes, three of them were killed. One of them was my nephew,' she answered.

'We've got to make them pay for what they did,' someone yelled angrily from the back of the group that now filled the room.

'All in good time,' the man closest to Gerry called back. 'It's defence we need now, not revenge. We have lodged an official complaint. We can consider legal action later.'

'We'll never get a fair hearing in one of their courts, and they won't recognise any decisions made by our court. What is the point?' another man replied.

'I think it is appropriate military action that we should be considering,' the voice from the back called. 'Playing by their rules will doom us to certain failure. We need to set a precedent, something for them to consider when next contemplating the murder of our people.'

'He's right about that I think,' the portly woman near Gerry said to the man beside her. 'If we show weakness now they'll feel they can walk over us with impunity in the future. Always they push their demands upon us, and every time we follow we diminish our settlements sovereignty. We are not governed by the home planet.'

'I do think that sometimes they need to be reminded of that fact, but it is beside the point. This isn't the time for doing anything rash,' the man near Gerry replied. By the tone in which he spoke, and the way people focussed on him, Gerry assumed he held some authority in this community. 'Our relationship with the home planet couldn't be any more strained than it is right now.'

There was a rising murmur through the group of people surrounding Gerry and Charmaine, but it was cut short when the door opened and a red-faced, panting teenager burst through the crowd holding a piece of paper outstretched before him.

'We've been sent instructions from Earth, sir,' the young man said, handing the man standing closest to Gerry the slip of paper.

'The U.S. Minister of Health and the Secretary-General of the United Nations have co-signed these demands. All off-planet and even shuttle flights are grounded, and all people on Clarkson are now in enforced quarantine,' he told them, after quickly reading the note. 'We are free to go where we please on this continent but all shuttles are to be grounded, and of course we can't leave the planet Incoming flights have been cancelled indefinitely. The troops that are on their way here will no longer be landing, but will stay in orbit waiting further developments.

'That's what we expected. It works in our favour', he added. 'Now they won't be able to make landfall here. Our independence has been our main goal, and we're getting much closer to that.'

'So this means you will be able to bring my crew back here, and David Oaks too? They've been living pretty rough out there,' Gerry said to him, hoping he wasn't overstepping his welcome.

'Of course, I'll send someone immediately,' the man replied with a smile, handing the slip of paper back to the boy and telling him to send his driver out there to pick them up at the campsite.

'You know where our camp is?' Gerry asked the man, as the youngster sped from the room to follow his instructions.

'Yes, we were told to avoid the area a few weeks ago by various officials on Earth. We knew something was going on there long before Charmaine contacted us with word that she and Gaston were here on Clarkson. My name's Mark Drake, by the way. I'm the Mayor of this community.'

Gerry shook his hand. 'I guess you know who I am by now.'

'Of course,' Drake replied. 'You can't realise how much you've helped us all. I can say for all of us here on Clarkson that we are deeply in your debt. We will ensure that you and your crew will live very comfortably here.'

'We haven't exactly given up yet. I think most of us are hoping that our condition will improve, and we will be allowed to return home to Earth,' Gerry advised him. 'I know the radiation effects dissipated in the first infected person to come here after they were exposed to it, and I'm hoping it will be the same for us.'

'I'm not interested in returning,' Charmaine said quietly. 'I'm staying here no matter what happens.'

'It's your only real option now, after what you have been involved in. You will be imprisoned for life if Earth authorities get hold of you,' Gerry said to her solemnly. 'I'll probably get the same treatment.'

Charmaine nodded and smiled at him, clearly unperturbed. 'It doesn't matter to me what they think of me on Earth. They have no power over me here, and this is my true home.'

'We should let them rest for a while,' the Mayor suggested to the group that surrounded them. 'They've had enough action for one day. Let's give them some space.'

People nodded and murmured assent, but before each person left the room, they would approach Gerry and Charmaine and shake their hands, and some of the women would embrace them. The room had almost emptied before Gerry realised what they had were doing. They were each deliberately exposing themselves to the radioactive material that enveloped their bodies. A sense of dread fell over him, and he imagined that many of them might die the same horrible death that their supervisor did at the early stages of their mission, when they were first exposed.

He greeted each of the remaining people robotically as they filed out, barely aware of the people he met, numb with an overriding sense of powerlessness. The gravity of what he and his crew had done welled up inside him, the realisation of the true extent of what they were involved in hitting him hard.

The Mayor was the last to leave, pointing to a cabinet near the door as he stepped out. 'Fresh clothing and water is here. Food is available, but I understand that you don't need it anymore. Make yourself at home. We'll talk again when you are rested and your friends are brought from the camp.'

Gerry nodded his thanks, and the door finally closed and he and Charmaine were alone.

'Where are we? Whose house is this?' Gerry asked her after a few seconds of silence. He felt for the firearm in his pockets but it wasn't there. Someone had taken it from him, but he didn't let it concern him for the moment.

'It was my fathers' house, but it's mine now. They kept it maintained for me after he died. I've been planning to return since I was eleven years old,' she answered, with a sigh.

'What about your mother? Is she still back on Earth?'

'No, she died when I was only a year old. A drug overdose. My father raised me until I was ten or so, and then he moved here, leaving me with his brother's family.'

'That must have been hard on you,' Gerry said, a little taken aback that such a highly educated and balanced woman came from such a dysfunctional background.

'Not as bad as it seems. I always had hope. I knew I would be living here one day, and it gave me something to aim for. I just wished he had lived long enough for us to spend some time together here. But I feel closer to him, just being here in the home he set up for us.'

Charmaine lifted her legs onto the bed and lay down beside him, and moving onto his side so he could see her, Gerry closed her hand in his. 'We should get cleaned up before we get too relaxed. I'm fetid.'

'Me too, but let's just lay here for a while. I know I won't be able to sleep, but the idea of some quiet time just to ourselves sounds wonderful.'

'Yeah,' Gerry replied, closing his eyes and willing his muscles to relax.

They stayed like that for about two hours, neither of them moving or speaking.

Though they could no longer sleep, they felt revitalised after their rest. They stayed alert the whole time, but calmed themselves by positive thoughts and using untaught meditation methods. They were learning to control their own state of mind, allowing it to rest for a time. Without this new-found ability, Gerry was sure he would have gone mad before now. A mind that never rests, a brain that is always calculating, could not possibly stay balanced. The very thought horrified him. People needed at least a few hours of mental respite from the rigours of life every few days.

Gerry rose first, and used the shower. The soap and the clean running water seemed to sluice off weeks of dirt and oily grime, and his mood was lightened considerably more when he put on the fresh clothing that had been left for him. There was a spring in his step when he returned to the bedroom.

'I'd almost forgotten there was someone handsome underneath all that mud and torn cloth,' Charmaine said, smiling at him as she rose from the bed. She picked a fresh towel from the pile and left the room for the shower.

Gerry flicked on a tiny radio on the bedside, and the music from the settlements radio station filled the room. Christian music from Earth was playing, but he left it on anyway, appreciating the sound regardless of the inane lyrics. Looking about, he noticed a piece of paper that seemed to have been slipped under the front door.

'*Your friends have been picked up from the camp and are staying at my residence. Come visit when you feel up to it. Dinner is at sundown if you can make it. Thank you. Mayor Drake,*' it read, and there was a simple hand-drawn map showing where his home was situated.

Gerry was greatly relieved to hear that the remainder of his crew were safe. Dinner at the Mayors' house didn't hold much appeal though, considering his complete inability to eat, but he would look forward to a reunion with his friends.

'We've still a few hours till we should visit the mayor, how about we go for a walk around the settlement?' Gerry asked Charmaine when she entered the room after her shower, handing her the note he had found.

'OK then, I'll be with you in a minute. It will be good to be able to walk around freely again,' Charmaine replied after she read the invitation, and sat down on the edge of the bed to brush her hair.

Gerry walked to the front door and realised that he hadn't seen any footwear with the clothing that had been left for them,

296

but when he stepped outside he was glad to find two new pairs of sandals on the doorstep. He was relieved that they wouldn't need to put their filthy old boots back on.

Looking over the property for the first time, Gerry took some deep breaths. The air was fresh, holding a soft scent of some herbs growing somewhere nearby. There were plantations of various citrus trees and vegetable plots surrounding the house. None of the plants in this garden could reproduce, their flight from Earth as seedlings destroying their DNA. Each new planting needed to be genetically assembled on this planet, without any original intact DNA available to the gardener. It wasn't difficult, but it was an expensive process, and Gerry realised that the property Charmaine had inherited was quite an investment. Her father must have invested a lifetime of pay cheques into this place.

The nearest house was barely visible, such was the distance, and the land between them looked amazingly fertile, bursting with healthy growth. Stepping out into the garden, Gerry looked over the skies, half-expecting to see another probe stalking him. There was none though, and he guessed that if they sent down another it would have better things to do now that monitor him. Now that probably hundreds of people had been exposed to the radioactive material, they had concerns that were more important on Clarkson than warranted by a couple of researchers who had absconded from quarantine. He had no doubt that they would come after him, but not yet. The risk of his gaolers contamination would not allow it.

When Charmaine came outside to join him, he admired her figure for a moment. The simple, locally made clothing, had been designed to cover her body almost completely, as Christian modesty stipulated, but it accentuated her curves and gave her a far more alluring look than the old coveralls and boots she had been wearing. A thin cord tied around her middle let him see the thinness of her waist and the curves of her hips, and he wished suddenly that they hadn't left the privacy of her house. He was keen to look around the settlement though, so he said nothing. They would have enough time to be alone when things had calmed down a little here. Their future still felt so full of uncertainties to Gerry.

They followed an overgrown driveway, obviously rarely used, probably due to the fact that there were very few cars here. Small animals scampered from them as they walked, some resembling lizards, others rodents. At some point Charmaine grabbed Gerry's hand and held it while they walked. She smiled when he looked at her, and he could see that she really was happy about being here, regardless of the circumstances. He was glad to see someone could be so happy when the situation was still so dangerous for them all, but he wondered if it did not arise from a little naivety on her part. Would she really be allowed to live here, happily ever after? He thought not. She had crimes to pay for, and they would not be forgotten. They would both be arrested as soon as it was practicable for Earth officials to do so.

'Do you hear that?' Charmaine said to him, craning her neck to look over the fields to the source of the sound. 'It's music.'

Gerry could just hear it, the melancholy tones of a church organ drifting along with the breeze. 'Sounds like church music. There might be a wedding or something happening.'

'Or a funeral,' Charmaine added quietly.

Gerry realised she was probably right. The radiation exposure may be taking its toll. To be burying people only hours after death would not be unusual here, on an off-planet settlement with little storage resources for food, let alone corpses. The thought of hundreds of people dying, in the manner that their supervisor had, appalled him. 'Let's hope not.'

They reached a well-kept road, which Gerry assumed would be the main road for the settlement, winding past all of the properties. He glanced quickly at the map he held in his hand and pointed the way. 'I don't think it's far to the Mayors home, but we can take a walk along the main street to get a bit of a feel of the layout of this place.'

'Sounds just fine to me,' Charmaine answered, and hand in hand, they strolled along the dusty dirt road.

Gerry needed to remind himself that they were not on Earth, such was the similarity. The properties they passed all had various plants from the home planet on display. The tropical climate here, as it was over most of the planet, obviously necessitated the growing of fauna from similarly hot and humid areas on Earth. They walked past rows of mango trees one moment, bananas the next, and then pawpaw and some types of plants Gerry couldn't

298

name. Rice fields lined the road as they neared the hub of the settlement, a few hundred homes and offices clustered together tightly, though by no means could it be considered a city. To Gerry, the place resembled some of the remote outstations back in Australia that he had visited as a youngster. The dwellings were all similar, very simple in construction.

As they walked up the gentle incline, Gerry noticed something not totally unexpected. Another surveillance probe had been dispatched from the gunship in orbit, and it now hovered high over the largest building, which Gerry assumed to be the administration office block. He could see people milling around at the front of the building, hundreds of tiny figures dressed in black.

'We should go see what's going on over there,' Gerry suggested to Charmaine. 'The people are out in force.'

'Do you think we should?' Charmaine replied.

'Why not?' Gerry asked her. 'It might be something that concerns us.'

'Exactly, it could be that they are at a funeral. Their exposure to the radioactive material will come at a huge cost. Everyone here knows and accepts that. Nevertheless, now might not be the time to interfere, while their grief is still so fresh.'

Gerry realised that she was right. The large building the people were congregating around was a church. That was from where the melancholy music emanated.

'Maybe we should go ask someone else what is going on,' Gerry suggested. 'I don't go to funerals as a rule, and walking into one uninvited isn't something I'd like to contemplate. Especially so, considering we were most likely the cause of their demise.'

'I don't like the way in which you lay blame on yourself for what is happening here on Clarkson, Gerry. You are a victim of our plans, while these people are all willing participants. If I were you I'd feel angry and used, definitely not blameworthy.'

'I made plenty of decisions during this mission that got us where we are today. I've played just as active a part as you have,' Gerry explained. 'If I'd kept us in quarantine near Earth, as ordered, this would never have happened.'

'Are you really so sure that we have done wrong to these people, giving them only what they sought, something which may benefit them as a society more than anything else possibly could?' Charmaine asked him.

'No, not a hundred percent sure, I must admit,' Gerry answered after a moments hesitation.

Charmaine pointed to a building that appeared to be a market, considering the advertising that adorned its walls, and tugged his hand to lead him in its direction. 'We'll ask someone here what has been happening.'

Gerry let himself be led into the store, and found it to be similar to a small corner shop back on Earth, though the variety of items on display was very much limited. Behind the counter was the portly woman he recognised from Charmaine's house, when he had regained consciousness after being burnt.

'Hello, we haven't been properly introduced,' Charmaine said to her. 'I'm Charmaine, and this is Gerry.'

Her smile was cheery and she seemed completely without fear of them as she outstretched her arm and shook hands with each of them. 'Nice to meet you, though I know all about you two already. We are all so grateful for what you have done for us. And that goes for your father too, god bless his soul.'

'You knew my father?' Charmaine asked.

'Of course, we arrived here within a couple of weeks of each other. He would stand right where you are every morning when he came to pick up the daily newsletter and we'd chat about old times. You were his favourite subject, you know.'

'I guess you would have heard that he died on the mission to bring the healing essence here,' Charmaine added.

'Yes dear. I'm so sorry for your loss. He didn't fail though. His plans have come into fruition. We are all very proud of him. Our whole community says a prayer for him every week at Mass.'

'Thank you,' was all Charmaine could think to say.

'We're worried about the side effects that some people suffer. Our supervisor died when he was exposed. There seems to be most of the settlement gathered around the church. What has happened?' Gerry inquired.

The woman nodded solemnly. 'Yes, there have been many deaths today. You have seen a funeral for some of them.'

'Do you have any idea yet what percentages of people are reacting badly to the exposure?' Charmaine asked her.

'People have been saying that it's about one in seven that are killed. It is a high price to pay, but I am sure that our future generations will appreciate our sacrifice. They've been given a future that they couldn't possibly have otherwise.'

'I hope you're right,' Gerry said, feeling nowhere near as confident as she appeared to be.

'While I think of it, since you're here you might as well get yourself something to eat for tonight,' the woman continued. 'Take your pick of anything in the store. It's on me. You probably won't have any of the local currency yet, so it's the least I can do.'

'Thanks very much, but we won't be eating at home tonight. The Mayor has invited us to dinner,' Charmaine explained.

'Oh, that's good. If there's anything you need though, don't hesitate to ask.'

'Thanks. We had best be going now. We are expected at the Mayors place soon. It was nice to meet you,' Charmaine said, and she and Gerry exited the store and walked back out onto the road.

The hand drawn map Gerry held showed the Mayors residence to be somewhere close to the church that he was so keen to avoid. However, as they neared the throngs of grieving people they heard a familiar voice call to them from the neighbouring property. It was Darren, who was waving them over. Thankfully, the crowd would not likely see them.

'You're at the right place,' Darren said to them with a smile. 'Dinner is waiting, though I've a feeling we won't be partaking.'

'A soft chair and a glass of iced water sounds like heaven to me. Just the warm shower and soft bed back at home made coming to this settlement worthwhile,' Charmaine added cheerily.

'Where are the others?' Gerry asked Darren, keen to get off the street.

'They're waiting inside, let's join them,' Darren replied, and led them down a narrow, paved path.

When they emerged from the thick garden path, they found themselves on the front lawn of the Mayor's home. The grass was lush and looked as good as any on Earth, but Gerry knew it would be some local equivalent that they had cultivated. It had the startling form of an English garden, and Gerry had to smile at the idea that people would attempt to bring the very appearance of their native birthplace with them to a new planet.

The house was larger than most that Gerry had seen during their walk, but was of the same simple construction. The large glass doors were wide open, and Darren led them up the steps and into the dim interior.

'Welcome Charmaine and Gerry. Please, take a seat at the table,' someone said. Gerry had to wait for a moment for his eyes to adjust to the dim lighting after coming in from the sunshine outside before he could properly see who had spoken, though finally he recognised the man he had met back at Charmaine's home where he regained consciousness.

'Thankyou sir, we appreciate the invitation,' Gerry said to the Mayor, stepping forward and shaking his hand. Jennifer and Gaston were seated at the table also, though there was no sign of David. Gerry remembered that his wife had been ill and assumed he would be at home with her.

To the right of the Mayor was someone Gerry did not recognise, a short, dark-haired man wearing a business suit and a serious demeanour, both of which seemed somehow pointless and out of place in this far-flung land. He too, stood and proffered his hand, which Gerry shook as the Mayor introduced him as Nigel Adams, the community's security advisor.

'Pleased to meet you,' Gerry said to Adams, but could not hide his surprise at finding such a person on this remote planet. 'You must have an easy job here on Clarkson.'

'Yes, it has been one of the quieter times in my life,' he replied with no change in expression as he shook Charmaine's hand also, and returned to his seat.

'Mr Adams has only been here for a few weeks. He came here as a consultant but he's decided to make this his permanent home,' the Mayor informed them.

'Forgive me for asking, and tell me to mind my own business if you like, but does your presence here have anything to do with our arrival?' Charmaine asked Adams, speaking exactly what Gerry had been thinking.

'I guess there is no reason why we should keep any information from you,' the Mayor said, speaking for his advisor, and waving Charmaine, Darren and Gerry to their seats at the long table at which Jennifer and even Gaston were already seated. 'You have proven yourselves as sympathetic to our cause. Am I right Mr Adams?'

The security man nodded almost imperceptibly, and the Mayor continued. 'Mr Adams is simply here to help us fulfil our goals without offending officials Earth-side too much. Our transition to a fertile community has frightened some people back on Earth, and gained the interest of those on other settlements. We need to be very careful.'

'I think it might be the methods that were used that frightened people most,' Gerry said, unable to keep his thoughts to himself. 'We came close to killing everyone on Earth during our mission. They should be afraid.'

'Your friends have informed me of a few problems on your journey,' the Mayor replied. 'I am sorry about that, but they couldn't have been foreseen. No one here expected anyone to be hurt, and our people stranded on that moon could do only so much to help you. We were in constant contact with them of course, but I'm afraid there was nothing we could do either. You know though that as part of our emigration agreement we agreed not to leave this planet. We were not permitted hyper-speed craft of our own. It was a one way ticket.'

Gerry could only nod, still amazed by the callous nature in which he and his crew had been used. He was sure that more than one government on Earth would like to see this man behind bars, there being little doubt that he was the mastermind behind their dangerous journey. Gerry could never trust someone so conniving and self-serving, and was beginning to feel uncomfortable sitting at his table.

'You became involved for the right reasons, Gerry,' Gaston said in his rasping voice, as if reading Gerry's thoughts. 'You saved my life and attempted to save my crew-mate. That is all. Your involvement ends now.'

'Gaston is right,' the Mayor added. 'Please don't feel guilt or responsibility for what has happened over the past month. We will make it clear to Earth-side officials that you were involuntarily involved'

They were interrupted by a miserable looking young man carrying a tray of drinks, which he placed on the table before them with a strained smile and left the room again, only to return with another huge tray covered in plates of various foods.

When the servant had disappeared back into the kitchen, the Mayor explained his workers demeanour. 'His brother died today

303

I'm afraid. The miraculous essence that will save our community has a bad effect on some. Perhaps their souls are tainted in some way.'

Gerry felt instantly angered, but controlled his response. 'Don't blame the individual. The substance killed our Supervisor too. He was a good man. Charmaine's father died the same way, while he was trying attempting to get you what you wanted.'

'I apologise Mr Handley, I spoke without thinking. I forget myself sometimes. These are exciting times,' the Mayor said with a smile, appearing anything but contrite.

'How are you feeling, by the way,' Jennifer asked the Mayor. 'It's been a few hours since your first exposure. You should begin to notice the symptoms soon.'

'I haven't noticed any change yet,' the Mayor replied. 'That's fine with me though. I've heard about your lack of appetite, so I would like to enjoy one last meal if I am given the time. I hope you don't mind me eating in front of you, but try any of the food or drink you would like. Perhaps there is something here that your stomachs will accept.'

Darren immediately reached forward and grabbed a glass and a bottle of some type of spirit, pouring himself a generous amount.

'Nice choice. That whiskey was distilled not far from here, aged for 17 years,' the mayor informed him, but was cut short as Darren gulped the amber liquid down, and a few seconds later it burst back out again in an awesome display of projectile vomiting. The security man was in the firing line, and caught most of it on his once impeccable suit.

Darren's face reddened as he wiped his chin. 'I'm real sorry about that.'

Passing Darren a venomous glance, the security man said nothing as he rose from his chair and walked from the room.

The Mayor was in fits of laughter, clutching his heaving belly. 'Don't worry about it, he's always been too uptight. Even more so at the moment. He's probably worrying about his flight tomorrow.'

'His flight? I thought all craft were grounded,' Gerry said.

The Mayor nodded. 'They are, technically. Nevertheless, there's just one more flight we need to make. I thought Charmaine would have told you about it.'

Gerry turned to her. 'Where's he going?'

'To the other settlement. There is another like this on the other side of the planet,' Charmaine informed him.

'He'll infect the people there too,' Gerry said, turning back to the Mayor.

'That's the idea,' the politician replied. 'We're counting on it.'

'Now that's just going too far,' Gerry said, surprised by the surge of anger that welled up within him. 'Risking the population of this settlement is bad enough, but deliberately exposing everyone else on the planet at this early stage would be a damn stupid thing to do. You should wait until you have observed the effects on this place.'

The Mayor held up a hand. 'Please, not too loud. This house is under surveillance. We have taken measures to ensure our privacy, but they have their limits.'

'How can you possible keep such a thing from Earth's officials anyway? They will track the ship, and once it leaves the quarantine area it will be shot down,' Gerry said.

'We've planned for that, but you're right, it will be a dangerous journey,' the Mayor replied, stuffing his mouth with a large forkful of meat that dripped gravy onto his chin.

'This situation is getting worse every day,' Gerry said, to no one in particular. 'Everyone here seems so flippant, though they're messing with something incredibly dangerous.'

'They are focussing on the positives,' Charmaine said quietly. 'The chance of long-term survival of the communities on Clarkson without the radiation exposure is almost nil, but they have been given the chance to have a future, and will make the work these people do during their lives mean something. They'll have another generation to benefit from what these people have done here.'

All Gerry could do was shake his head, and resign himself to the fact that this madness was now almost totally out of his control.

Dinner remained a solemn affair, each of them with so much to consider. The Mayor was the only one who ate, but by the pallid sheen to his skin when he excused himself from the room hinted that he would not be keeping it down for long.

Gerry and Charmaine spoke only a few words during their walk back to her new home.

'This is all going too far, you realise that, don't you?' he asked her.

'Neither of us knows for sure whether or not this will all turn out well for us. Let's just wait and see. Leave it be now Gerry'

He smiled and hugged her tighter, however, Gerry could not just leave it be.

TWENTY-ONE

'It's not easy when the road is your driver...'
Leo Sayer – When I Need You

Distancing himself from a problem he had a hand in creating, in Gerry's mind, was not a realistic option. These people were intent on spreading the infectious material as far as they could. It was so unscientific, so illogical, that it dumbfounded Gerry that these people could be so reckless. Nevertheless, Gerry was to discover that he had severely underestimated the extremes that the Mayor and his off-siders would go to secure independence for Clarkson.

In the early hours of the morning, Gerry slipped quietly from the bed he and Charmaine shared. Though of course unable to sleep, Gerry knew she would be too exhausted to want to follow him. 'I'm going to take a shower and sit outside for a bit.'

'OK Gerry,' she whispered back with a lazy smile. 'I'll just stay here and bathe in the afterglow if that's alright with you?'

Gathering his clothes from the floor, Gerry took them to the bathroom with him and had a shower, then quickly dressed himself in the local clothing he had been given. He checked that his hand-held computer was still in the pocket. It was.

The air was crisp and cool as he stepped out the back door of Charmaine's house. The garden was dense, overgrown by years of neglect. There would be little chance of him being seen. He listened for Charmaine's footfalls inside, but there were none.

Convinced that she had stayed in bed, Gerry weaved his way into the foliage, careful to make as little sound as possible. When he reached the edge of the property he stopped and retrieved the computer from his pocket. He switched it on, and with a couple of taps he had turned on the devices networking capabilities. He saw the probe listed as one of the possible contacts, and sent a simple message.

'WE NEED TO TALK.' He didn't bother telling them to keep it quiet. He knew they would.

In a few seconds, there was a soft hum from above, the probe having tracked his location instantly using his computers signal. It was too high though; probably wary of an attack, but when Gerry waved it down it approached to within two metres of his head.

'Someone is in that house, I can't talk for long,' Gerry said quietly.

'Go ahead then,' the voice from the probe whispered.

'Who is it that I am talking to, exactly?' Gerry inquired.

'Commander Lorens. We've met before.'

Gerry was a little startled by the fact. The same man had ordered him down to a planet to help destroy some vermin. Though these vermin had villages, housing, and other evidence of an advanced society. The job had plagued Gerry ever since. 'Yes, I remember. It's been a while between massacres.'

'I know that wasn't in your job description, but you were a big help. We needed everyone we could get down there to successfully complete the mission,' the Commander replied.

'Never mind. Do you know about the flight tomorrow, to the other settlement?' Gerry asked, eager to change the subject.

'We do. We have been given an ultimatum. Let it reach its destination or all life on Earth will be killed. Our hands are tied.'

'What the fuck?' Gerry said. 'They are threatening Earth? How do they expect to achieve that?'

'They have control of the hyper-speed drive on Clavus. They have had it aimed at us for a decade, and there has always been too much risk involved in approaching it to destroy it. Gaston seems to have automated the ships systems while he was stranded aboard. He has turned the ship into what is now, purely a weapon.'

'Shit. This is getting ridiculous. We were wondering why the drive was aimed in the direction of Earth early in our mission. Why didn't you tell us this then?'

'We couldn't risk the information being leaked to the general public. We both know that even entangled particle communications are not one hundred percent secure. The panic that might ensue would not help any of us. However, now we are in a position to act. The shuttle leaves at first light. Will you help us?'

'I don't see that I have a choice now,' Gerry answered quietly, though without hesitation.

'The major problem we have is that we don't know where the computer is located that Gaston will use to remotely fire the engines toward us,' the voice from the probe advised Gerry. 'He has kept it off-line so we can't trace it. We would have destroyed it if we knew its position.'

'Do you want me to find it and destroy it?' Gerry asked.

'If you are left with no better option, yes. But a more desirable outcome would be for you to reprogram the ships systems so that the hyper-speed drive becomes permanently inoperable.'

308

'That could be done from the computer here on Clarkson?' Gerry asked.

'Yes, Gaston has given himself full remote control access to the ships systems.'

'He would have set some type of password, and if he programmed the ships systems himself, how can I be sure that I'll be able to understand the methods he used? Software written by someone for their own one-off use will hardly be user-friendly,' Gerry whispered.

'You'll have to allow him to connect to the ship before you act.'

'That's risky, but it does seem like the best course of action,' Gerry answered. 'But how will I find him?'

'We have been tracking his movements,' the man on Earth told Gerry quietly, his voice rasping through the probes speakers. 'He is home now, so you will need to follow him from there in the morning. I expect that he will lead you to the computer. We will help you.'

'It probably won't be held in and of the officials' residences or offices. They would be the first places you would attack if things escalated into direct conflict,' Gerry surmised.

'Yes. Very likely somewhere non-threatening to us, and out of the way.'

'Dawn isn't long away. You should lead me to Gaston now. He might leave early, we can't risk losing track of him,' Gerry advised the military official back on Earth.

'Yes, follow the probe,' was the answer he received, and the device immediately began to drift across the garden, following the overgrown walking track to the back fence of the property.

Gerry followed, careful not to step on anything that would make noise. Charmaine must not discover what he was about to do, else she would surely try to stop him. He had never taken sides in this situation, only done what was needed to survive. Nevertheless, his own welfare, and even that of his crew, was a minor thing to risk considering the possible outcome if Gaston and his supporters had their way. Their intent to spread the radioactive material at any cost, even the death of the home planet, was too dangerous to permit. Gerry decided to do whatever was required to nullify the threat to his planet of birth.

The probe waited for Gerry as he parted two strands of fence wire and slipped through, into the scrub-land that surrounded Charmaine's home.

'We are scanning the area thoroughly. You are the only person in this settlement that is outdoors at the moment. You cannot be seen by anyone. Walk quickly,' the Commander said to him through the probe.

'How can you be so sure?' Gerry asked.

'The probes sensors operate well on clear nights like this, and we are receiving a good picture from the gunship in orbit above you. You're standing out very clearly on our screens.'

It didn't take long to reach the more densely populated hub of the settlement, but no one was out on the streets.

'The house Gaston is staying at is 80 metres further down this street. Stay in the cover at the side of the road as you go there. I'll check on the surrounds,' the voice from the probe told him.

Gerry simply nodded and the device shot upward with a hum. Doing as instructed, he made his way quietly through the vegetation that lined the road. There was a light in the distance, the glow from an open window. In less than a minute, he spanned the distance and stopped on the overgrown verge of the property, where he sat down to watch and wait. He needed to know where the computer was that Gaston would use to connect to the altered hyper-speed craft. He could see his silhouette through the window, limping about the room, obviously busy with something. At this hour, it did seem a little unusual to Gerry, especially for someone still recuperating from horrific injuries.

Suddenly there was the sound of a jet engine firing up somewhere nearby, shattering the silence. The probe appeared beside him with a whoosh of air.

'This is emergency, Handley. You need to get in there now. Gaston must be able to connect to the hyper-speed crafts systems from his home. Their shuttle has just departed, and he's still in there. It's headed toward the second settlement. We will be destroying it soon. You only have a few minutes left to take control of the computer terminal.'

'Alright, I'll go in now. Watch my back,' Gerry whispered.

There was no cover around the house, so he had to risk simply keeping low to the ground while he sprinted across the bare yard. There were no sounds of alarm from inside, so he had probably made it unseen. Gerry moved to the window and peered within. He could see Gaston at the far end of the room, seated in front of a small computer. He was flicking switches, powering up the equipment that was attached to it. He would have to hurry.

A few steps to the right and he was at the front door, where he carefully turned the handle, keeping as quiet as possible. It only turned a small way and then stopped. It had been locked, which Gerry thought strange on such a small close-knit community.

'There's another window at the side of the house. Try that,' Commander Lorens' voice suggested from the probe. It was hovering above him, above the roof-line so that nobody inside could see it.

Gerry did as suggested, kneeling and trying to pry the window open when he got there, but it would not move. 'I'm going to have to smash my way in.'

'Yes. But get in there fast. You won't have much time.'

Gerry nodded agreement, and looked about for something with which to smash the glass. There wasn't anything to hit the window with or throw at it, the area was completely bare earth.

'Damn it,' Gerry muttered, pulling the right sleeve of his coveralls down as far as it would go and grabbed the cuff in his fist. In one smooth movement, he stood up and sent his fist through the window, then slammed his arm about in the window space to break away the remaining glass.

As he expected, when he withdrew his arm it was covered in blood, and it poured down his hand in huge quantities. If it continued for too long he would fall unconscious from blood loss, so he thrust his upper body through the opening without hesitation. He could see the flashing blue light running across his arm as he pulled himself into the house, making his body twitch slightly, but he had no time to observe its other effects. As soon as he had hit the floor he was up and running for Gaston.

The room where Gaston sat was unsealed, the door wide open. He was very confident, Gerry thought to himself as he ran into the room. Too confident.

It was a good thing that Gerry had entered the room so quickly. It spoiled Gaston's aim. Noticing the gun too late to stop, Gerry felt a huge blow to his abdomen as the weapon discharged. Gerry had momentum though, and as he fell forward, he slammed into Gaston, who was still in his seat. As he went down Gerry noticed that the gun he had just been shot with was the very one he had brought with him from their shuttle. They had taken it and now used it against him.

This gave Gerry a surge of anger that helped sustained him long enough to twist the gun from Gaston's hand and press his forearm against his throat, rendering him immediately immobile. He tossed the gun aside, out of Gaston's reach, and as the sense of relief struck him because he had survived and stopped Gaston, the pain struck too.

Waves of dizziness overcame him, and he didn't know how long he lay there. Flashes of electric blue blinded him, yet he wasn't even sure if his eyes were open. Unsure whether or not he had lost consciousness for a time, Gerry's vision began to return, along with his ability to move.

As his eyes focussed, he saw Gaston, still pinned to the floor with his arm still choking him. His face had turned purple, and Gerry realised that he could not breathe.

'Sorry about that, but I obviously could not let you go through with it,' Gerry said to him as he released the pressure he had on Gaston's throat.

There was a distant explosion that rattled the ceiling. The shuttle full of radiation-effected settlers had just been shot down. Gerry pushed himself back, and used the wall to help him get to his feet. He weaved a little as he said to Gaston, 'It's time to make a mess of your damn control room.'

'No,' Gaston cried, trying to sit upright. Gerry grabbed the legs of a nearby table and turned it over, and then lowered it across Gaston's body, effectively pinning him to the floor under its weight.

'There is another computer,' Gaston groaned as Gerry painfully lifted a wooden chair and swung it up over his head, ready to smash the computer equipment. 'A backup in case something happened to this one. An operator will be on his way to it now. You cannot stop him.'

The importance of what Gaston had just said struck Gerry like a hammer blow. Even though he might be lying, the risk that he wasn't was too much to accept. His mind raced for a moment, rapid-fire thoughts and solutions assaulting him. And when the altered mind-set stopped, Gerry knew what needed to be done. 'Sadly then, I'm just going to have to fire the drive toward this planet, and then destroy the moon the ship is on by switching to full drive power. It's the best solution you've left me with. You people here are just too dangerous, and so is that hyper-speed craft you've turned into a weapon.'

He waited for a response from Gaston, something to give him reprieve from the act he was about to commit, but none was forthcoming. He took a deep breath, annoyed that his hands were shaking slightly as he lowered them onto the keyboard.

It took less than a minute to programme the hyper-speed drive to fire its emissions at the very planet he was now on, and to set it to switch to full power after a few minutes. Afterwards, he spent another few minutes quietly destroying the computer equipment. The instructions he had sent could never be rescinded, but he would ensure that if anything went wrong, the remote weapon would never again be controlled from this terminal.

Gerry had set the hyper-speed drive in the remote ship to fire, to destroy all life on Clarkson, and then the very moon it rested upon. He would be destroying the strange life on the moon that lived somehow without an obvious food source; he would be destroying all life on this planet, including Charmaine's and his own.

He had found a way of removing some of the risks involved in the spread of the radioactive material, and he knew he had to make the most of his opportunity, no matter the personal sacrifice and the sacrifice of this colony. It was his time to take full responsibility for the predicament that confronted humanity. To wipe the slate clean. He felt that, for the human race, the status-quo, the predictability, was not something to be desired, rarely so in fact, but the circumstances that had been unleashed upon them held too many dangers, too many unknowns. Too many new threats.

There would be no pain. The sheer magnitude of the energy that he had directed at them would kill them in an instant after striking the planet. Gerry saw no point in frightening Charmaine with the terrible details concerning what he had done. What point would it serve? It would be the most terrible lie of his life. However, like placing the hood over the head of a person about to be executed, it was all he had to give.

'Goodbye Gaston. We only have about a week to live. Try to enjoy the time we have left.'

'But why?' Gaston asked Gerry, lifting his head to look him in the eye.

'You wanted to give your people the power to reproduce, at any cost, but threatening destruction of the home planet, or even just holding the power to do so, was just too much for me. You are dangerous extremists. You could have decided on a safer way of building an empire.'

'Do we all need to die just because we weren't humble enough for you?' Gaston said with a hiss.

'In this case, yes, I am afraid so.'

When he exited the house, leaving Gaston still pinned to the floor by the heavy table, Gerry found the probe waiting for him.

'Thank you, Mr Handley. You have stopped the biggest threat to humanity in known history. Your name will be remembered.'

'So I guess there is no way off this planet. The crew and I are going to die here,' Gerry said.

'That shuttle we destroyed was the only one on Clarkson, I'm afraid.' Commander Lorens said through the probes speaker. 'And the nearest hyper-speed ship is more than two weeks away.'

'That's OK,' Gerry said, already resigned to the fact that there would be no rescue of him and his crew. Even if they could get them off the doomed planet, they would not. Can you keep Charmaine and myself safe for our remaining time here? The settlers will be angry. They might come after us.'

'They will all be dead in a week. They will have other things on their mind, but we will do everything we can to protect you from them if the need arises. It's the least we can do.'

313

'Thank you,' Gerry replied simply. 'Take care of the rest of my crew too, if you will. They've been through a lot.'

The walk to Charmaine's new home was a poignant one for Gerry, and the sorrow he felt as he realised that every living thing he laid his eyes upon would soon die, seemed to tear painfully at his innards. There was no turning back now though. The lethal burst of radiation was surging toward them now, and nothing could stop it.

When she met him at the gate with a smile that held so much promise, the claws that seemed to dig at his very mind tore so deeply that he gasped. He greeted her with a long, passionate embrace though, and they sat together and talked of the future, a future that did not hold any mysteries. Strangely, for the first time in Gerry's life he was thoroughly contented. With no possible way to improve his life, to shape his future, he felt suffused with a sense of stress-relieving resignation. The best he could do with the remainder of his life was to mindlessly enjoy himself, and help his friends do the same. It was a wonderful conclusion to a relentlessly unsettled existence. To Gerry it felt a reward an immense, lifelong weight, lifted from his shoulders.

During the night, Darren and Jennifer burst through the door, panting furiously and trying to talk at the same time. Gerry showed them to seats and soon had the full story.

The settlers had found out from Gaston what he had done, and a mob had gathered in the front yard of the Mayor's house, calling for them to come out. When they did emerge, they were only abused and threatened. Many of the people carried weapons, and when missiles began to be thrown through the windows of the house, the Mayor came down from his room, and had a talk with some of the people. Jennifer and Darren could not hear what they spoke about, but when he returned he immediately ordered them out of his house, without explanation.

'We were chased here by about a hundred of the townspeople,' Jennifer said finally. 'For some reason they think we are going to try to kill them!'

Gerry could only nod, realising that they still had no idea of what he had done. They knew nothing of the certain death he had arranged for them all. He and Charmaine made up beds for them in a spare room, telling them they could stay there for as long as they needed, and that they were now under the military protection of the United Nations, so they were completely safe from the angry hordes. They relaxed after a while, and to Gerry, they soon seemed more comfortable here than they had been since the beginning of their ill-fated research mission.

On Earth their own threat had been annulled, though here on Clarkson, more than once Gerry thought he heard screams of pain from someone far away, and he wondered if the settlers were coming for their revenge. Nobody came within sight of the house though, and if he and his friends were under attack, the gunship in orbit above was effectively, and unobtrusively, keeping them safe.

Charmaine noticed nothing out of order. Sadly though, she would never know how grateful the people that once knew her on the home planet were, for the sacrifice she was unwittingly about to make. She would never know that she held within her the only girl ever conceived under the light of an alien sun.

She and Gerry enjoyed their last days and nights together, their passing so sudden that neither of them were aware of the end when it came.